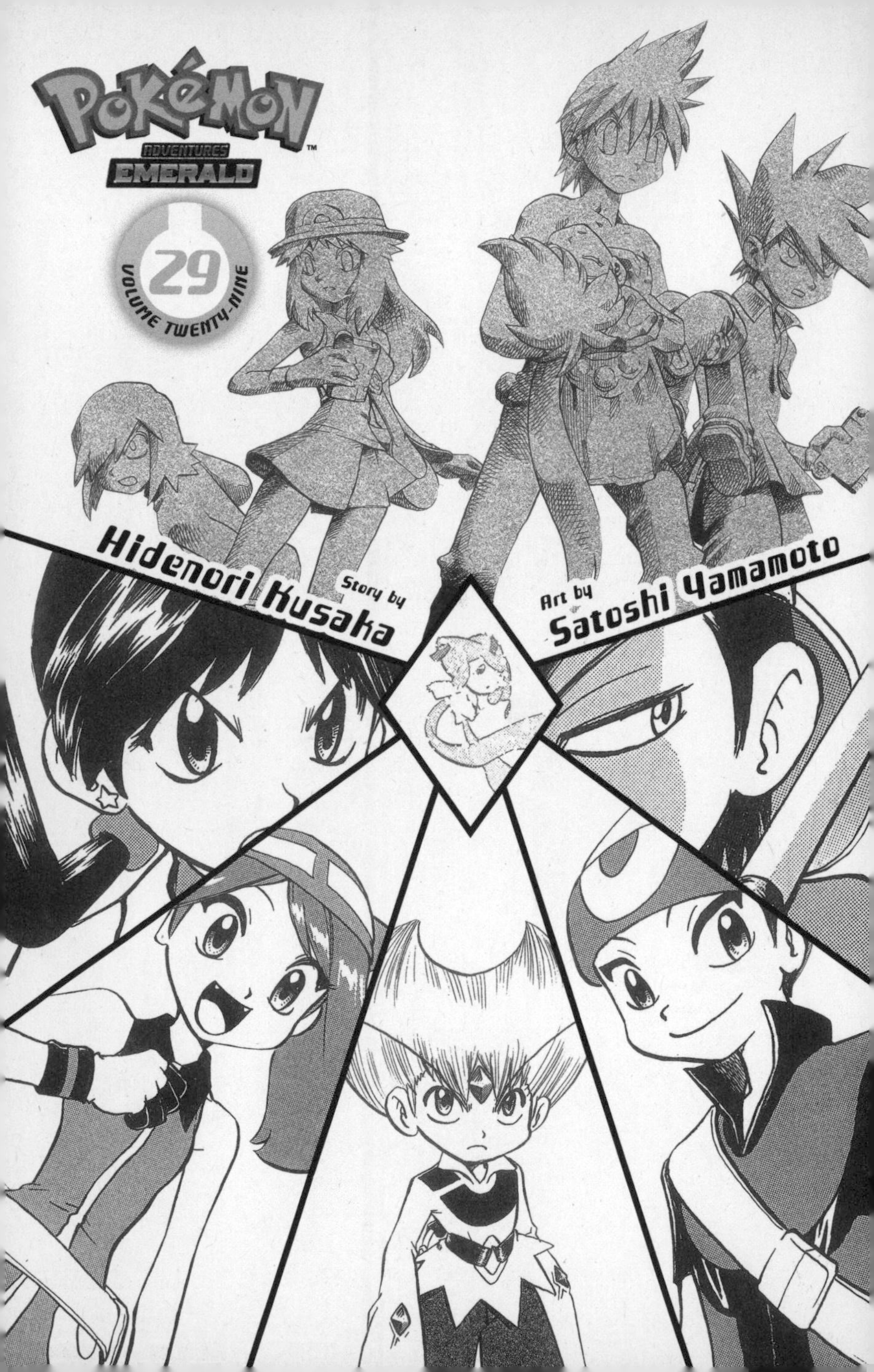
POKÉMON
ADVENTURES
EMERALD
29
VOLUME TWENTY-NINE
Story by
Hidenori Kusaka
Art by
Satoshi Yamamoto

SPECIAL OBJECT

The Pokédex holders and their stories

Kanto region

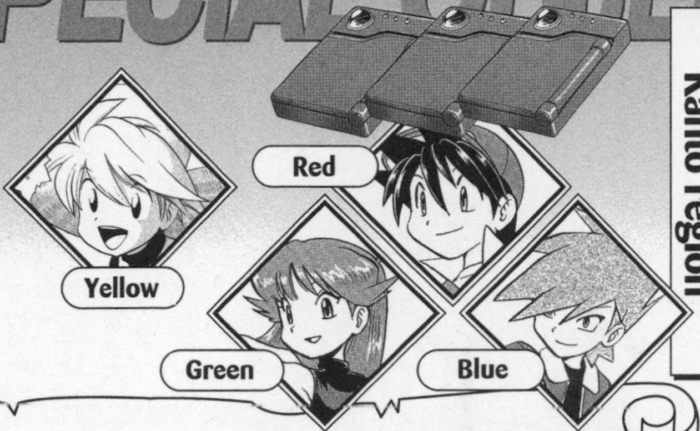
Red
Yellow
Green
Blue

1st Chapter

Red, a young boy from Pallet Town, receives a Pokédex from Professor Oak and heads out on a Pokémon training journey. Along the way, he meets two other Trainers–Blue, who becomes his rival, and Green. Red fights evil Team Rocket with his new friends and then becomes Champion of the Pokémon League.

2nd Chapter

Two years later, Red suddenly disappears, and Yellow, a mysterious new Trainer, appears at Professor Oak's laboratory in search of him.

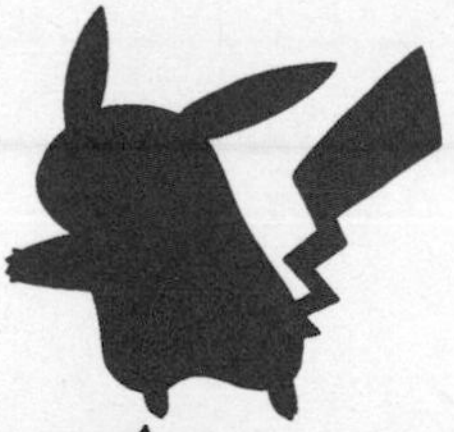

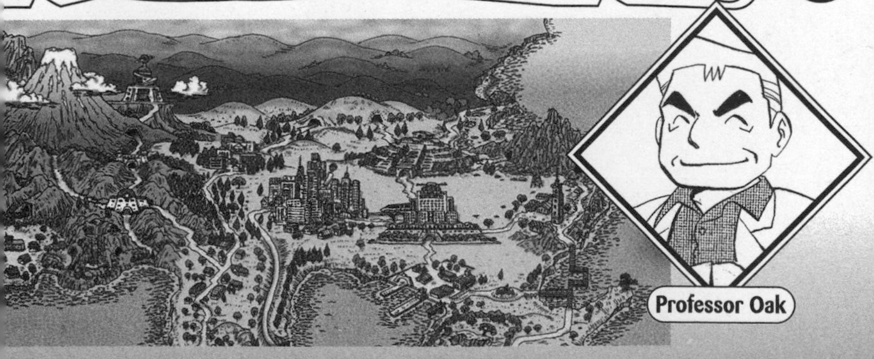
Professor Oak

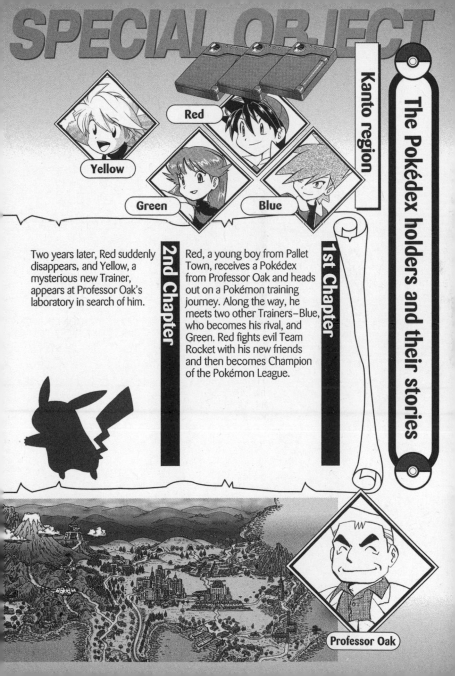

POKÉMON

Johto region

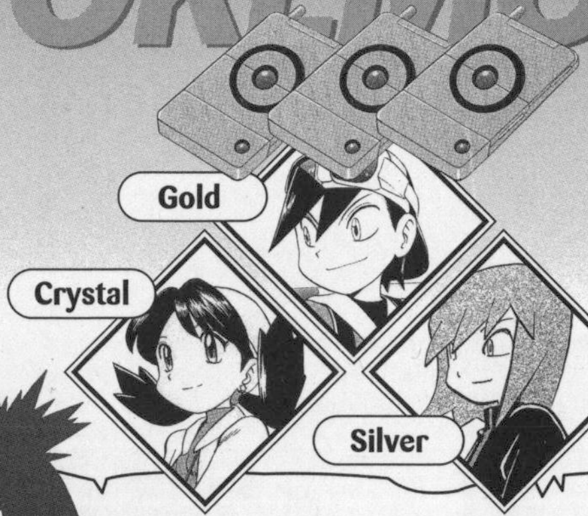
Gold
Crystal
Silver

3rd Chapter

Standing in Yellow's way is the Kanto Elite Four, led by Lance. In a major battle at Cerise Island, Yellow manages to stymie the group's evil ambitions.

A year later, Gold, a boy living in New Bark Town in a house full of Pokémon, sets out on a journey in pursuit of Silver, a Trainer who stole a Totodile from Professor Elm's laboratory. The two don't get along at first, but eventually they become partners fighting side by side. During their journey, they meet Crystal, the Trainer whom Professor Elm entrusts with the completion of his Pokédex. Together, the trio succeed in shattering the evil scheme of the Mask of Ice, a villain who leads what remains of Team Rocket.

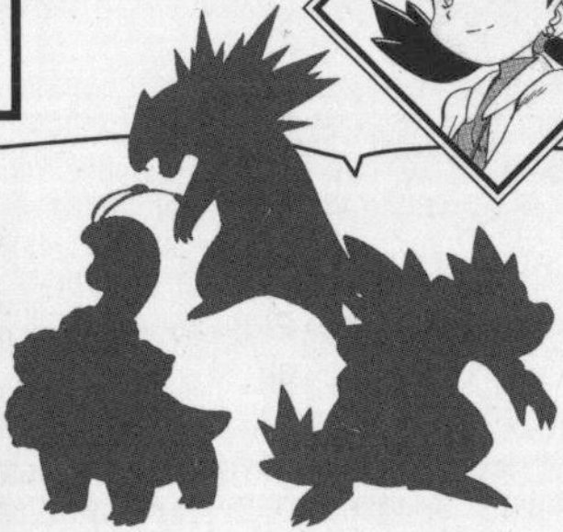

Hoenn region

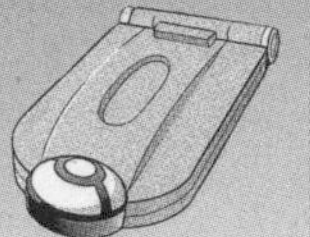

4th Chapter

Pokémon Trainer Ruby has a passion for Pokémon Contests. He runs away from home right after his family moves to Littleroot Town. He meets a wild girl named Sapphire, and they pledge to compete with each other in an 80-day challenge to...

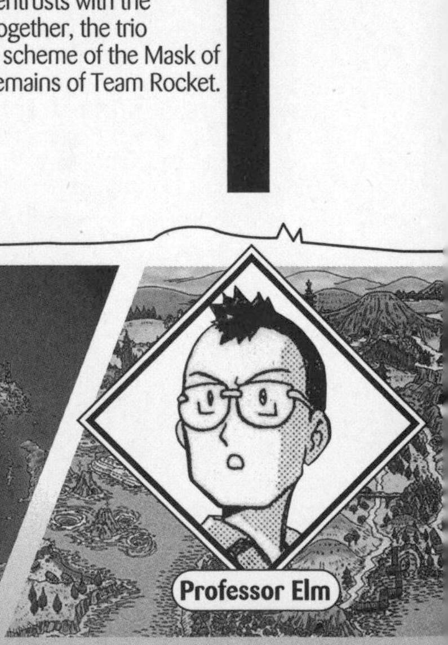
Professor Elm

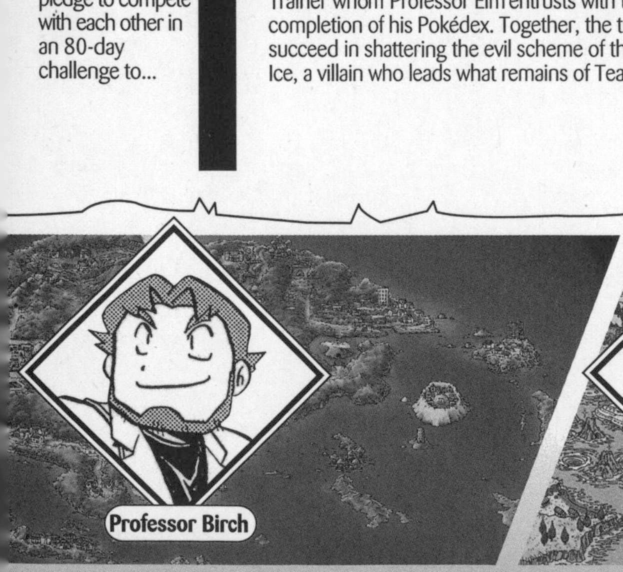
Professor Birch

SPECIAL OBJECT

Kanto region

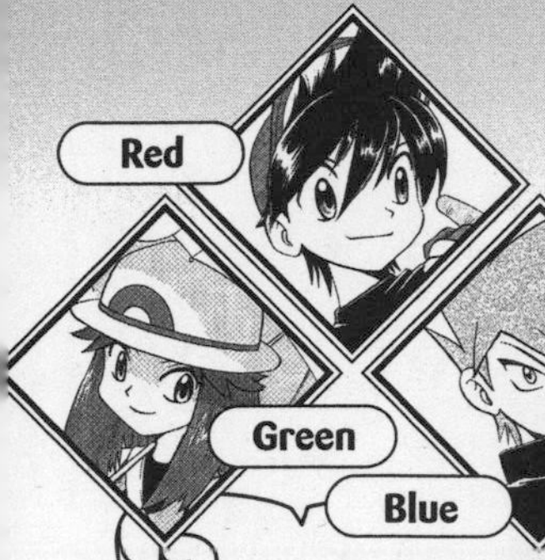
Red
Green
Blue

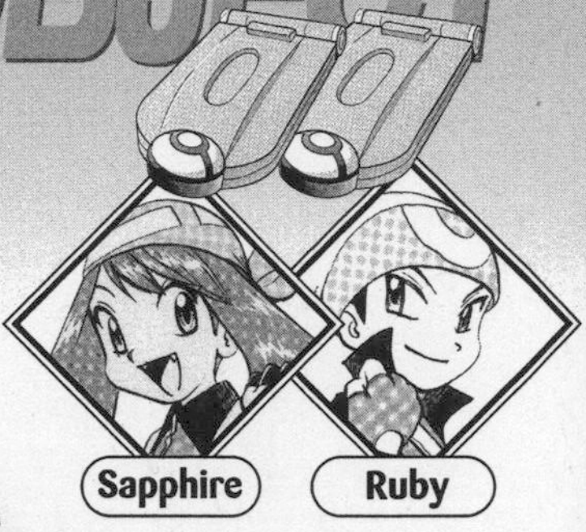
Sapphire
Ruby

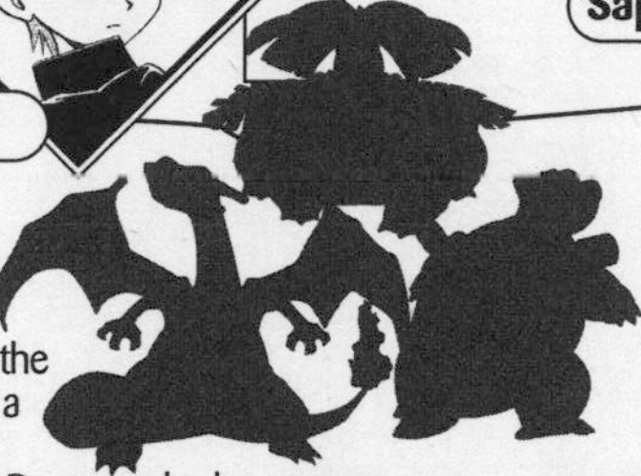

5th Chapter

Six months later, a new adventure unfolds for Red and his friends on the Sevii Islands. After a deadly battle, Red manages to defeat Deoxys, who has fallen into the hands of Giovanni. Silver, in search of his true identity, is faced with the shocking truth that Giovanni is his father. Red and his friends manage to safely land the Team Rocket airship, which was flying out of control thanks to Carr, one of the Three Beasts, who betrayed Team Rocket. But then another of the Three Beasts, Sird, appears, and in a mysterious flash of light the five Pokédex holders—Red, Blue, Green, Yellow and Silver—are petrified. Literally!

...win every Pokémon Contest and every Pokémon Gym Battle, respectively. Meanwhile, in the Hoenn region, Team Aqua and Team Magma set their evil plot in motion. As a result, Legendary Pokémon Groudon and Kyogre are awakened and inflict catastrophic climate changes on Hoenn. In the end, thanks to Ruby and Sapphire's heroic efforts, the two legendary Pokémon go back into hibernation.

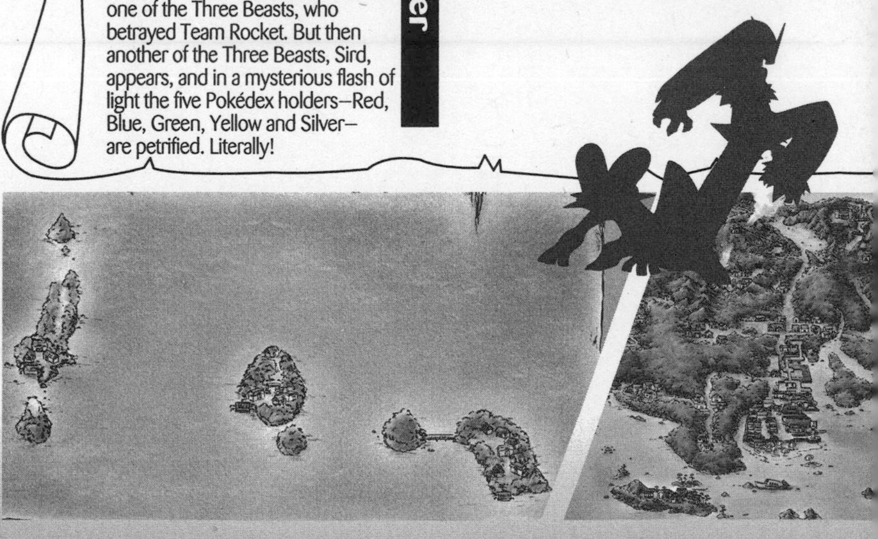

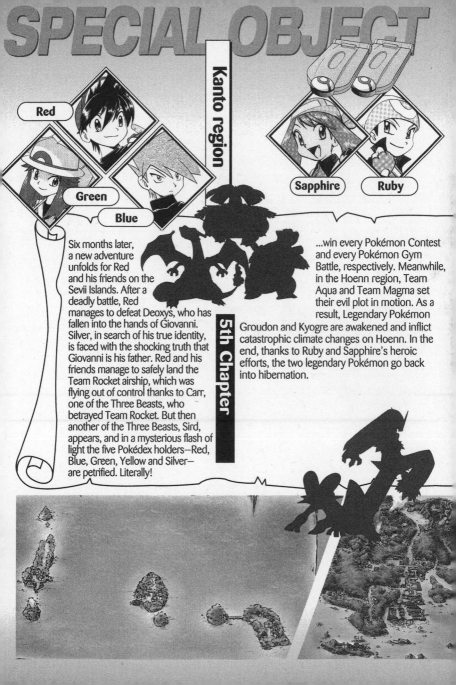

POKÉMON ADVENTURES EMERALD

VOLUME TWENTY-NINE 29

CONTENTS

POKÉMON

Hoenn region

Emerald

6th Chapter

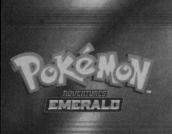

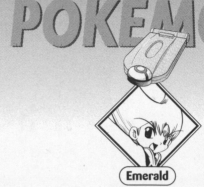

A few months later, a young Trainer named Emerald crashes the press opening of a new Pokémon facility, the Battle Frontier, and challenges the facility's Frontier Brains. Emerald has just seven days to defeat them all! Simultaneously, Emerald must capture and protect Jirachi, the Wish Pokémon, who can grant any wish and awakens every thousand years for only seven days—in this case, the same seven as Emerald's challenge. But Jirachi falls into the hands of the enemy, armor-clad "Guile"—who is actually Archie, the former leader of Team Aqua. Can Emerald stop Archie before he wishes his diabolical ambitions into reality...?!

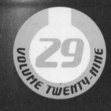

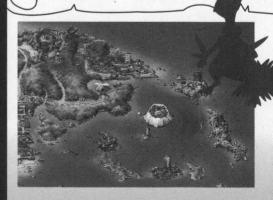

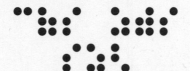

The Final Battle I

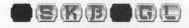

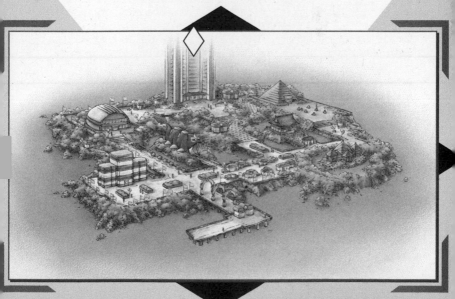

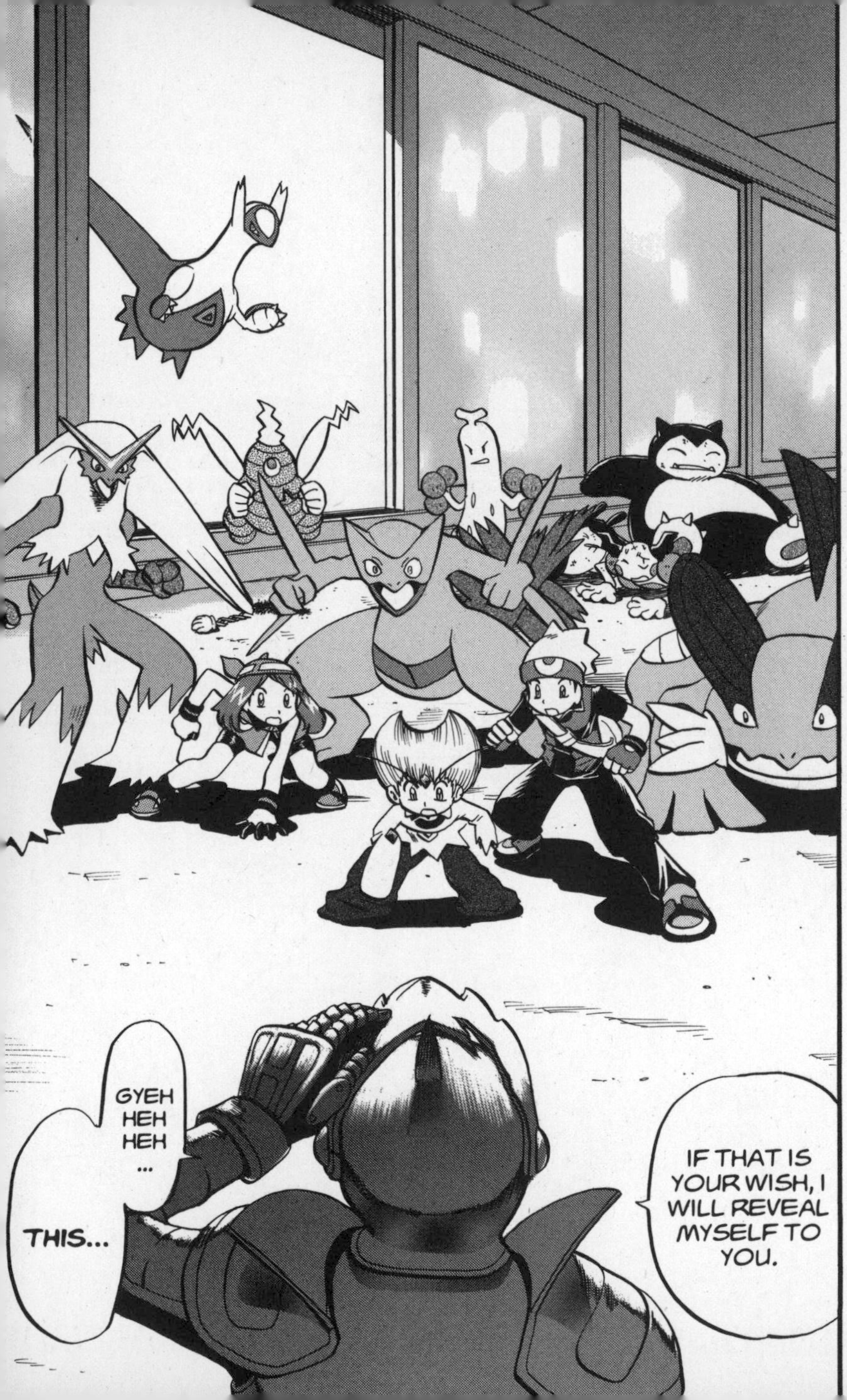
IF THAT IS YOUR WISH, I WILL REVEAL MYSELF TO YOU.
GYEH HEH HEH ...
THIS...

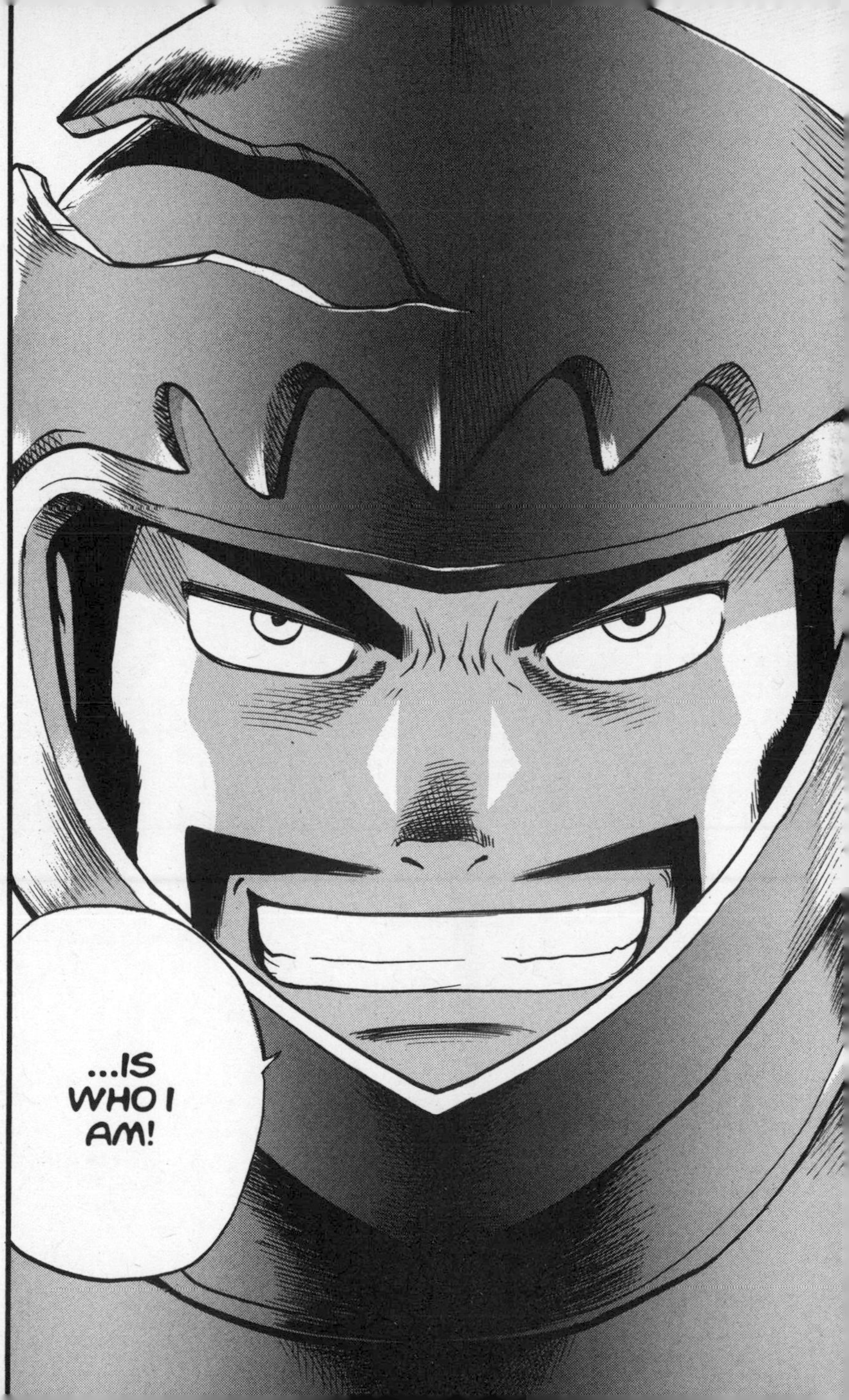
...IS WHO I AM!

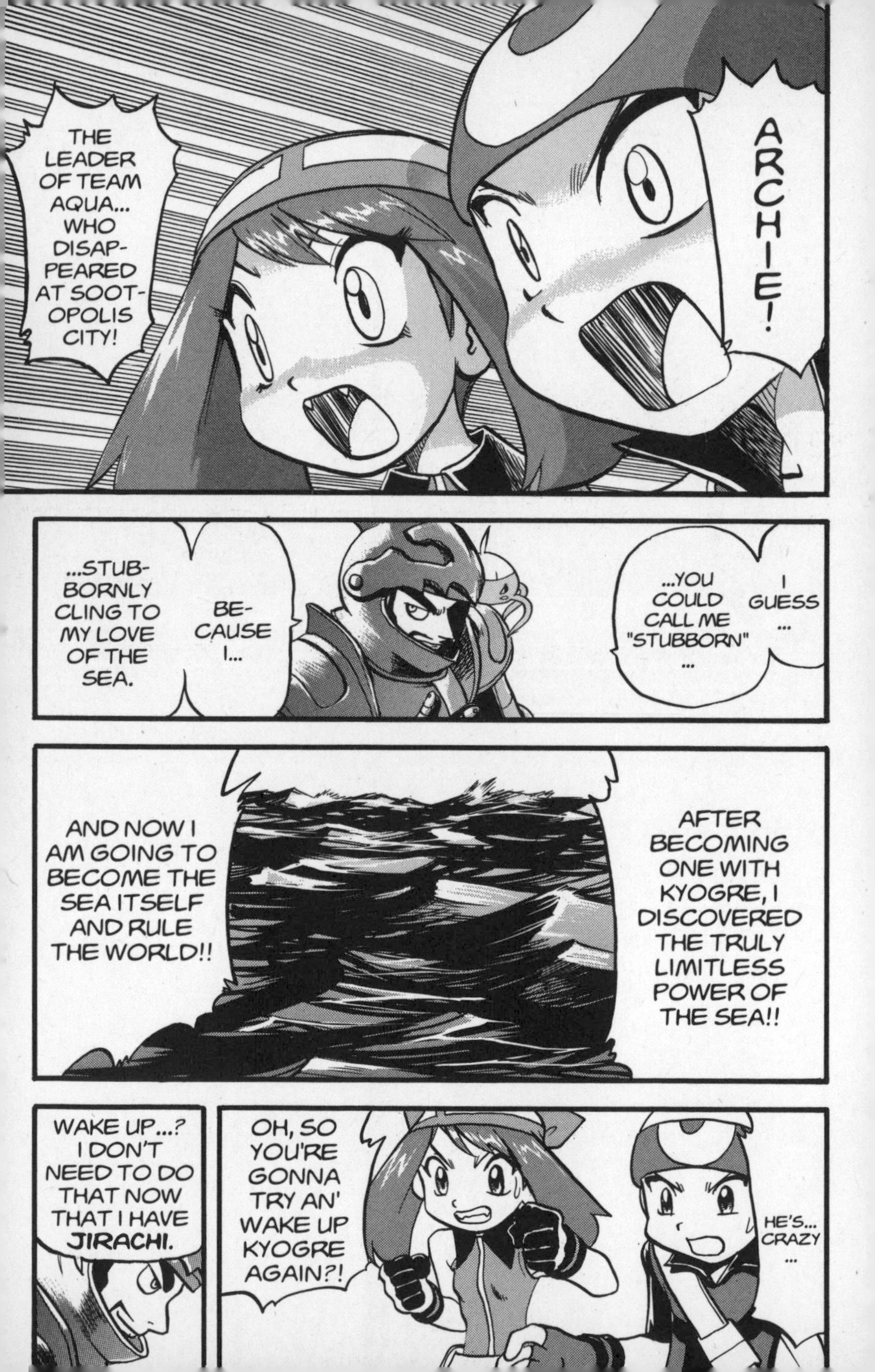
ARCHIE!
THE LEADER OF TEAM AQUA... WHO DISAPPEARED AT SOOTOPOLIS CITY!
I GUESS ...
...YOU COULD CALL ME "STUBBORN" ...
BECAUSE I...
...STUBBORNLY CLING TO MY LOVE OF THE SEA.
AFTER BECOMING ONE WITH KYOGRE, I DISCOVERED THE TRULY LIMITLESS POWER OF THE SEA!!
AND NOW I AM GOING TO BECOME THE SEA ITSELF AND RULE THE WORLD!!
HE'S... CRAZY ...
OH, SO YOU'RE GONNA TRY AN' WAKE UP KYOGRE AGAIN?!
WAKE UP...? I DON'T NEED TO DO THAT NOW THAT I HAVE **JIRACHI**.

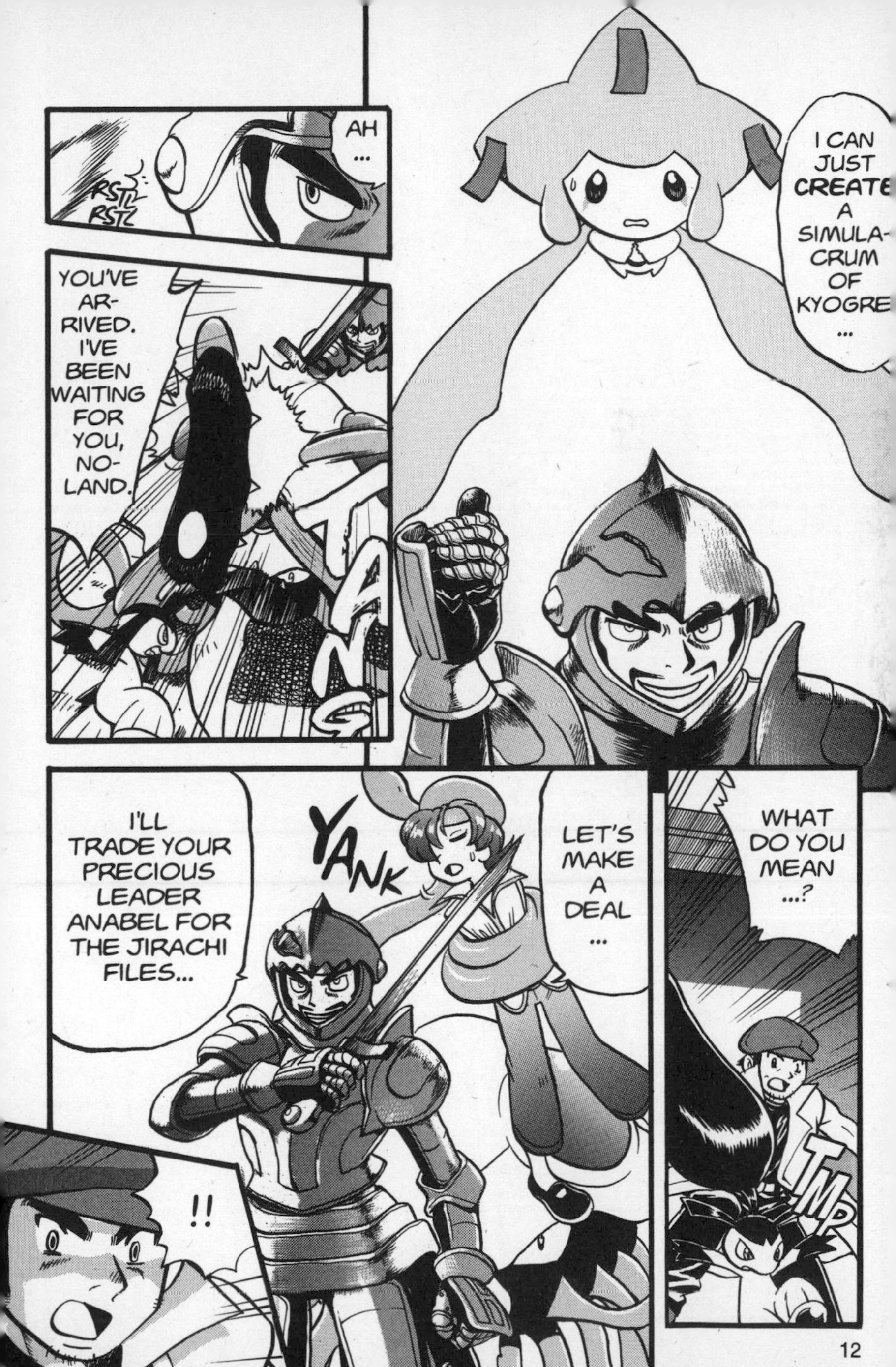
I CAN JUST CREATE A SIMULACRUM OF KYOGRE ...
AH ...
RSTL RSTL
YOU'VE ARRIVED. I'VE BEEN WAITING FOR YOU, NOLAND.
WHAT DO YOU MEAN ...?
TMP
LET'S MAKE A DEAL ...
YANK
I'LL TRADE YOUR PRECIOUS LEADER ANABEL FOR THE JIRACHI FILES...
!!

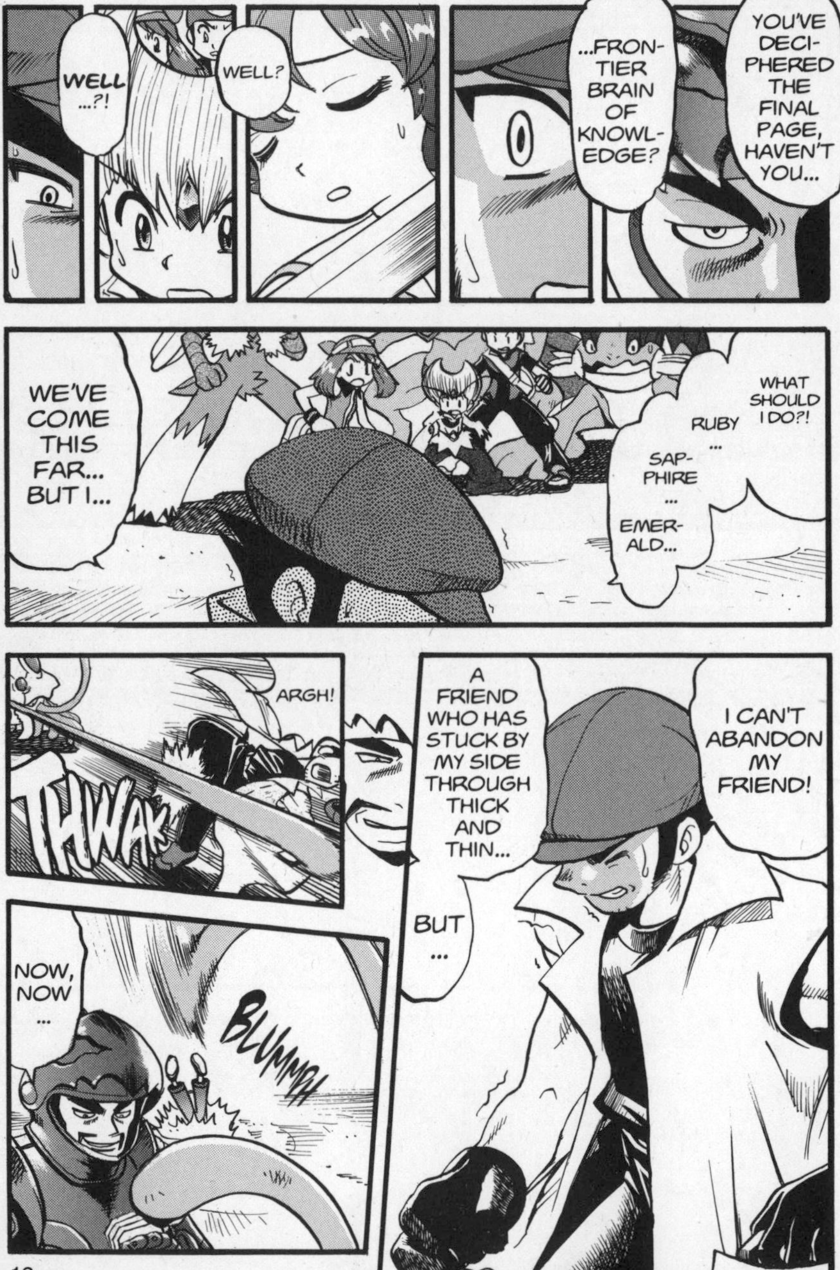
YOU'VE DECIPHERED THE FINAL PAGE, HAVEN'T YOU...
...FRONTIER BRAIN OF KNOWLEDGE?
WELL?
WELL ...?!
WHAT SHOULD I DO?!
RUBY ...
SAPPHIRE ...
EMERALD...
WE'VE COME THIS FAR... BUT I...
I CAN'T ABANDON MY FRIEND!
A FRIEND WHO HAS STUCK BY MY SIDE THROUGH THICK AND THIN...
BUT ...
ARGH!
THWAK
NOW, NOW ...
BLUMMPH

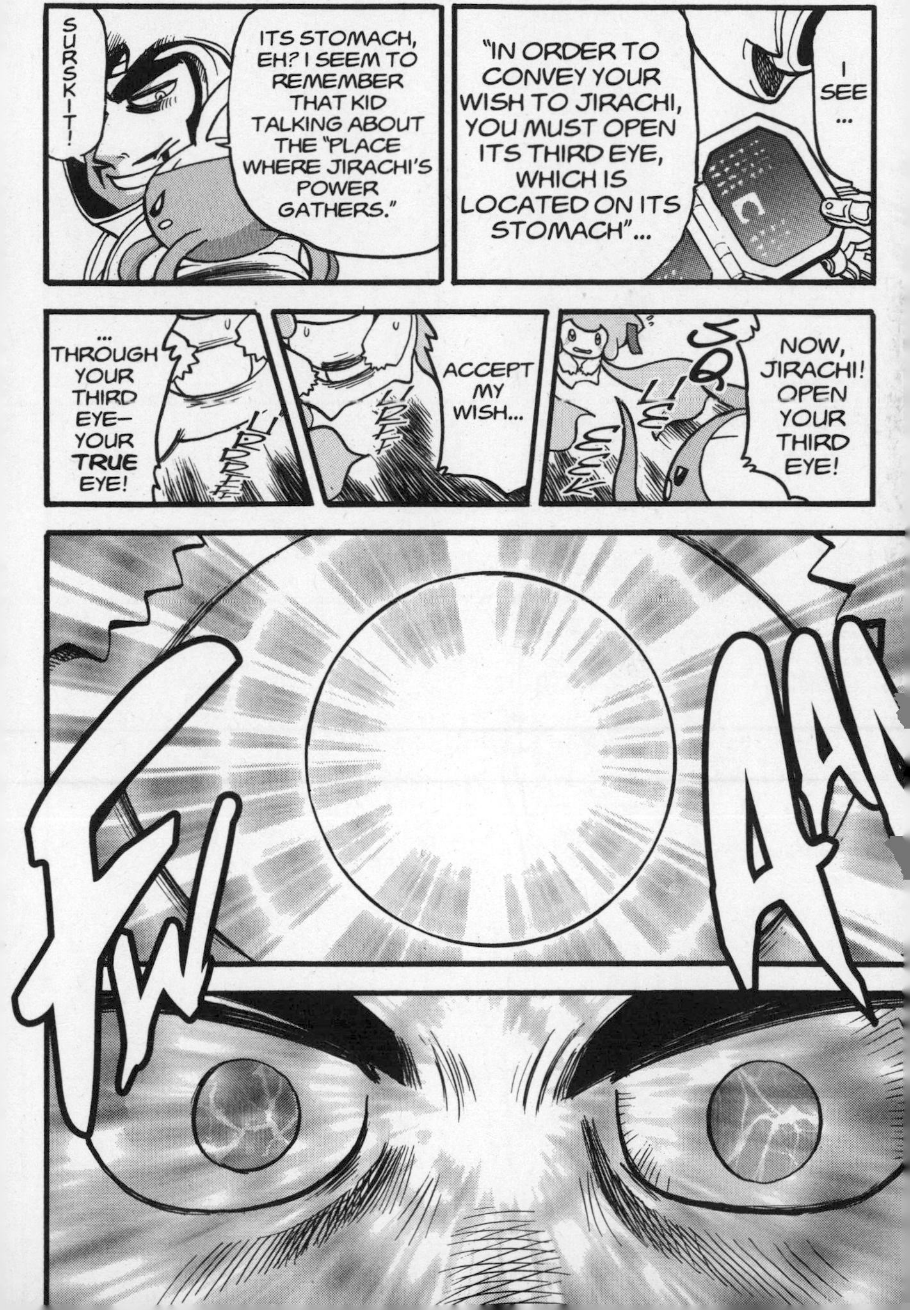
I SEE...
"IN ORDER TO CONVEY YOUR WISH TO JIRACHI, YOU MUST OPEN ITS THIRD EYE, WHICH IS LOCATED ON ITS STOMACH"...
ITS STOMACH, EH? I SEEM TO REMEMBER THAT KID TALKING ABOUT THE "PLACE WHERE JIRACHI'S POWER GATHERS."
SURSKIT!
NOW, JIRACHI! OPEN YOUR THIRD EYE!
ACCEPT MY WISH...
...THROUGH YOUR THIRD EYE—YOUR **TRUE** EYE!

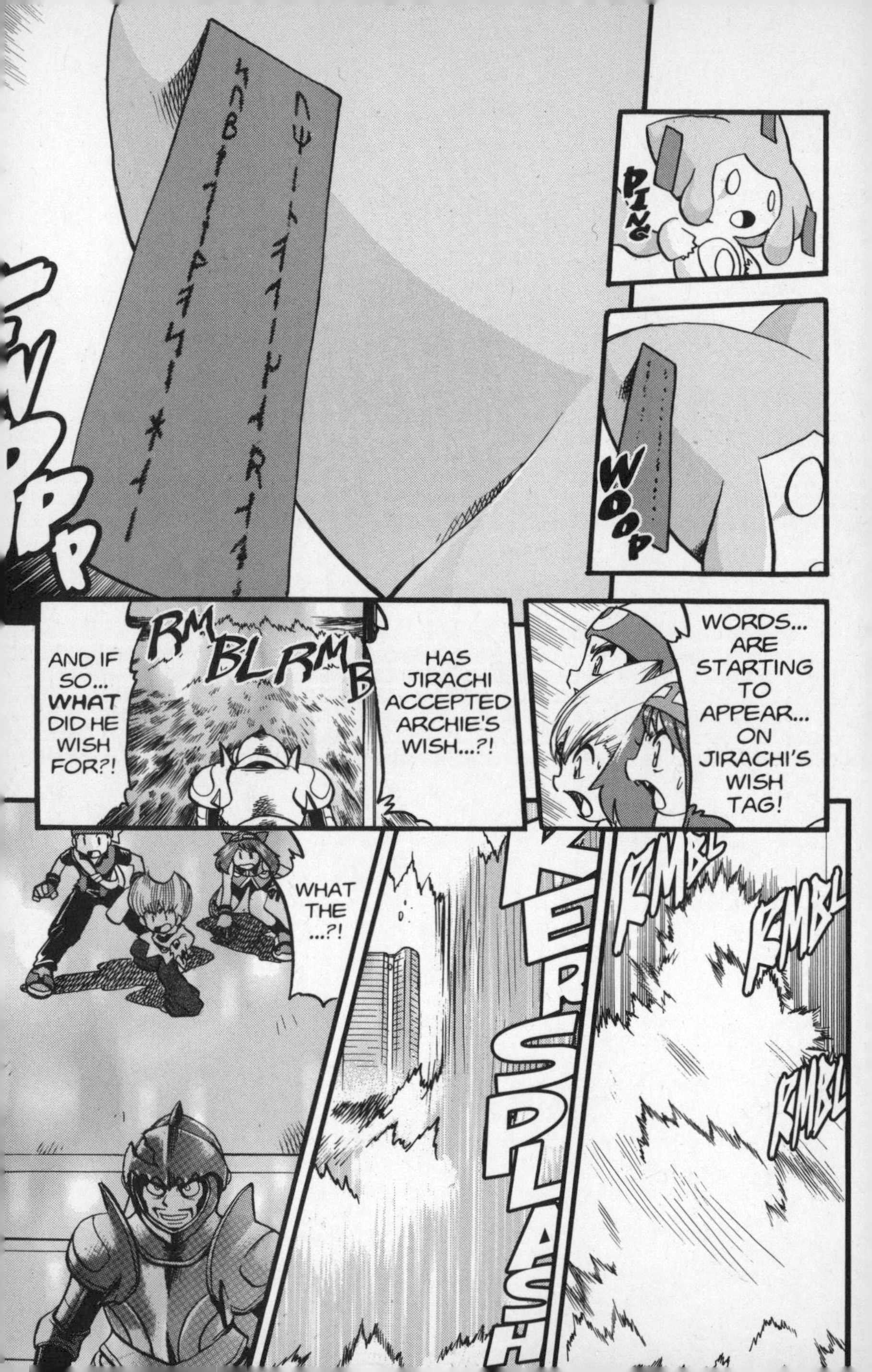
PING
WOOOP
WORDS... ARE STARTING TO APPEAR... ON JIRACHI'S WISH TAG!
HAS JIRACHI ACCEPTED ARCHIE'S WISH...?!
RM BLRM B
AND IF SO... WHAT DID HE WISH FOR?!
RMBL
RMBL
RMBL
KERSPLASH
WHAT THE ...?!

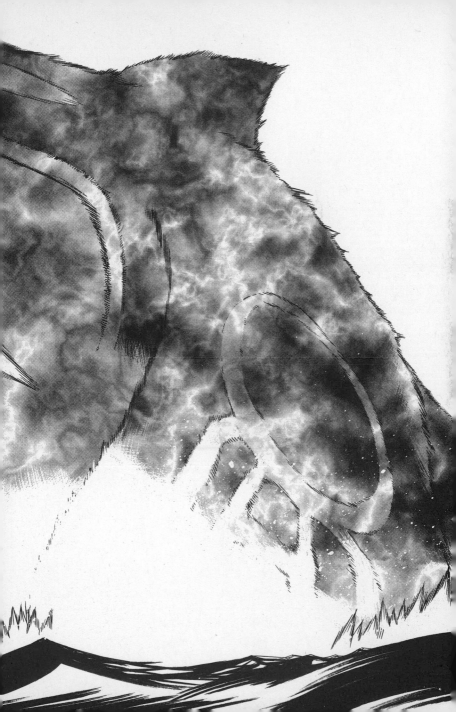

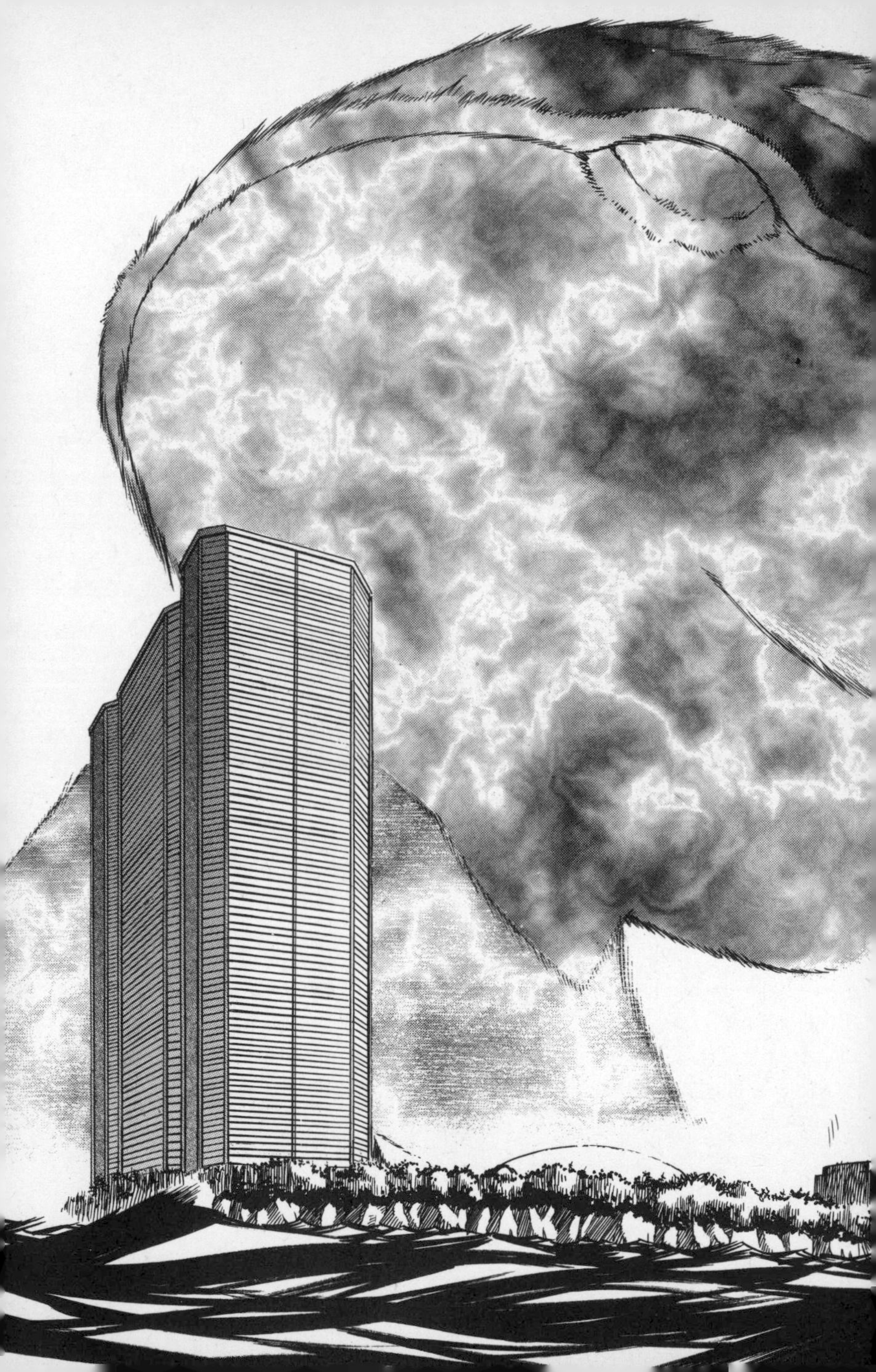

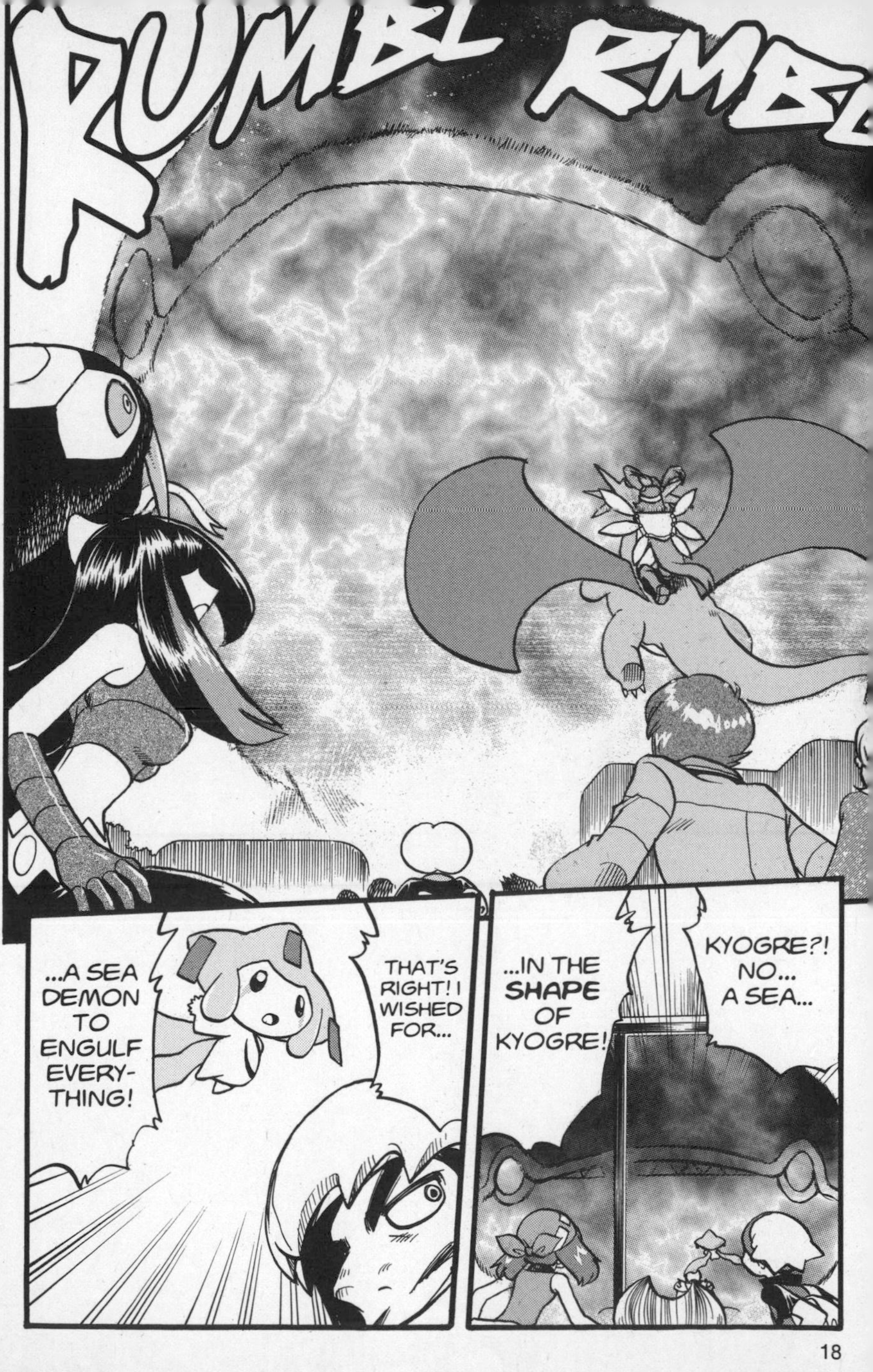
RUMBL RMBL
KYOGRE?! NO... A SEA...
...IN THE SHAPE OF KYOGRE!
THAT'S RIGHT! I WISHED FOR...
...A SEA DEMON TO ENGULF EVERY-THING!

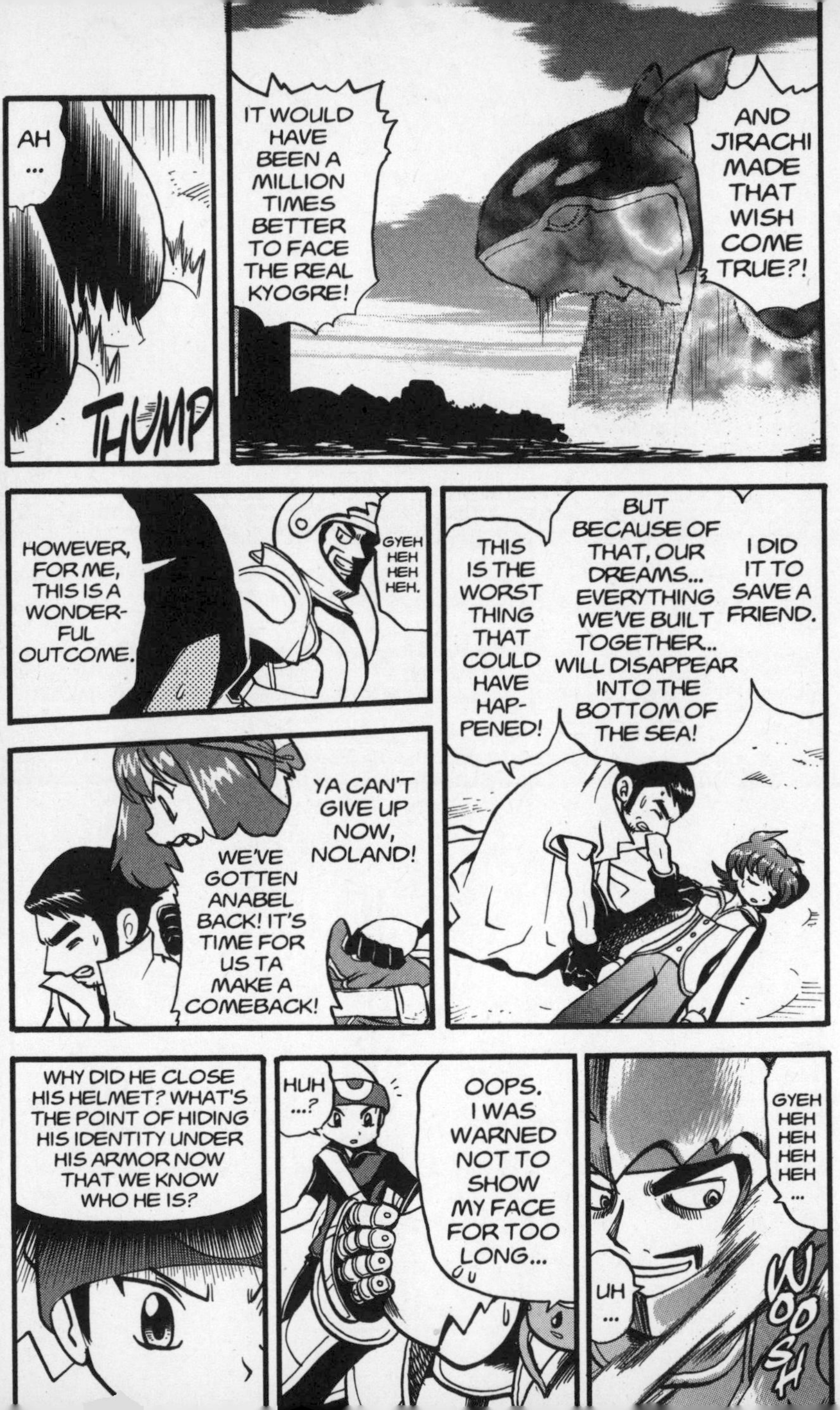
AND JIRACHI MADE THAT WISH COME TRUE?!
IT WOULD HAVE BEEN A MILLION TIMES BETTER TO FACE THE REAL KYOGRE!
AH ...
THUMP
I DID IT TO SAVE A FRIEND.
BUT BECAUSE OF THAT, OUR DREAMS... EVERYTHING WE'VE BUILT TOGETHER... WILL DISAPPEAR INTO THE BOTTOM OF THE SEA!
THIS IS THE WORST THING THAT COULD HAVE HAP-PENED!
GYEH HEH HEH HEH.
HOWEVER, FOR ME, THIS IS A WONDER-FUL OUTCOME.
YA CAN'T GIVE UP NOW, NOLAND!
WE'VE GOTTEN ANABEL BACK! IT'S TIME FOR US TA MAKE A COMEBACK!
GYEH HEH HEH HEH HEH ...
UH ...
WOOSH
OOPS. I WAS WARNED NOT TO SHOW MY FACE FOR TOO LONG...
HUH ...?
WHY DID HE CLOSE HIS HELMET? WHAT'S THE POINT OF HIDING HIS IDENTITY UNDER HIS ARMOR NOW THAT WE KNOW WHO HE IS?

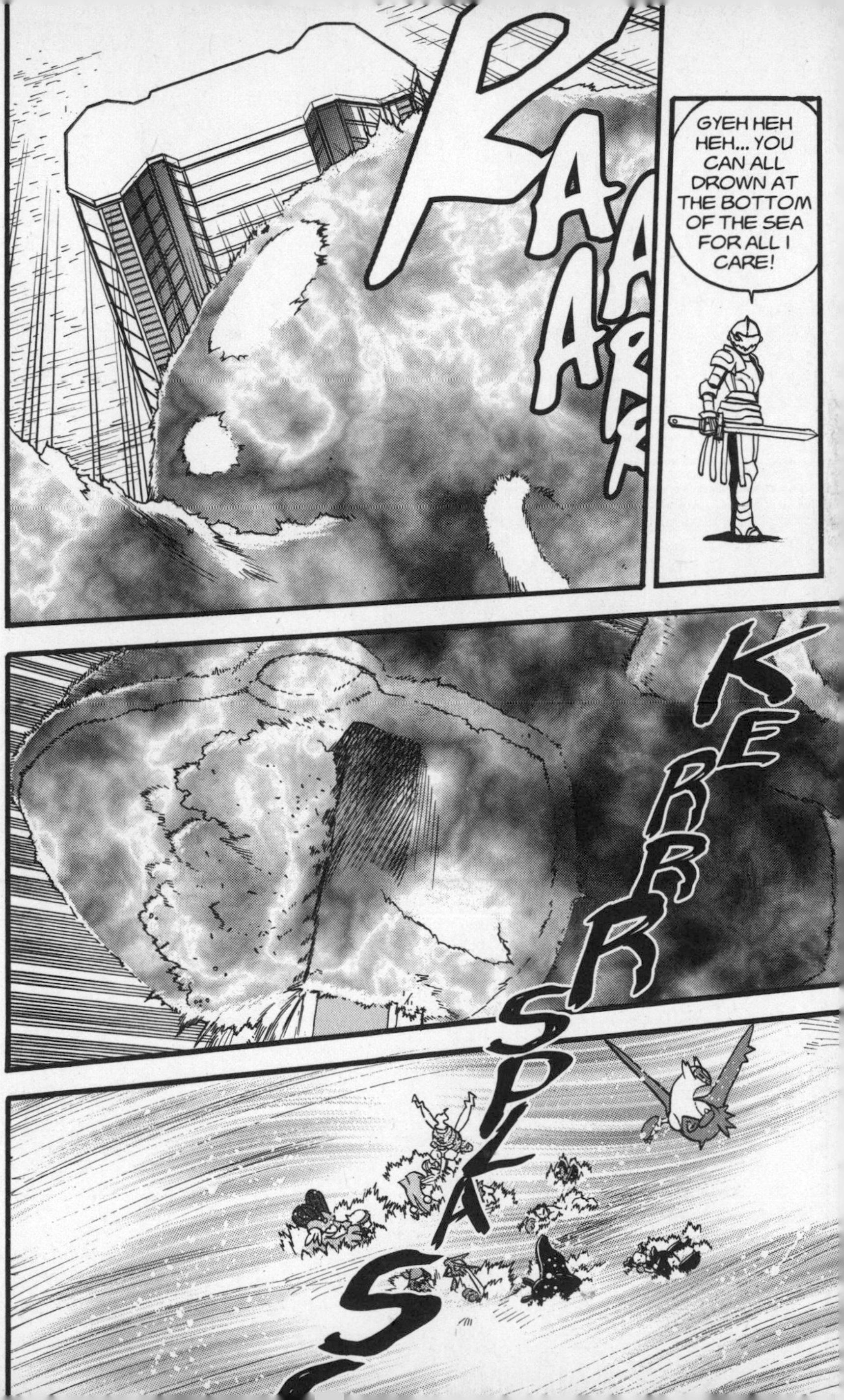
GYEH HEH HEH... YOU CAN ALL DROWN AT THE BOTTOM OF THE SEA FOR ALL I CARE!
KERRRR
SPLAS

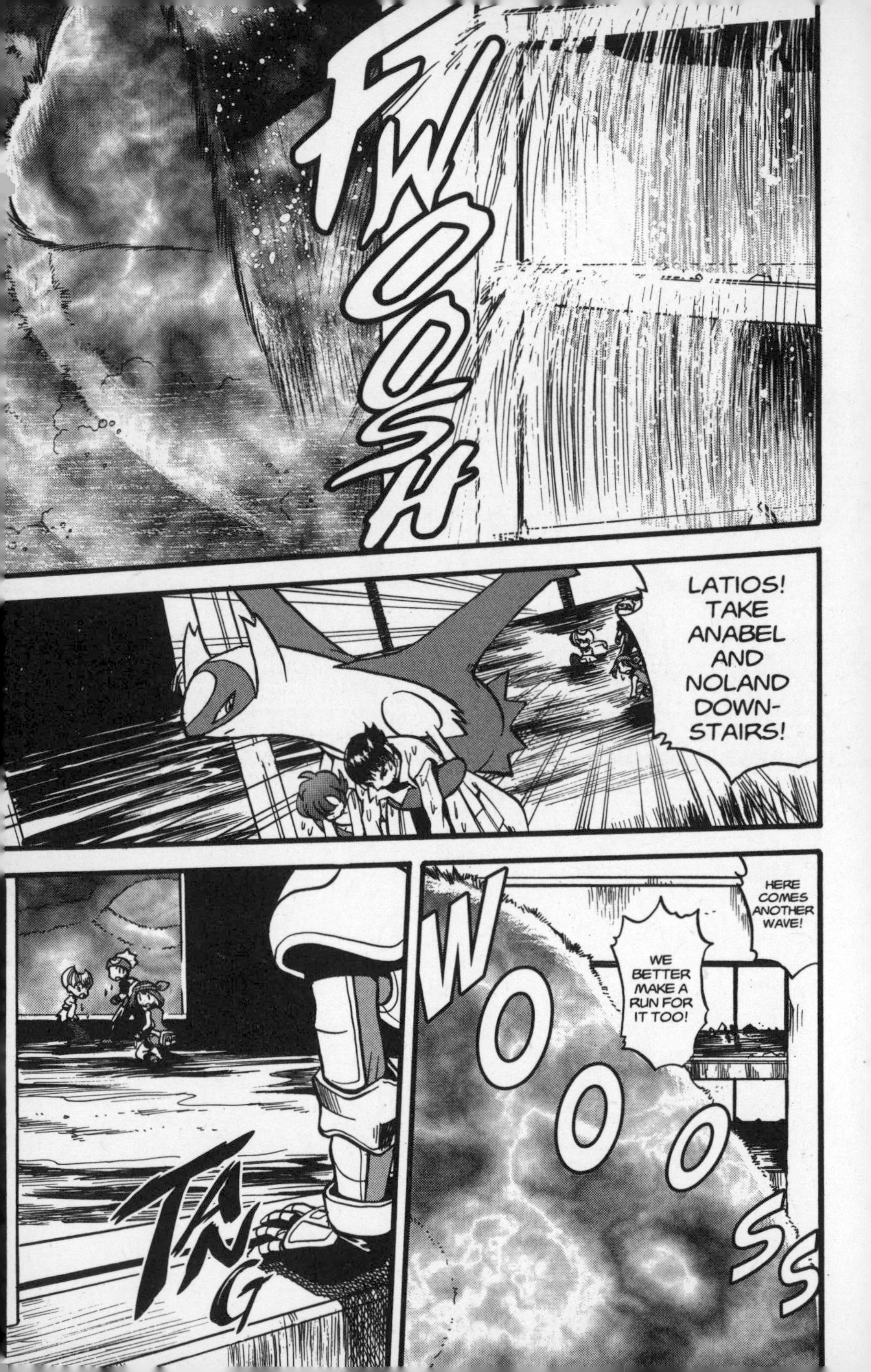
FWOOOSH
LATIOS! TAKE ANABEL AND NOLAND DOWN-STAIRS!
HERE COMES ANOTHER WAVE!
WE BETTER MAKE A RUN FOR IT TOO!
WOOOOSS
TANG

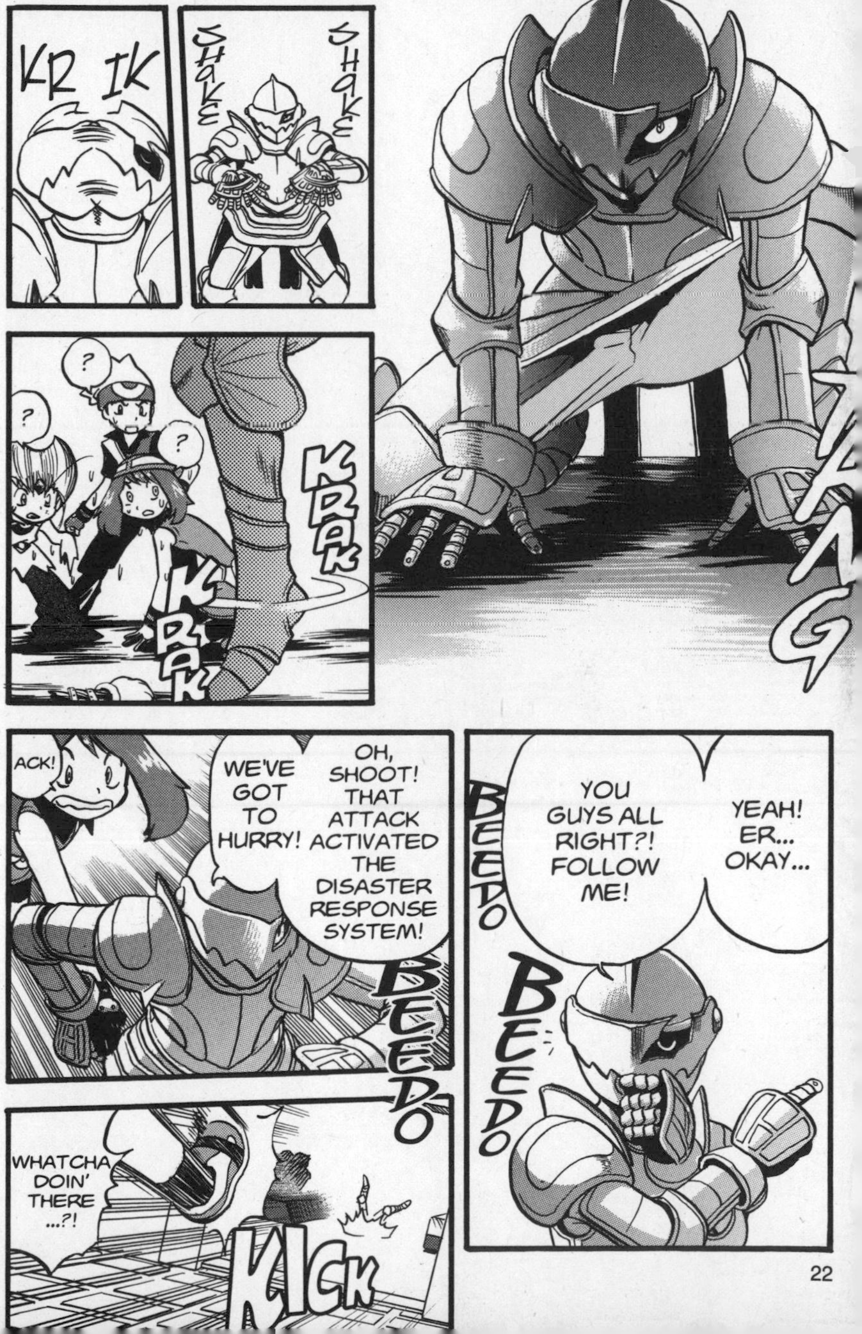
SHAKE SHAKE
KR IK
KRAK
KRAK
YOU GUYS ALL RIGHT?! FOLLOW ME!
YEAH! ER... OKAY...
BEEDO
BEEDO
BEEDO
OH, SHOOT! THAT ATTACK ACTIVATED THE DISASTER RESPONSE SYSTEM!
WE'VE GOT TO HURRY!
ACK!
WHATCHA DOIN' THERE ...?!
KICK

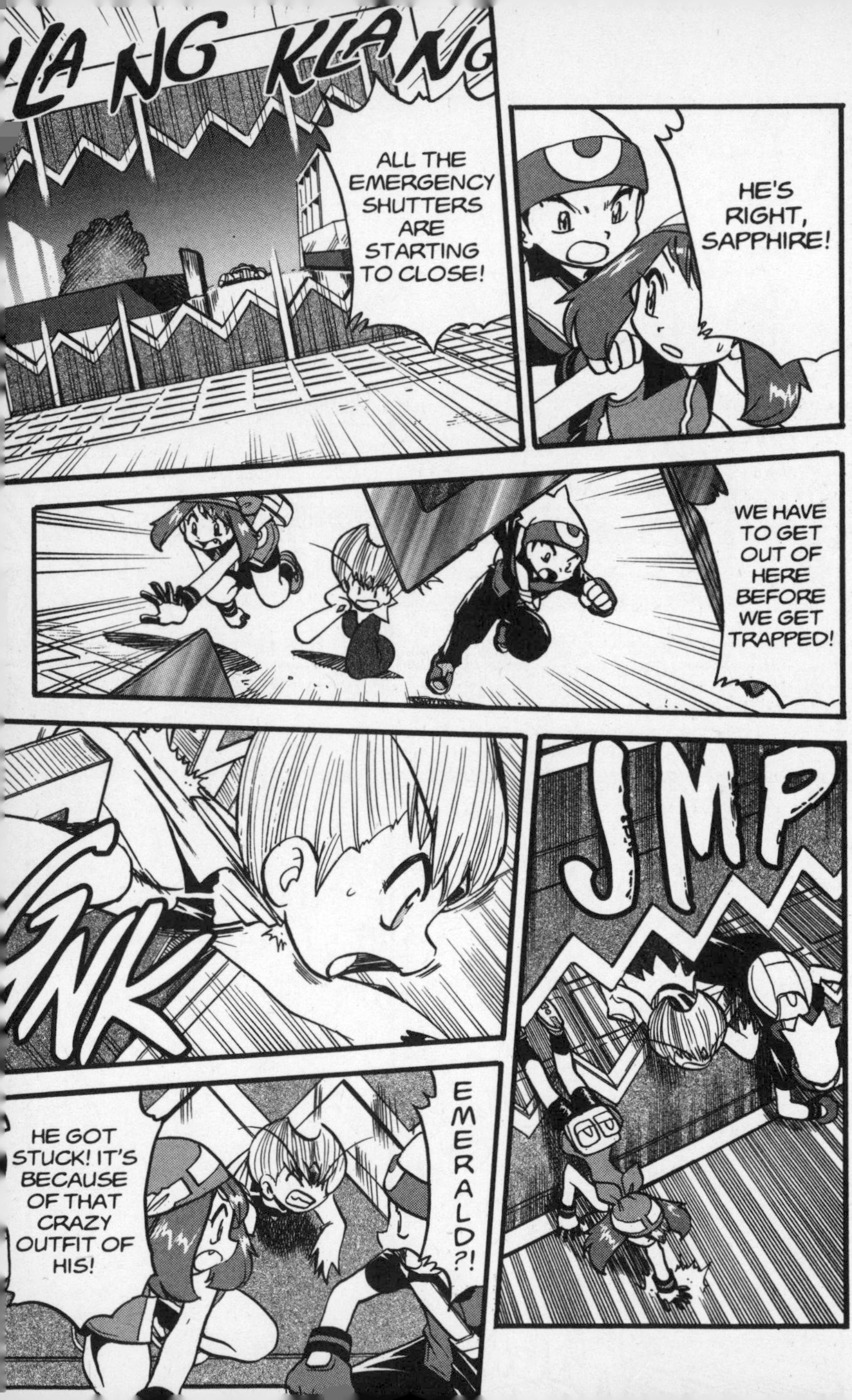
HE'S RIGHT, SAPPHIRE!
LANG KLANG
ALL THE EMERGENCY SHUTTERS ARE STARTING TO CLOSE!
WE HAVE TO GET OUT OF HERE BEFORE WE GET TRAPPED!
JMP
NK
EMERALD?!
HE GOT STUCK! IT'S BECAUSE OF THAT CRAZY OUTFIT OF HIS!

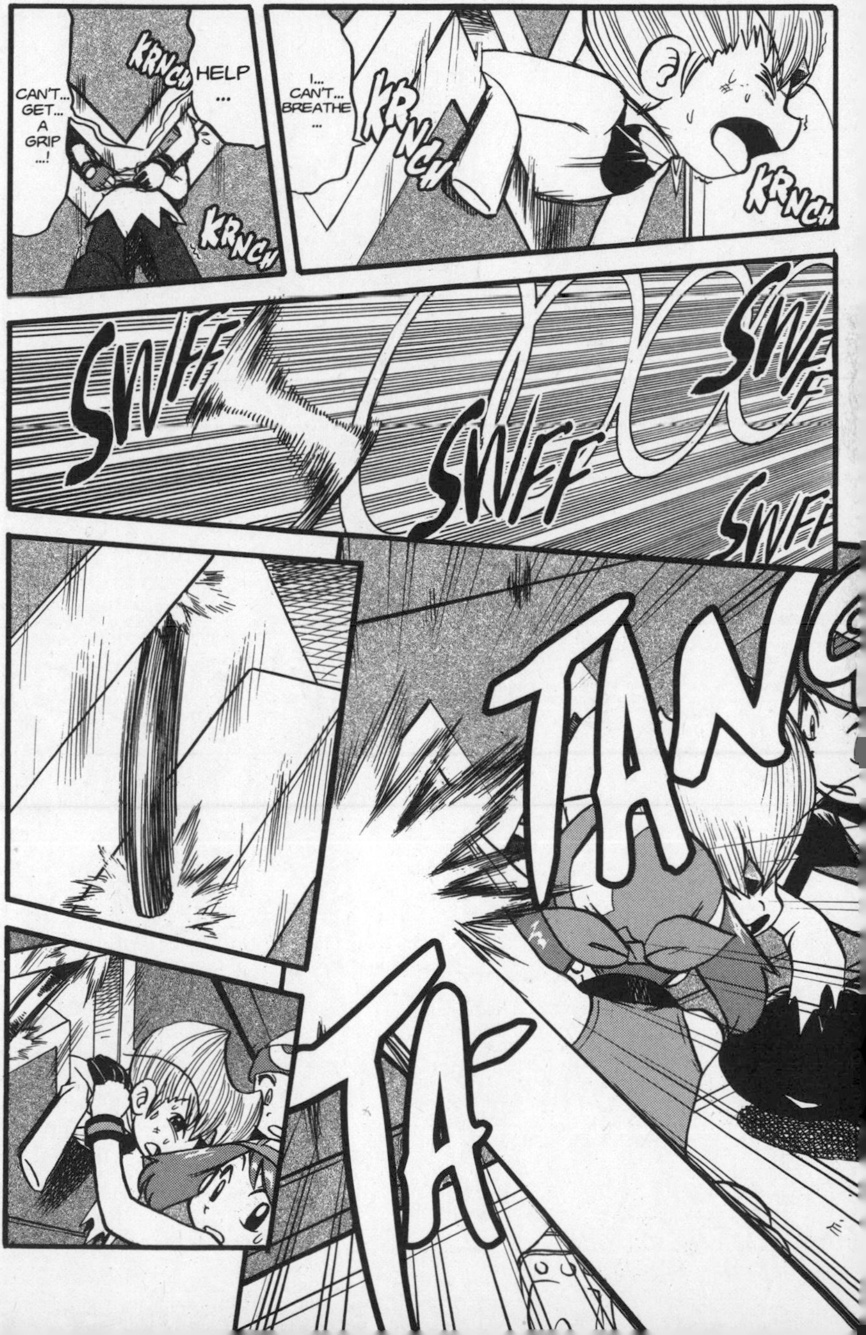
KRNCH
I... CAN'T... BREATHE...
KRNCH
KRNCH
HELP...
CAN'T... GET... A GRIP...!
KRNCH
SWFF
SWFF
SWFF
SWFF
TAN
TA

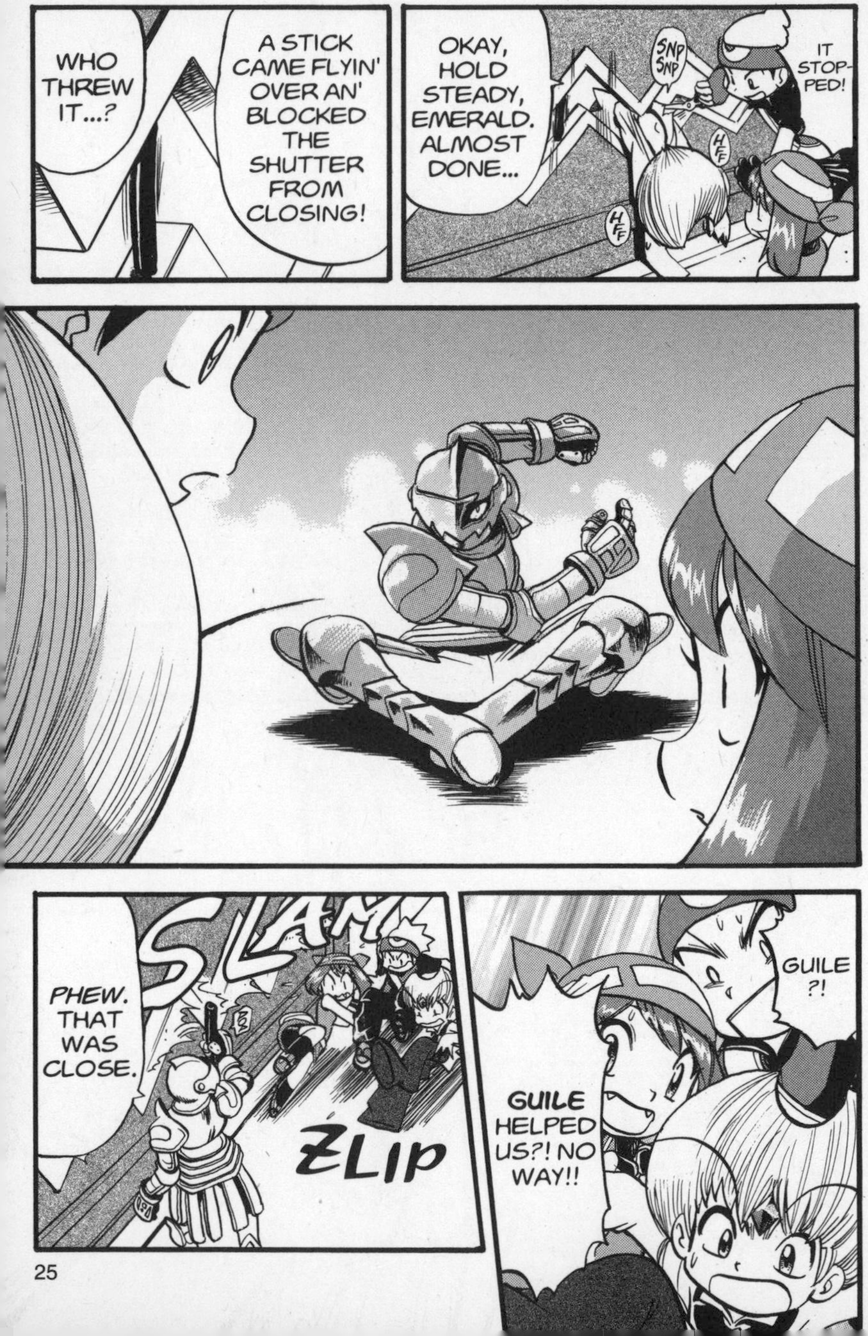
IT STOP-PED!
SNP SNP
OKAY, HOLD STEADY, EMERALD. ALMOST DONE...
HFF
HFF
A STICK CAME FLYIN' OVER AN' BLOCKED THE SHUTTER FROM CLOSING!
WHO THREW IT...?
GUILE ?!
GUILE HELPED US?! NO WAY!!
SLAM
PHEW. THAT WAS CLOSE.
ZLIP

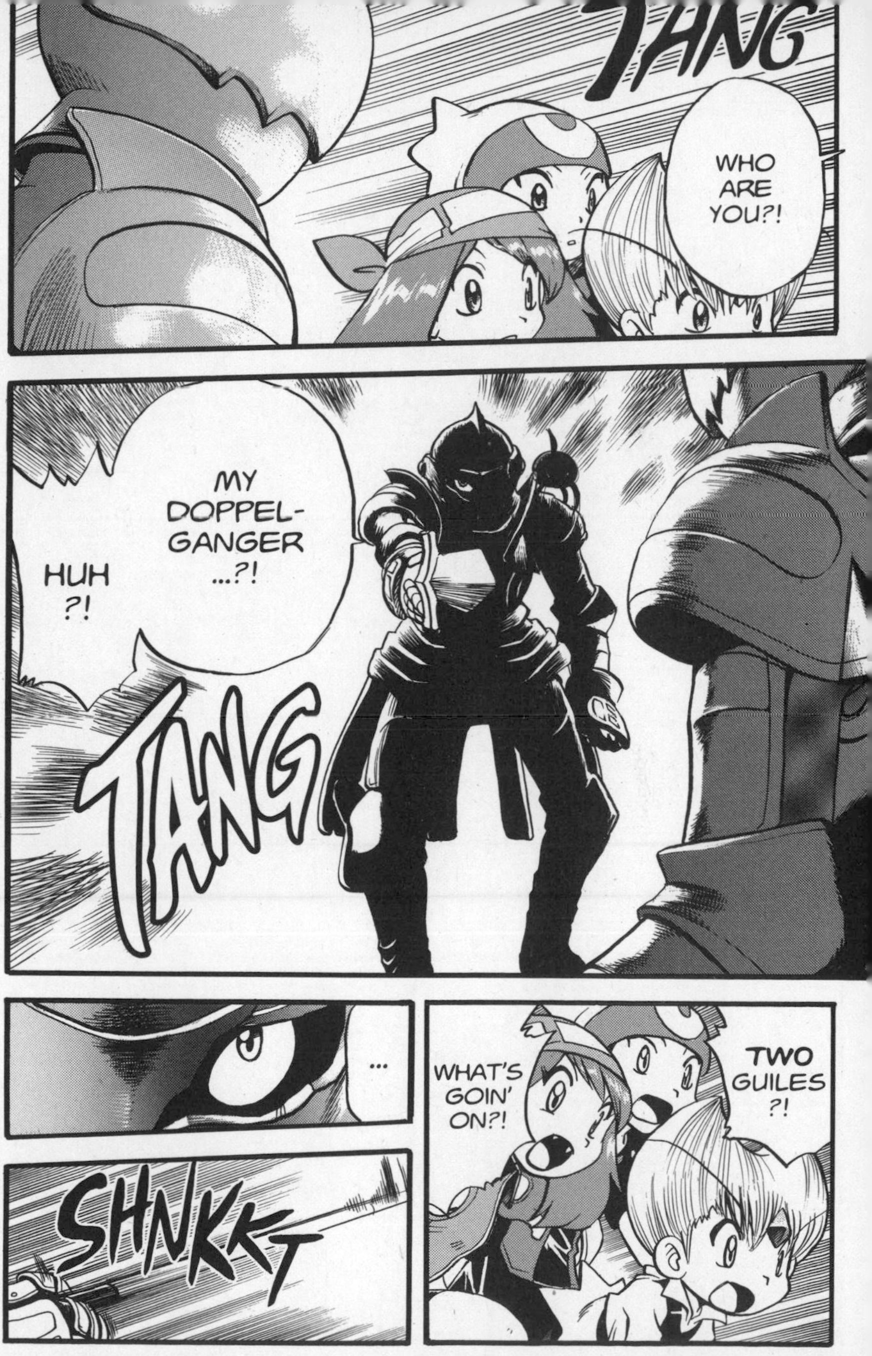
TANG
WHO ARE YOU?!
MY DOPPEL-GANGER ...?!
HUH ?!
TANG
TWO GUILES ?!
WHAT'S GOIN' ON?!
...
SHNKKT

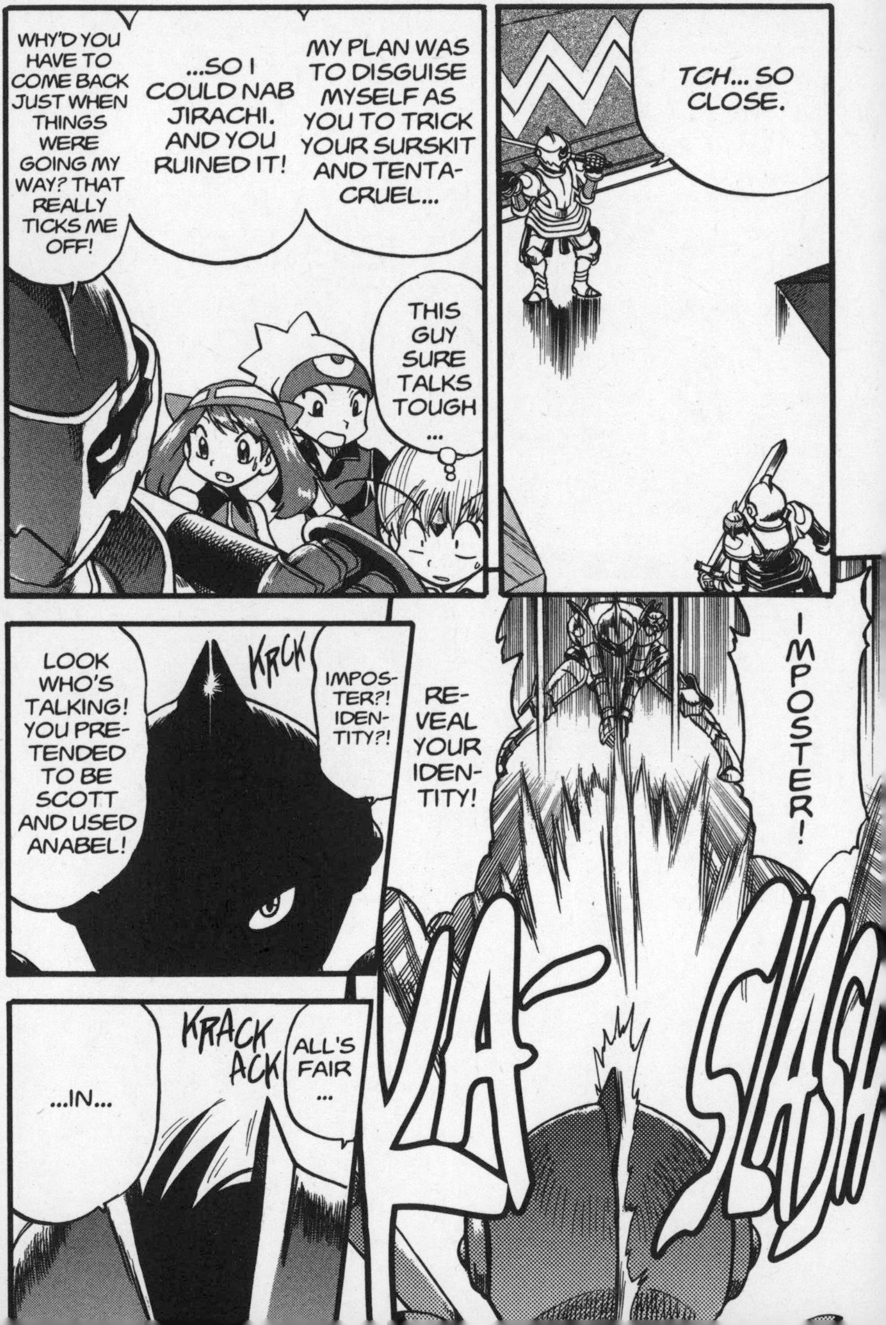
TCH... SO CLOSE.
MY PLAN WAS TO DISGUISE MYSELF AS YOU TO TRICK YOUR SURSKIT AND TENTA-CRUEL...
...SO I COULD NAB JIRACHI. AND YOU RUINED IT!
WHY'D YOU HAVE TO COME BACK JUST WHEN THINGS WERE GOING MY WAY? THAT REALLY TICKS ME OFF!
THIS GUY SURE TALKS TOUGH ...
IMPOSTER!
KA-
SLASH
REVEAL YOUR IDENTITY!
KRCK
IMPOSTER?! IDENTITY?!
LOOK WHO'S TALKING! YOU PRETENDED TO BE SCOTT AND USED ANABEL!
KRACK ACK
ALL'S FAIR ...
...IN...

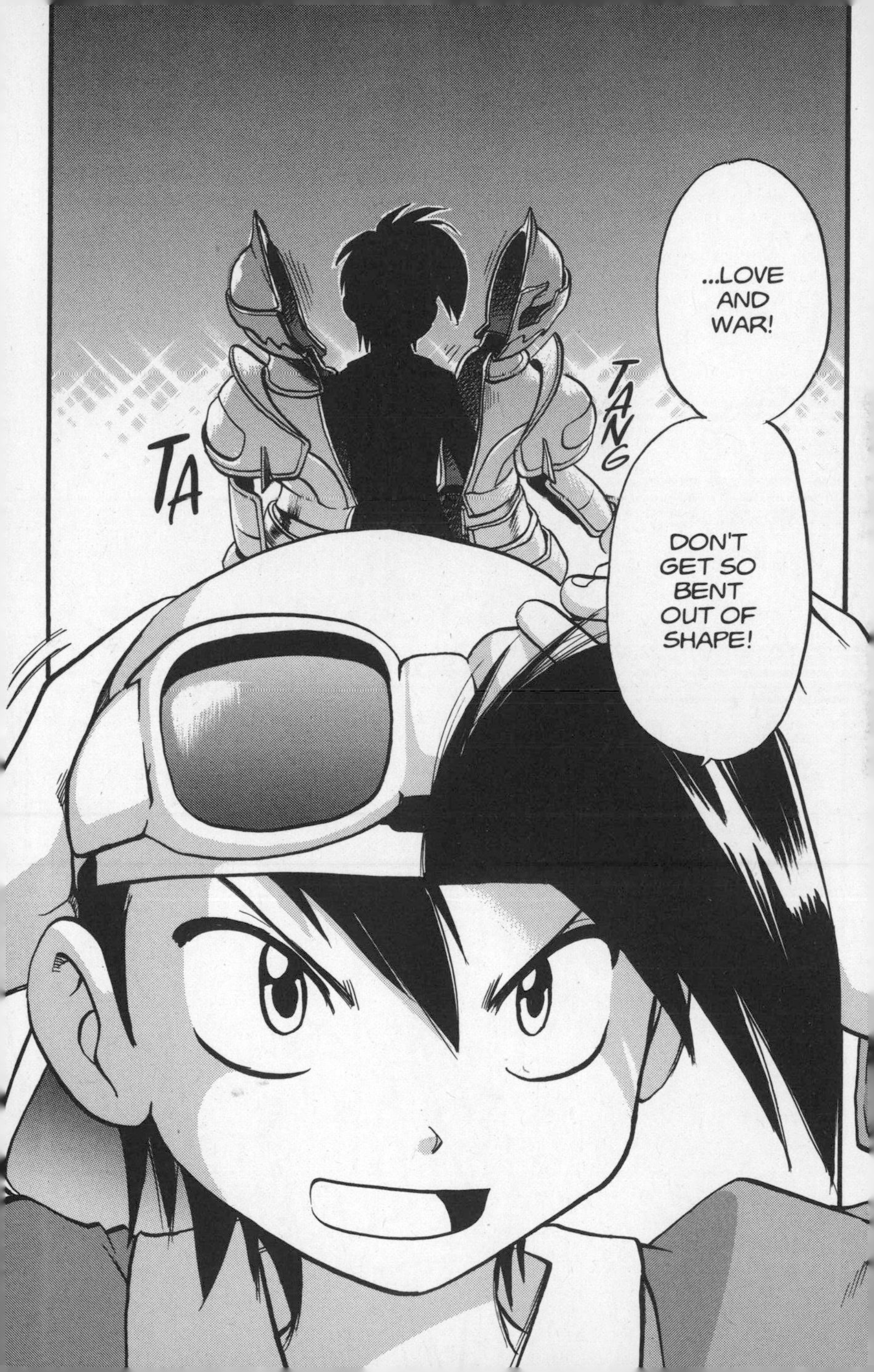

...LOVE AND WAR!
TANG
TA
DON'T GET SO BENT OUT OF SHAPE!

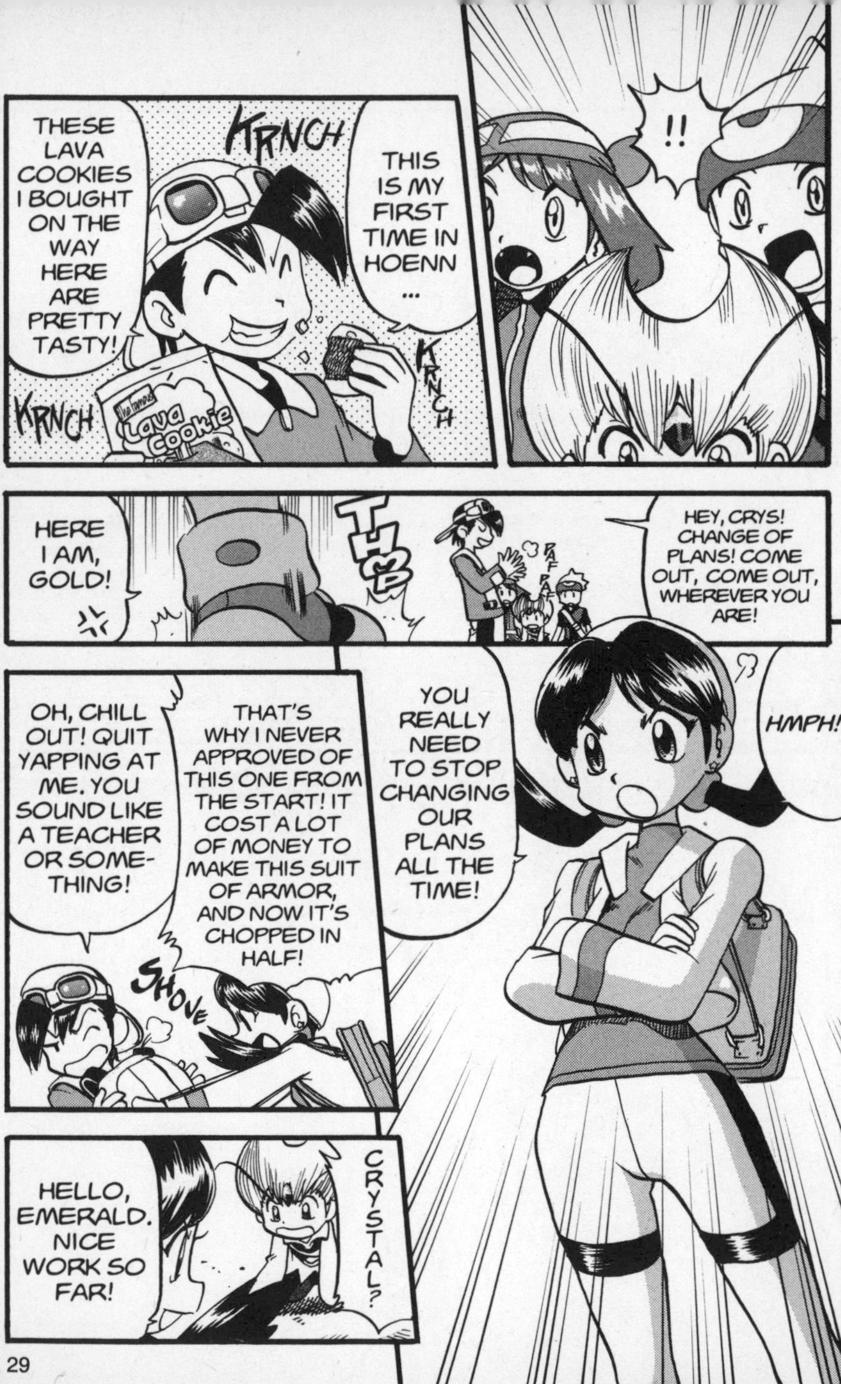
!!
THIS IS MY FIRST TIME IN HOENN ...
KRNCH
KRNCH
THESE LAVA COOKIES I BOUGHT ON THE WAY HERE ARE PRETTY TASTY!
The Famous Lava Cookie
KRNCH
HEY, CRYS! CHANGE OF PLANS! COME OUT, COME OUT, WHEREVER YOU ARE!
PAF PAF
THWP
HERE I AM, GOLD!
HMPH!
YOU REALLY NEED TO STOP CHANGING OUR PLANS ALL THE TIME!
THAT'S WHY I NEVER APPROVED OF THIS ONE FROM THE START! IT COST A LOT OF MONEY TO MAKE THIS SUIT OF ARMOR, AND NOW IT'S CHOPPED IN HALF!
OH, CHILL OUT! QUIT YAPPING AT ME. YOU SOUND LIKE A TEACHER OR SOME-THING!
SHOVE
CRYSTAL?
...
HELLO, EMERALD. NICE WORK SO FAR!

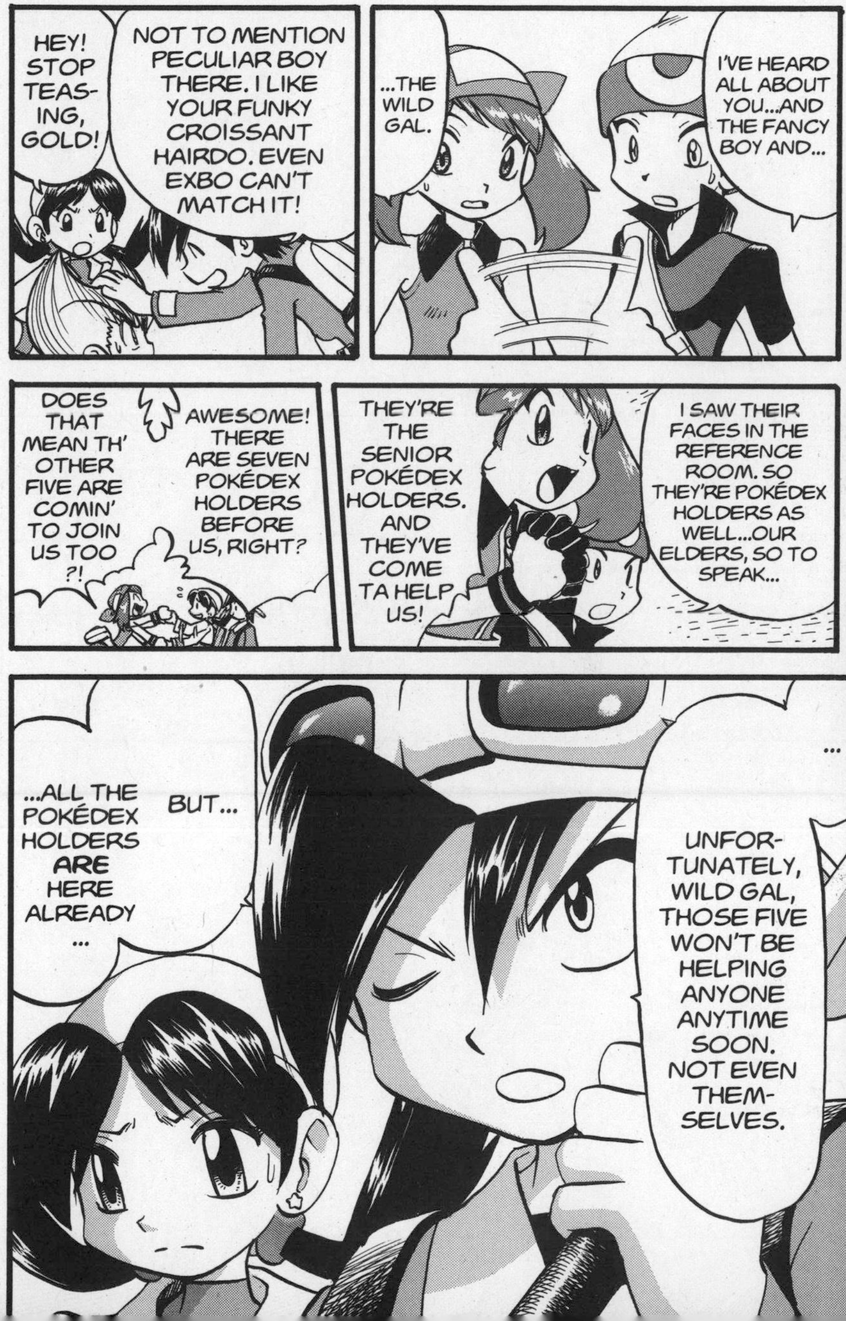
I'VE HEARD ALL ABOUT YOU...AND THE FANCY BOY AND...
...THE WILD GAL.
NOT TO MENTION PECULIAR BOY THERE. I LIKE YOUR FUNKY CROISSANT HAIRDO. EVEN EXBO CAN'T MATCH IT!
HEY! STOP TEAS-ING, GOLD!
I SAW THEIR FACES IN THE REFERENCE ROOM. SO THEY'RE POKÉDEX HOLDERS AS WELL...OUR ELDERS, SO TO SPEAK...
THEY'RE THE SENIOR POKÉDEX HOLDERS. AND THEY'VE COME TA HELP US!
AWESOME! THERE ARE SEVEN POKÉDEX HOLDERS BEFORE US, RIGHT?
DOES THAT MEAN TH' OTHER FIVE ARE COMIN' TO JOIN US TOO ?!
...
UNFOR-TUNATELY, WILD GAL, THOSE FIVE WON'T BE HELPING ANYONE ANYTIME SOON. NOT EVEN THEM-SELVES.
BUT...
...ALL THE POKÉDEX HOLDERS **ARE** HERE ALREADY ...

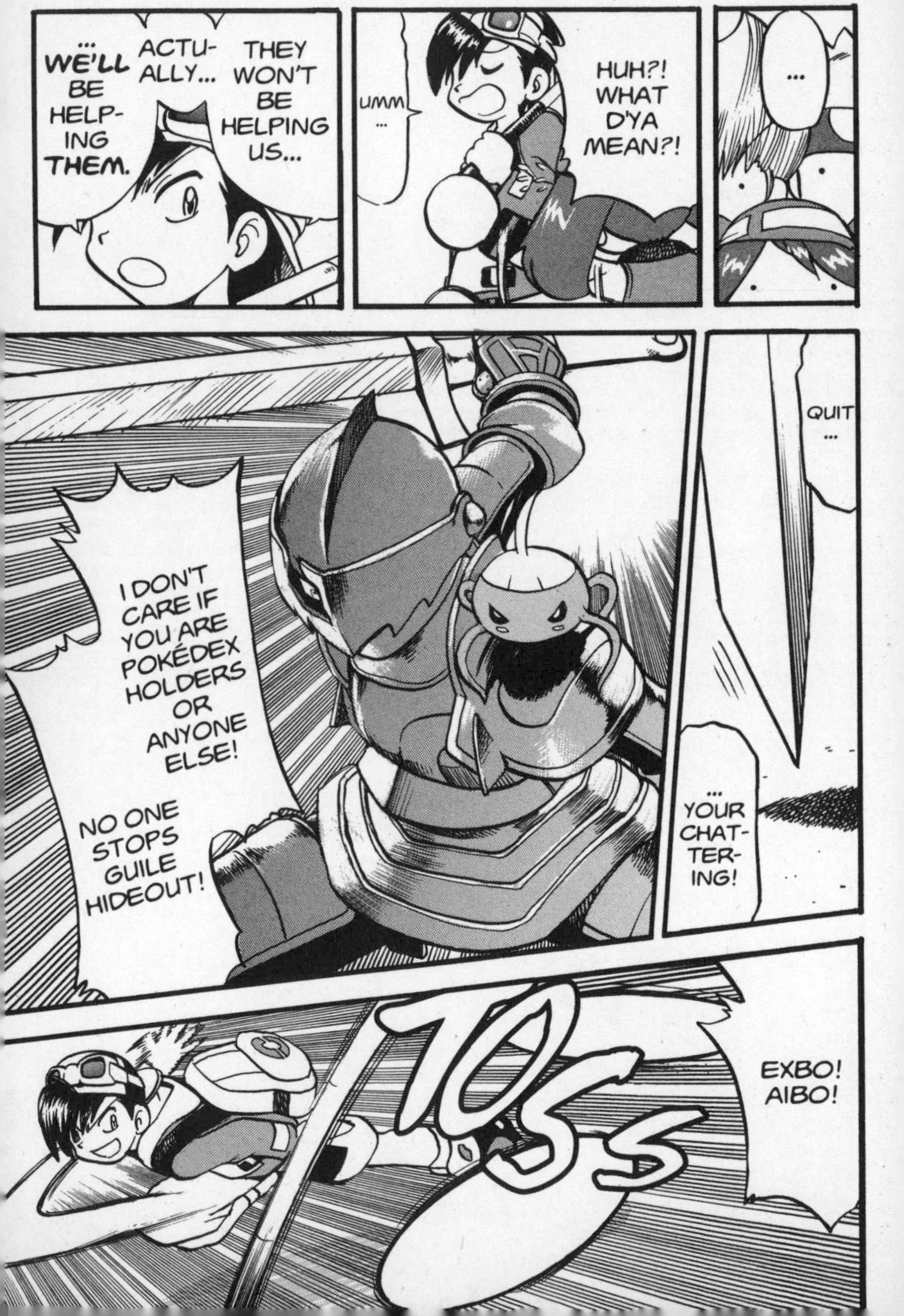
...
HUH?! WHAT D'YA MEAN?!
UMM ...
ACTUALLY...
THEY WON'T BE HELPING US...
... WE'LL BE HELPING THEM.
QUIT ...
... YOUR CHATTERING!
I DON'T CARE IF YOU ARE POKÉDEX HOLDERS OR ANYONE ELSE!
NO ONE STOPS GUILE HIDEOUT!
EXBO! AIBO!
TOSS

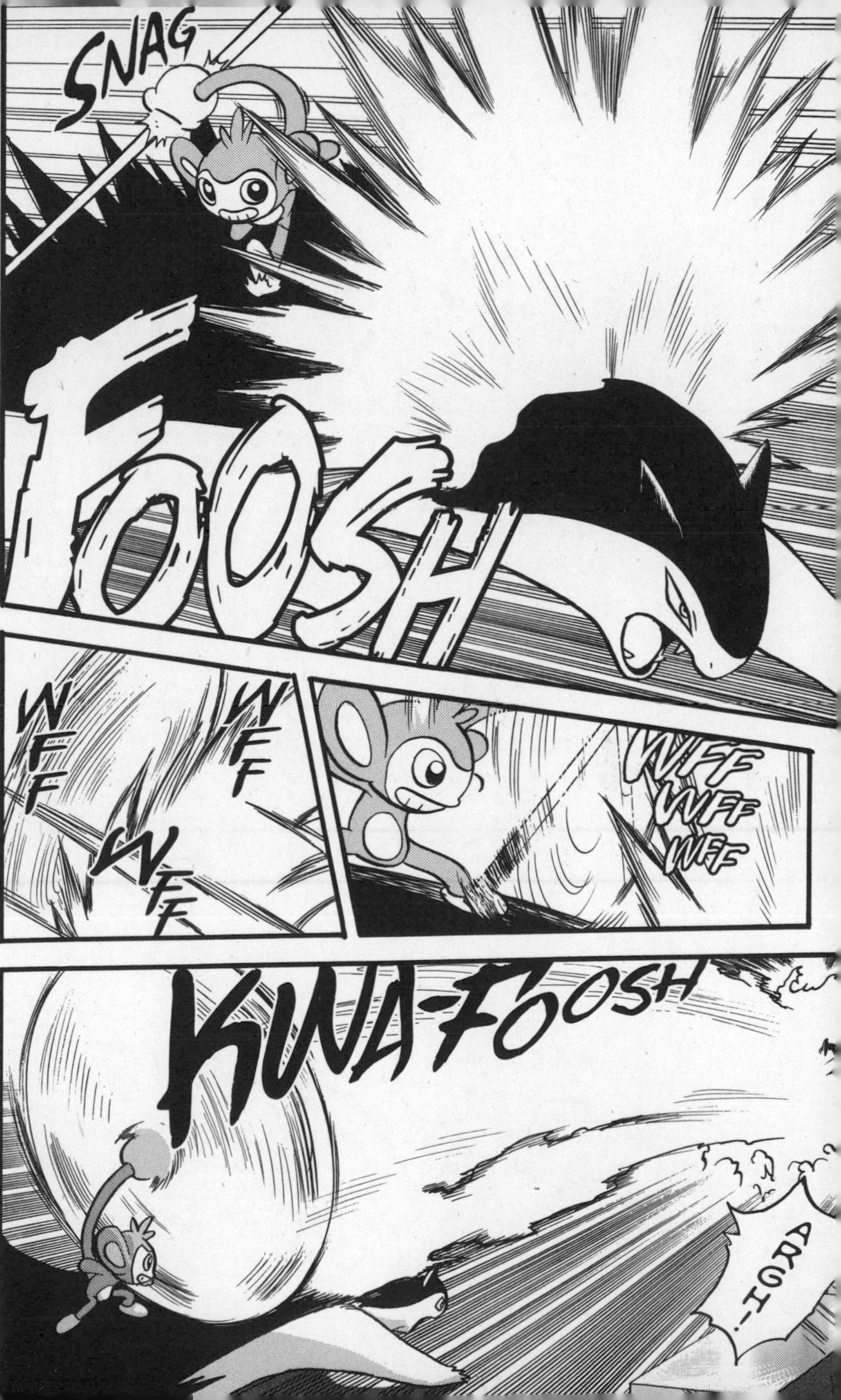
SNAG
FOOSH
WFF WFF WFF
WFF WFF WFF
KWA-FOOSH
ARGH--!

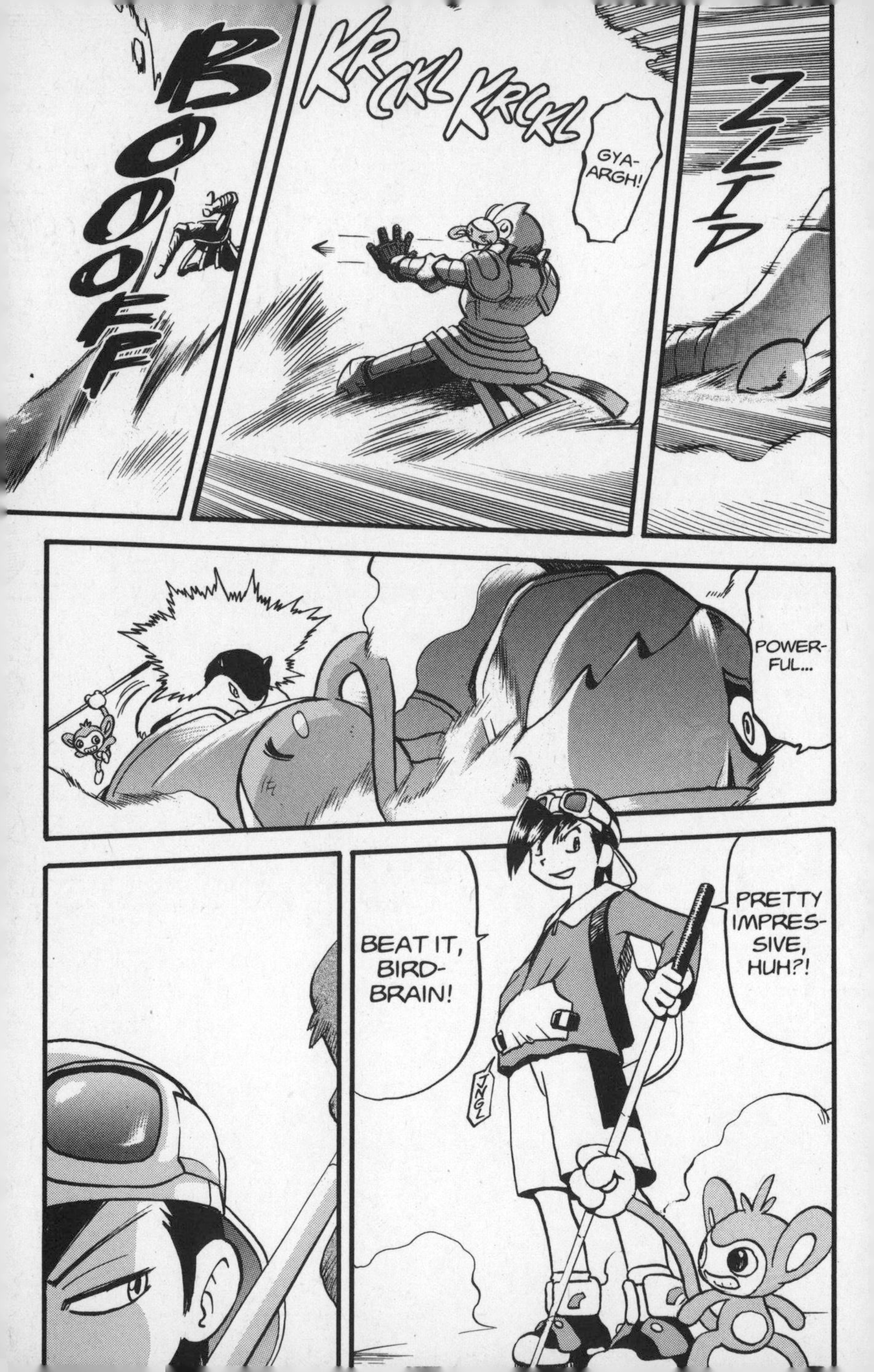
ZZIP
KRCKL KRCKL
GYA-ARGH!
BOOOFF
POWER-FUL...
PRETTY IMPRES-SIVE, HUH?!
BEAT IT, BIRD-BRAIN!
JNGL

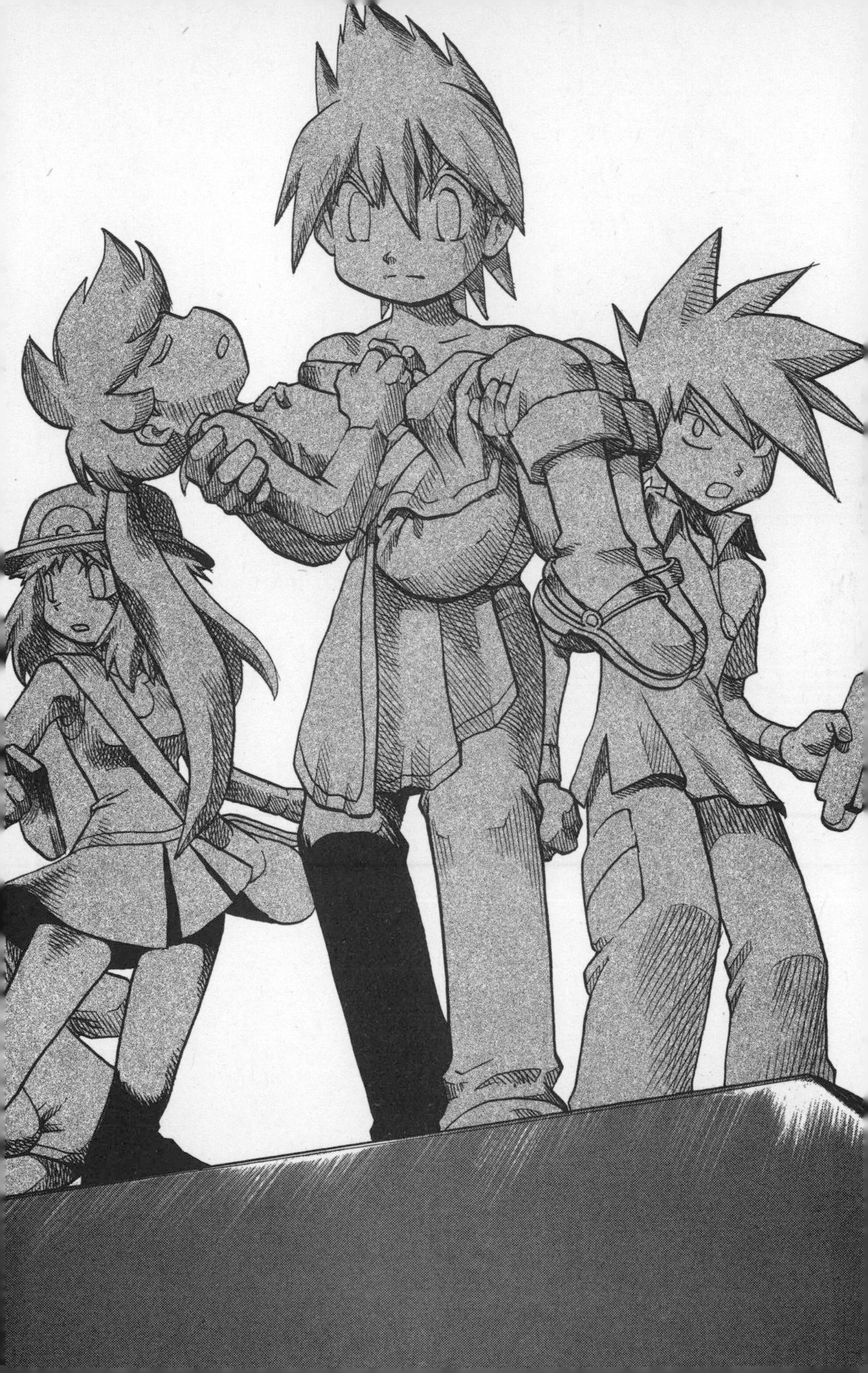

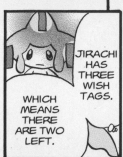

JIRACHI HAS THREE WISH TAGS.

WHICH MEANS THERE ARE TWO LEFT.

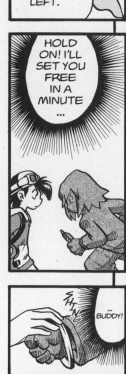

HOLD ON! I'LL SET YOU FREE IN A MINUTE...

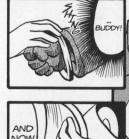

SHTNG

...BUDDY!

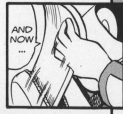

AND NOW...

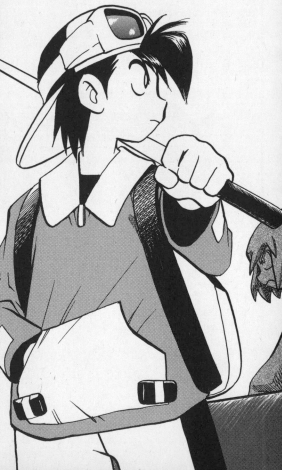

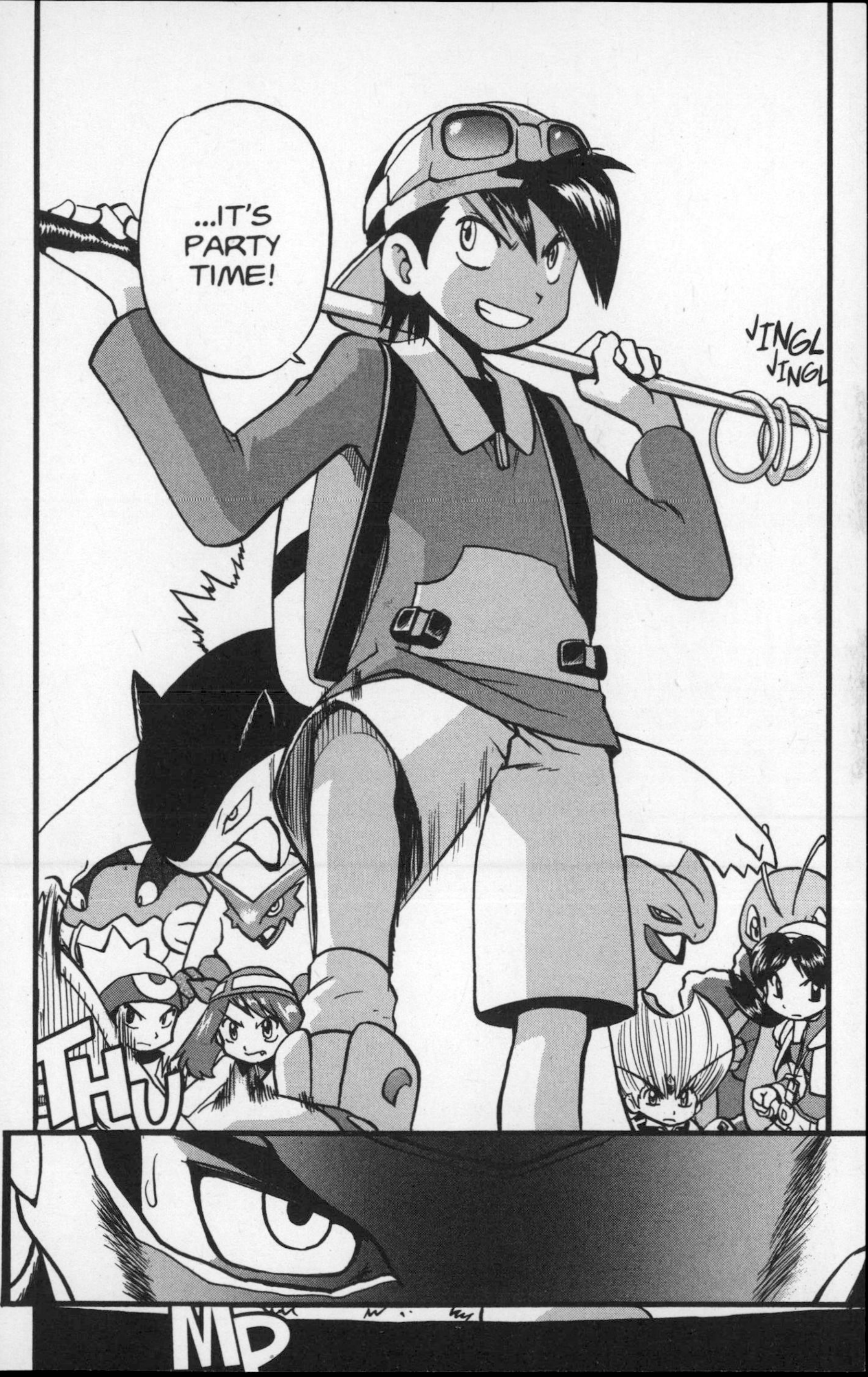
...IT'S PARTY TIME!
JINGL JINGL
THU
MP

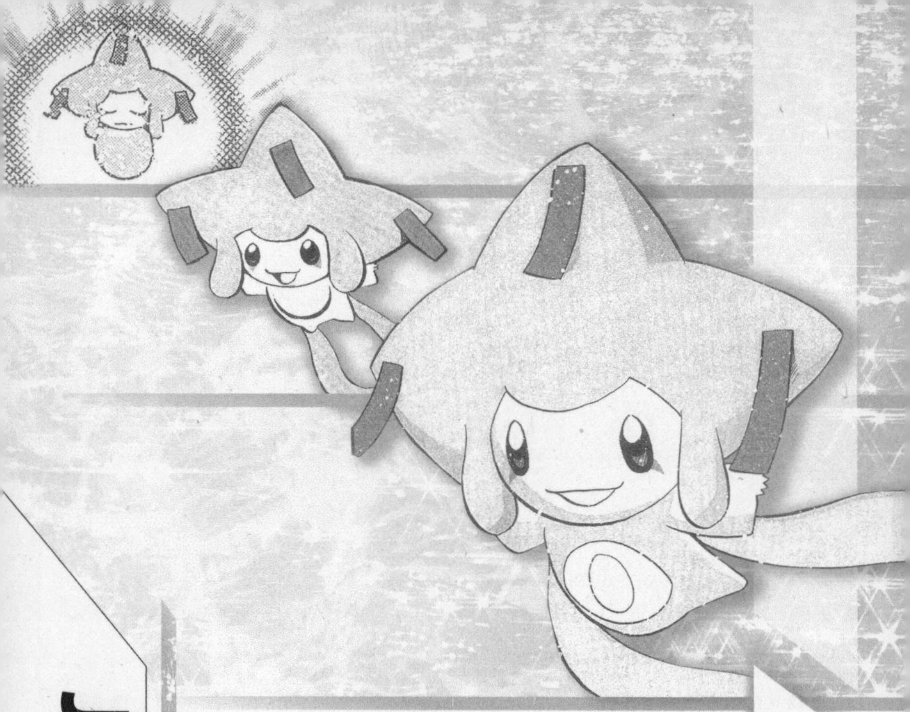

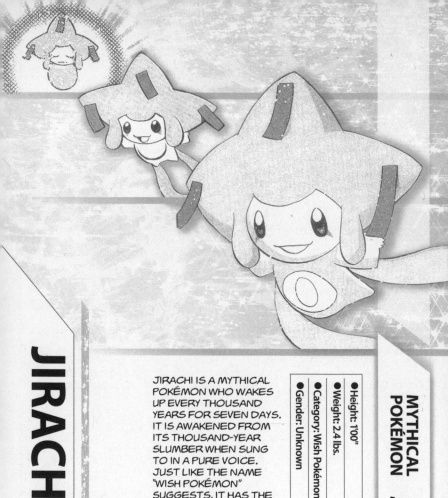

MYTHICAL POKÉMON

JIRACHI

1

- Height: 1'00"
- Weight: 2.4 lbs.
- Category: Wish Pokémon
- Gender: Unknown

JIRACHI IS A MYTHICAL POKÉMON WHO WAKES UP EVERY THOUSAND YEARS FOR SEVEN DAYS. IT IS AWAKENED FROM ITS THOUSAND-YEAR SLUMBER WHEN SUNG TO IN A PURE VOICE. JUST LIKE THE NAME "WISH POKÉMON" SUGGESTS, IT HAS THE POWER TO MAKE ANY WISH COME TRUE. THE WISHER MUST LOOK INTO JIRACHI'S THIRD EYE (TRUE EYE) LOCATED ON ITS STOMACH TO CONVEY THEIR WISH. THE TAGS HANGING FROM ITS HEAD ARE WISH TAGS WHERE THE WISHES WILL BE INSCRIBED.

JIRACHI

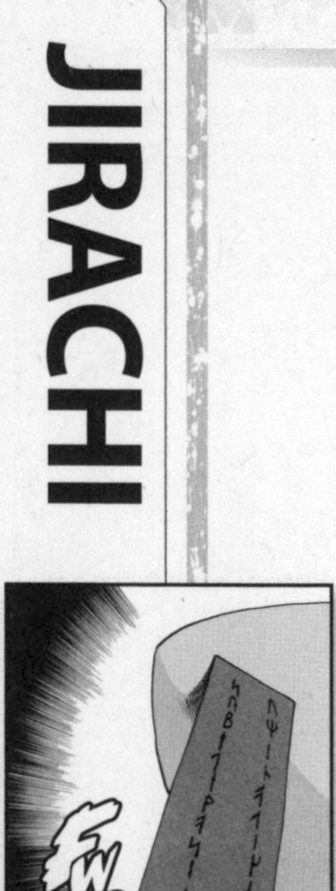
FWPP

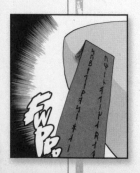

The Final Battle II

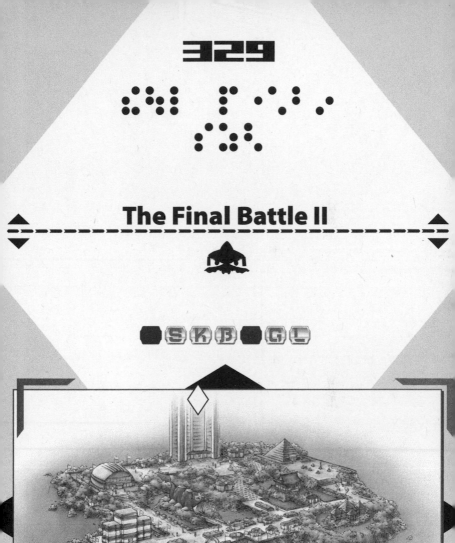

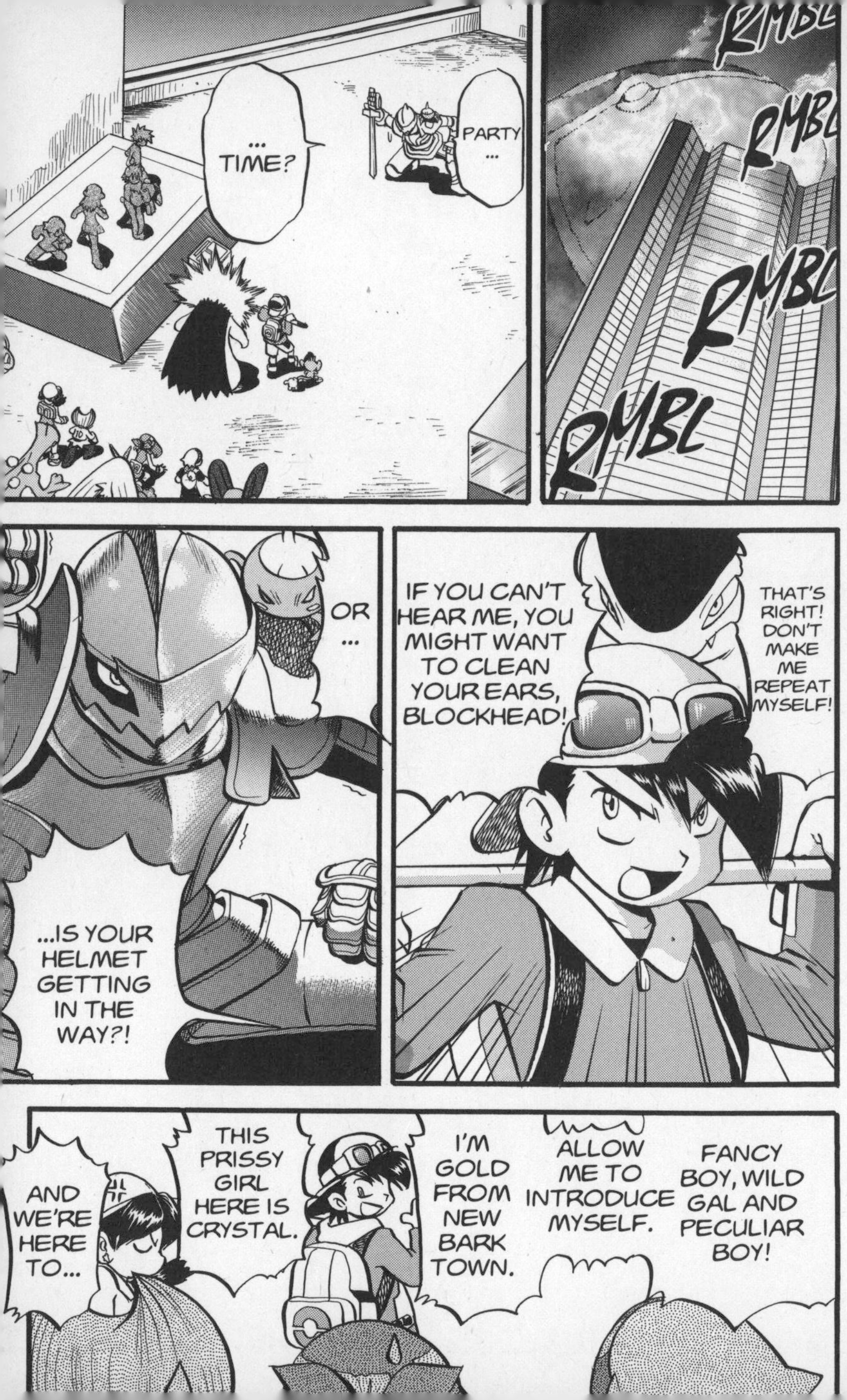
RMBL
RMBL
RMBL
RMBL
PARTY ...
... TIME?
THAT'S RIGHT! DON'T MAKE ME REPEAT MYSELF!
IF YOU CAN'T HEAR ME, YOU MIGHT WANT TO CLEAN YOUR EARS, BLOCKHEAD!
OR ...
...IS YOUR HELMET GETTING IN THE WAY?!
FANCY BOY, WILD GAL AND PECULIAR BOY!
ALLOW ME TO INTRODUCE MYSELF.
I'M GOLD FROM NEW BARK TOWN.
THIS PRISSY GIRL HERE IS CRYSTAL.
AND WE'RE HERE TO...

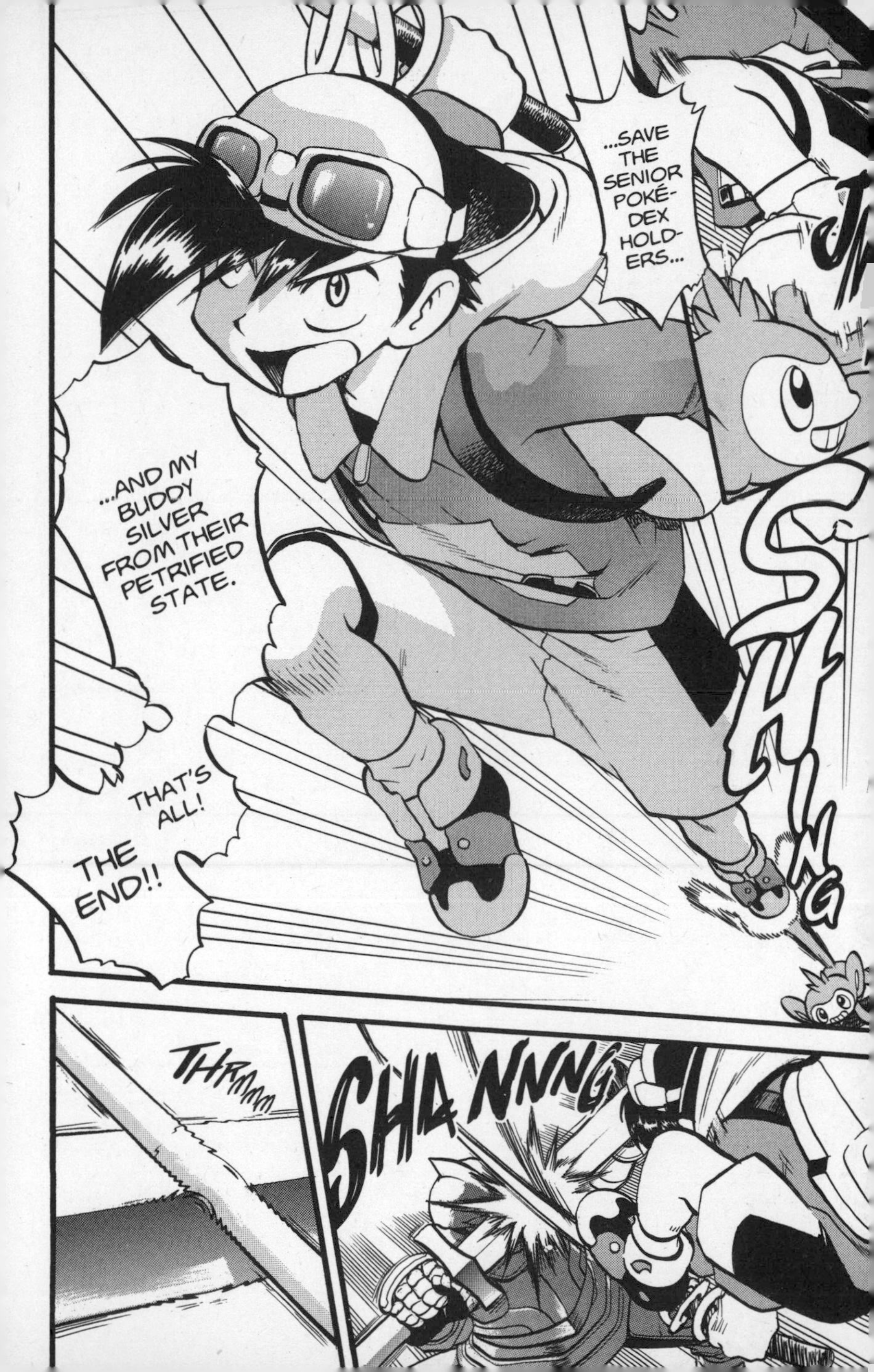
...SAVE THE SENIOR POKÉ-DEX HOLD-ERS...
...AND MY BUDDY SILVER FROM THEIR PETRIFIED STATE.
THAT'S ALL!
THE END!!
SHING
SHANNNG
THRMMM

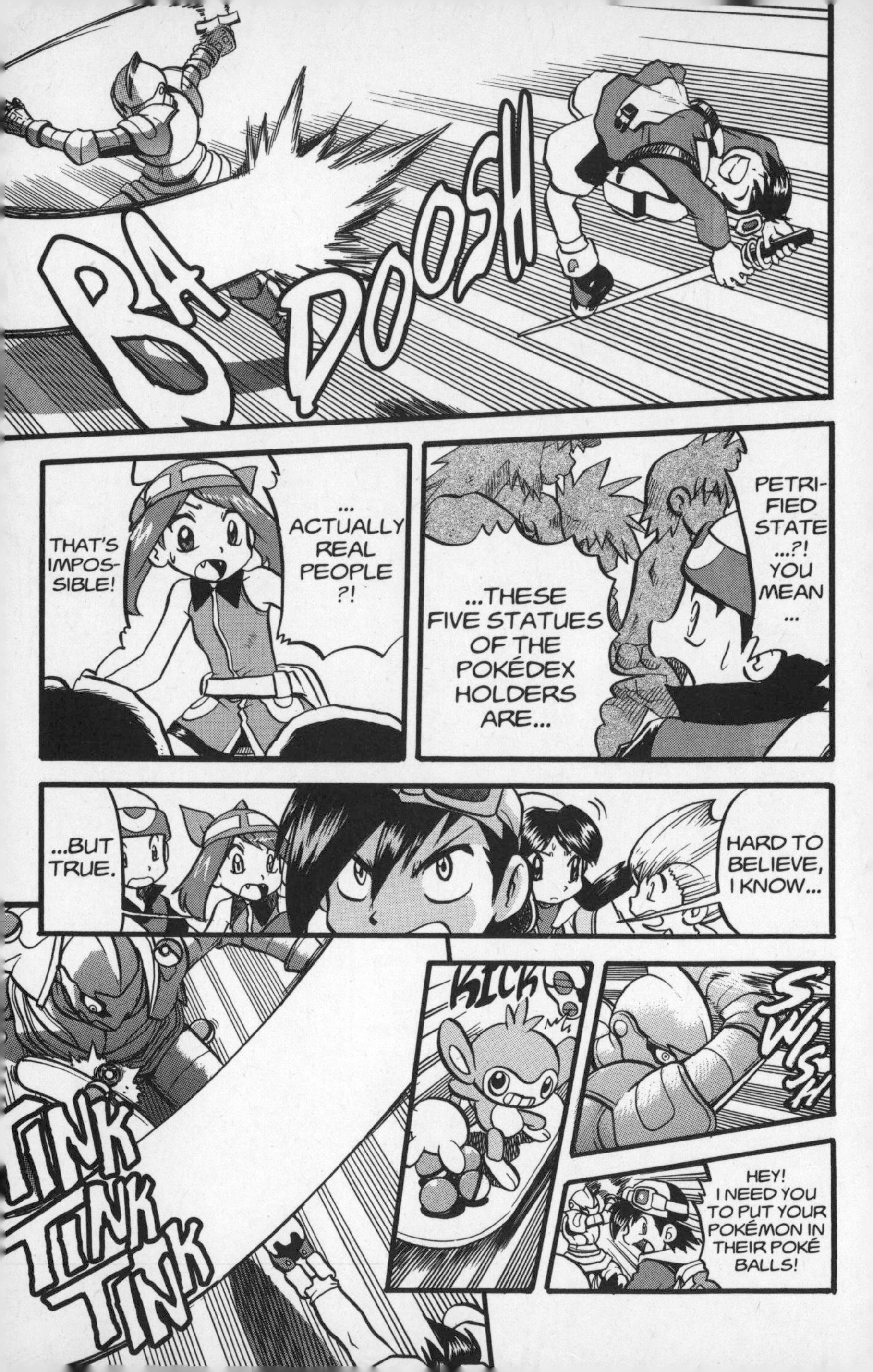
BA
DOOSH
PETRIFIED STATE ...?! YOU MEAN ...
...THESE FIVE STATUES OF THE POKÉDEX HOLDERS ARE...
... ACTUALLY REAL PEOPLE ?!
THAT'S IMPOSSIBLE!
HARD TO BELIEVE, I KNOW...
...BUT TRUE.
SWISH
HEY! I NEED YOU TO PUT YOUR POKÉMON IN THEIR POKÉ BALLS!
KICK
TINK TINK TINK

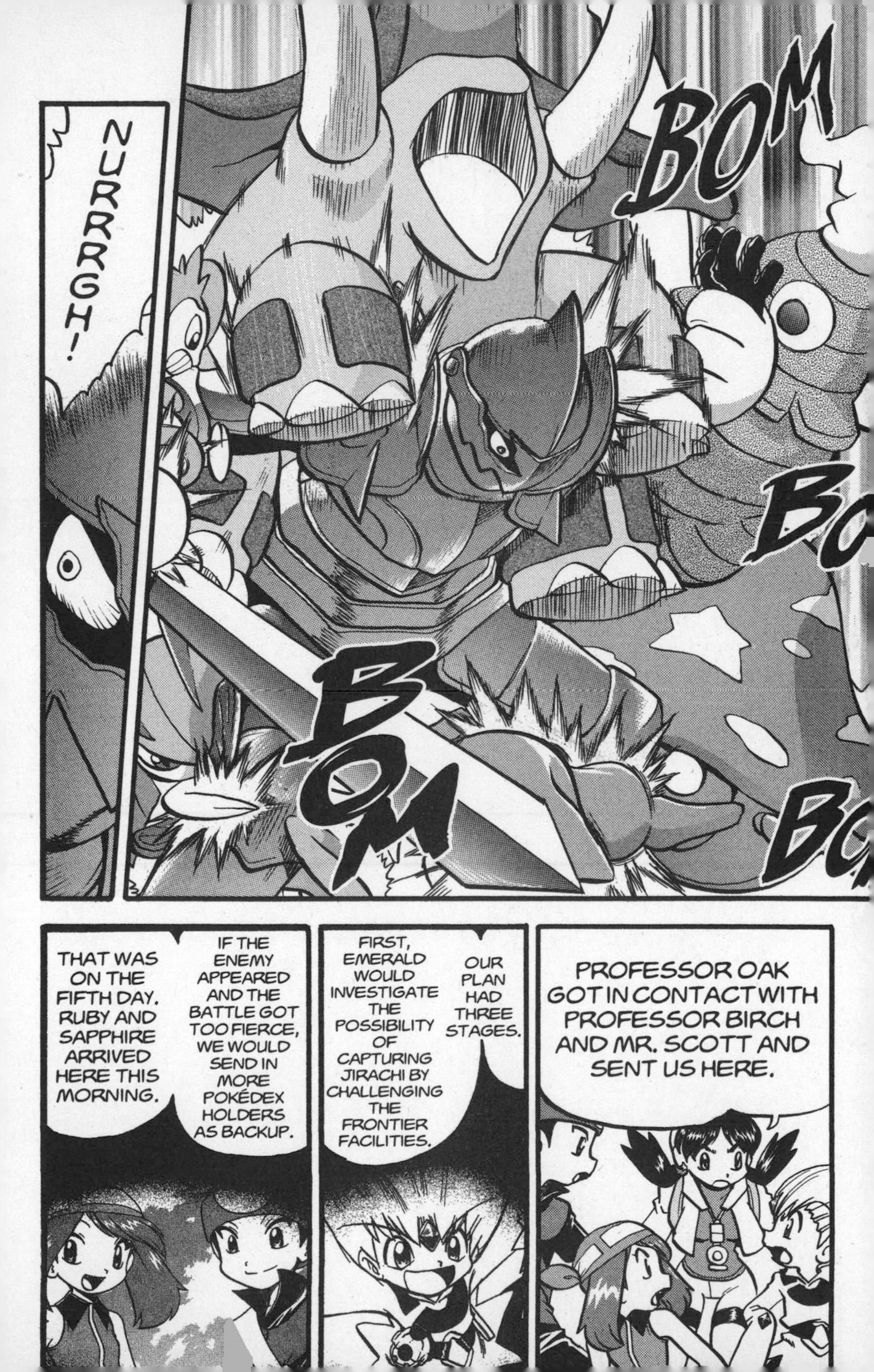
BOM
BO
BO
BOM
NURRRGH!
PROFESSOR OAK GOT IN CONTACT WITH PROFESSOR BIRCH AND MR. SCOTT AND SENT US HERE.
OUR PLAN HAD THREE STAGES.
FIRST, EMERALD WOULD INVESTIGATE THE POSSIBILITY OF CAPTURING JIRACHI BY CHALLENGING THE FRONTIER FACILITIES.
IF THE ENEMY APPEARED AND THE BATTLE GOT TOO FIERCE, WE WOULD SEND IN MORE POKÉDEX HOLDERS AS BACKUP.
THAT WAS ON THE FIFTH DAY. RUBY AND SAPPHIRE ARRIVED HERE THIS MORNING.

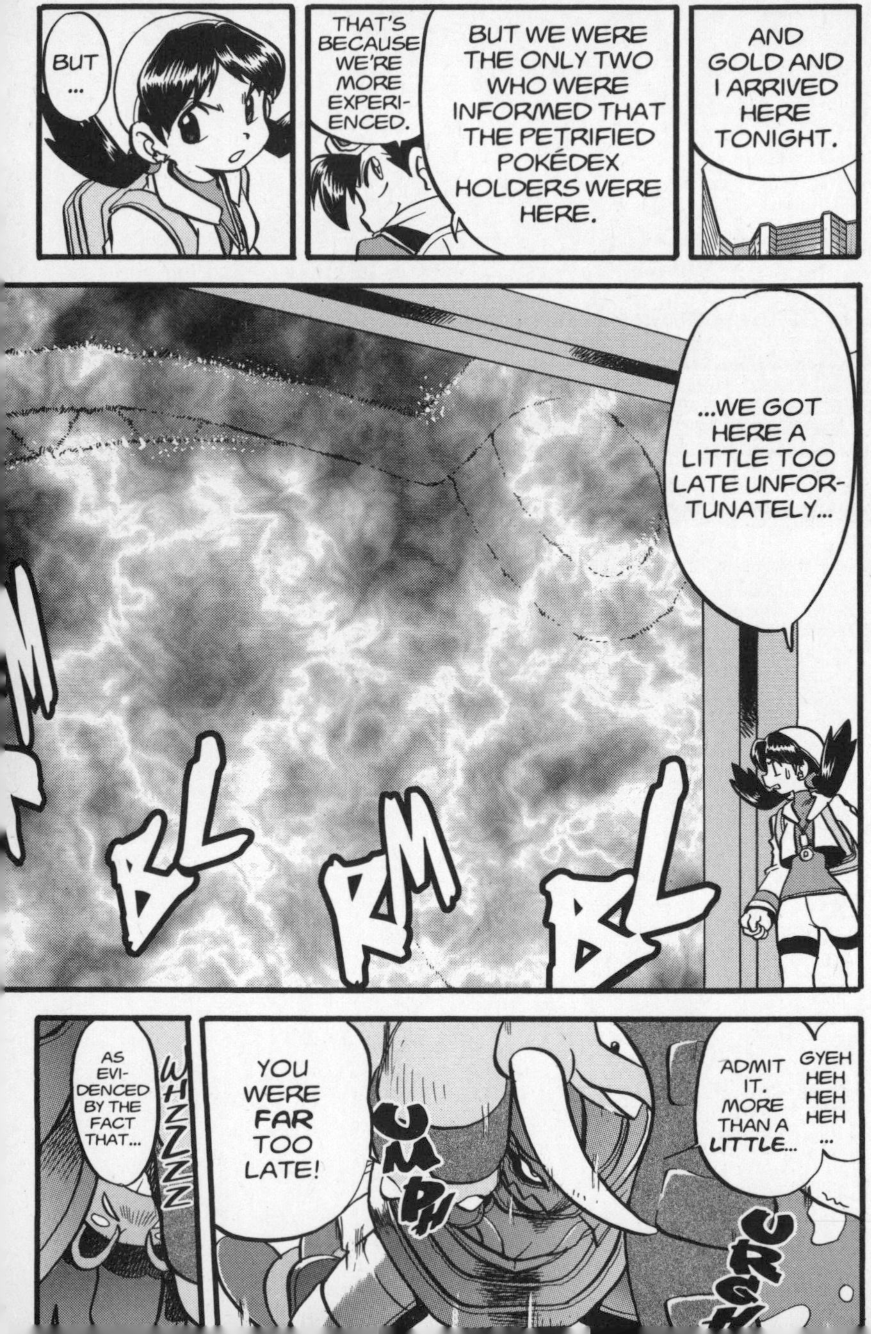
AND GOLD AND I ARRIVED HERE TONIGHT.
BUT WE WERE THE ONLY TWO WHO WERE INFORMED THAT THE PETRIFIED POKÉDEX HOLDERS WERE HERE.
THAT'S BECAUSE WE'RE MORE EXPERI-ENCED.
BUT ...
...WE GOT HERE A LITTLE TOO LATE UNFOR-TUNATELY...
BL RM BL
GYEH HEH HEH HEH ...
ADMIT IT. MORE THAN A LITTLE...
URGH
YOU WERE FAR TOO LATE!
UMPH
WHZZZZ
AS EVI-DENCED BY THE FACT THAT...

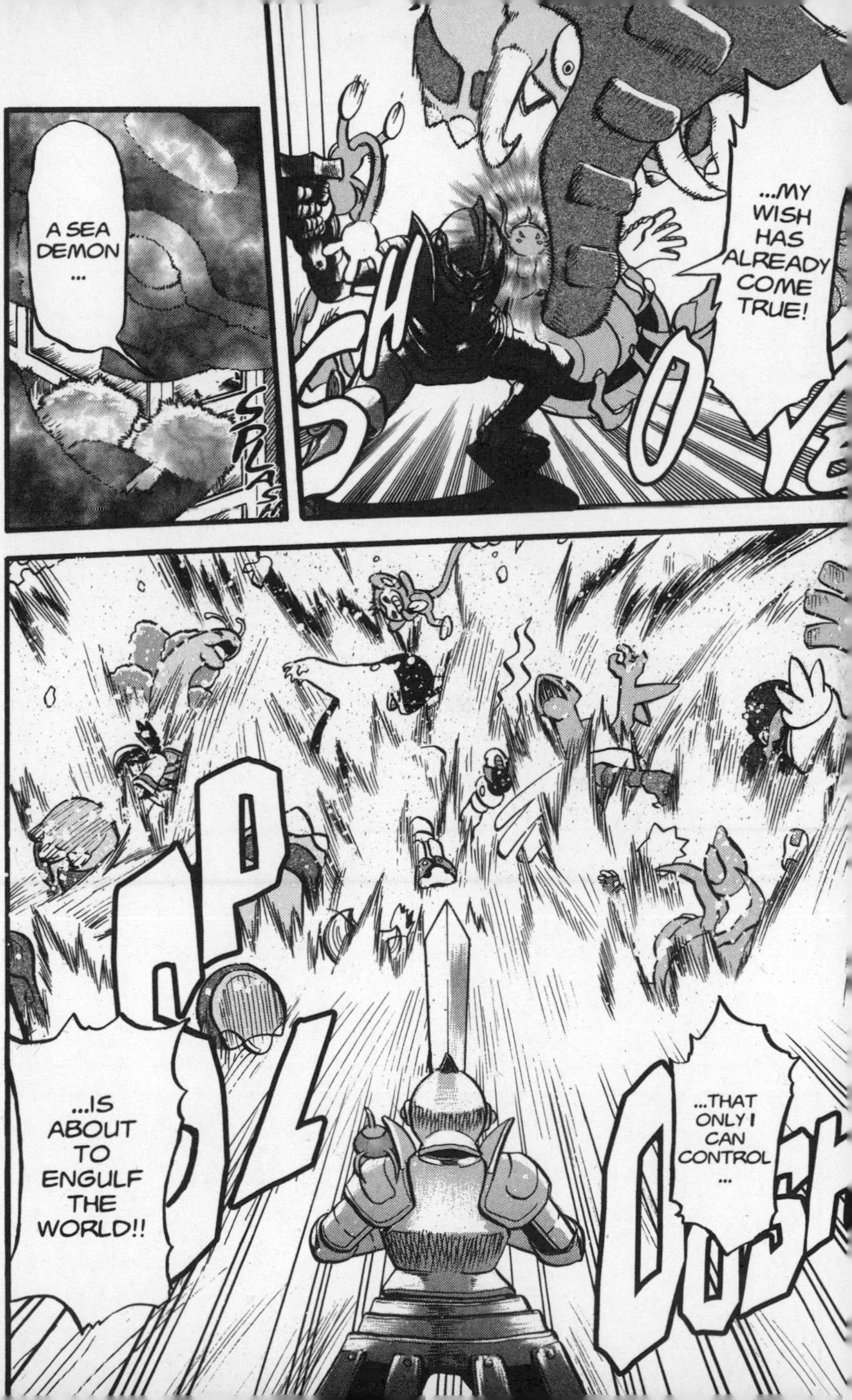
...MY WISH HAS ALREADY COME TRUE!
A SEA DEMON ...
SPLASH
...THAT ONLY I CAN CONTROL ...
...IS ABOUT TO ENGULF THE WORLD!!

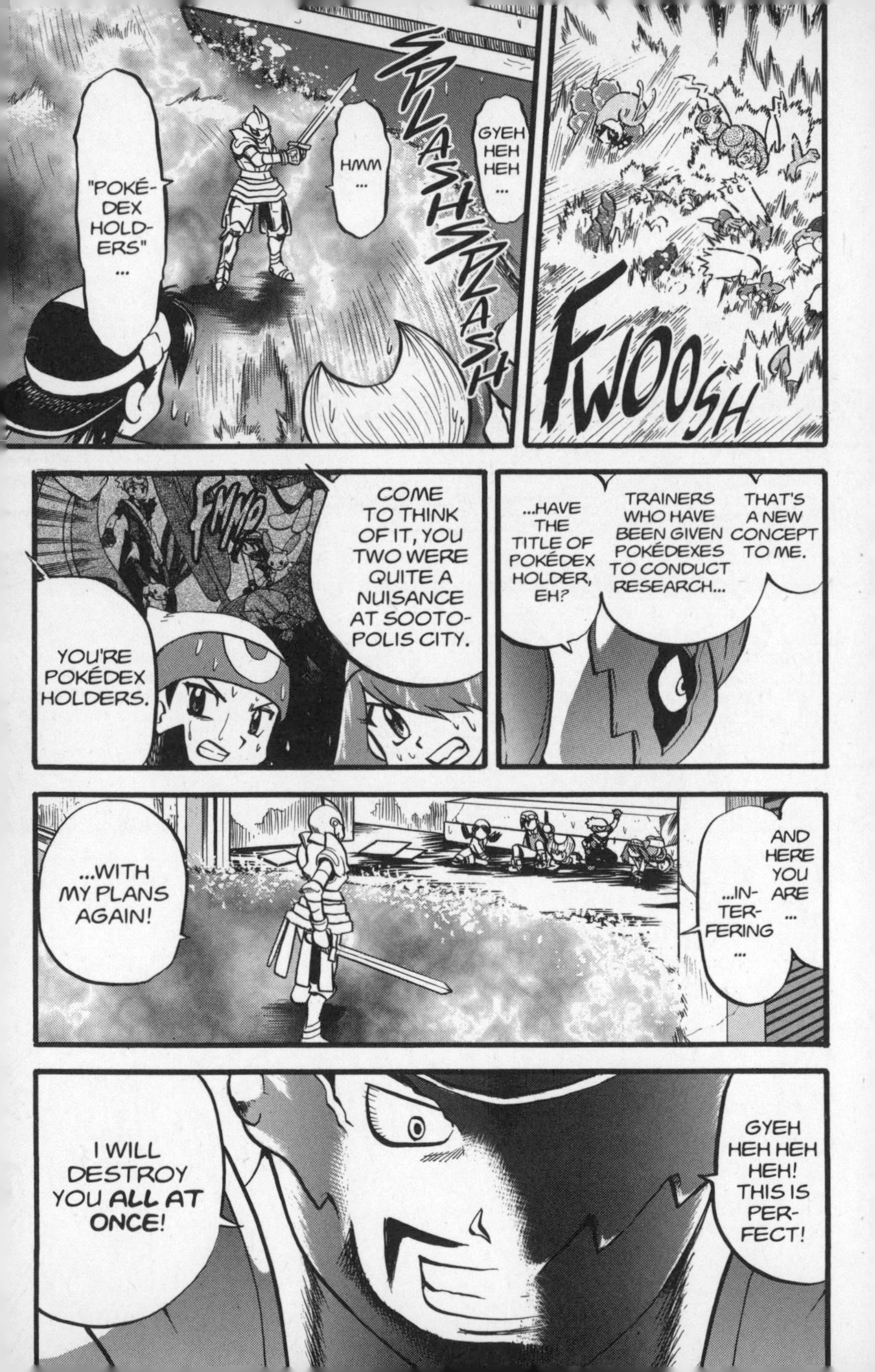
FWOOSH
GYEH HEH HEH ...
SPLASHSPLASH
HMM ...
"POKÉDEX HOLDERS" ...
THAT'S A NEW CONCEPT TO ME.
TRAINERS WHO HAVE BEEN GIVEN POKÉDEXES TO CONDUCT RESEARCH...
...HAVE THE TITLE OF POKÉDEX HOLDER, EH?
COME TO THINK OF IT, YOU TWO WERE QUITE A NUISANCE AT SOOTOPOLIS CITY.
YOU'RE POKÉDEX HOLDERS.
AND HERE YOU ARE ...
...INTERFERING ...
...WITH MY PLANS AGAIN!
GYEH HEH HEH HEH! THIS IS PERFECT!
I WILL DESTROY YOU **ALL AT ONCE**!

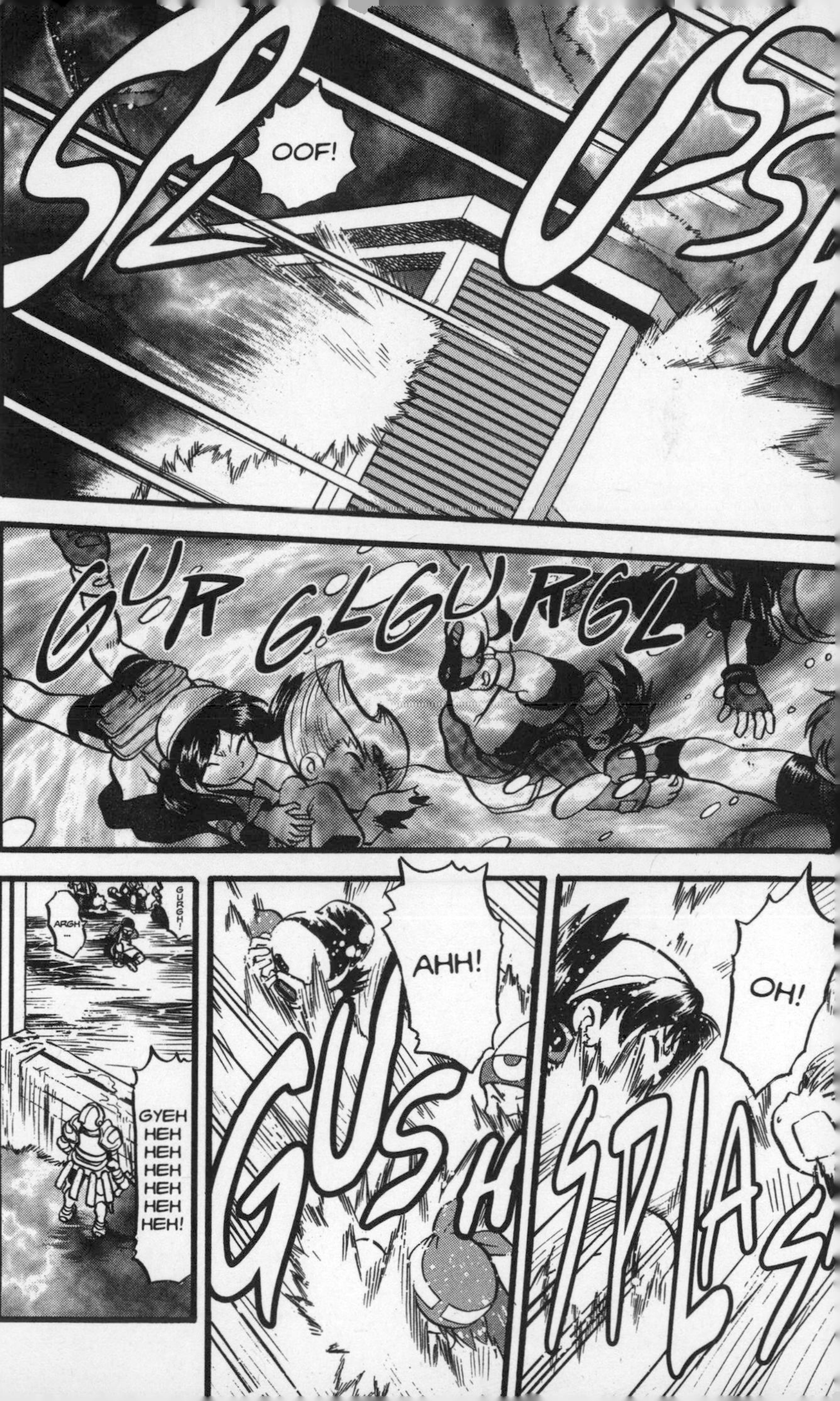
SLUSH
OOF!
GUR GLGURGL
OH!
SPLAS
AHH!
GUSH
GURGH!
ARGH...
GYEH HEH HEH HEH HEH HEH HEH!

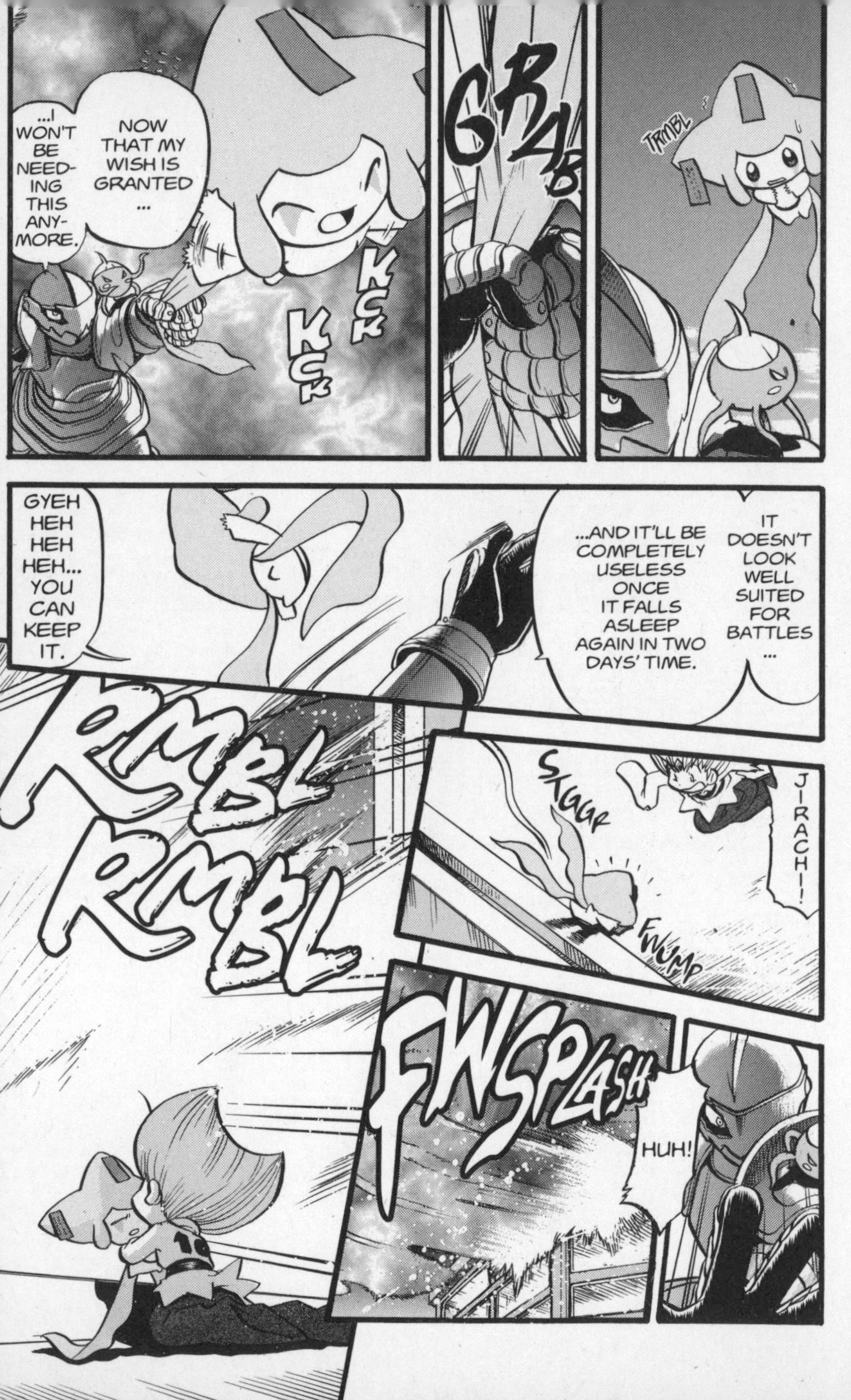
TRMBL
GRAB
NOW THAT MY WISH IS GRANTED...
...I WON'T BE NEEDING THIS ANYMORE.
KCK KCK
IT DOESN'T LOOK WELL SUITED FOR BATTLES...
...AND IT'LL BE COMPLETELY USELESS ONCE IT FALLS ASLEEP AGAIN IN TWO DAYS' TIME.
GYEH HEH HEH HEH... YOU CAN KEEP IT.
JIRACHI!
SKGGR
FWUMP
RMBL RMBL
HUH!
FWSPLASH

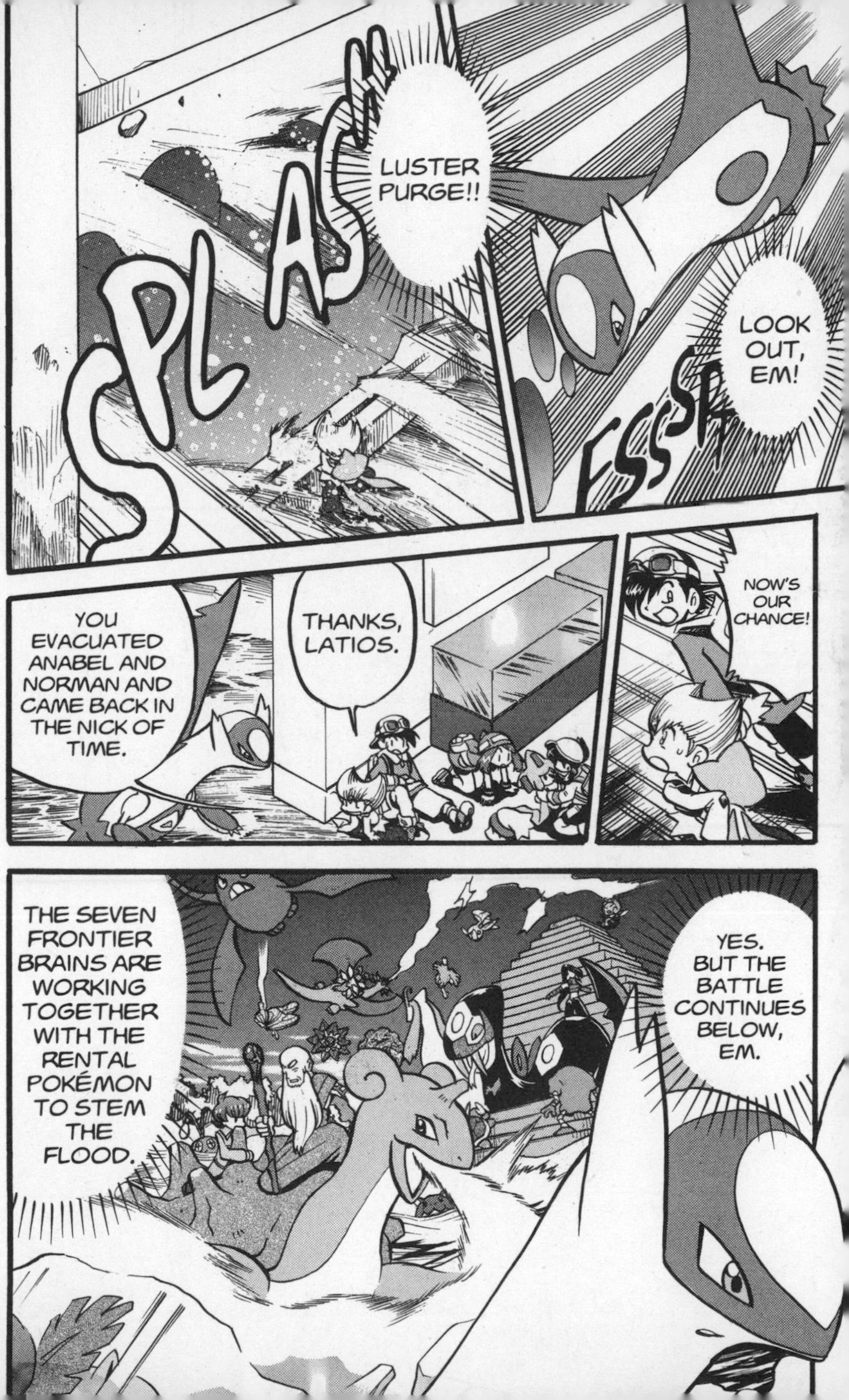
ESSSH
LOOK OUT, EM!
LUSTER PURGE!!
SPLASH
NOW'S OUR CHANCE!
THANKS, LATIOS.
YOU EVACUATED ANABEL AND NORMAN AND CAME BACK IN THE NICK OF TIME.
YES. BUT THE BATTLE CONTINUES BELOW, EM.
THE SEVEN FRONTIER BRAINS ARE WORKING TOGETHER WITH THE RENTAL POKÉMON TO STEM THE FLOOD.

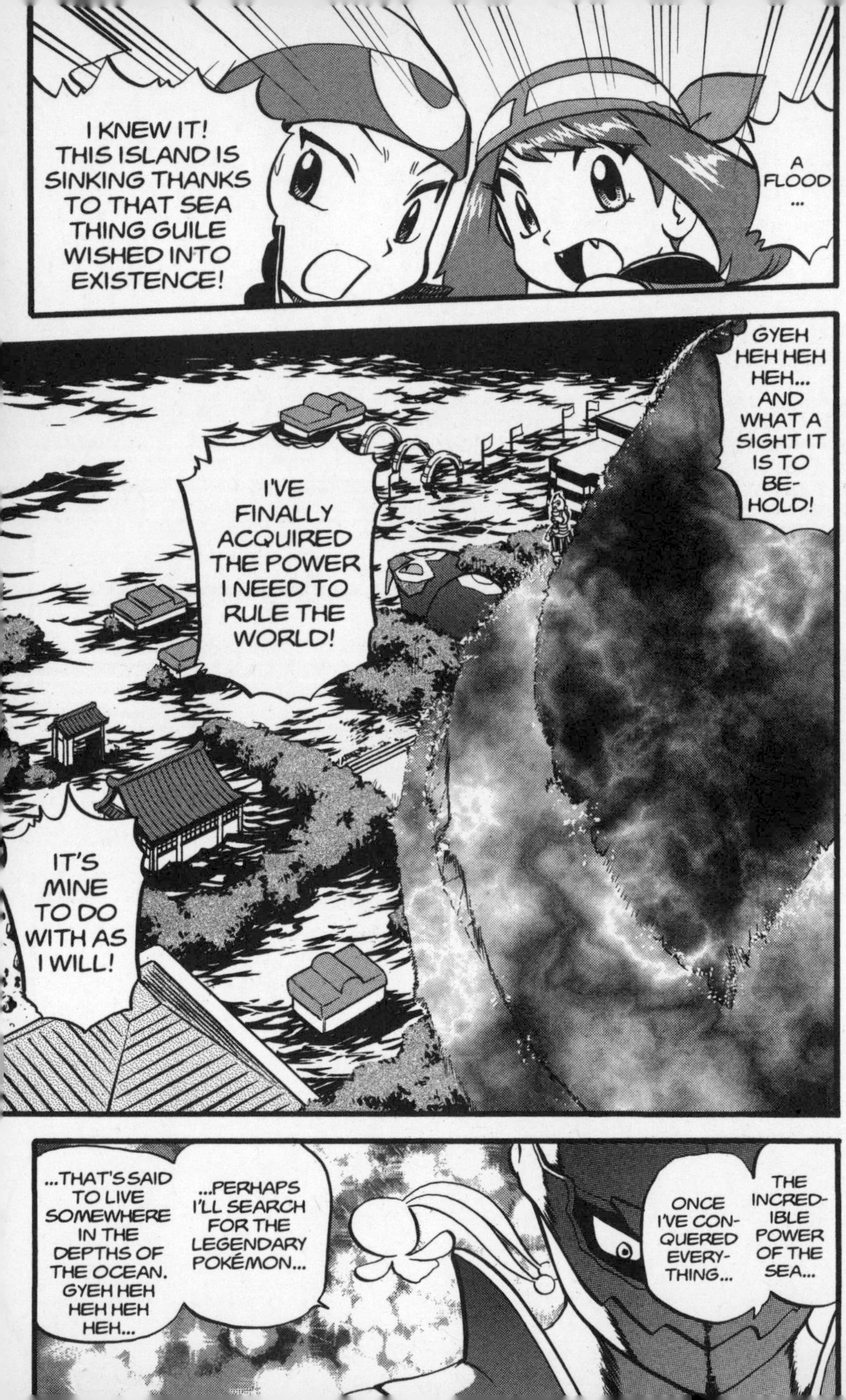
A FLOOD ...
I KNEW IT! THIS ISLAND IS SINKING THANKS TO THAT SEA THING GUILE WISHED INTO EXISTENCE!
GYEH HEH HEH HEH... AND WHAT A SIGHT IT IS TO BEHOLD!
I'VE FINALLY ACQUIRED THE POWER I NEED TO RULE THE WORLD!
IT'S MINE TO DO WITH AS I WILL!
THE INCREDIBLE POWER OF THE SEA...
ONCE I'VE CONQUERED EVERYTHING...
...PERHAPS I'LL SEARCH FOR THE LEGENDARY POKÉMON...
...THAT'S SAID TO LIVE SOMEWHERE IN THE DEPTHS OF THE OCEAN. GYEH HEH HEH HEH HEH...

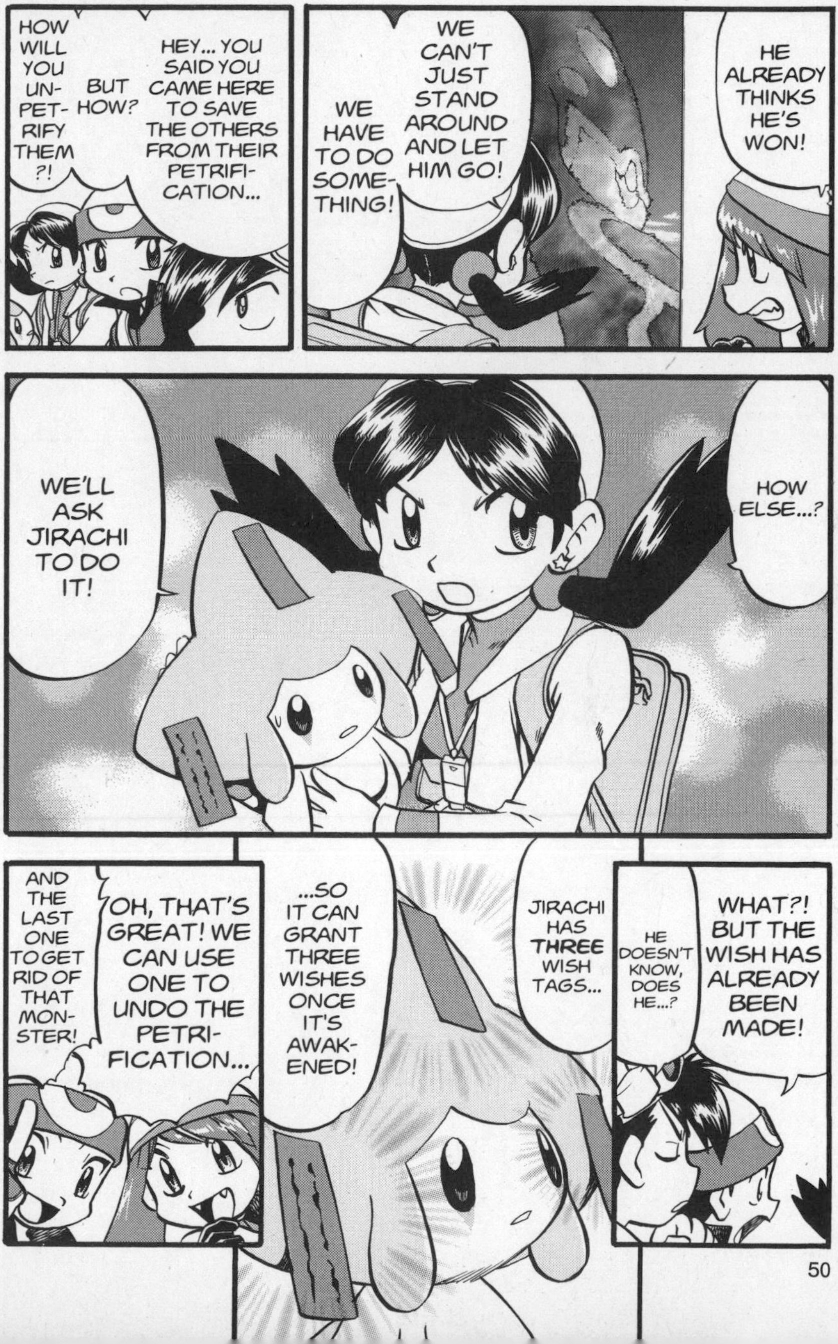
HE ALREADY THINKS HE'S WON!
WE CAN'T JUST STAND AROUND AND LET HIM GO!
WE HAVE TO DO SOMETHING!
HEY... YOU SAID YOU CAME HERE TO SAVE THE OTHERS FROM THEIR PETRIFICATION...
BUT HOW?
HOW WILL YOU UNPETRIFY THEM?!
HOW ELSE...?
WE'LL ASK JIRACHI TO DO IT!
WHAT?! BUT THE WISH HAS ALREADY BEEN MADE!
HE DOESN'T KNOW, DOES HE...?
JIRACHI HAS **THREE** WISH TAGS...
...SO IT CAN GRANT THREE WISHES ONCE IT'S AWAKENED!
OH, THAT'S GREAT! WE CAN USE ONE TO UNDO THE PETRIFICATION...
AND THE LAST ONE TO GET RID OF THAT MONSTER!

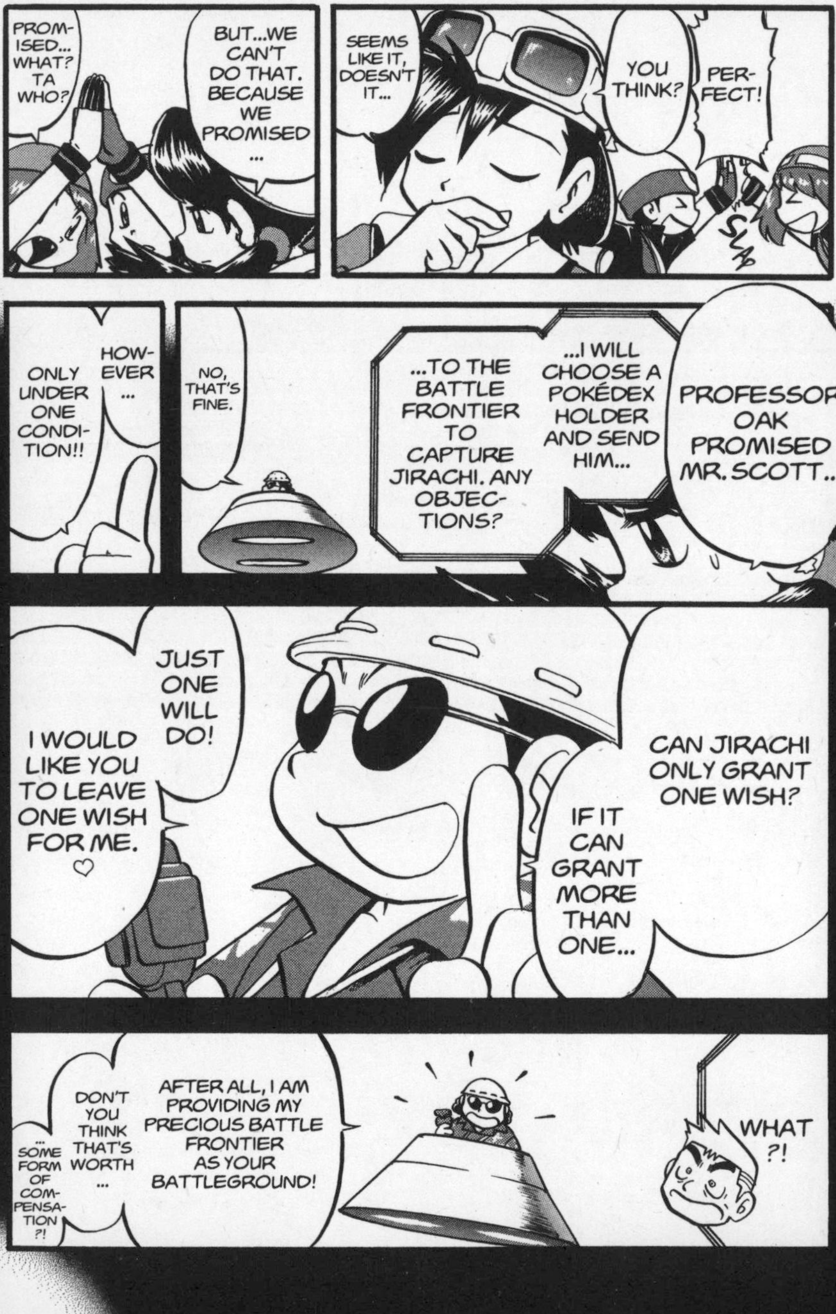
PERFECT!
YOU THINK?
SEEMS LIKE IT, DOESN'T IT...
SLAP
BUT...WE CAN'T DO THAT. BECAUSE WE PROMISED...
PROMISED... WHAT? TA WHO?
PROFESSOR OAK PROMISED MR. SCOTT...
...I WILL CHOOSE A POKÉDEX HOLDER AND SEND HIM...
...TO THE BATTLE FRONTIER TO CAPTURE JIRACHI. ANY OBJECTIONS?
NO, THAT'S FINE.
HOWEVER...
ONLY UNDER ONE CONDITION!!
CAN JIRACHI ONLY GRANT ONE WISH?
IF IT CAN GRANT MORE THAN ONE...
JUST ONE WILL DO!
I WOULD LIKE YOU TO LEAVE ONE WISH FOR ME. ♡
WHAT?!
AFTER ALL, I AM PROVIDING MY PRECIOUS BATTLE FRONTIER AS YOUR BATTLEGROUND!
DON'T YOU THINK THAT'S WORTH...
...SOME FORM OF COMPENSATION?!

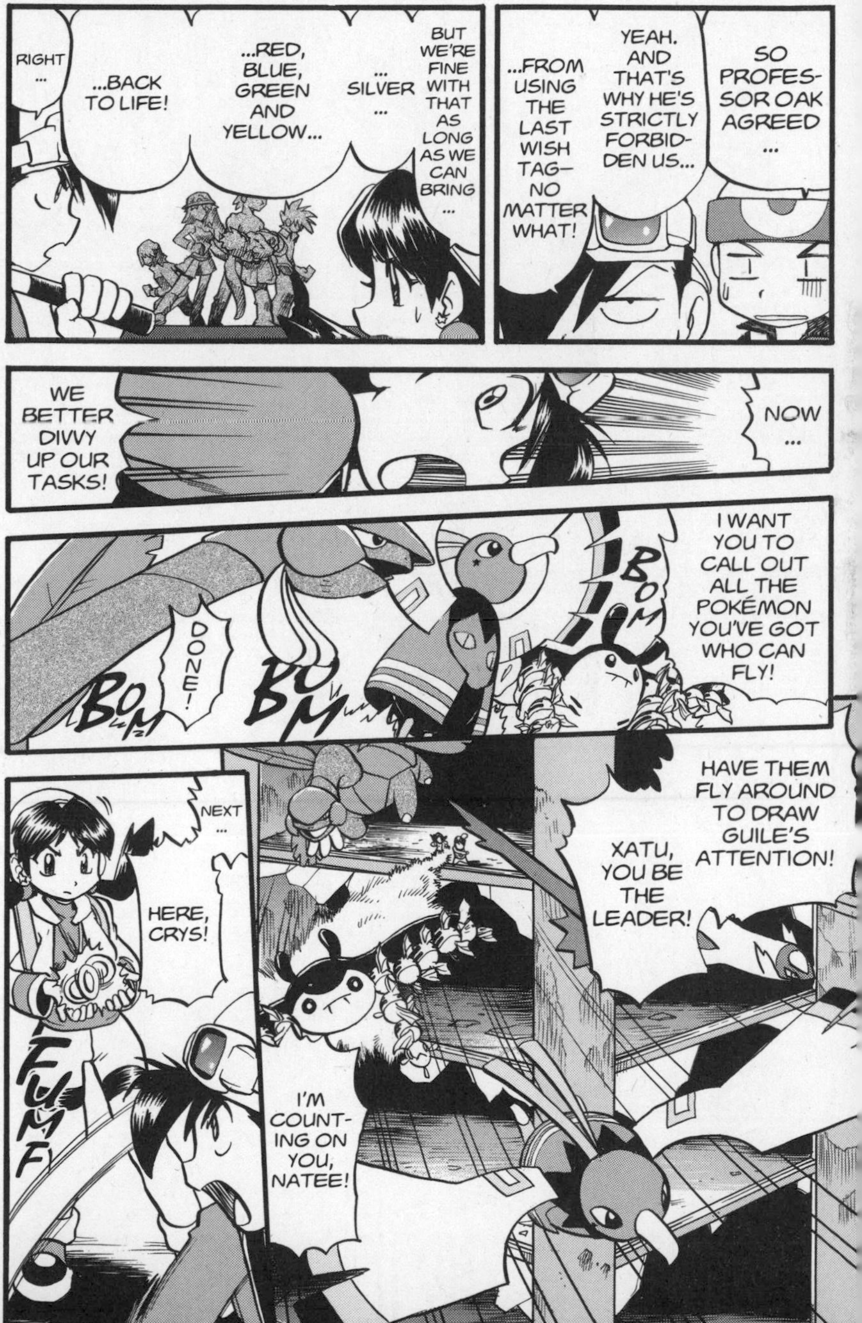
SO PROFES-SOR OAK AGREED ...
YEAH. AND THAT'S WHY HE'S STRICTLY FORBID-DEN US...
...FROM USING THE LAST WISH TAG— NO MATTER WHAT!
BUT WE'RE FINE WITH THAT AS LONG AS WE CAN BRING ...
... SILVER ...
...RED, BLUE, GREEN AND YELLOW...
...BACK TO LIFE!
RIGHT ...
NOW ...
WE BETTER DIVVY UP OUR TASKS!
I WANT YOU TO CALL OUT ALL THE POKÉMON YOU'VE GOT WHO CAN FLY!
BOM
BOM
DONE!
BOM
HAVE THEM FLY AROUND TO DRAW GUILE'S ATTENTION!
XATU, YOU BE THE LEADER!
I'M COUNT-ING ON YOU, NATEE!
NEXT ...
HERE, CRYS!
FUMF

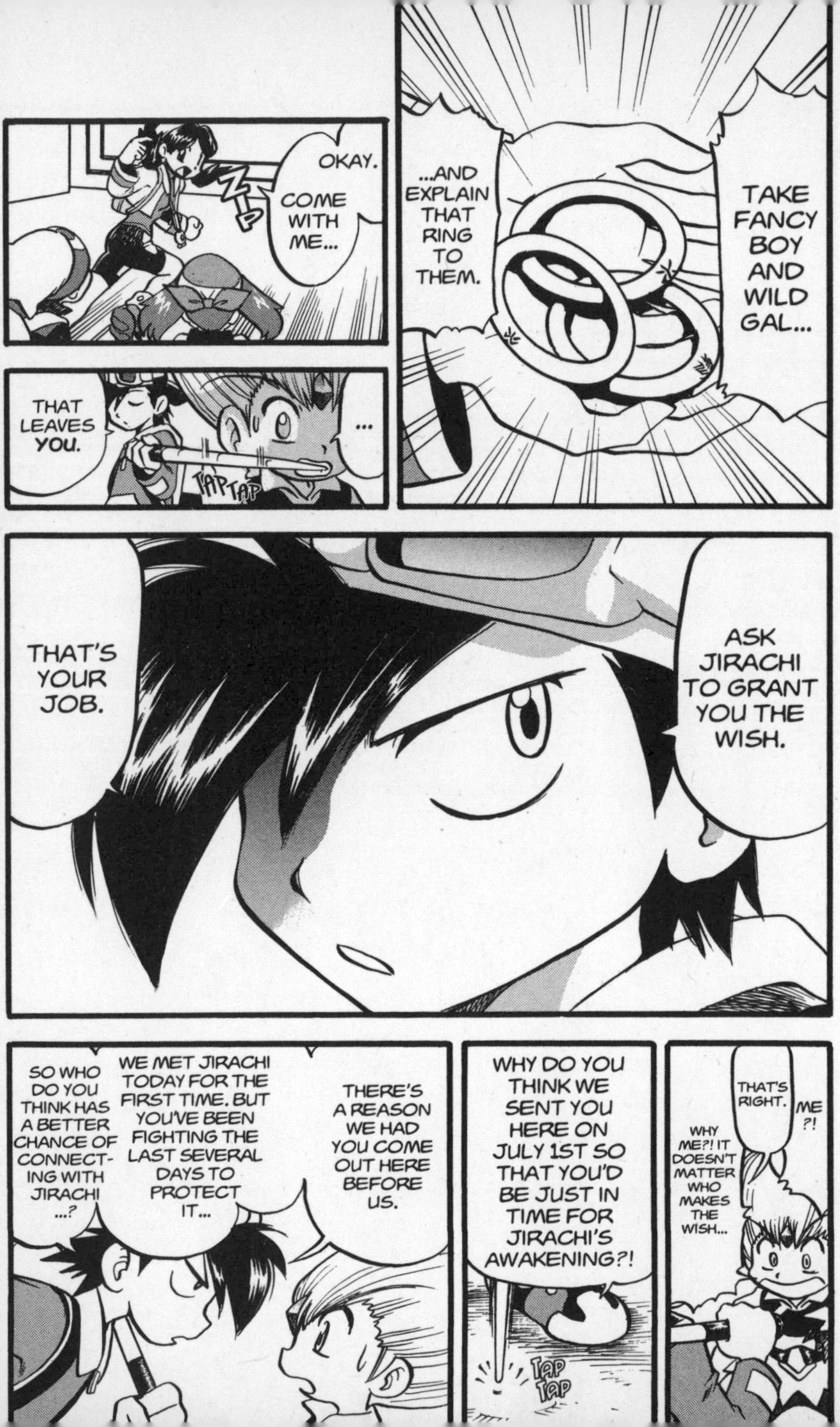
TAKE FANCY BOY AND WILD GAL...
...AND EXPLAIN THAT RING TO THEM.
OKAY. COME WITH ME...
ZIP
...
THAT LEAVES YOU.
TAP TAP
ASK JIRACHI TO GRANT YOU THE WISH.
THAT'S YOUR JOB.
THAT'S RIGHT.
ME?!
WHY ME?! IT DOESN'T MATTER WHO MAKES THE WISH...
WHY DO YOU THINK WE SENT YOU HERE ON JULY 1ST SO THAT YOU'D BE JUST IN TIME FOR JIRACHI'S AWAKENING?!
TAP TAP
THERE'S A REASON WE HAD YOU COME OUT HERE BEFORE US.
WE MET JIRACHI TODAY FOR THE FIRST TIME. BUT YOU'VE BEEN FIGHTING THE LAST SEVERAL DAYS TO PROTECT IT...
SO WHO DO YOU THINK HAS A BETTER CHANCE OF CONNECTING WITH JIRACHI ...?

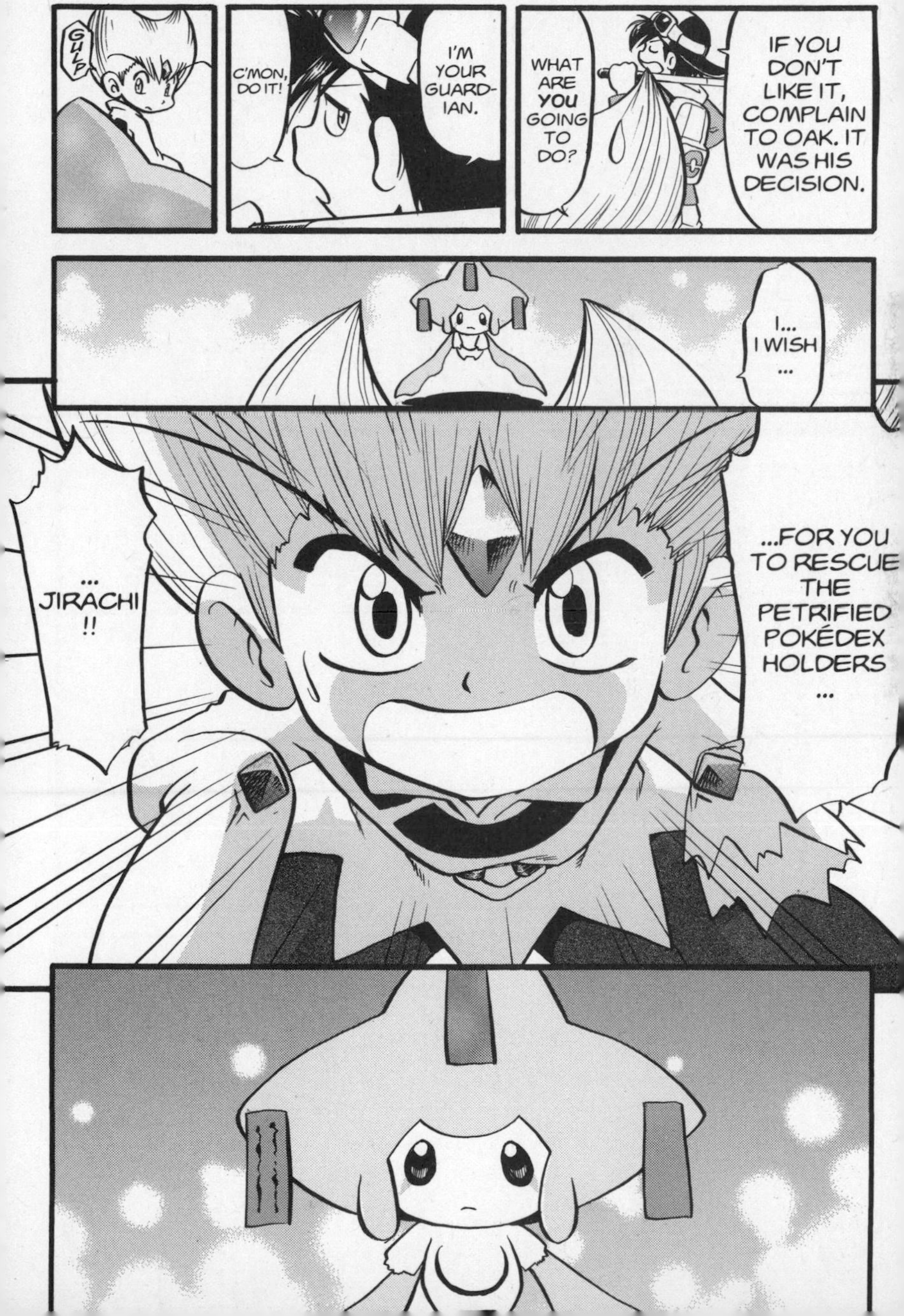
IF YOU DON'T LIKE IT, COMPLAIN TO OAK. IT WAS HIS DECISION.
WHAT ARE YOU GOING TO DO?
I'M YOUR GUARD-IAN.
C'MON, DO IT!
GULP
I... I WISH ...
...FOR YOU TO RESCUE THE PETRIFIED POKÉDEX HOLDERS ...
... JIRACHI !!

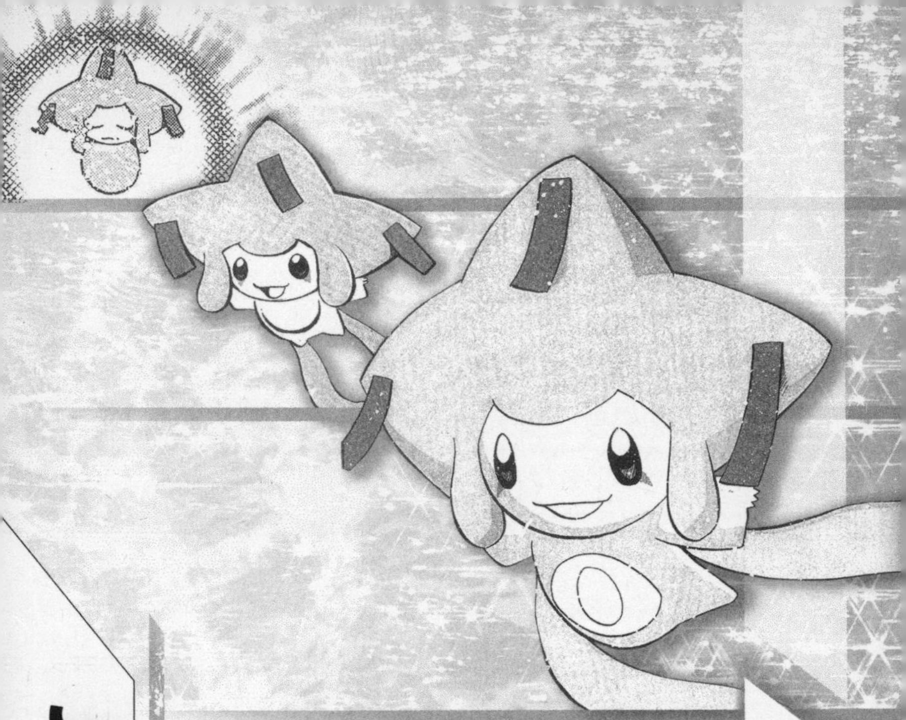

MYTHICAL POKÉMON

JIRACHI 2

- Type: Steel/Psychic
- Ability: Serene Grace
- Pokédex Number Hoenn: 201/National: 385

AFTER AWAKENING FOR SEVEN DAYS (OR SOONER ONCE ALL ITS WISH TAGS HAVE BEEN USED), JIRACHI WILL GO BACK TO SLEEP FOR ANOTHER THOUSAND YEARS. A TOUGH CRYSTAL-LIKE PROTECTIVE SUBSTANCE SURROUNDS ITS BODY WHILE JIRACHI IS ASLEEP; WHEN ENDANGERED, JIRACHI IS ALSO CAPABLE OF FIGHTING WHILE ASLEEP. DOOM DESIRE IS JIRACHI'S SIGNATURE ATTACK.

JIRACHI

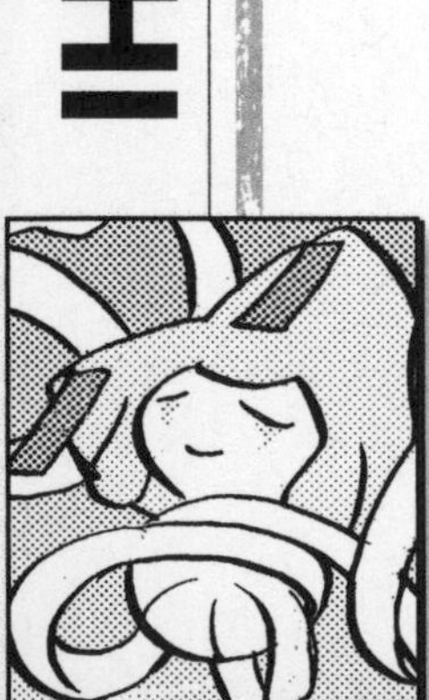

330

The Final Battle III

POKÉMON ADVENTURES•THE SIXTH CHAPTER•EMERALD

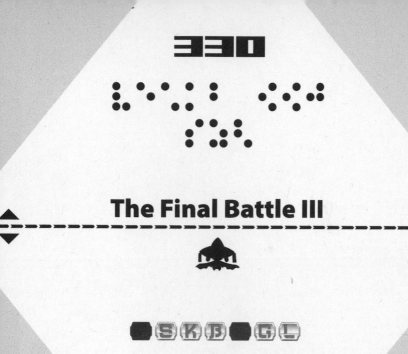

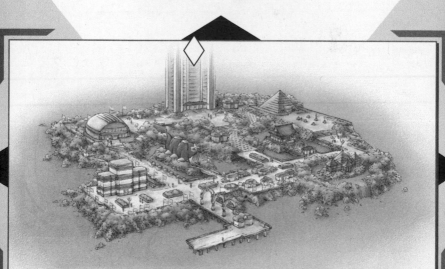

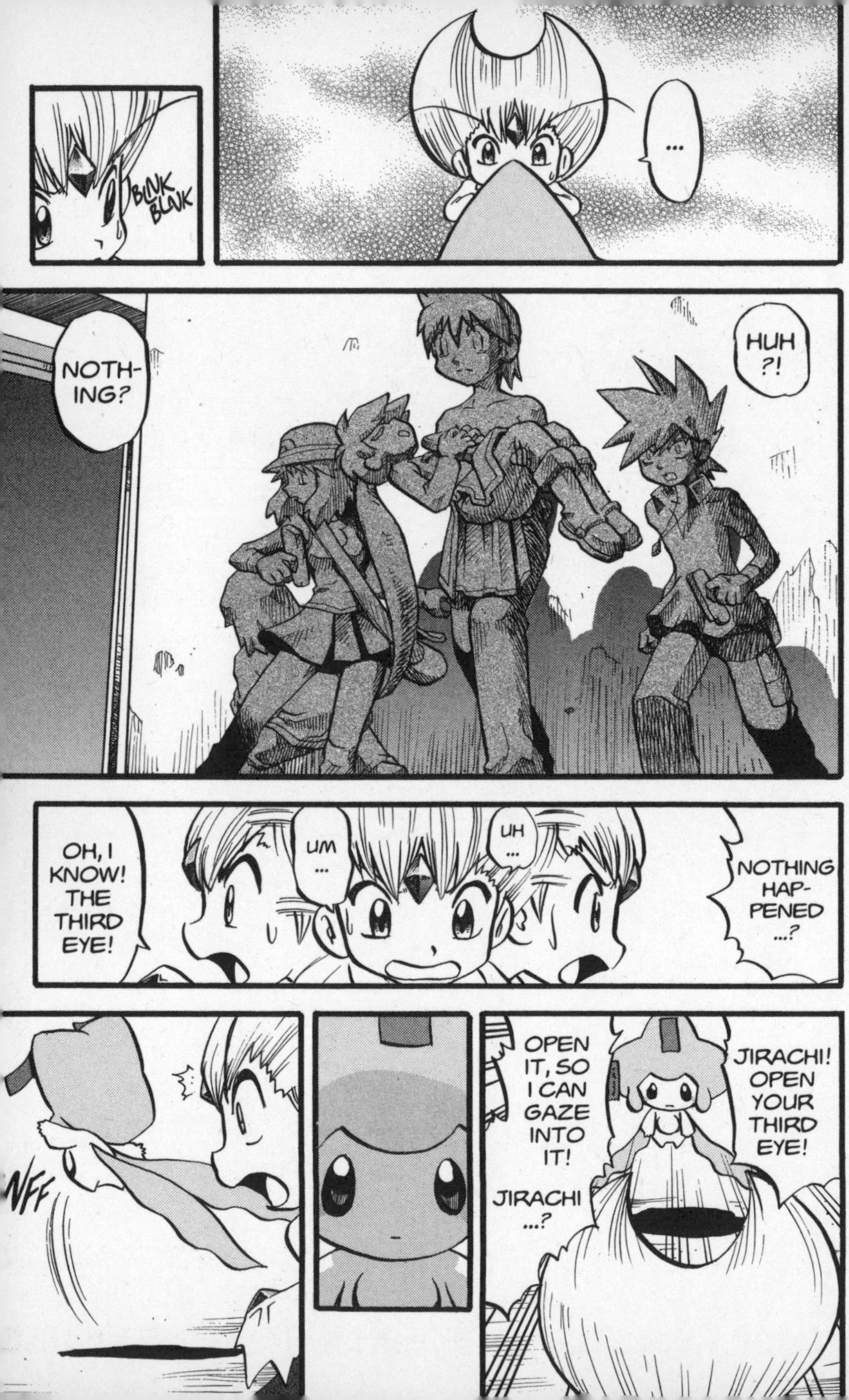
...
BLNK BLNK
HUH ?!
NOTH-ING?
NOTHING HAP-PENED ...?
UH ...
UM ...
OH, I KNOW! THE THIRD EYE!
JIRACHI! OPEN YOUR THIRD EYE!
OPEN IT, SO I CAN GAZE INTO IT!
JIRACHI ...?
NFF

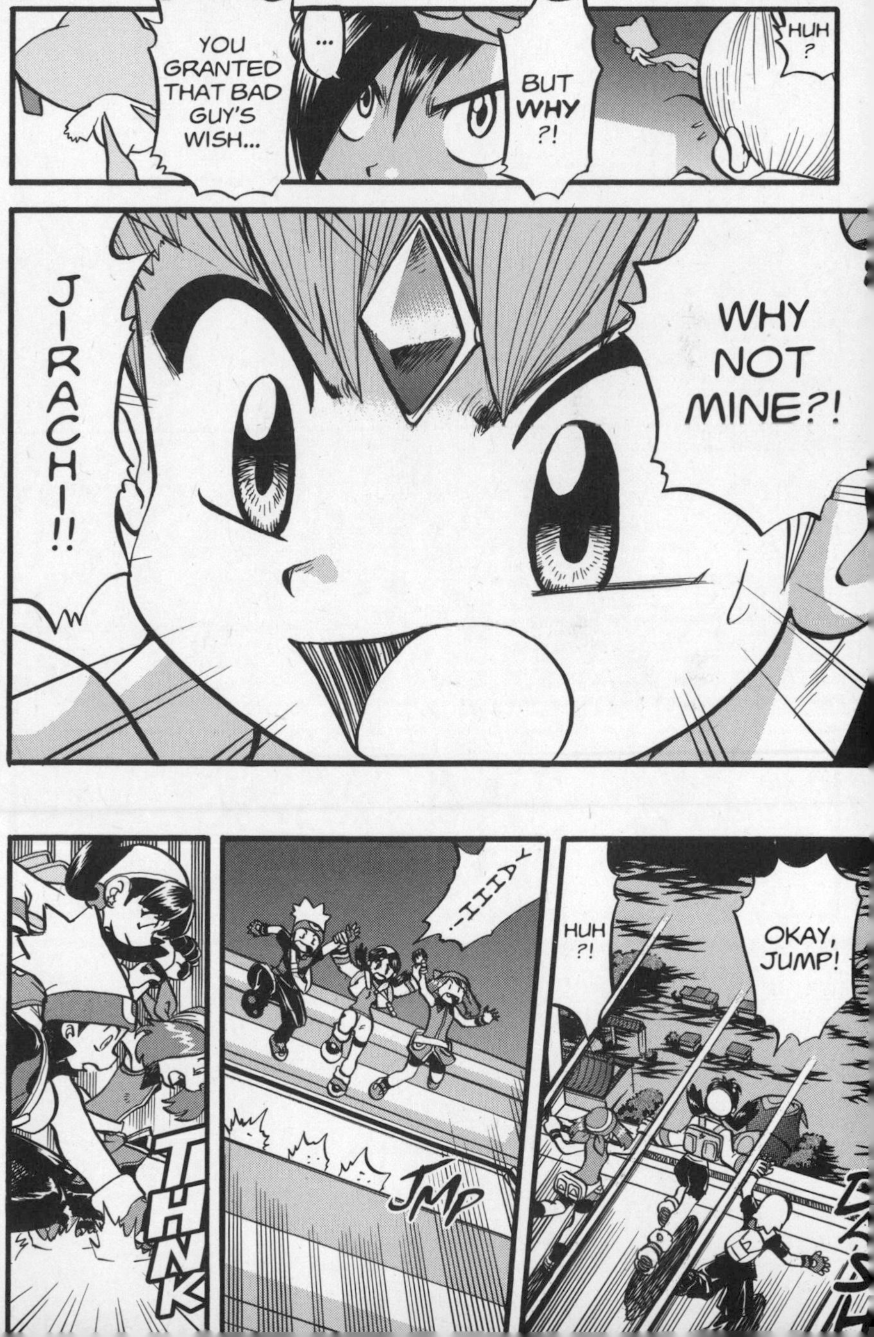
HUH?
BUT WHY?!
...
YOU GRANTED THAT BAD GUY'S WISH...
WHY NOT MINE?!
JIRACHI!!
OKAY, JUMP!
HUH?!
JMP
THNK

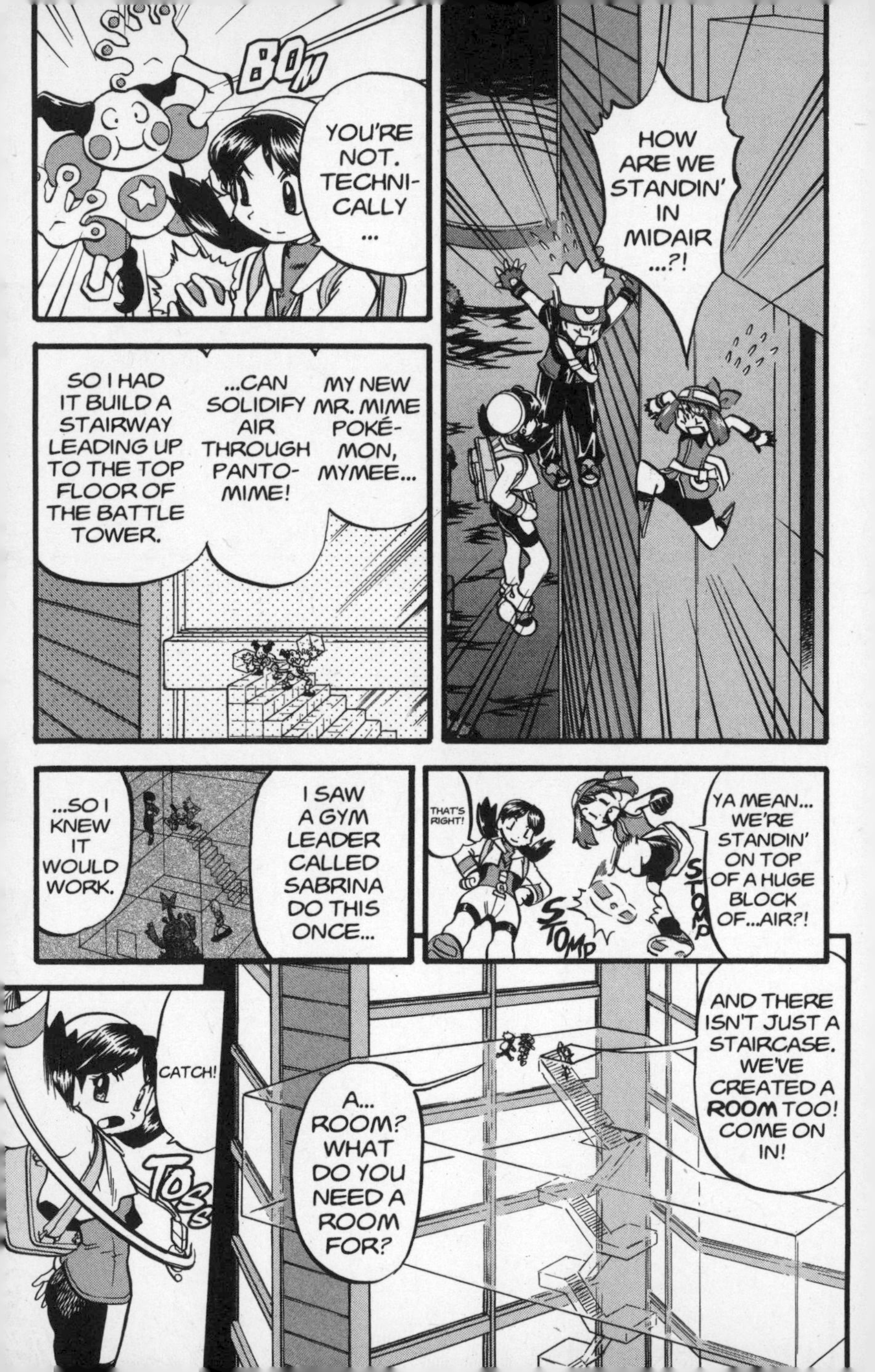
HOW ARE WE STANDIN' IN MIDAIR ...?!
BOM
YOU'RE NOT. TECHNICALLY ...
MY NEW MR. MIME POKÉMON, MYMEE...
...CAN SOLIDIFY AIR THROUGH PANTOMIME!
SO I HAD IT BUILD A STAIRWAY LEADING UP TO THE TOP FLOOR OF THE BATTLE TOWER.
YA MEAN... WE'RE STANDIN' ON TOP OF A HUGE BLOCK OF...AIR?!
STOMP
STOMP
THAT'S RIGHT!
I SAW A GYM LEADER CALLED SABRINA DO THIS ONCE...
...SO I KNEW IT WOULD WORK.
AND THERE ISN'T JUST A STAIRCASE. WE'VE CREATED A **ROOM** TOO! COME ON IN!
A... ROOM? WHAT DO YOU NEED A ROOM FOR?
CATCH!
TOSS

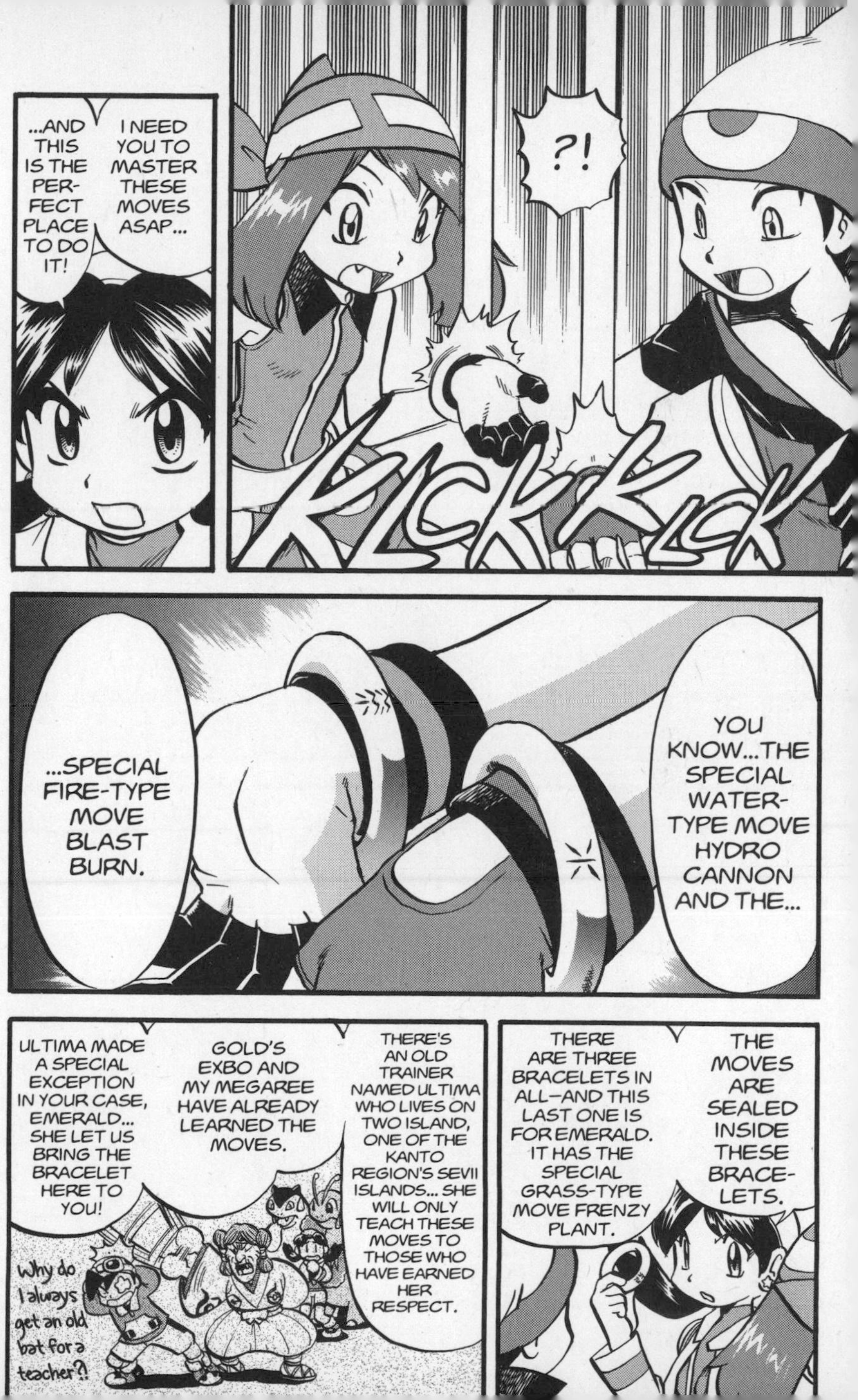
?!
KLICK KLICK
I NEED YOU TO MASTER THESE MOVES ASAP...
...AND THIS IS THE PERFECT PLACE TO DO IT!
YOU KNOW...THE SPECIAL WATER-TYPE MOVE HYDRO CANNON AND THE...
...SPECIAL FIRE-TYPE MOVE BLAST BURN.
THE MOVES ARE SEALED INSIDE THESE BRACELETS.
THERE ARE THREE BRACELETS IN ALL—AND THIS LAST ONE IS FOR EMERALD. IT HAS THE SPECIAL GRASS-TYPE MOVE FRENZY PLANT.
THERE'S AN OLD TRAINER NAMED ULTIMA WHO LIVES ON TWO ISLAND, ONE OF THE KANTO REGION'S SEVII ISLANDS... SHE WILL ONLY TEACH THESE MOVES TO THOSE WHO HAVE EARNED HER RESPECT.
GOLD'S EXBO AND MY MEGAREE HAVE ALREADY LEARNED THE MOVES.
ULTIMA MADE A SPECIAL EXCEPTION IN YOUR CASE, EMERALD... SHE LET US BRING THE BRACELET HERE TO YOU!
Why do I always get an old bat for a teacher?!

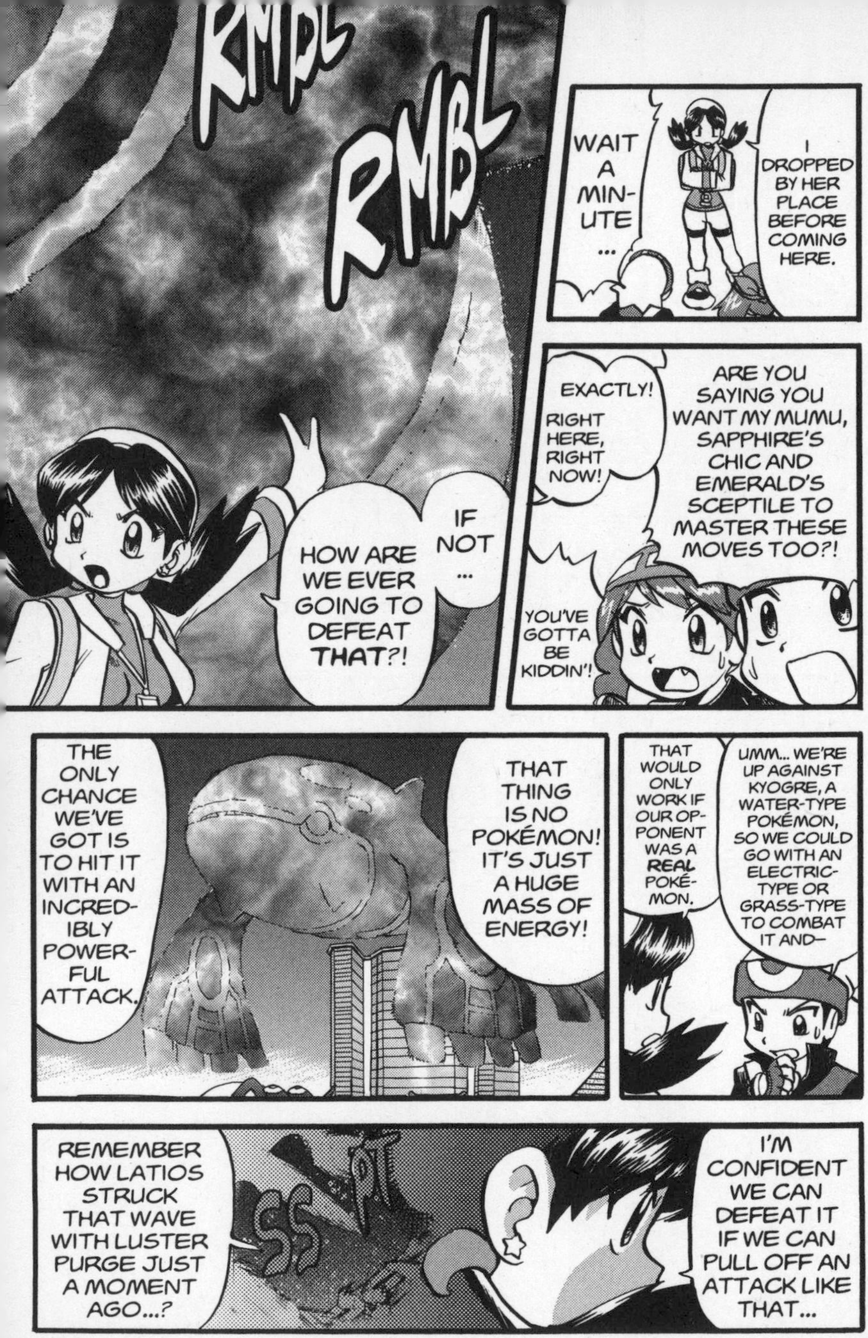
I DROPPED BY HER PLACE BEFORE COMING HERE.
WAIT A MIN-UTE...
ARE YOU SAYING YOU WANT MY MUMU, SAPPHIRE'S CHIC AND EMERALD'S SCEPTILE TO MASTER THESE MOVES TOO?!
EXACTLY!
RIGHT HERE, RIGHT NOW!
YOU'VE GOTTA BE KIDDIN'!
RMBL
RMBL
IF NOT...
HOW ARE WE EVER GOING TO DEFEAT THAT?!
UMM... WE'RE UP AGAINST KYOGRE, A WATER-TYPE POKÉMON, SO WE COULD GO WITH AN ELECTRIC-TYPE OR GRASS-TYPE TO COMBAT IT AND—
THAT WOULD ONLY WORK IF OUR OP-PONENT WAS A REAL POKÉ-MON.
THAT THING IS NO POKÉMON! IT'S JUST A HUGE MASS OF ENERGY!
THE ONLY CHANCE WE'VE GOT IS TO HIT IT WITH AN INCRED-IBLY POWER-FUL ATTACK.
I'M CONFIDENT WE CAN DEFEAT IT IF WE CAN PULL OFF AN ATTACK LIKE THAT...
REMEMBER HOW LATIOS STRUCK THAT WAVE WITH LUSTER PURGE JUST A MOMENT AGO...?

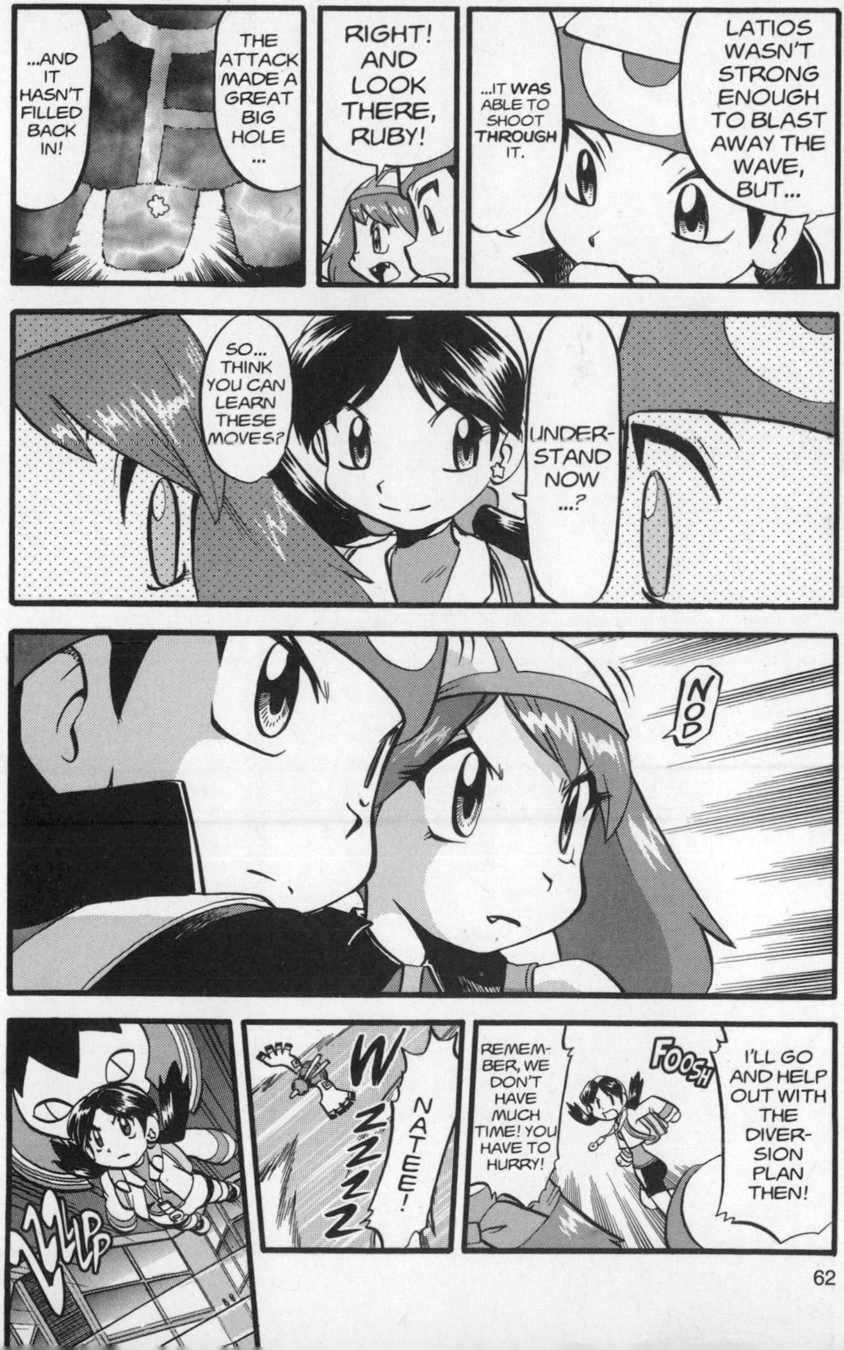
LATIOS WASN'T STRONG ENOUGH TO BLAST AWAY THE WAVE, BUT...
...IT WAS ABLE TO SHOOT THROUGH IT.
RIGHT! AND LOOK THERE, RUBY!
THE ATTACK MADE A GREAT BIG HOLE ...
...AND IT HASN'T FILLED BACK IN!
UNDER-STAND NOW ...?
SO... THINK YOU CAN LEARN THESE MOVES?
NOD
I'LL GO AND HELP OUT WITH THE DIVER-SION PLAN THEN!
FOOSH
REMEM-BER, WE DON'T HAVE MUCH TIME! YOU HAVE TO HURRY!
NATEE!
WZZZZZ

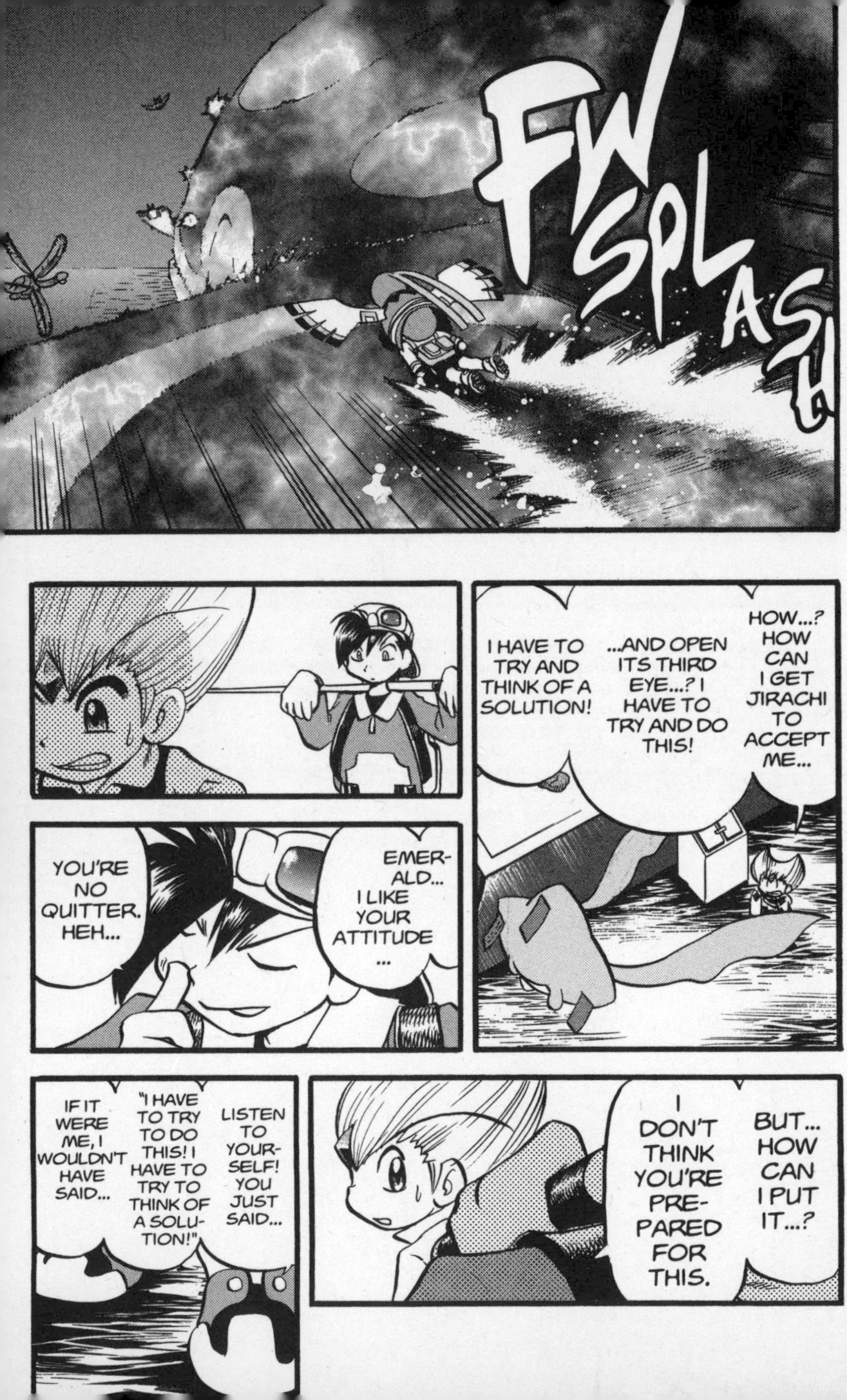
FW
SPLASH
HOW...? HOW CAN I GET JIRACHI TO ACCEPT ME...
...AND OPEN ITS THIRD EYE...? I HAVE TO TRY AND DO THIS!
I HAVE TO TRY AND THINK OF A SOLUTION!
EMERALD... I LIKE YOUR ATTITUDE...
YOU'RE NO QUITTER. HEH...
BUT... HOW CAN I PUT IT...?
I DON'T THINK YOU'RE PREPARED FOR THIS.
LISTEN TO YOURSELF! YOU JUST SAID...
"I HAVE TO TRY TO DO THIS! I HAVE TO TRY TO THINK OF A SOLUTION!"
IF IT WERE ME, I WOULDN'T HAVE SAID...

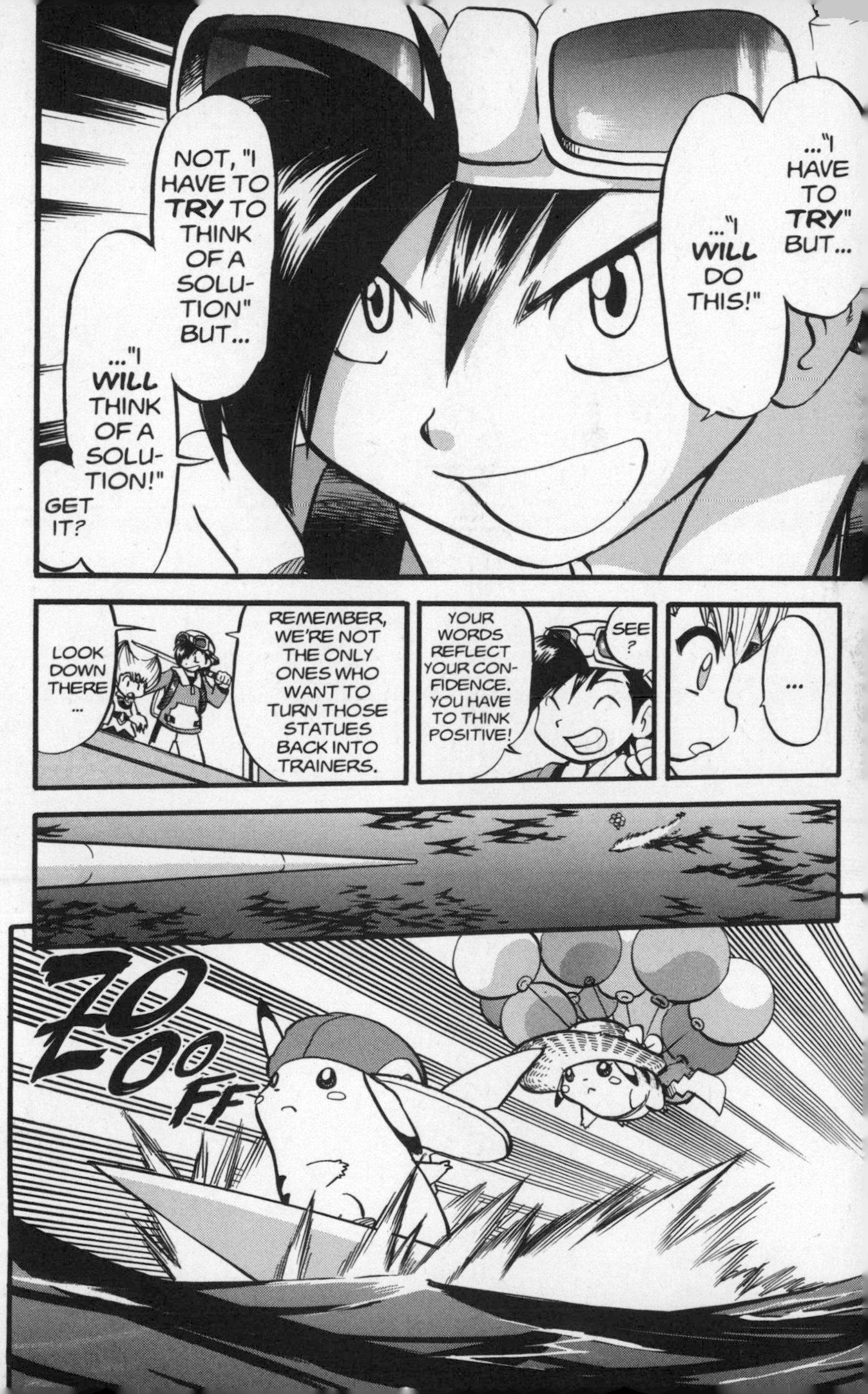
..."I HAVE TO TRY" BUT...
..."I WILL DO THIS!"
NOT, "I HAVE TO TRY TO THINK OF A SOLUTION" BUT...
..."I WILL THINK OF A SOLUTION!"
GET IT?
...
SEE?
YOUR WORDS REFLECT YOUR CONFIDENCE. YOU HAVE TO THINK POSITIVE!
REMEMBER, WE'RE NOT THE ONLY ONES WHO WANT TO TURN THOSE STATUES BACK INTO TRAINERS.
LOOK DOWN THERE ...
ZOOOFF

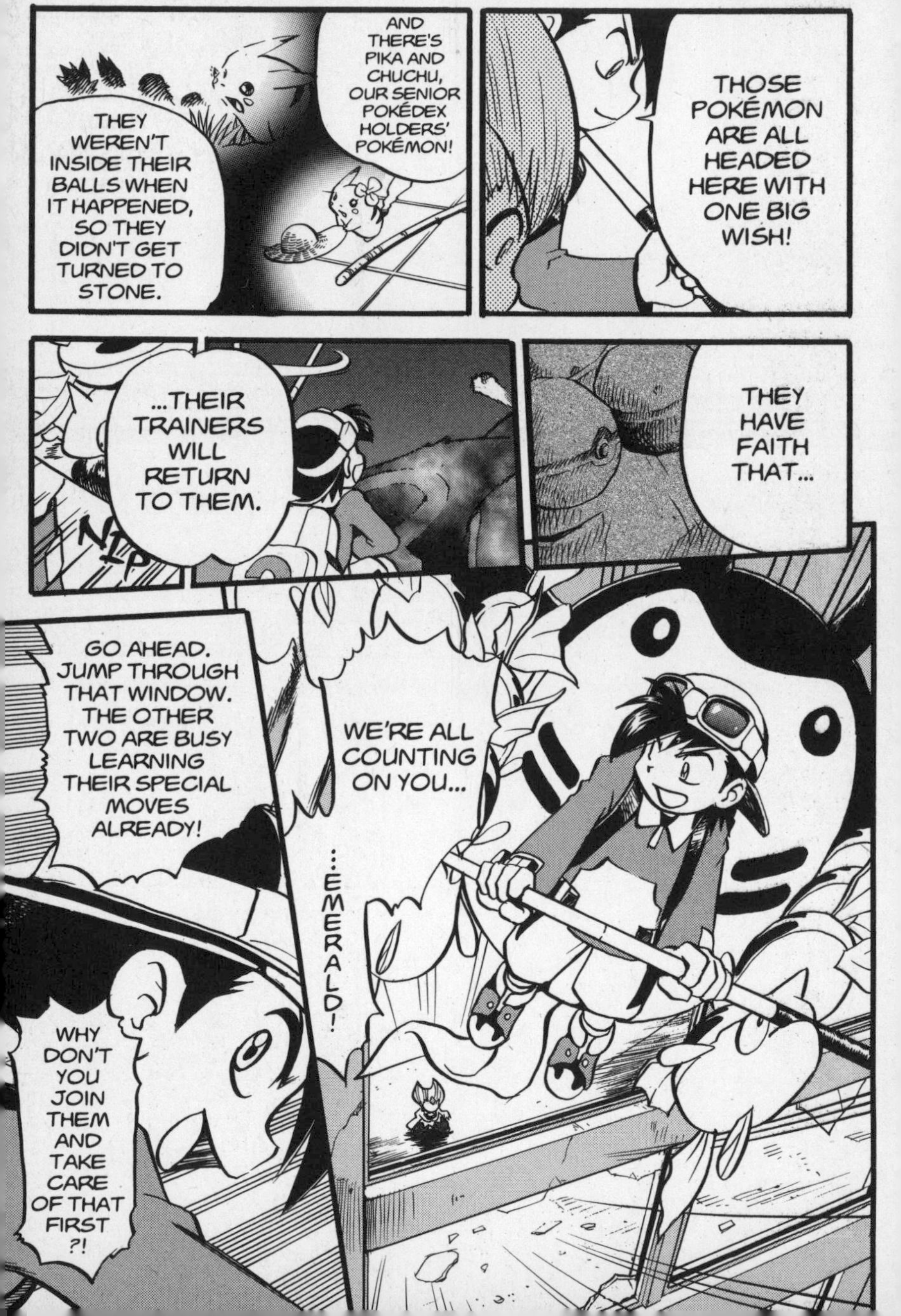
THOSE POKÉMON ARE ALL HEADED HERE WITH ONE BIG WISH!
AND THERE'S PIKA AND CHUCHU, OUR SENIOR POKÉDEX HOLDERS' POKÉMON!
THEY WEREN'T INSIDE THEIR BALLS WHEN IT HAPPENED, SO THEY DIDN'T GET TURNED TO STONE.
THEY HAVE FAITH THAT...
...THEIR TRAINERS WILL RETURN TO THEM.
NIP
WE'RE ALL COUNTING ON YOU...
...EMERALD!
GO AHEAD. JUMP THROUGH THAT WINDOW. THE OTHER TWO ARE BUSY LEARNING THEIR SPECIAL MOVES ALREADY!
WHY DON'T YOU JOIN THEM AND TAKE CARE OF THAT FIRST?!

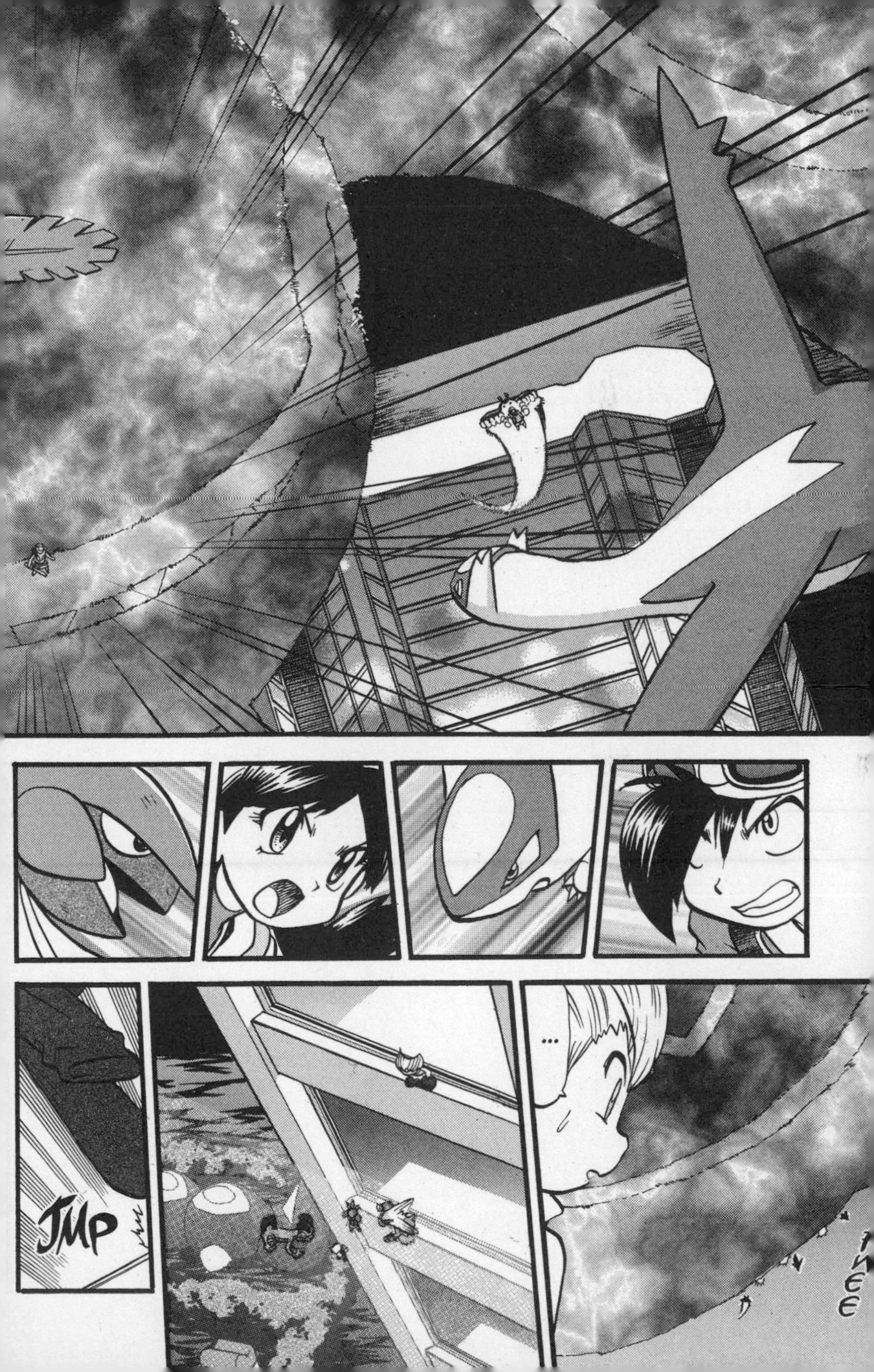
...
FWEE
JMP

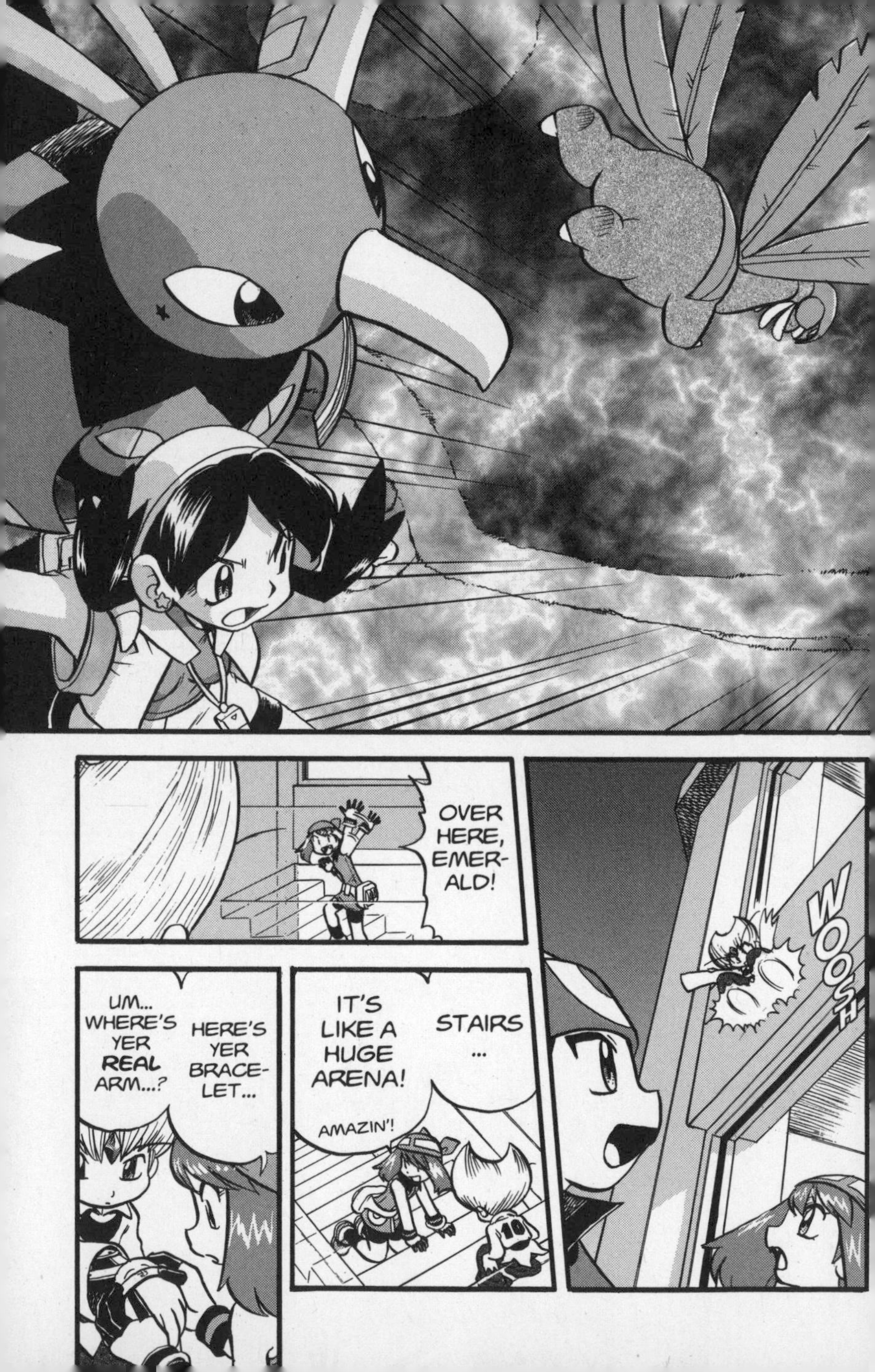
WOOOSH
OVER HERE, EMER-ALD!
STAIRS ...
IT'S LIKE A HUGE ARENA!
AMAZIN'!
HERE'S YER BRACE-LET...
UM... WHERE'S YER **REAL** ARM...?

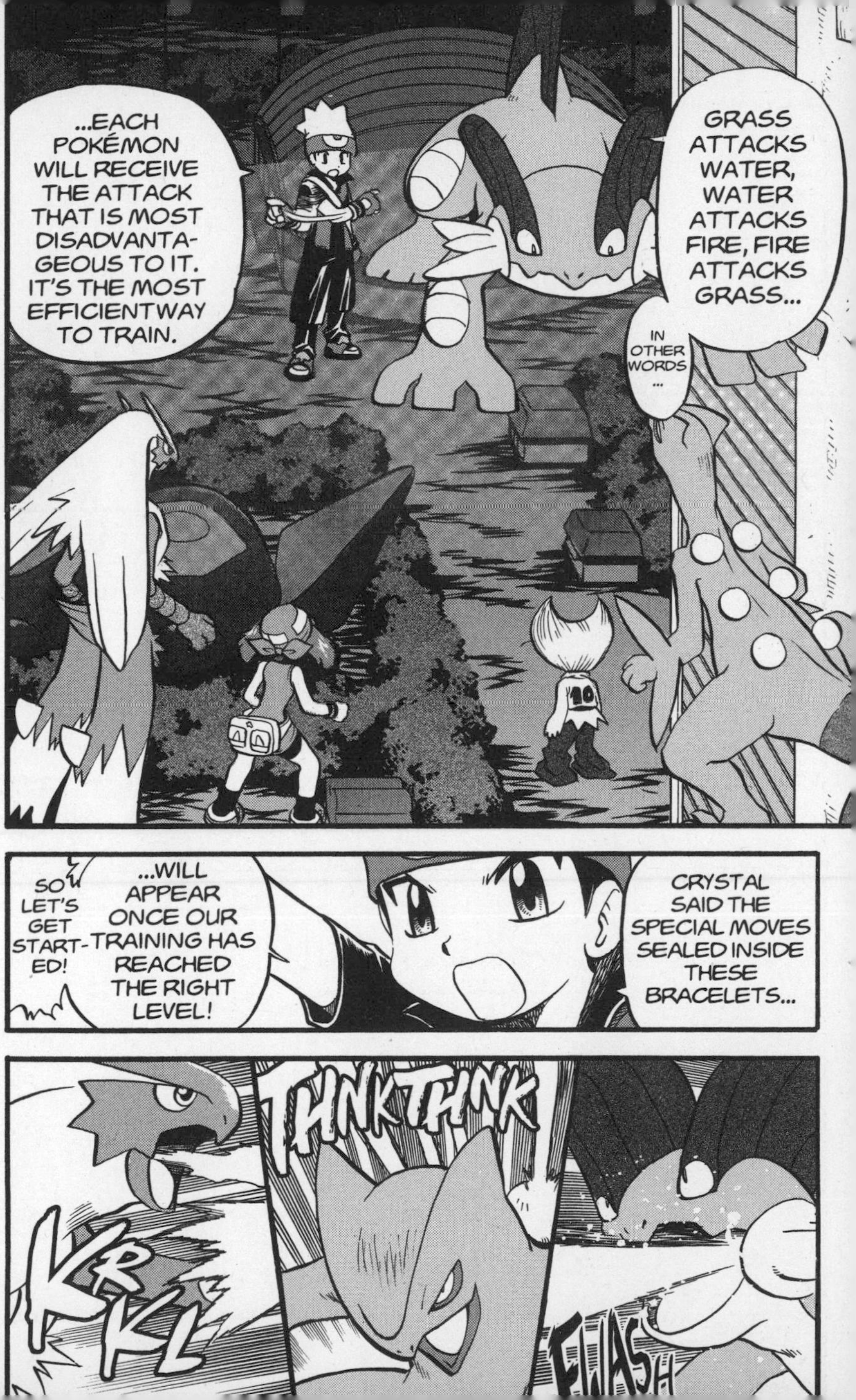
GRASS ATTACKS WATER, WATER ATTACKS FIRE, FIRE ATTACKS GRASS...
IN OTHER WORDS...
...EACH POKÉMON WILL RECEIVE THE ATTACK THAT IS MOST DISADVANTAGEOUS TO IT. IT'S THE MOST EFFICIENT WAY TO TRAIN.
CRYSTAL SAID THE SPECIAL MOVES SEALED INSIDE THESE BRACELETS...
...WILL APPEAR ONCE OUR TRAINING HAS REACHED THE RIGHT LEVEL!
SO LET'S GET STARTED!
THNK THNK
FWASH
KRKL

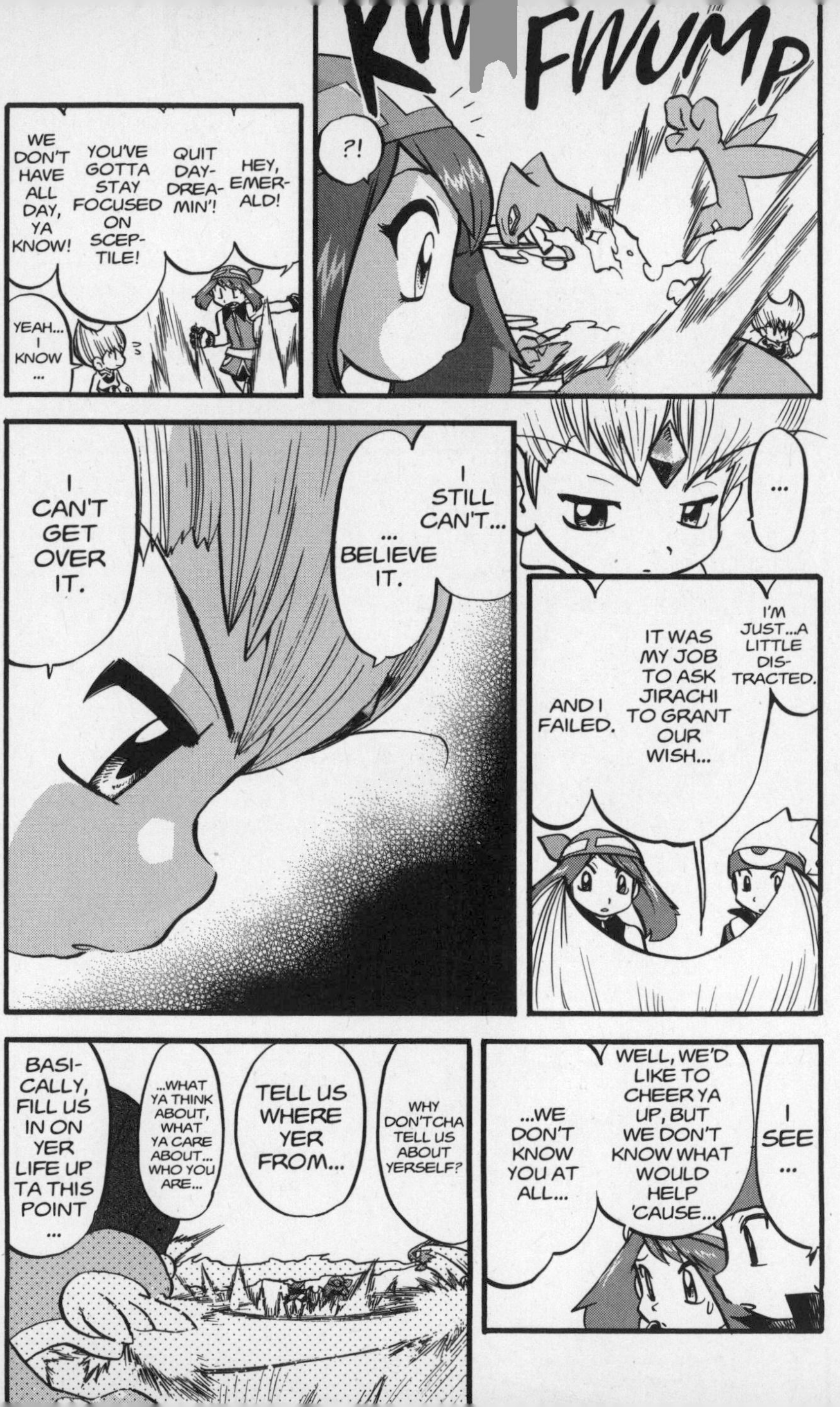
FWUMP
?!
HEY, EMERALD!
QUIT DAYDREAMIN'!
YOU'VE GOTTA STAY FOCUSED ON SCEPTILE!
WE DON'T HAVE ALL DAY, YA KNOW!
YEAH... I KNOW...
...
I'M JUST...A LITTLE DISTRACTED.
IT WAS MY JOB TO ASK JIRACHI TO GRANT OUR WISH...
AND I FAILED.
I STILL CAN'T... ...BELIEVE IT.
I CAN'T GET OVER IT.
I SEE...
WELL, WE'D LIKE TO CHEER YA UP, BUT WE DON'T KNOW WHAT WOULD HELP 'CAUSE...
...WE DON'T KNOW YOU AT ALL...
WHY DON'TCHA TELL US ABOUT YERSELF?
TELL US WHERE YER FROM...
...WHAT YA THINK ABOUT, WHAT YA CARE ABOUT... WHO YOU ARE...
BASICALLY, FILL US IN ON YER LIFE UP TA THIS POINT...

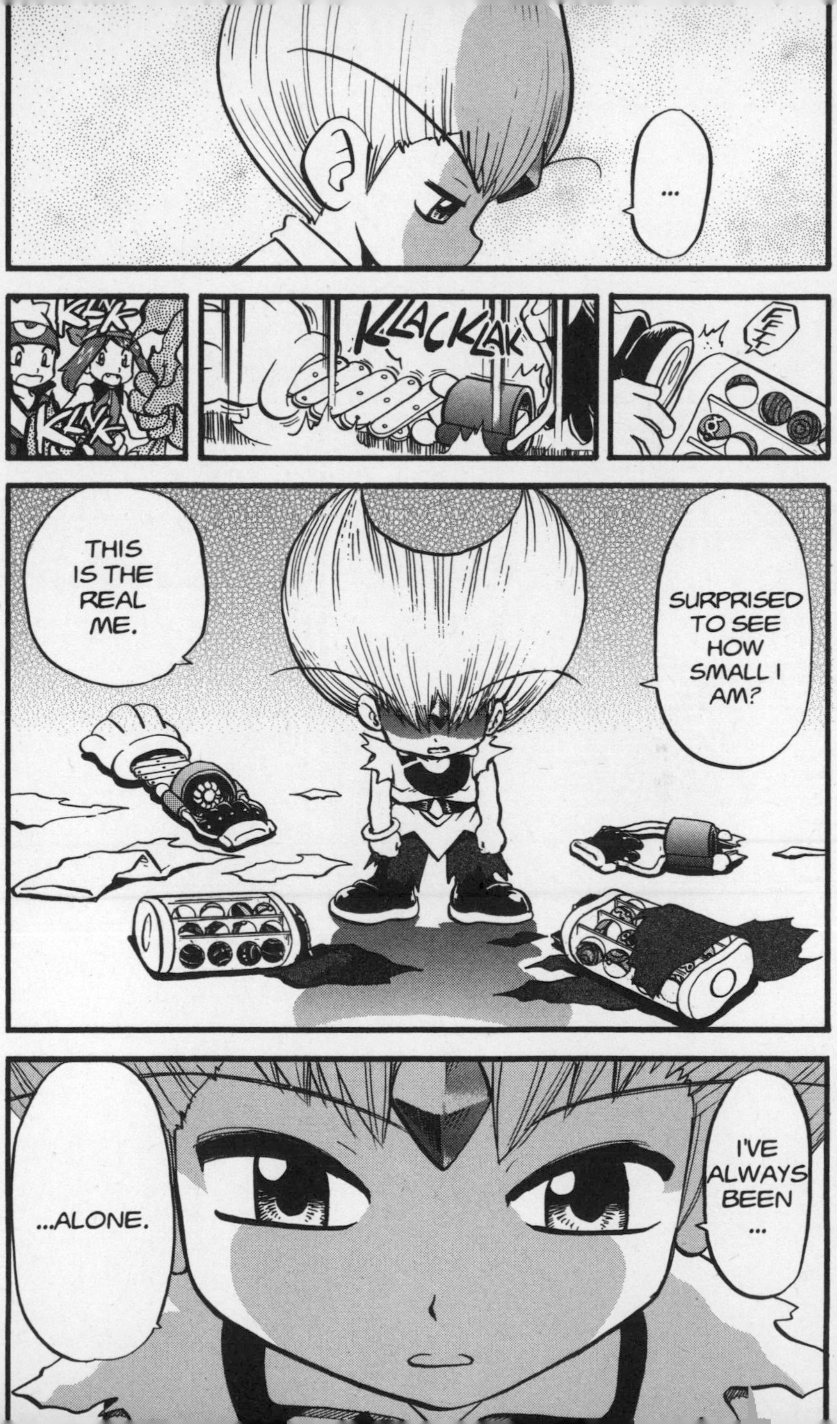
...
KLACKLAK
KLNK
KLNK
SURPRISED TO SEE HOW SMALL I AM?
THIS IS THE REAL ME.
I'VE ALWAYS BEEN ...
...ALONE.

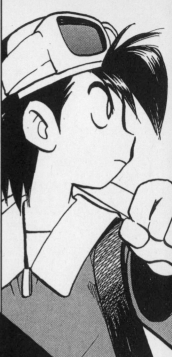

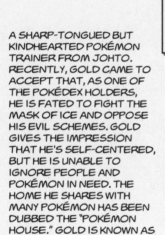

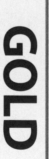

CHARACTER PROFILE / GOLD

A SHARP-TONGUED BUT KINDHEARTED POKÉMON TRAINER FROM JOHTO. RECENTLY, GOLD CAME TO ACCEPT THAT, AS ONE OF THE POKÉDEX HOLDERS, HE IS FATED TO FIGHT THE MASK OF ICE AND OPPOSE HIS EVIL SCHEMES. GOLD GIVES THE IMPRESSION THAT HE'S SELF-CENTERED, BUT HE IS UNABLE TO IGNORE PEOPLE AND POKÉMON IN NEED. THE HOME HE SHARES WITH MANY POKÉMON HAS BEEN DUBBED THE "POKÉMON HOUSE." GOLD IS KNOWN AS THE "HATCHER."

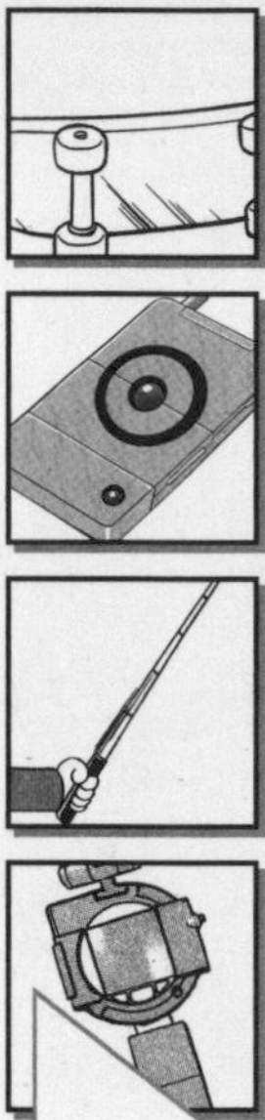

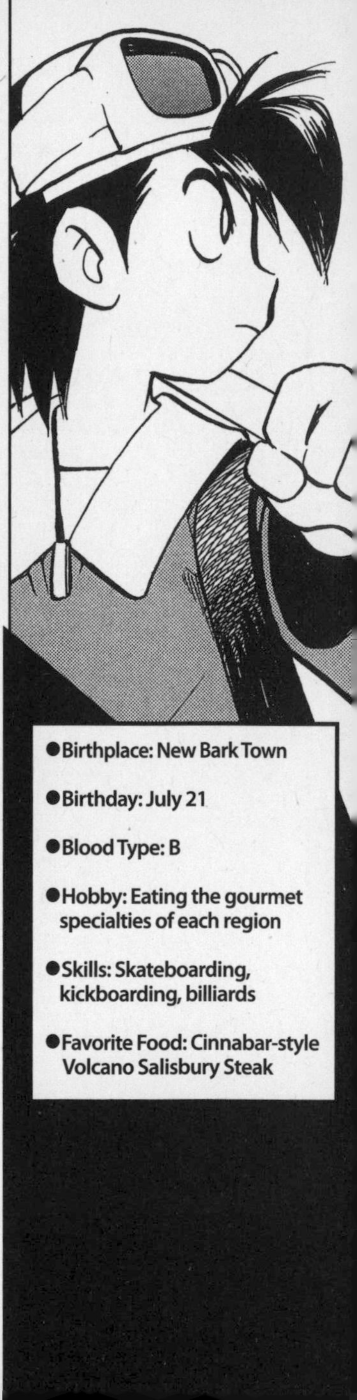

GOLD

- ●Birthplace: New Bark Town

- ●Birthday: July 21

- ●Blood Type: B

- ●Hobby: Eating the gourmet specialties of each region

- ●Skills: Skateboarding, kickboarding, billiards

- ●Favorite Food: Cinnabar-style Volcano Salisbury Steak

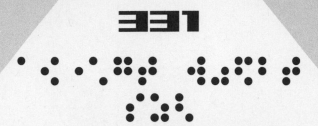

331

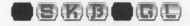

The Final Battle IV

●⊙⑤⑧Ⓑ●⑤ⓁⓁ

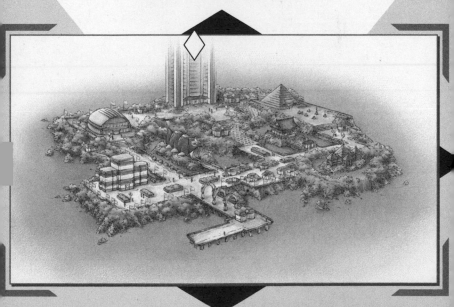

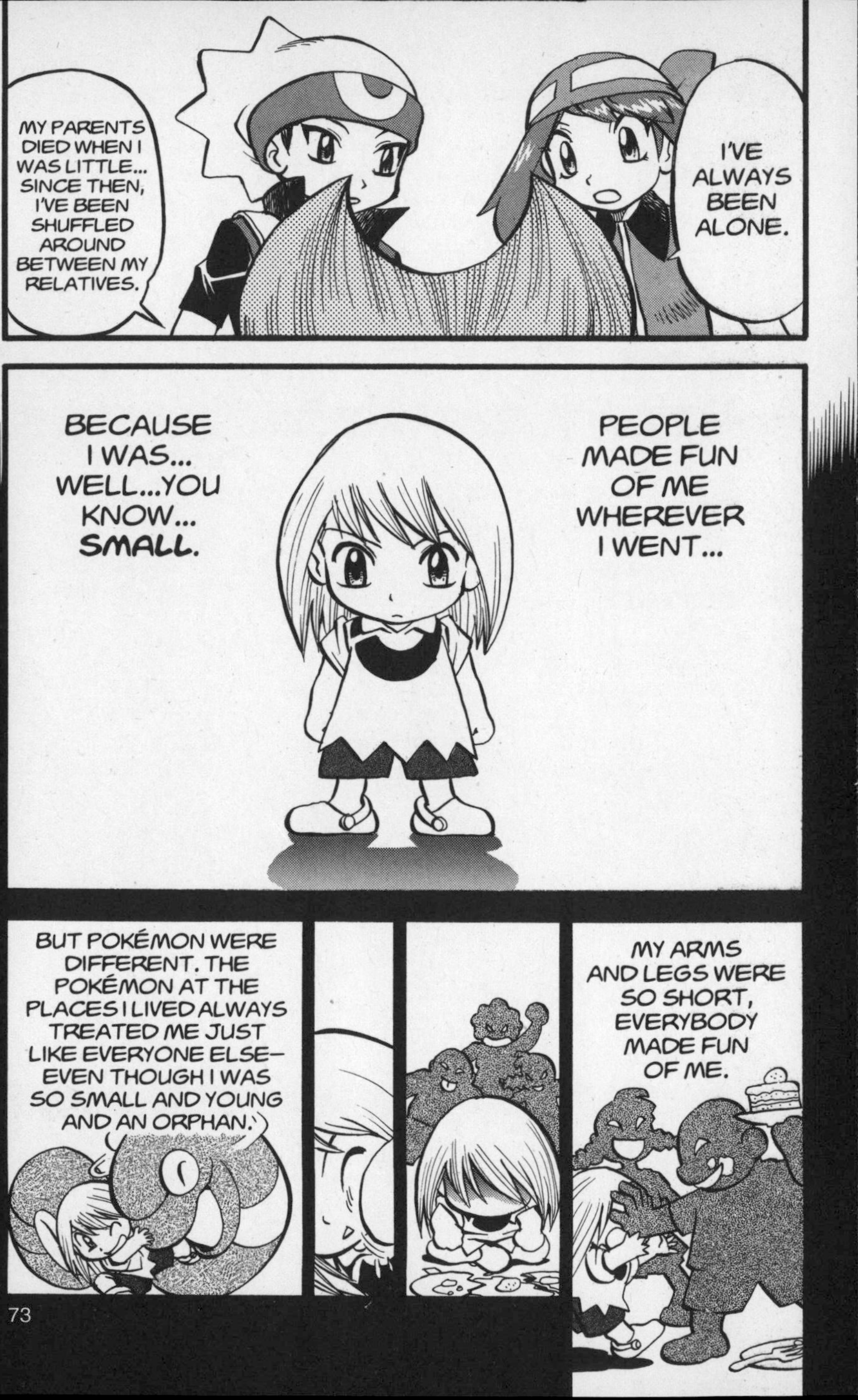
I'VE ALWAYS BEEN ALONE.
MY PARENTS DIED WHEN I WAS LITTLE... SINCE THEN, I'VE BEEN SHUFFLED AROUND BETWEEN MY RELATIVES.
PEOPLE MADE FUN OF ME WHEREVER I WENT...
BECAUSE I WAS... WELL...YOU KNOW... **SMALL.**
MY ARMS AND LEGS WERE SO SHORT, EVERYBODY MADE FUN OF ME.
BUT POKÉMON WERE DIFFERENT. THE POKÉMON AT THE PLACES I LIVED ALWAYS TREATED ME JUST LIKE EVERYONE ELSE—EVEN THOUGH I WAS SO SMALL AND YOUNG AND AN ORPHAN.

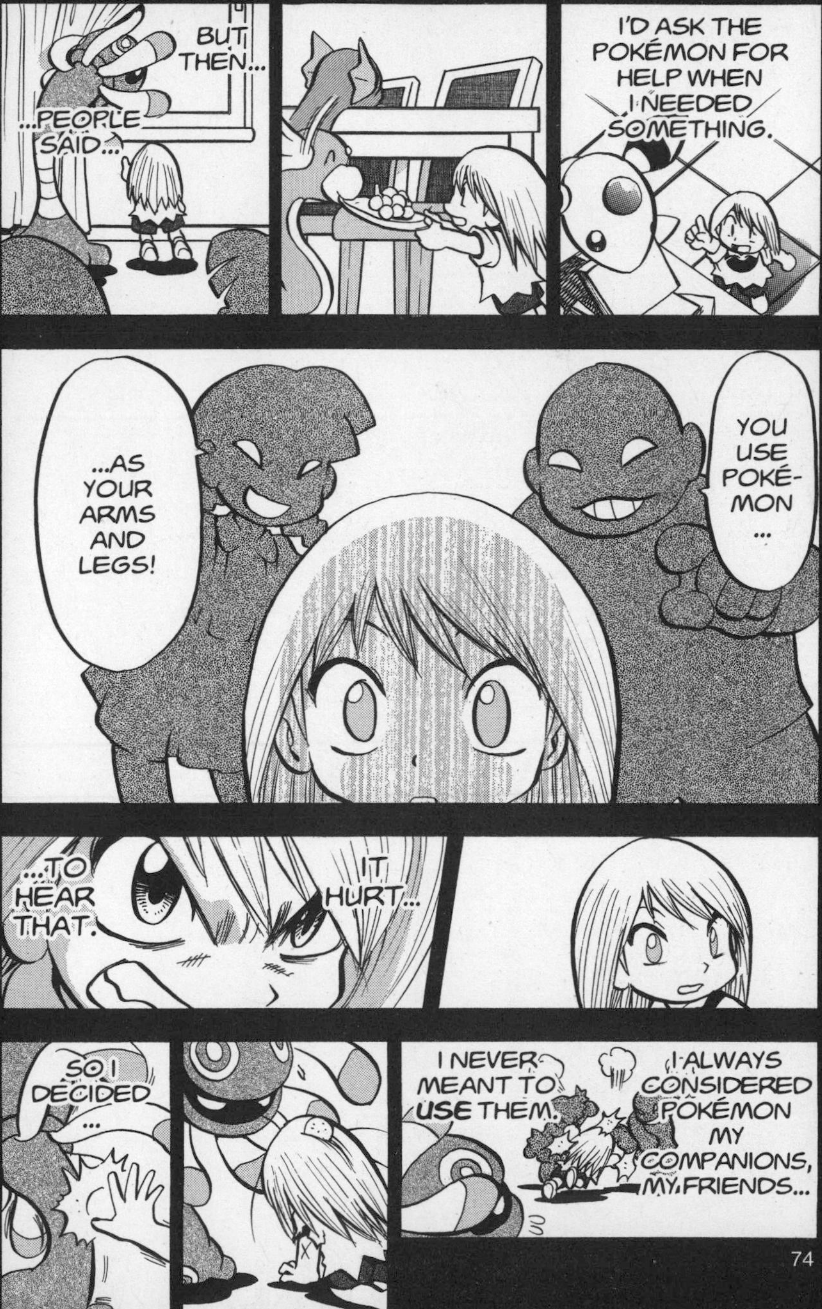
I'D ASK THE POKÉMON FOR HELP WHEN I NEEDED SOMETHING.
BUT THEN...
...PEOPLE SAID...
YOU USE POKÉMON...
...AS YOUR ARMS AND LEGS!
IT HURT...
...TO HEAR THAT.
I ALWAYS CONSIDERED POKÉMON MY COMPANIONS, MY FRIENDS...
I NEVER MEANT TO USE THEM.
SO I DECIDED...

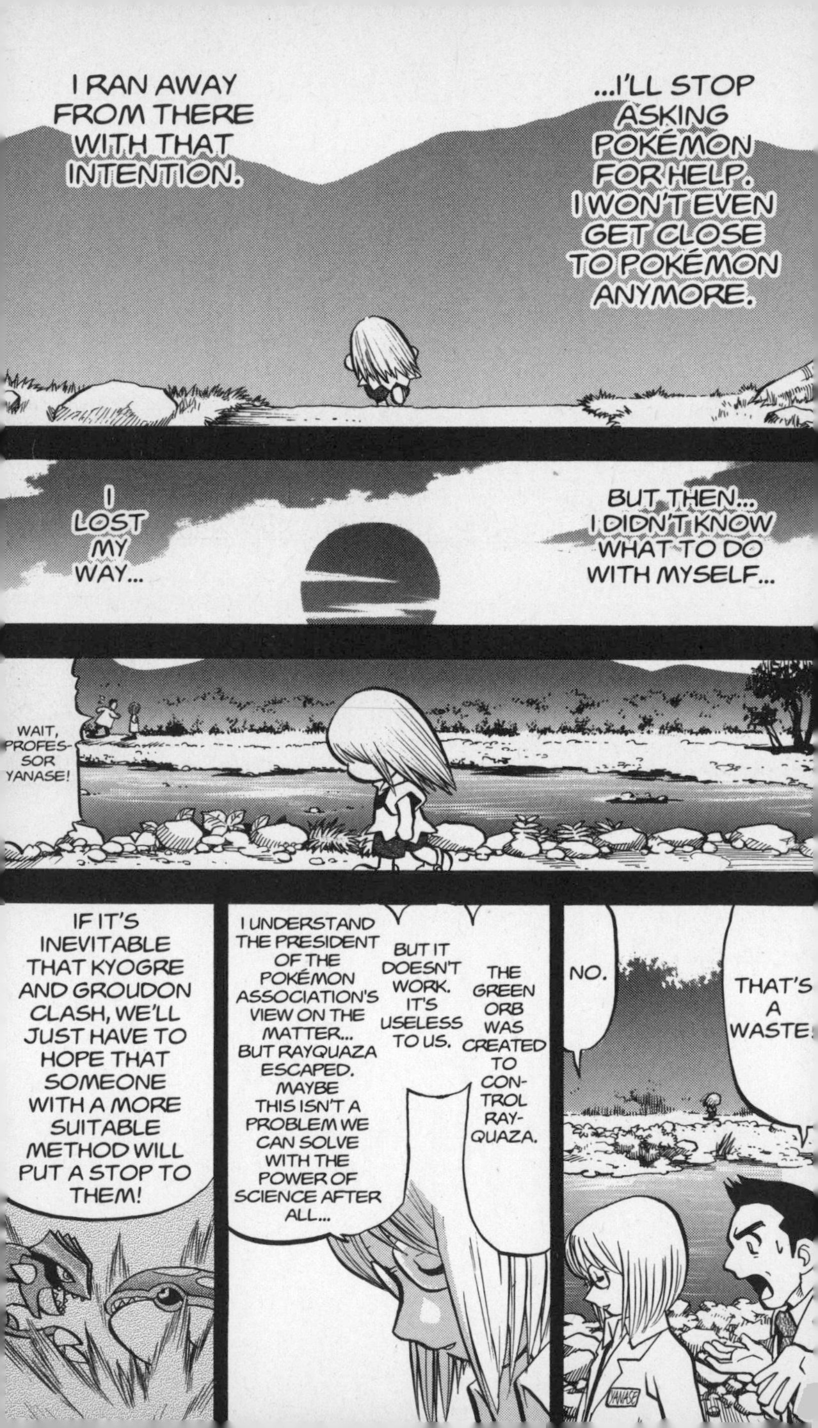
...I'LL STOP ASKING POKÉMON FOR HELP. I WON'T EVEN GET CLOSE TO POKÉMON ANYMORE.
I RAN AWAY FROM THERE WITH THAT INTENTION.
BUT THEN... I DIDN'T KNOW WHAT TO DO WITH MYSELF...
I LOST MY WAY...
WAIT, PROFES-SOR YANASE!
THAT'S A WASTE.
NO.
YANASE
THE GREEN ORB WAS CREATED TO CON-TROL RAY-QUAZA.
BUT IT DOESN'T WORK. IT'S USELESS TO US.
I UNDERSTAND THE PRESIDENT OF THE POKÉMON ASSOCIATION'S VIEW ON THE MATTER... BUT RAYQUAZA ESCAPED. MAYBE THIS ISN'T A PROBLEM WE CAN SOLVE WITH THE POWER OF SCIENCE AFTER ALL...
IF IT'S INEVITABLE THAT KYOGRE AND GROUDON CLASH, WE'LL JUST HAVE TO HOPE THAT SOMEONE WITH A MORE SUITABLE METHOD WILL PUT A STOP TO THEM!

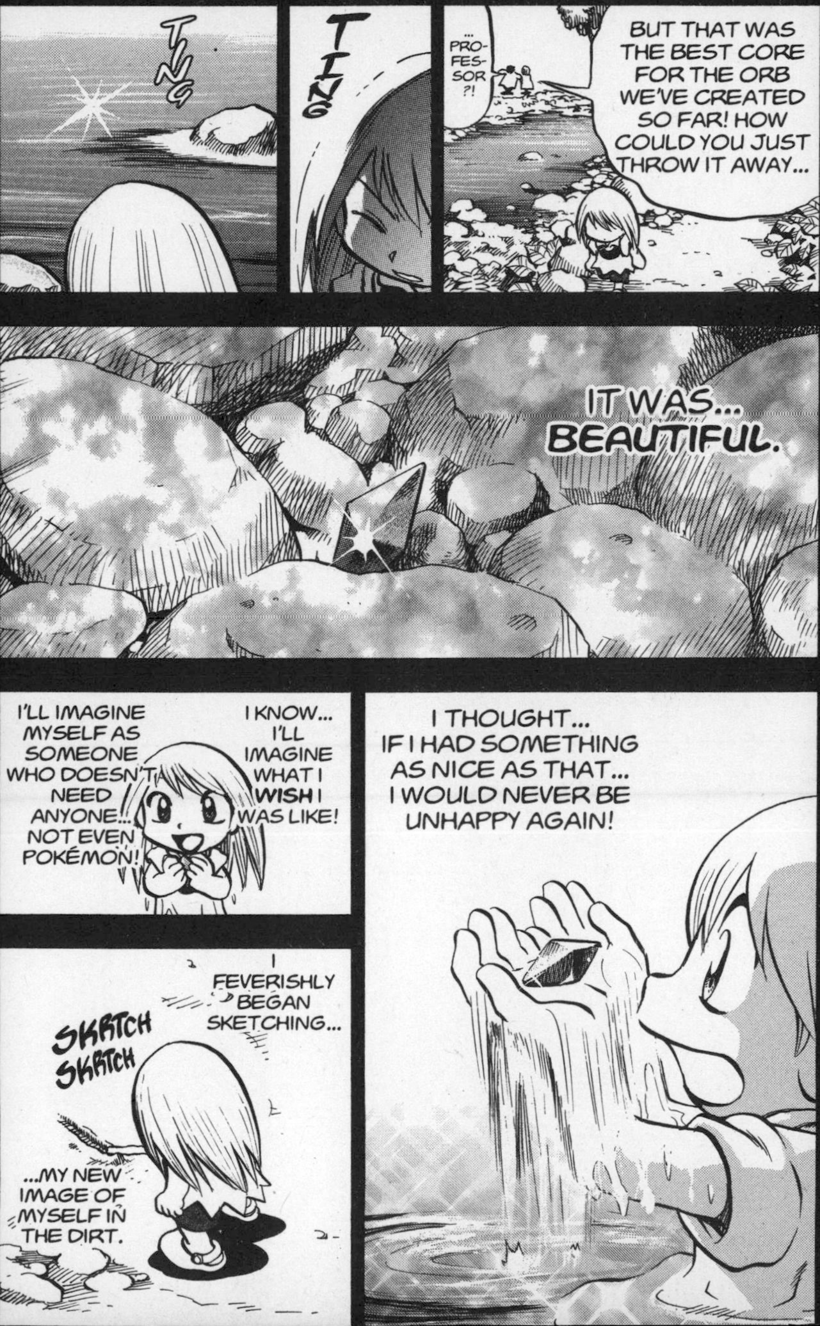
BUT THAT WAS THE BEST CORE FOR THE ORB WE'VE CREATED SO FAR! HOW COULD YOU JUST THROW IT AWAY...
...PROFESSOR?!
TING
TING
IT WAS... BEAUTIFUL.
I THOUGHT... IF I HAD SOMETHING AS NICE AS THAT... I WOULD NEVER BE UNHAPPY AGAIN!
I KNOW... I'LL IMAGINE WHAT I WISH I WAS LIKE!
I'LL IMAGINE MYSELF AS SOMEONE WHO DOESN'T NEED ANYONE... NOT EVEN POKÉMON!
I FEVERISHLY BEGAN SKETCHING...
SKRTCH SKRTCH
...MY NEW IMAGE OF MYSELF IN THE DIRT.

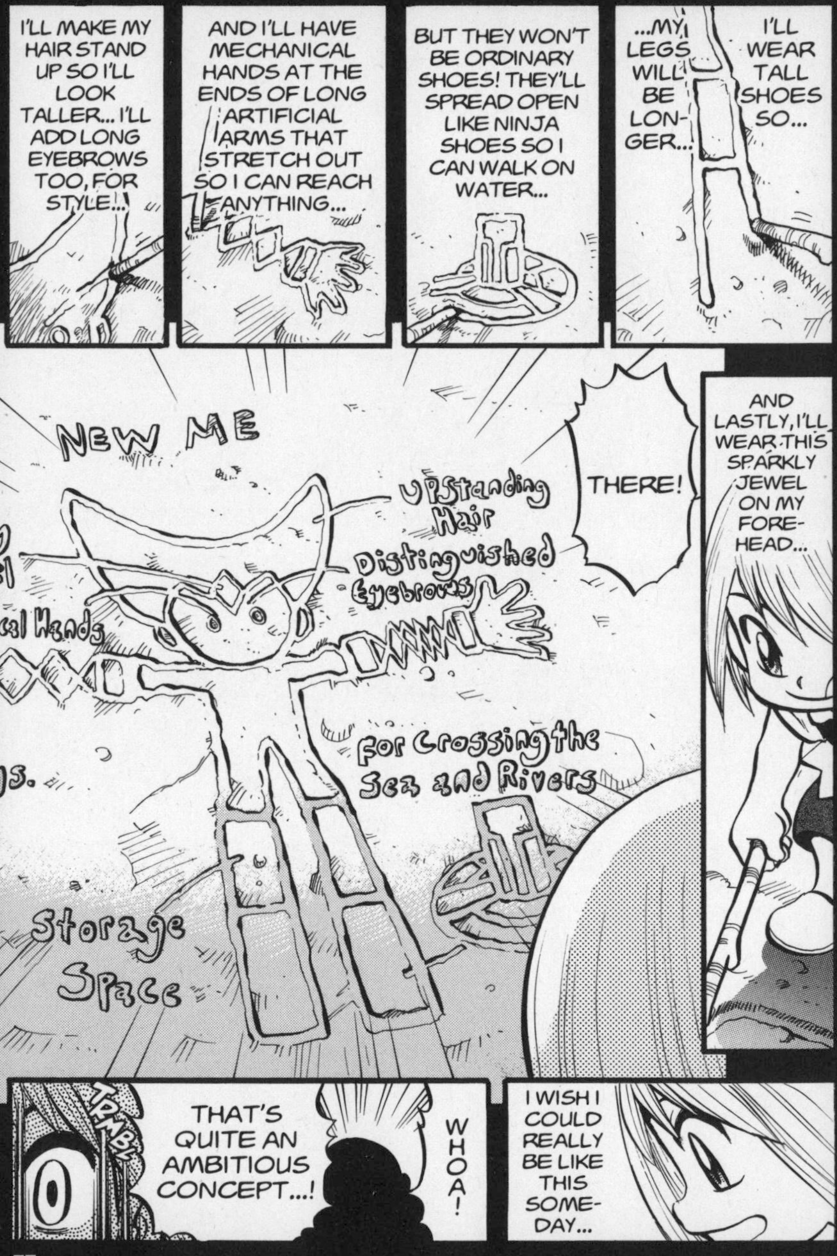
I'LL WEAR TALL SHOES SO...
...MY LEGS WILL BE LONGER...
BUT THEY WON'T BE ORDINARY SHOES! THEY'LL SPREAD OPEN LIKE NINJA SHOES SO I CAN WALK ON WATER...
AND I'LL HAVE MECHANICAL HANDS AT THE ENDS OF LONG ARTIFICIAL ARMS THAT STRETCH OUT SO I CAN REACH ANYTHING...
I'LL MAKE MY HAIR STAND UP SO I'LL LOOK TALLER... I'LL ADD LONG EYEBROWS TOO, FOR STYLE...
AND LASTLY, I'LL WEAR THIS SPARKLY JEWEL ON MY FOREHEAD...
THERE!
NEW ME
Upstanding Hair
Distinguished Eyebrows
For Crossing the Sea and Rivers
Storage Space
I WISH I COULD REALLY BE LIKE THIS SOMEDAY...
WHOA!
THAT'S QUITE AN AMBITIOUS CONCEPT...!

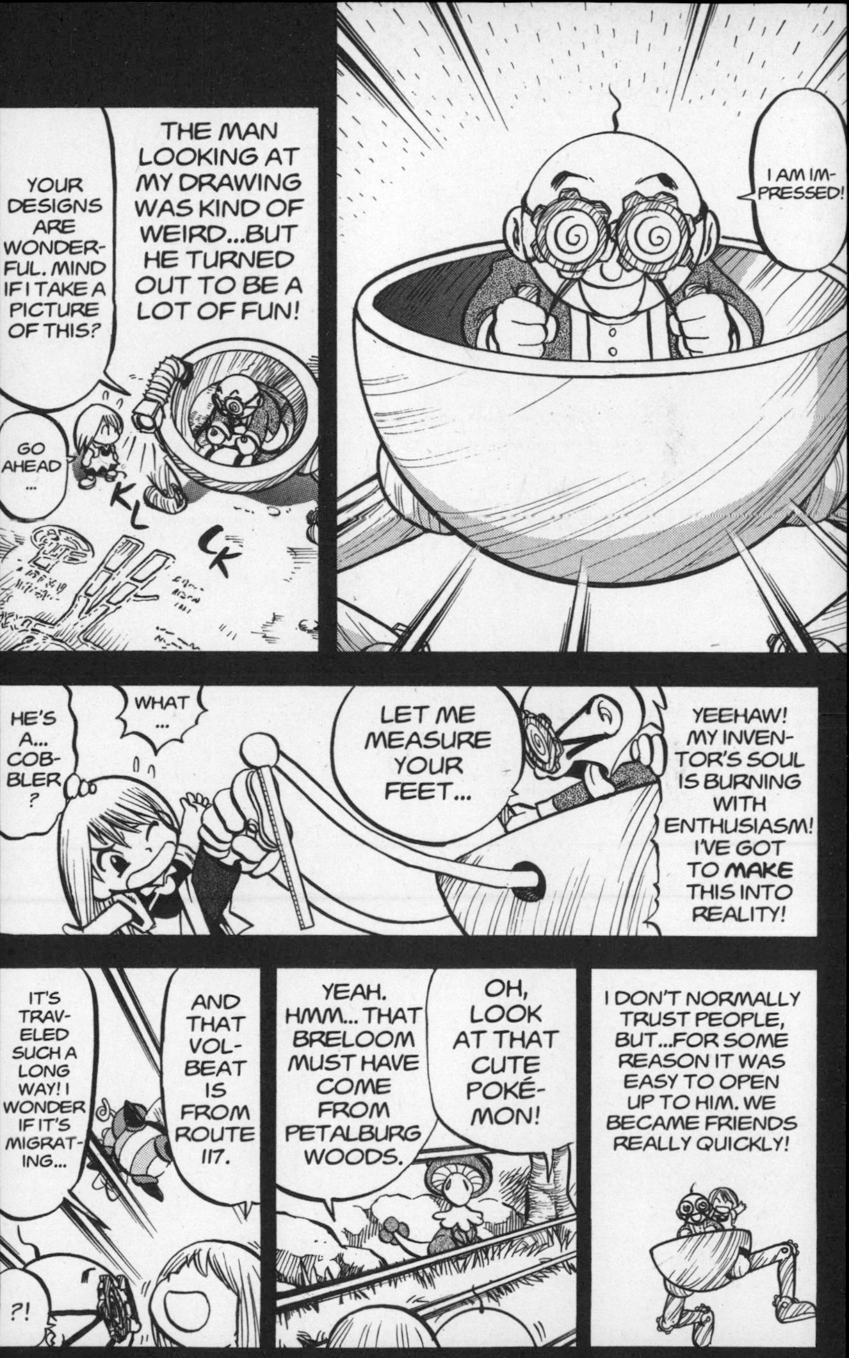
I AM IMPRESSED!
THE MAN LOOKING AT MY DRAWING WAS KIND OF WEIRD...BUT HE TURNED OUT TO BE A LOT OF FUN!
YOUR DESIGNS ARE WONDERFUL. MIND IF I TAKE A PICTURE OF THIS?
GO AHEAD ...
KL
CK
YEEHAW! MY INVENTOR'S SOUL IS BURNING WITH ENTHUSIASM! I'VE GOT TO MAKE THIS INTO REALITY!
LET ME MEASURE YOUR FEET...
WHAT ...
HE'S A... COBBLER?
I DON'T NORMALLY TRUST PEOPLE, BUT...FOR SOME REASON IT WAS EASY TO OPEN UP TO HIM. WE BECAME FRIENDS REALLY QUICKLY!
OH, LOOK AT THAT CUTE POKÉMON!
YEAH. HMM... THAT BRELOOM MUST HAVE COME FROM PETALBURG WOODS.
AND THAT VOLBEAT IS FROM ROUTE 117.
IT'S TRAVELED SUCH A LONG WAY! I WONDER IF IT'S MIGRATING...
?!

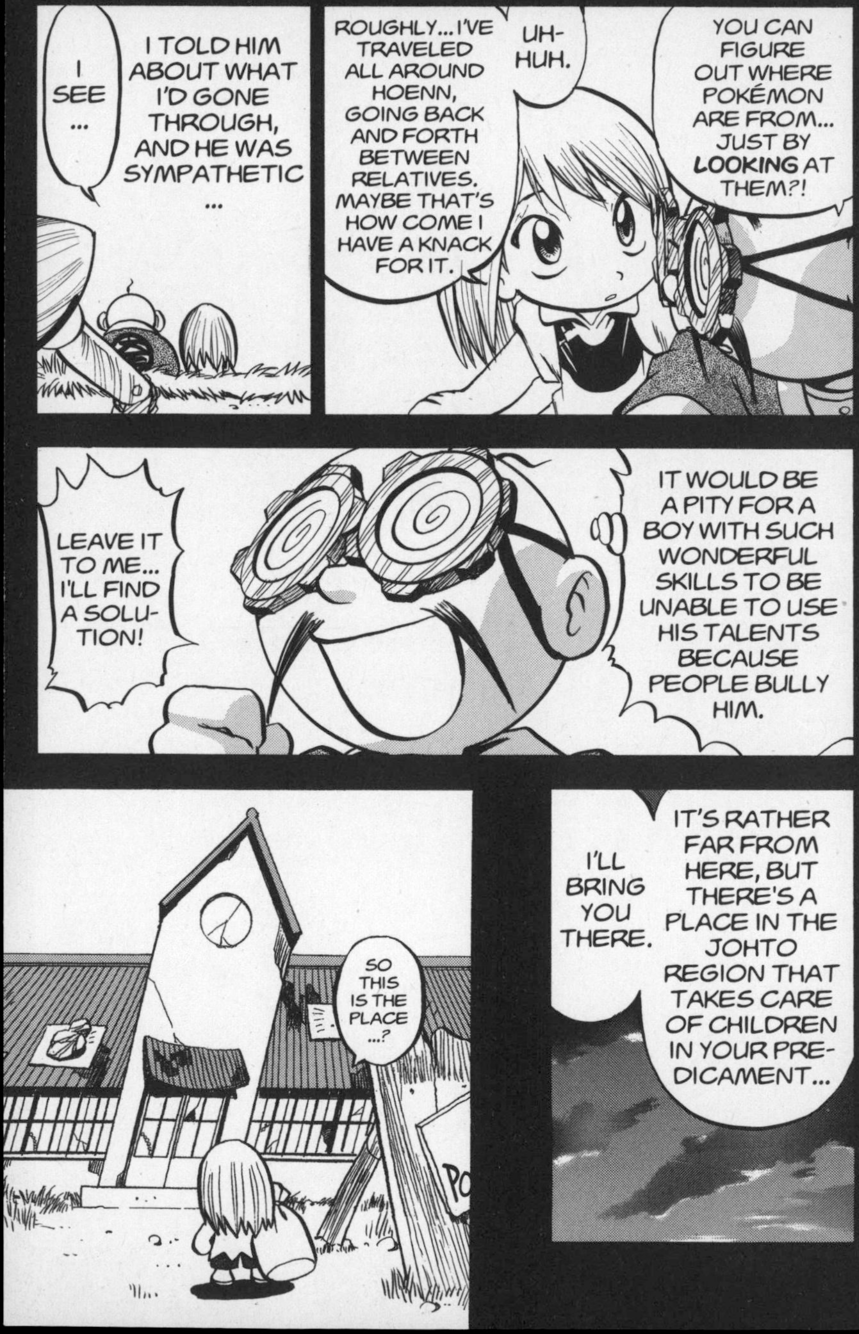
YOU CAN FIGURE OUT WHERE POKÉMON ARE FROM... JUST BY **LOOKING** AT THEM?!
UH-HUH.
ROUGHLY... I'VE TRAVELED ALL AROUND HOENN, GOING BACK AND FORTH BETWEEN RELATIVES. MAYBE THAT'S HOW COME I HAVE A KNACK FOR IT.
I TOLD HIM ABOUT WHAT I'D GONE THROUGH, AND HE WAS SYMPATHETIC ...
I SEE ...
IT WOULD BE A PITY FOR A BOY WITH SUCH WONDERFUL SKILLS TO BE UNABLE TO USE HIS TALENTS BECAUSE PEOPLE BULLY HIM.
LEAVE IT TO ME... I'LL FIND A SOLU-TION!
IT'S RATHER FAR FROM HERE, BUT THERE'S A PLACE IN THE JOHTO REGION THAT TAKES CARE OF CHILDREN IN YOUR PRE-DICAMENT...
I'LL BRING YOU THERE.
SO THIS IS THE PLACE ...?

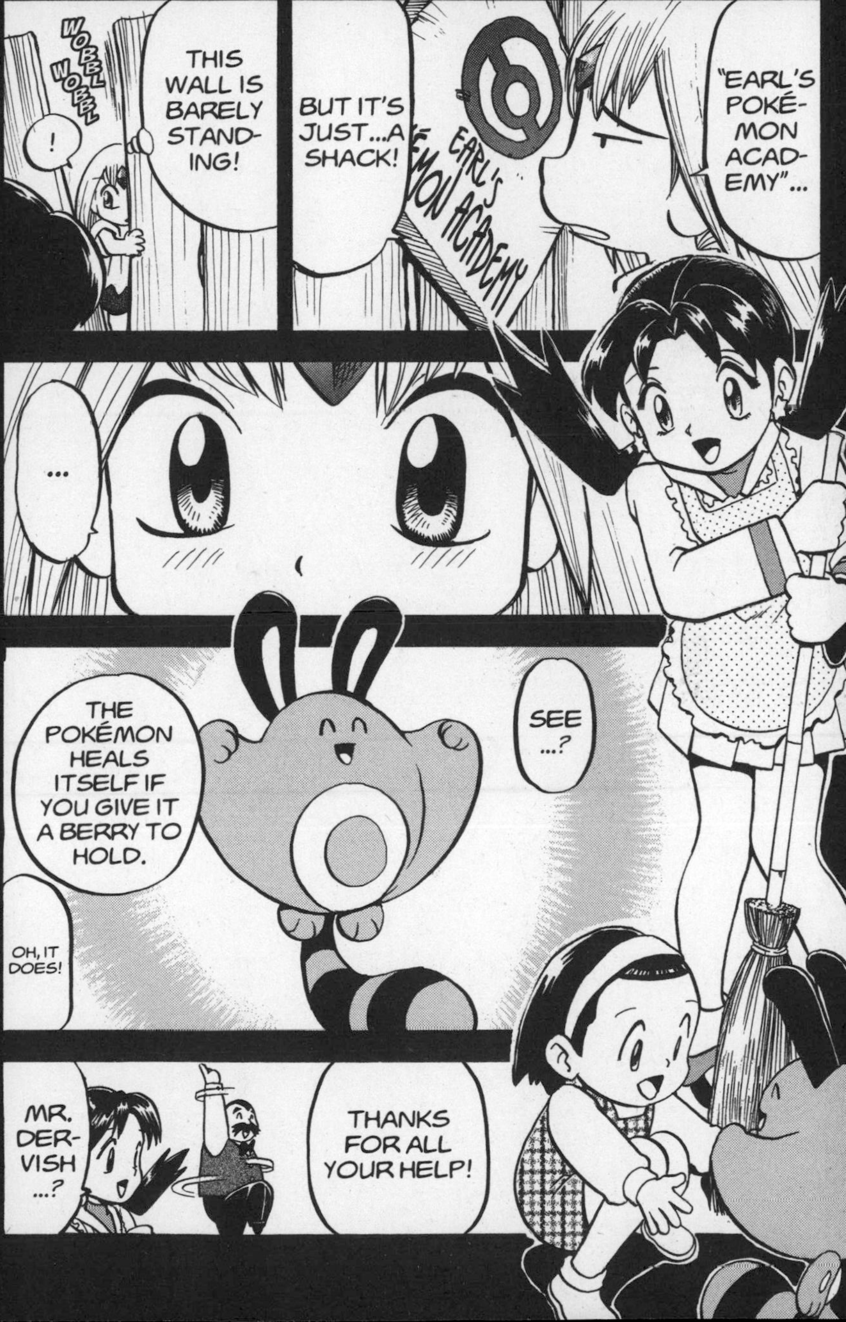
"EARL'S POKÉMON ACADEMY"...
BUT IT'S JUST...A SHACK!
THIS WALL IS BARELY STANDING!
WOBBL WOBBL
!
...
SEE ...?
THE POKÉMON HEALS ITSELF IF YOU GIVE IT A BERRY TO HOLD.
OH, IT DOES!
THANKS FOR ALL YOUR HELP!
MR. DERVISH ...?

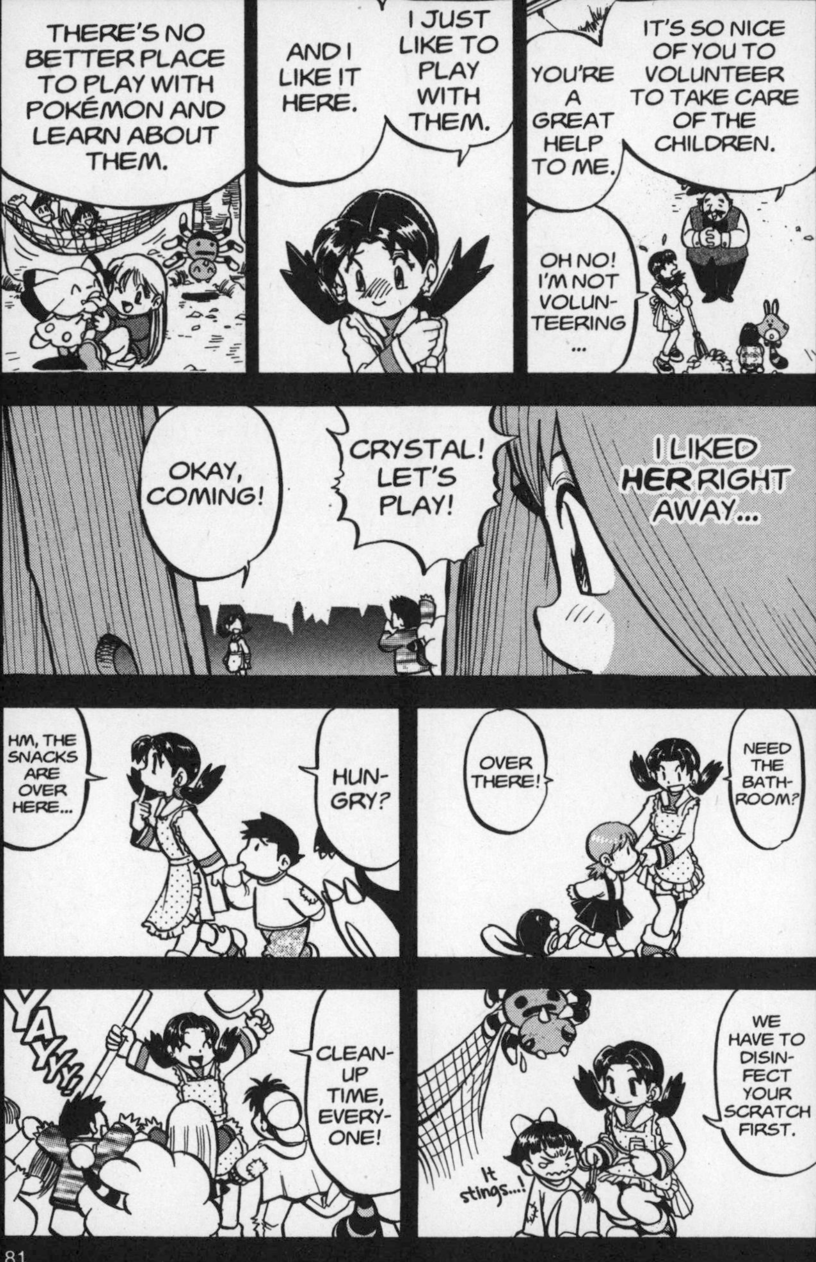

THERE'S NO BETTER PLACE TO PLAY WITH POKÉMON AND LEARN ABOUT THEM.
AND I LIKE IT HERE.
I JUST LIKE TO PLAY WITH THEM.
IT'S SO NICE OF YOU TO VOLUNTEER TO TAKE CARE OF THE CHILDREN.
YOU'RE A GREAT HELP TO ME.
OH NO! I'M NOT VOLUNTEERING ...
I LIKED HER RIGHT AWAY...
CRYSTAL! LET'S PLAY!
OKAY, COMING!
HUNGRY?
HM, THE SNACKS ARE OVER HERE...
NEED THE BATHROOM?
OVER THERE!
YAY!
CLEAN-UP TIME, EVERYONE!
WE HAVE TO DISINFECT YOUR SCRATCH FIRST.
It stings...!

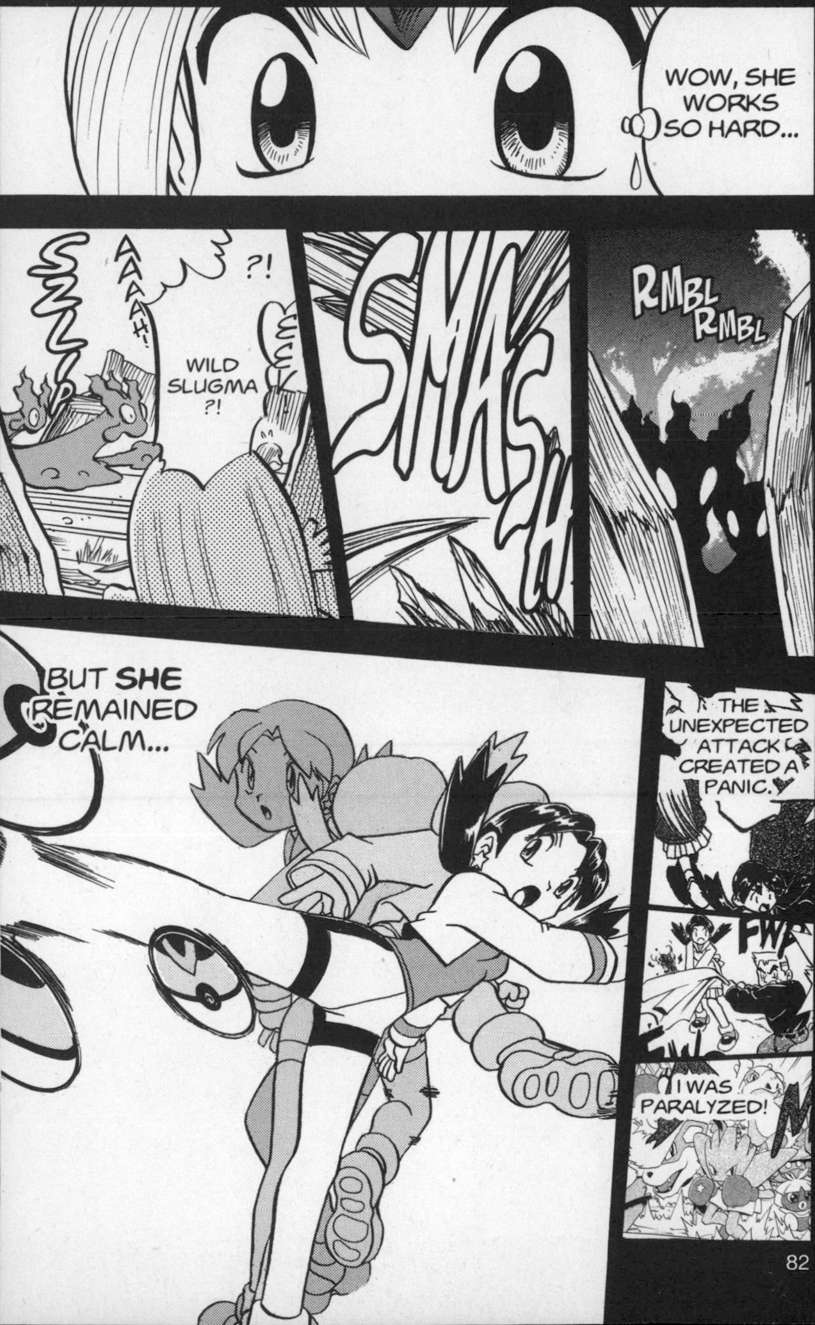
WOW, SHE WORKS SO HARD...
RMBL RMBL
SMASH
?!
AAAAH!
WILD SLUGMA ?!
THE UNEXPECTED ATTACK CREATED A PANIC.
FWP
I WAS PARALYZED!
BUT SHE REMAINED CALM...

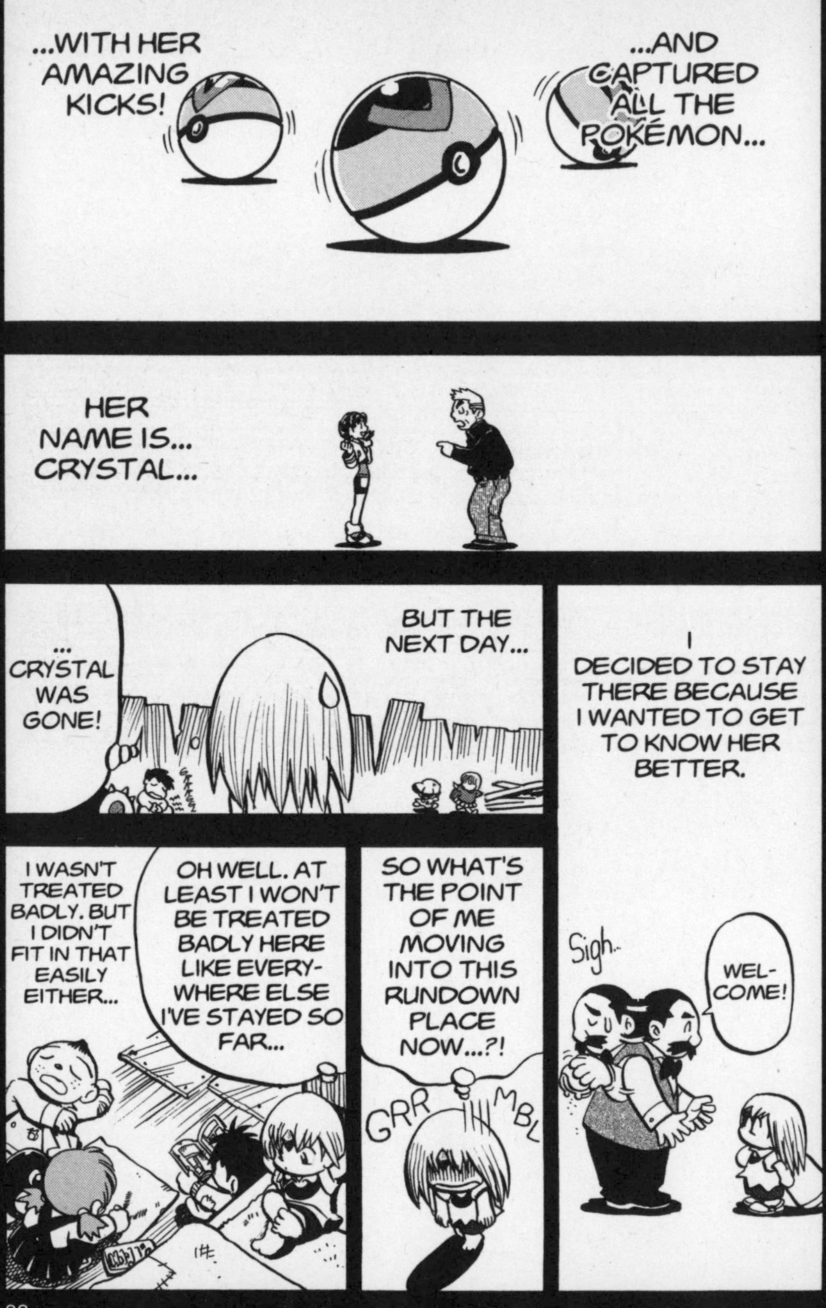
...AND CAPTURED ALL THE POKÉMON...
...WITH HER AMAZING KICKS!
HER NAME IS... CRYSTAL...
I DECIDED TO STAY THERE BECAUSE I WANTED TO GET TO KNOW HER BETTER.
BUT THE NEXT DAY...
... CRYSTAL WAS GONE!
WEL-COME!
Sigh..
SO WHAT'S THE POINT OF ME MOVING INTO THIS RUNDOWN PLACE NOW...?!
GRR
MBL
OH WELL. AT LEAST I WON'T BE TREATED BADLY HERE LIKE EVERY-WHERE ELSE I'VE STAYED SO FAR...
I WASN'T TREATED BADLY. BUT I DIDN'T FIT IN THAT EASILY EITHER...

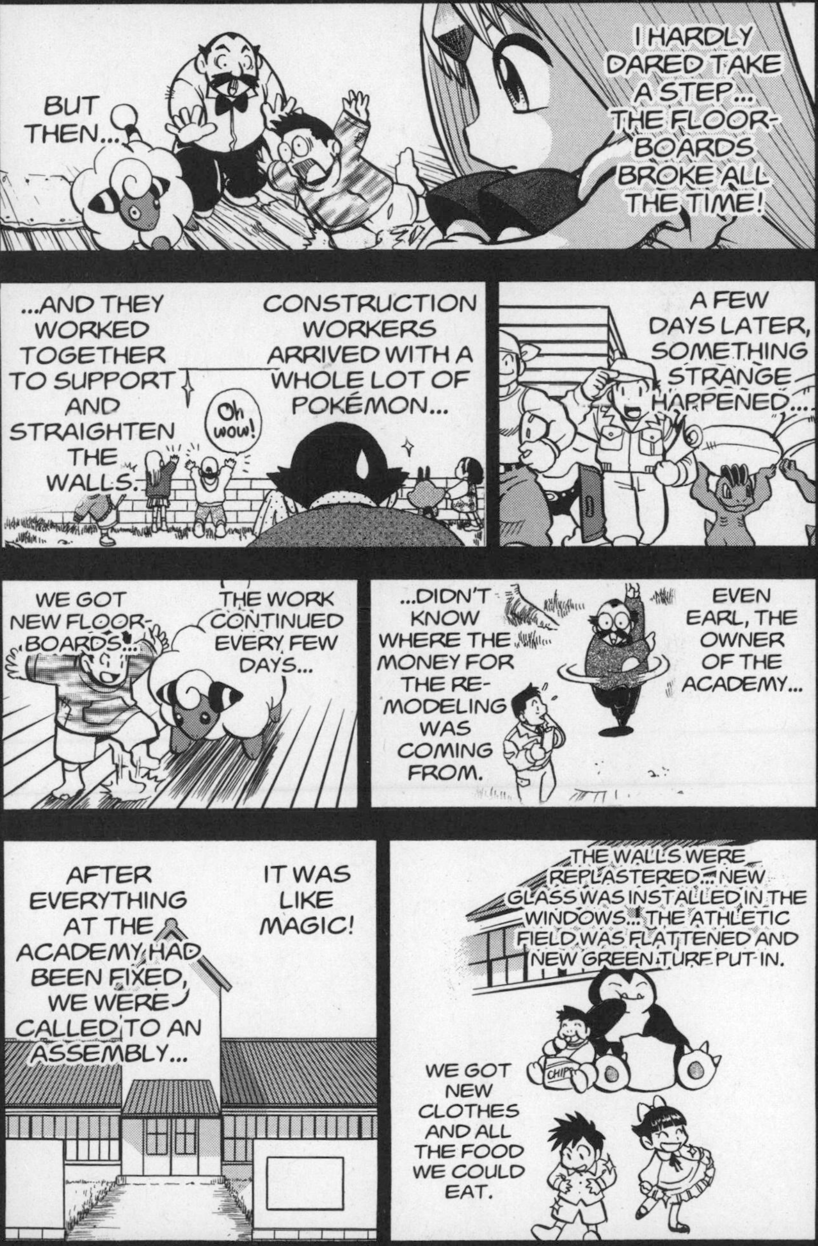
I HARDLY DARED TAKE A STEP... THE FLOOR-BOARDS BROKE ALL THE TIME!
BUT THEN...
A FEW DAYS LATER, SOMETHING STRANGE HAPPENED...
CONSTRUCTION WORKERS ARRIVED WITH A WHOLE LOT OF POKÉMON...
...AND THEY WORKED TOGETHER TO SUPPORT AND STRAIGHTEN THE WALLS.
Oh wow!
EVEN EARL, THE OWNER OF THE ACADEMY...
...DIDN'T KNOW WHERE THE MONEY FOR THE RE-MODELING WAS COMING FROM.
THE WORK CONTINUED EVERY FEW DAYS...
WE GOT NEW FLOOR-BOARDS...
THE WALLS WERE REPLASTERED... NEW GLASS WAS INSTALLED IN THE WINDOWS... THE ATHLETIC FIELD WAS FLATTENED AND NEW GREEN TURF PUT IN.
CHIPS
WE GOT NEW CLOTHES AND ALL THE FOOD WE COULD EAT.
IT WAS LIKE MAGIC!
AFTER EVERYTHING AT THE ACADEMY HAD BEEN FIXED, WE WERE CALLED TO AN ASSEMBLY...

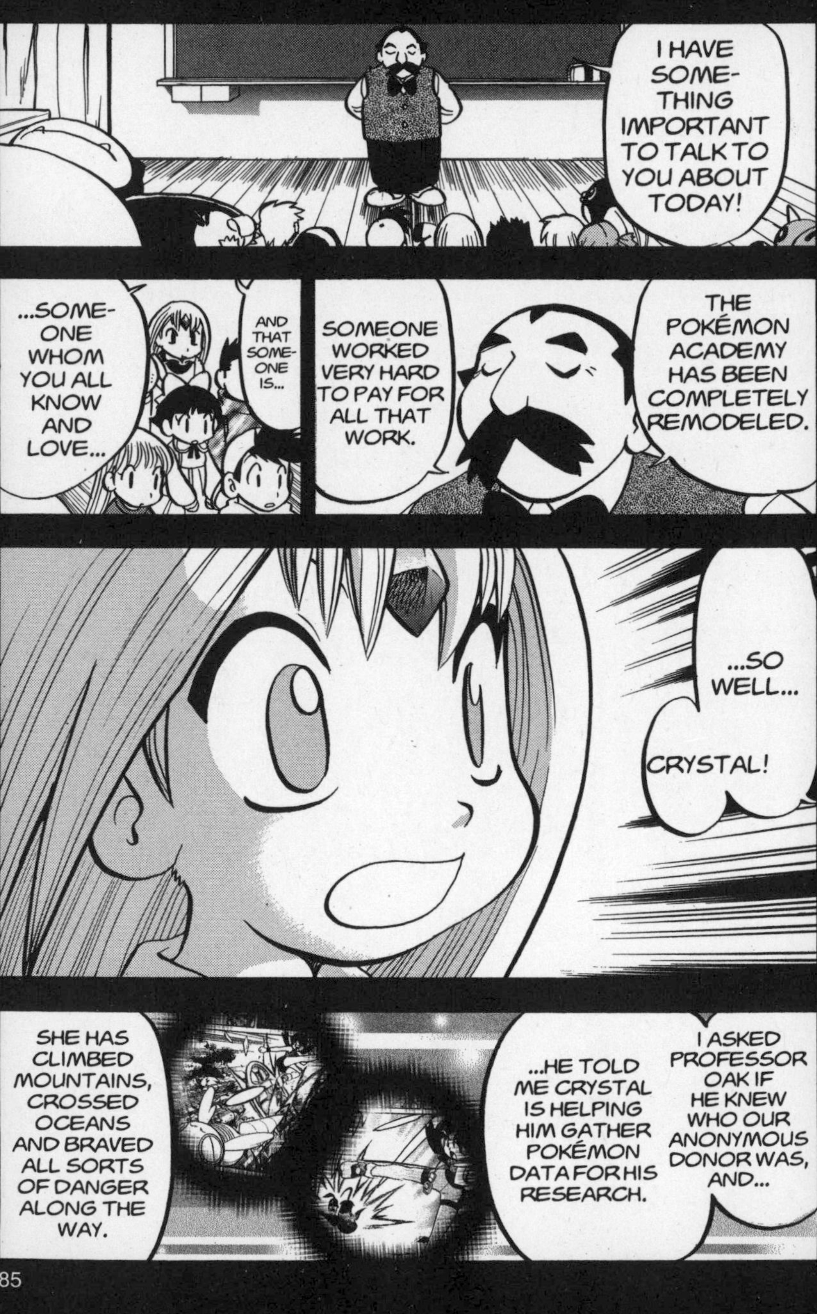
I HAVE SOMETHING IMPORTANT TO TALK TO YOU ABOUT TODAY!
THE POKÉMON ACADEMY HAS BEEN COMPLETELY REMODELED.
SOMEONE WORKED VERY HARD TO PAY FOR ALL THAT WORK.
AND THAT SOMEONE IS...
...SOMEONE WHOM YOU ALL KNOW AND LOVE...
...SO WELL...
CRYSTAL!
I ASKED PROFESSOR OAK IF HE KNEW WHO OUR ANONYMOUS DONOR WAS, AND...
...HE TOLD ME CRYSTAL IS HELPING HIM GATHER POKÉMON DATA FOR HIS RESEARCH.
SHE HAS CLIMBED MOUNTAINS, CROSSED OCEANS AND BRAVED ALL SORTS OF DANGER ALONG THE WAY.

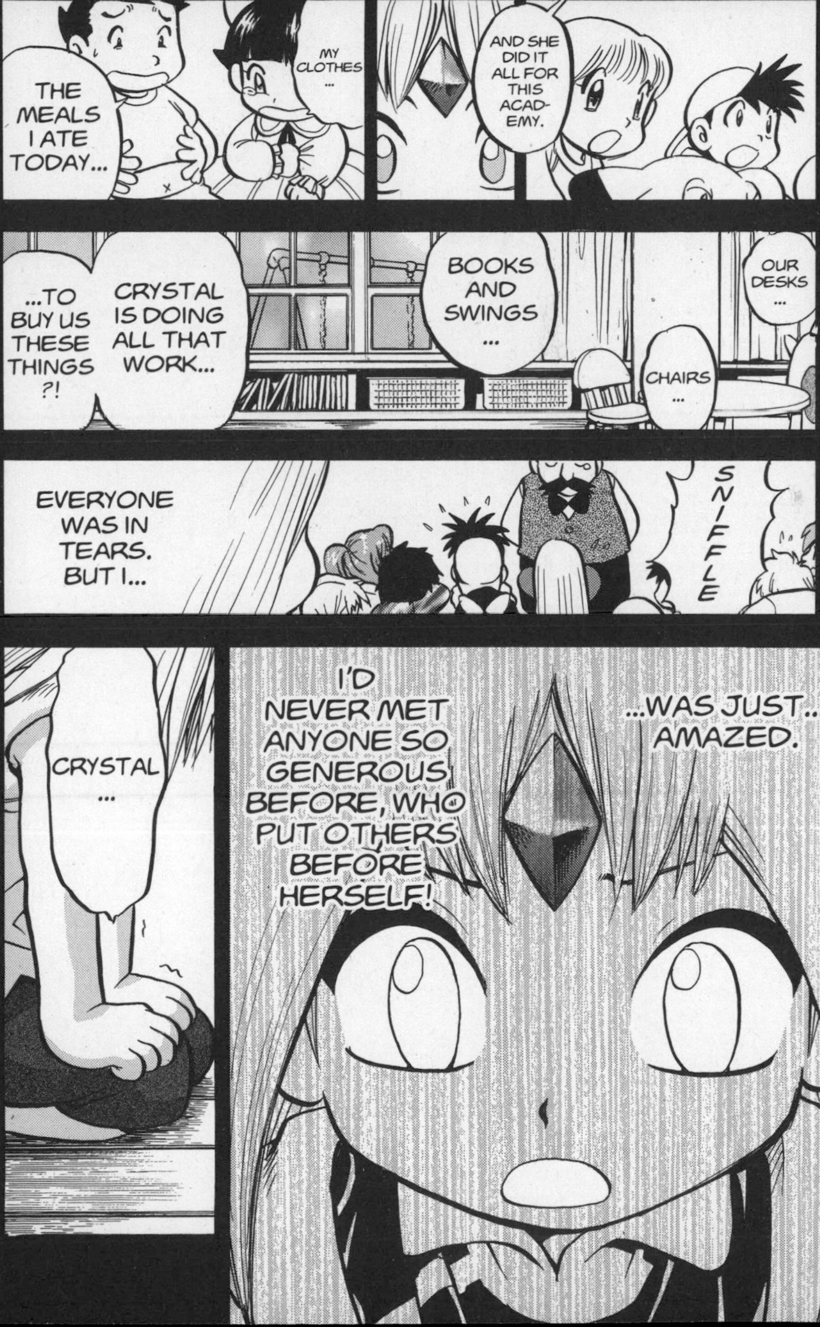

AND SHE DID IT ALL FOR THIS ACADEMY.
MY CLOTHES...
THE MEALS I ATE TODAY...
OUR DESKS...
CHAIRS...
BOOKS AND SWINGS...
CRYSTAL IS DOING ALL THAT WORK...
...TO BUY US THESE THINGS?!
SNIFFLE
EVERYONE WAS IN TEARS. BUT I...
...WAS JUST... AMAZED.
I'D NEVER MET ANYONE SO GENEROUS BEFORE, WHO PUT OTHERS BEFORE HERSELF!
CRYSTAL...

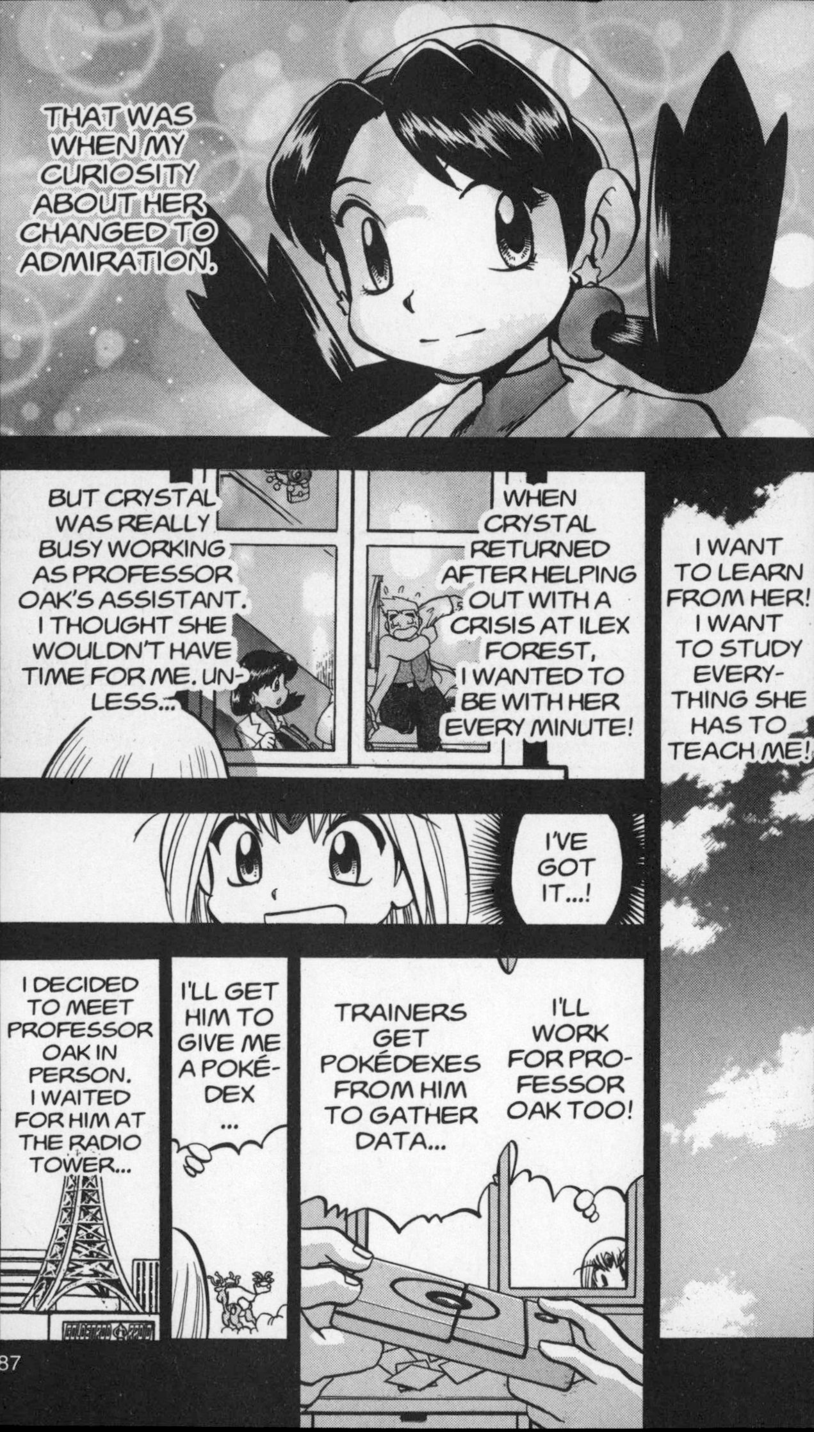
THAT WAS WHEN MY CURIOSITY ABOUT HER CHANGED TO ADMIRATION.
I WANT TO LEARN FROM HER! I WANT TO STUDY EVERY-THING SHE HAS TO TEACH ME!
WHEN CRYSTAL RETURNED AFTER HELPING OUT WITH A CRISIS AT ILEX FOREST, I WANTED TO BE WITH HER EVERY MINUTE!
BUT CRYSTAL WAS REALLY BUSY WORKING AS PROFESSOR OAK'S ASSISTANT. I THOUGHT SHE WOULDN'T HAVE TIME FOR ME. UN-LESS...
I'VE GOT IT...!
I'LL WORK FOR PRO-FESSOR OAK TOO!
TRAINERS GET POKÉDEXES FROM HIM TO GATHER DATA...
I'LL GET HIM TO GIVE ME A POKÉ-DEX ...
I DECIDED TO MEET PROFESSOR OAK IN PERSON. I WAITED FOR HIM AT THE RADIO TOWER...

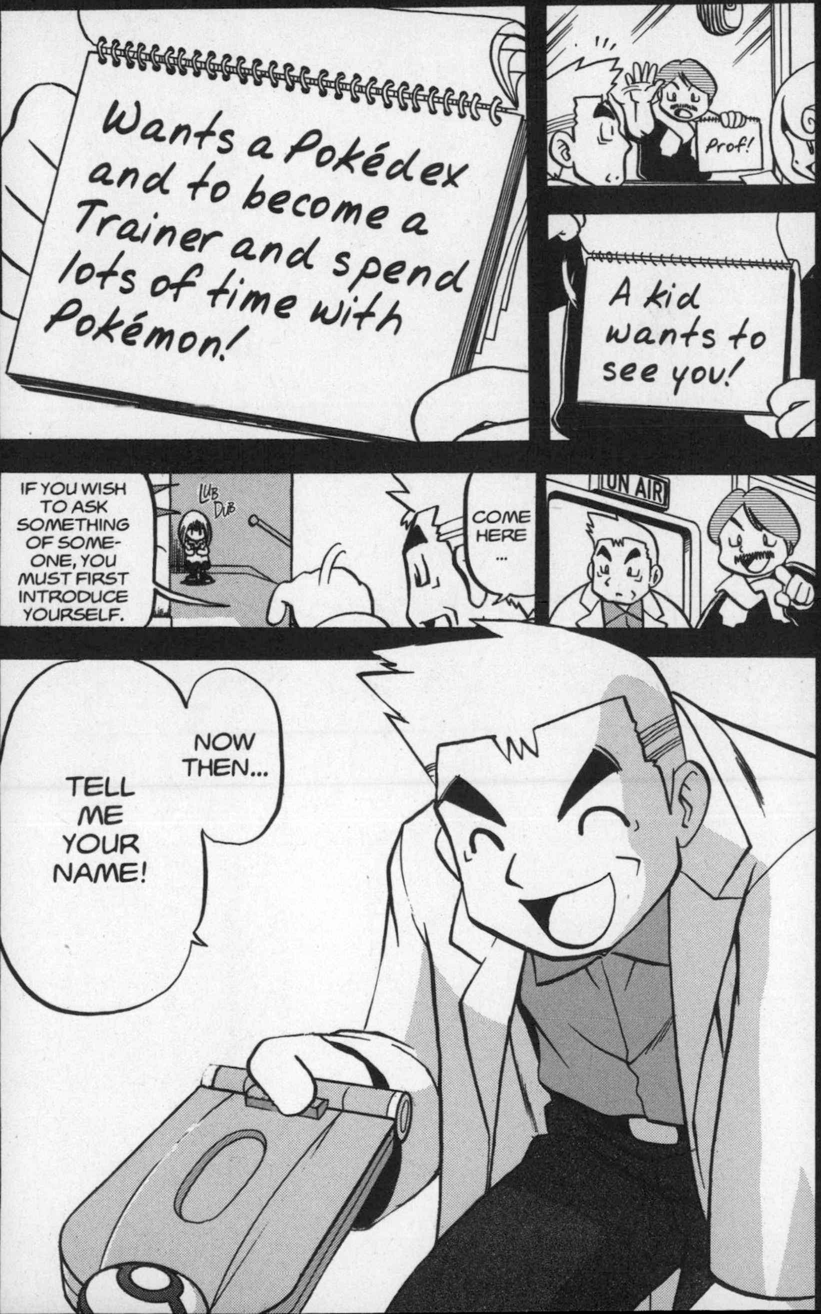
Prof!
A kid wants to see you!
Wants a Pokédex and to become a Trainer and spend lots of time with Pokémon!
ON AIR
COME HERE ...
LUB DUB
IF YOU WISH TO ASK SOMETHING OF SOME-ONE, YOU MUST FIRST INTRODUCE YOURSELF.
NOW THEN...
TELL ME YOUR NAME!

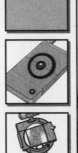

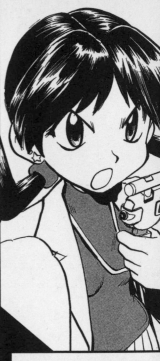

CHARACTER PROFILE / CRYSTAL

PROFESSOR OAK GAVE CRYSTAL A POKÉDEX AND ASKED HER TO FILL IT WITH DATA ABOUT POKÉMON. SHE IS KNOWN AS THE "CATCHER." CRYSTAL IS A KIND GIRL WHO TAKES CARE OF EVERYONE. SHE IS DEVOTED TO HER VOLUNTEER WORK AT EARL'S POKÉMON ACADEMY, BUT SHE CAN ALSO BE A WORKAHOLIC WHEN IT COMES TO CAPTURING POKÉMON WITH HER TEAM. SHE IS CURRENTLY WORKING AT PROFESSOR OAK'S LABORATORY AS HIS ASSISTANT.

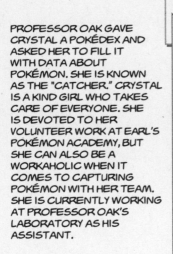

CRYSTAL

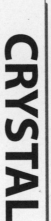

- Birthplace: Violet City
- Birthday: April 30
- Blood Type: A
- Family: Mother
- Skill: Apricorn picking
- Hobby: Reading

332

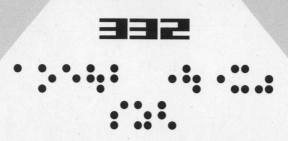

The Final Battle V

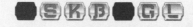

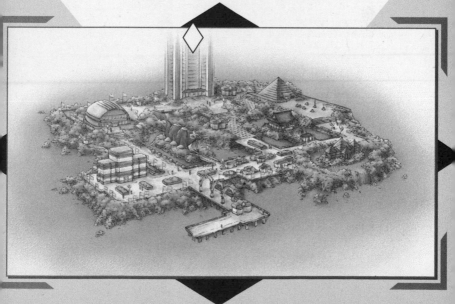

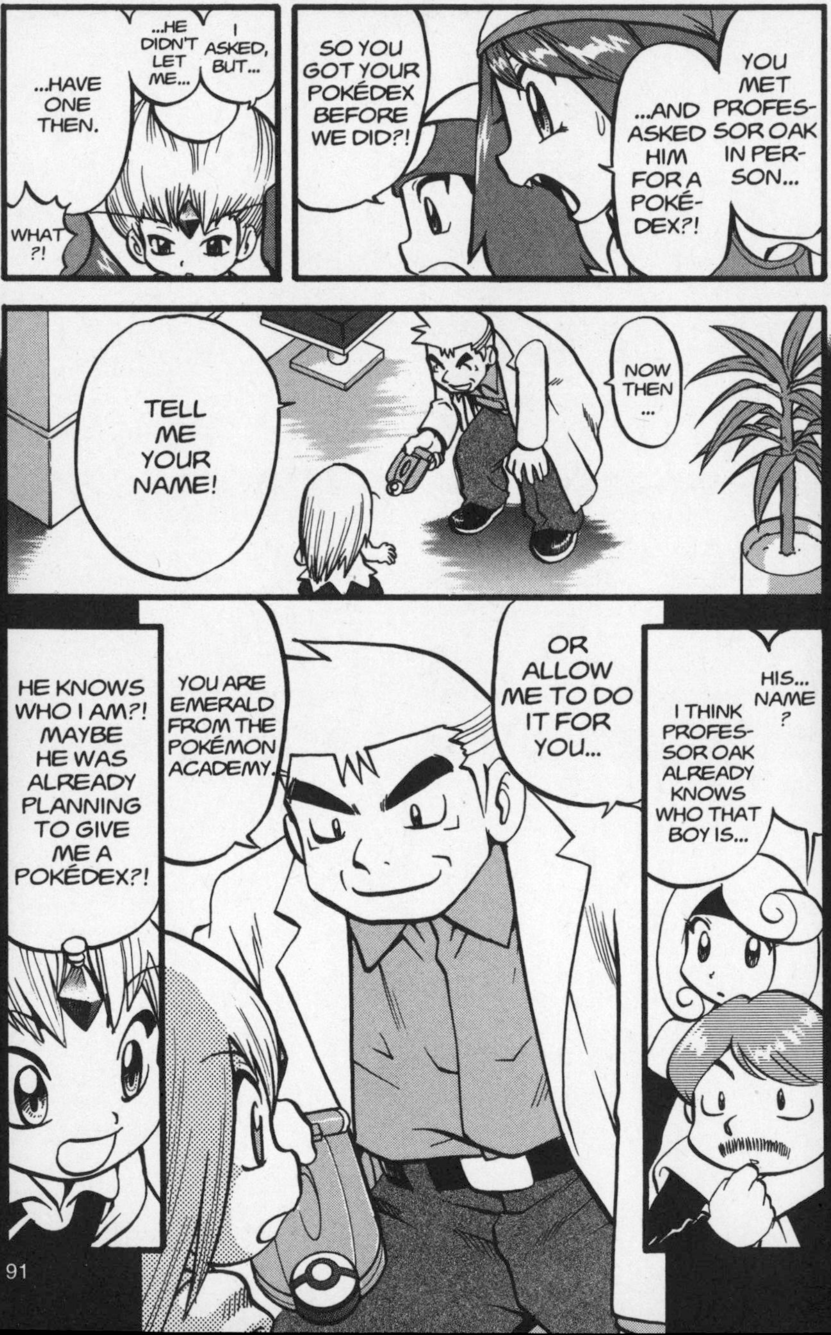
YOU MET PROFESSOR OAK IN PERSON...
...AND ASKED HIM FOR A POKÉDEX?!
SO YOU GOT YOUR POKÉDEX BEFORE WE DID?!
I ASKED, BUT...
...HE DIDN'T LET ME...
...HAVE ONE THEN.
WHAT?!
NOW THEN...
TELL ME YOUR NAME!
HIS... NAME?
I THINK PROFESSOR OAK ALREADY KNOWS WHO THAT BOY IS...
OR ALLOW ME TO DO IT FOR YOU...
YOU ARE EMERALD FROM THE POKÉMON ACADEMY.
HE KNOWS WHO I AM?! MAYBE HE WAS ALREADY PLANNING TO GIVE ME A POKÉDEX?!

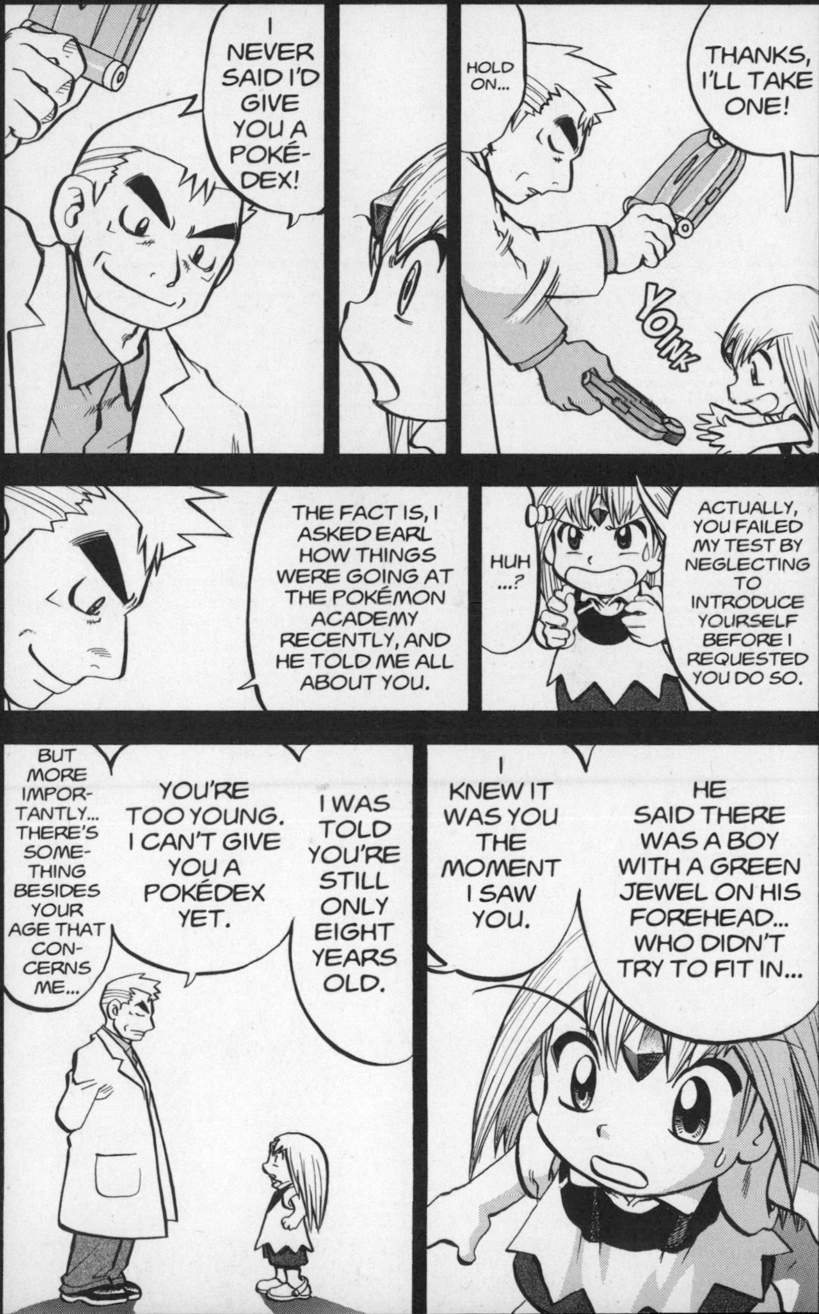
THANKS, I'LL TAKE ONE!
HOLD ON...
YOINK
I NEVER SAID I'D GIVE YOU A POKÉDEX!
ACTUALLY, YOU FAILED MY TEST BY NEGLECTING TO INTRODUCE YOURSELF BEFORE I REQUESTED YOU DO SO.
HUH ...?
THE FACT IS, I ASKED EARL HOW THINGS WERE GOING AT THE POKÉMON ACADEMY RECENTLY, AND HE TOLD ME ALL ABOUT YOU.
HE SAID THERE WAS A BOY WITH A GREEN JEWEL ON HIS FOREHEAD... WHO DIDN'T TRY TO FIT IN...
I KNEW IT WAS YOU THE MOMENT I SAW YOU.
I WAS TOLD YOU'RE STILL ONLY EIGHT YEARS OLD.
YOU'RE TOO YOUNG. I CAN'T GIVE YOU A POKÉDEX YET.
BUT MORE IMPORTANTLY... THERE'S SOMETHING BESIDES YOUR AGE THAT CONCERNS ME...

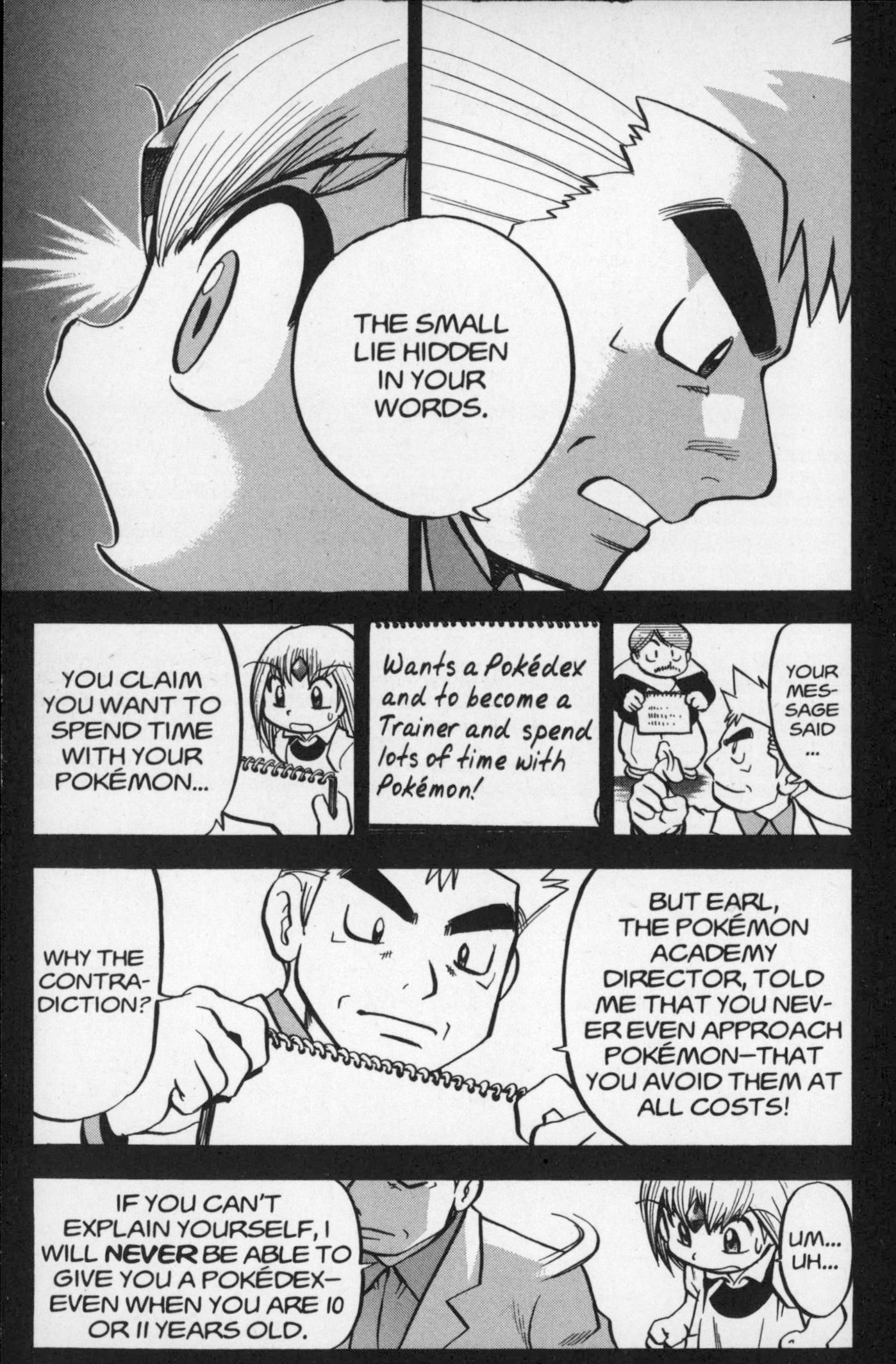
THE SMALL LIE HIDDEN IN YOUR WORDS.
YOUR MES-SAGE SAID ...
Wants a Pokédex and to become a Trainer and spend lots of time with Pokémon!
YOU CLAIM YOU WANT TO SPEND TIME WITH YOUR POKÉMON...
BUT EARL, THE POKÉMON ACADEMY DIRECTOR, TOLD ME THAT YOU NEV-ER EVEN APPROACH POKÉMON—THAT YOU AVOID THEM AT ALL COSTS!
WHY THE CONTRA-DICTION?
UM... UH...
IF YOU CAN'T EXPLAIN YOURSELF, I WILL **NEVER** BE ABLE TO GIVE YOU A POKÉDEX—EVEN WHEN YOU ARE 10 OR 11 YEARS OLD.

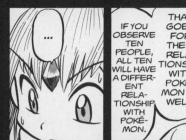

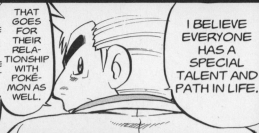

I BELIEVE EVERYONE HAS A SPECIAL TALENT AND PATH IN LIFE.
THAT GOES FOR THEIR RELATIONSHIP WITH POKÉMON AS WELL.
IF YOU OBSERVE TEN PEOPLE, ALL TEN WILL HAVE A DIFFERENT RELATIONSHIP WITH POKÉMON.
...
YOU MUST FIND YOUR OWN PATH.
BLIP
I WILL CONSIDER GIVING YOU A POKÉDEX IF, AND ONLY IF, YOU DISCOVER YOUR PATH.
UNTIL THEN, I WILL REGISTER YOU AS A TEMPORARY TRAINER.
MY PATH... MY SPECIAL TALENT...
AND MY RELATIONSHIP WITH POKÉMON...
THERE WAS ONLY ONE PERSON I COULD ASK FOR ADVICE...
WHAT DO YOU THINK?
LET'S SEE ...
HE SAID IT IN A ROUNDABOUT WAY, BUT...
...I THINK WHAT PROFESSOR OAK IS BASICALLY ASKING IS...

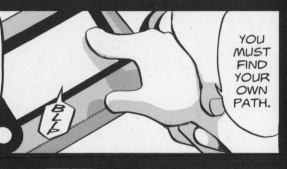

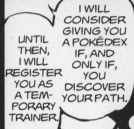

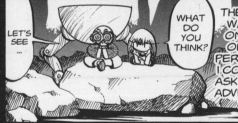

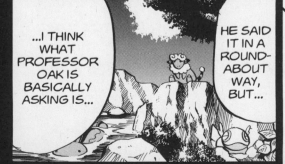

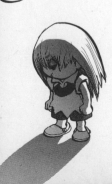

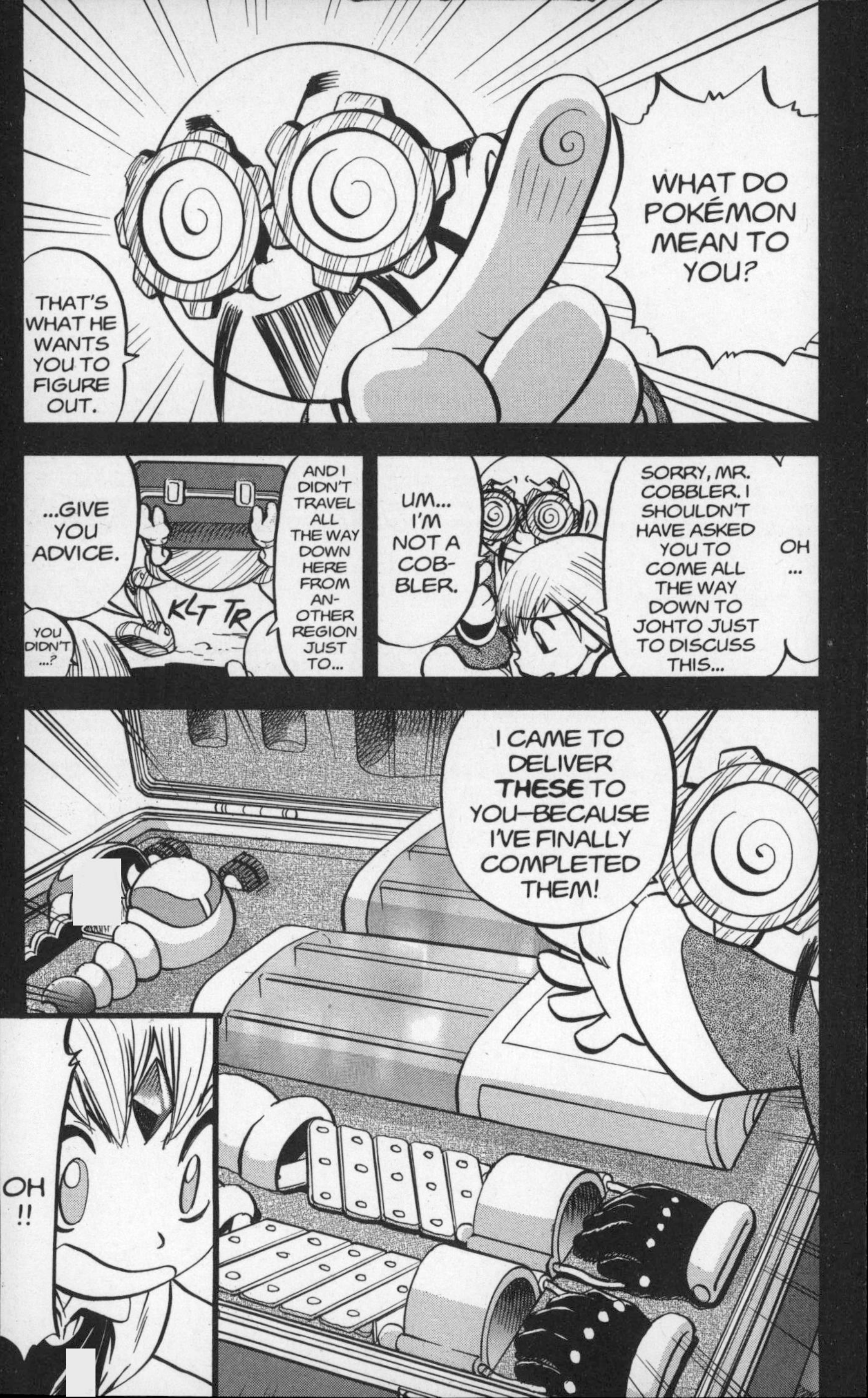
WHAT DO POKÉMON MEAN TO YOU?
THAT'S WHAT HE WANTS YOU TO FIGURE OUT.
OH ...
SORRY, MR. COBBLER. I SHOULDN'T HAVE ASKED YOU TO COME ALL THE WAY DOWN TO JOHTO JUST TO DISCUSS THIS...
UM... I'M NOT A COBBLER.
AND I DIDN'T TRAVEL ALL THE WAY DOWN HERE FROM ANOTHER REGION JUST TO...
...GIVE YOU ADVICE.
KLT TR
YOU DIDN'T ...?
I CAME TO DELIVER **THESE** TO YOU—BECAUSE I'VE FINALLY COMPLETED THEM!
OH !!

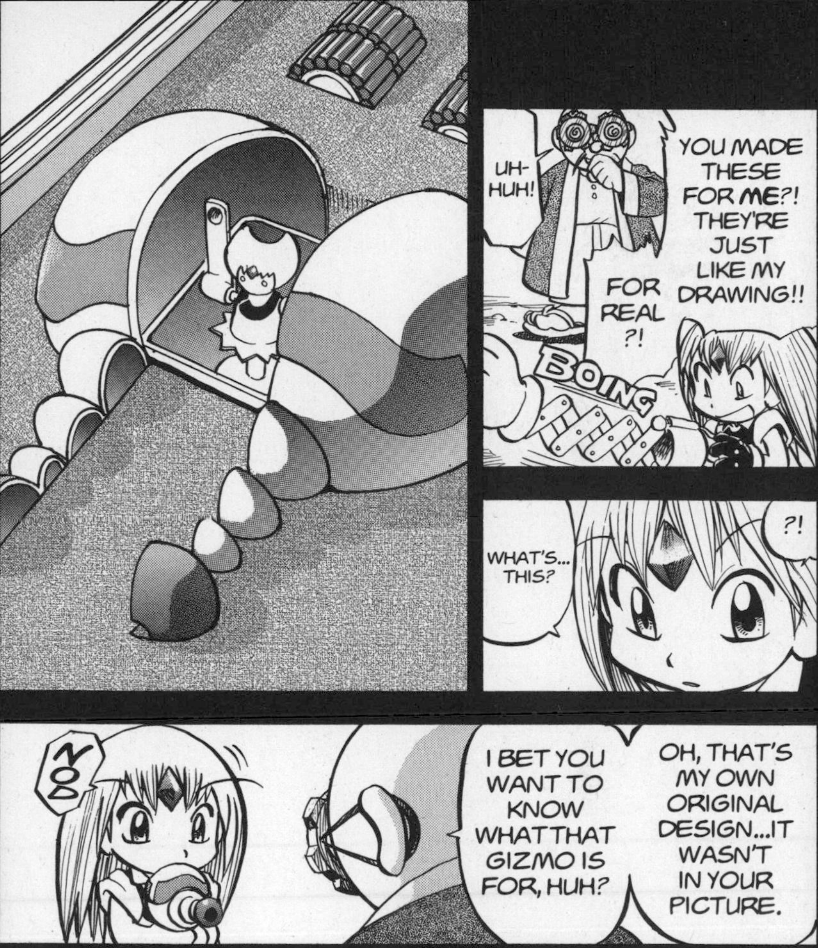
YOU MADE THESE FOR ME?! THEY'RE JUST LIKE MY DRAWING!!
UH-HUH!
FOR REAL ?!
BOING
?!
WHAT'S... THIS?
OH, THAT'S MY OWN ORIGINAL DESIGN...IT WASN'T IN YOUR PICTURE.
I BET YOU WANT TO KNOW WHAT THAT GIZMO IS FOR, HUH?
NOD

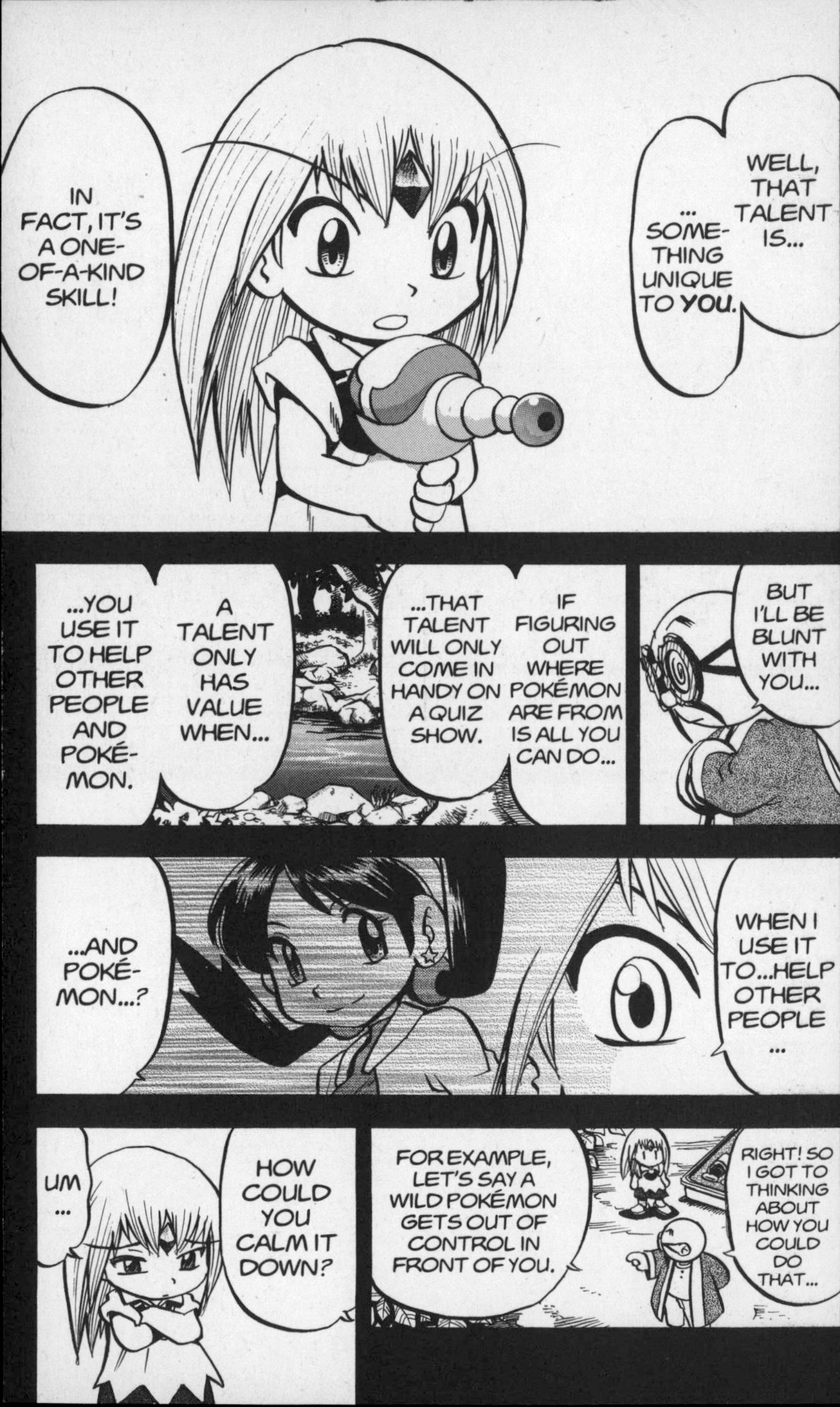
WELL, THAT TALENT IS...
...SOME-THING UNIQUE TO **YOU**.
IN FACT, IT'S A ONE-OF-A-KIND SKILL!
BUT I'LL BE BLUNT WITH YOU...
IF FIGURING OUT WHERE POKÉMON ARE FROM IS ALL YOU CAN DO...
...THAT TALENT WILL ONLY COME IN HANDY ON A QUIZ SHOW.
A TALENT ONLY HAS VALUE WHEN...
...YOU USE IT TO HELP OTHER PEOPLE AND POKÉ-MON.
WHEN I USE IT TO...HELP OTHER PEOPLE...
...AND POKÉ-MON...?
RIGHT! SO I GOT TO THINKING ABOUT HOW YOU COULD DO THAT...
FOR EXAMPLE, LET'S SAY A WILD POKÉMON GETS OUT OF CONTROL IN FRONT OF YOU.
HOW COULD YOU CALM IT DOWN?
UM...

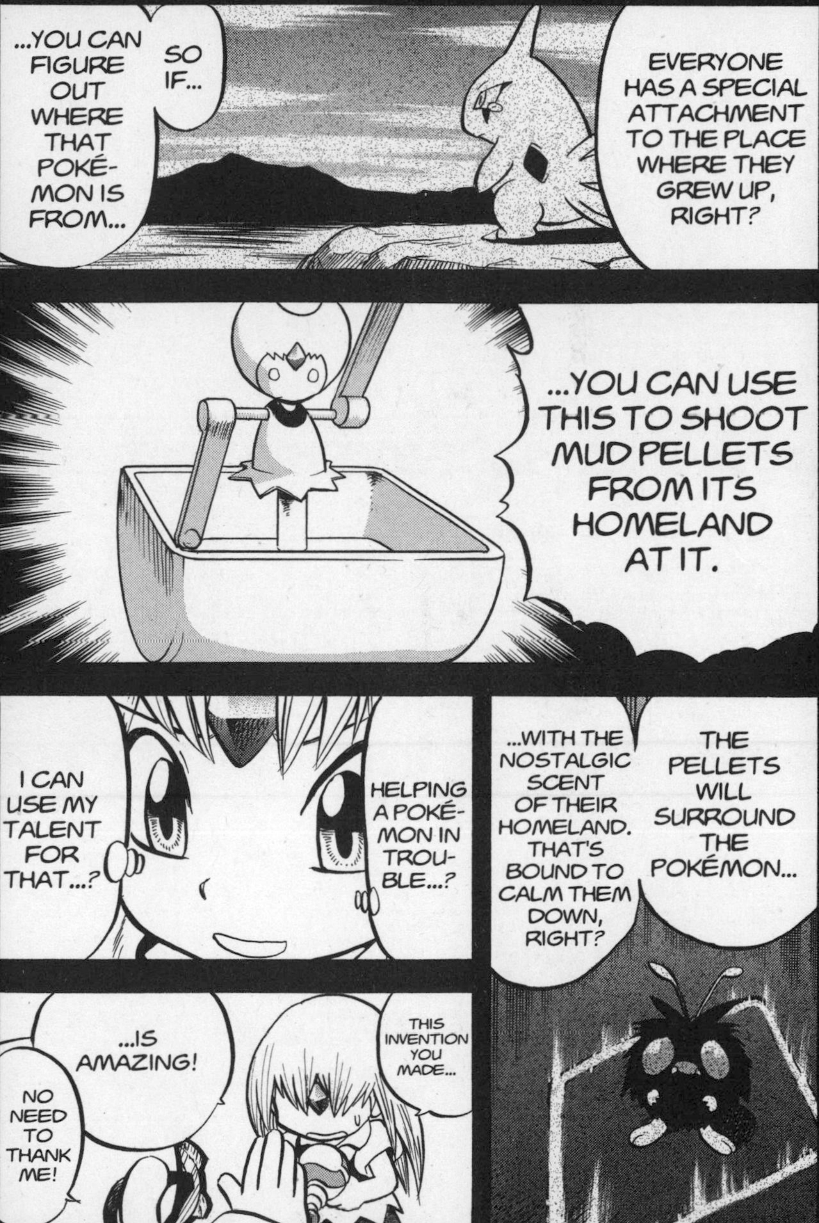
EVERYONE HAS A SPECIAL ATTACHMENT TO THE PLACE WHERE THEY GREW UP, RIGHT?
SO IF...
...YOU CAN FIGURE OUT WHERE THAT POKÉMON IS FROM...
...YOU CAN USE THIS TO SHOOT MUD PELLETS FROM ITS HOMELAND AT IT.
THE PELLETS WILL SURROUND THE POKÉMON...
...WITH THE NOSTALGIC SCENT OF THEIR HOMELAND. THAT'S BOUND TO CALM THEM DOWN, RIGHT?
HELPING A POKÉMON IN TROUBLE...?
I CAN USE MY TALENT FOR THAT...?
THIS INVENTION YOU MADE...
...IS AMAZING!
NO NEED TO THANK ME!

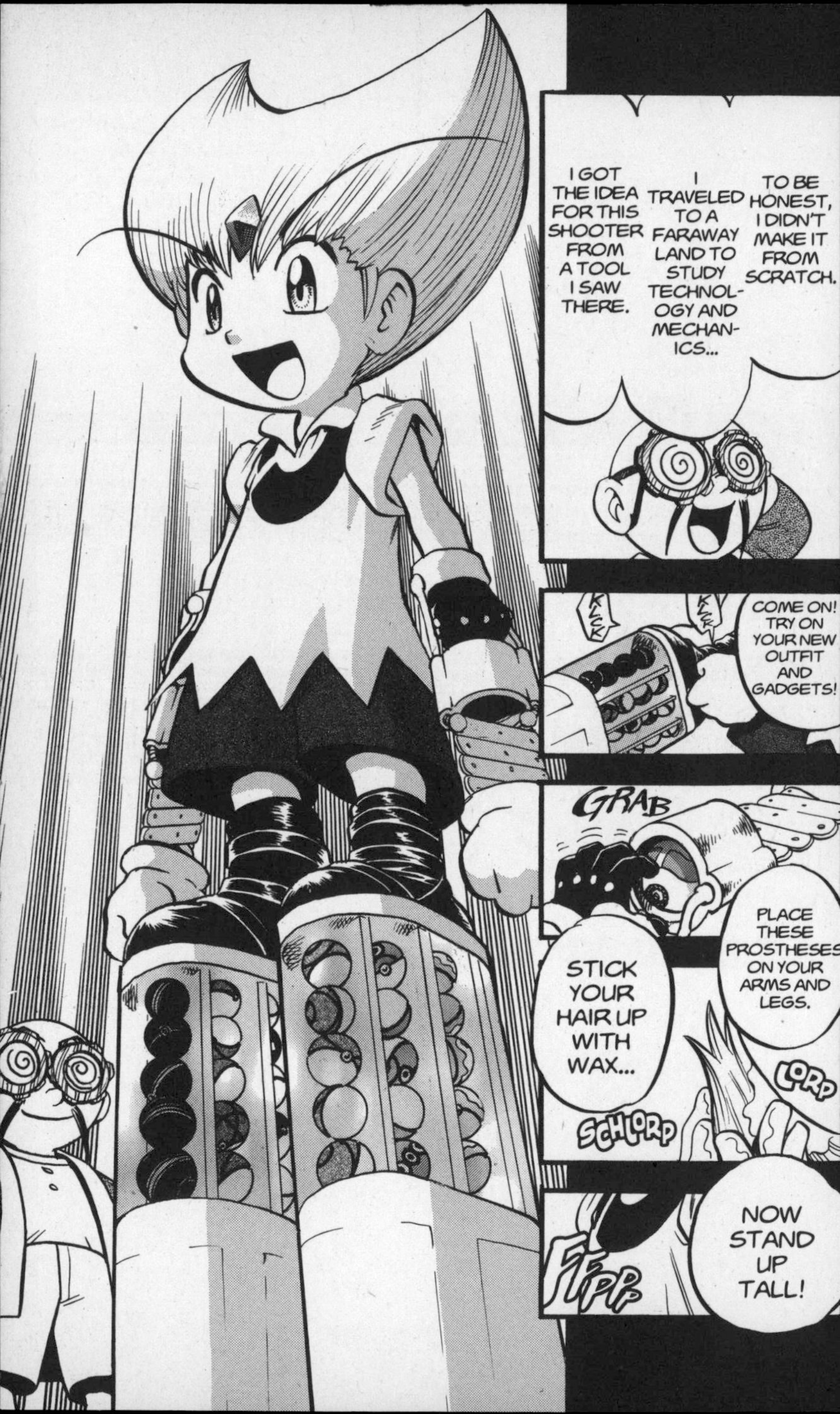

TO BE HONEST, I DIDN'T MAKE IT FROM SCRATCH.
I TRAVELED TO A FARAWAY LAND TO STUDY TECHNOLOGY AND MECHANICS...
I GOT THE IDEA FOR THIS SHOOTER FROM A TOOL I SAW THERE.
COME ON! TRY ON YOUR NEW OUTFIT AND GADGETS!
KLICK
KLICK
GRAB
PLACE THESE PROSTHESES ON YOUR ARMS AND LEGS.
STICK YOUR HAIR UP WITH WAX...
LORP
SCHLORP
NOW STAND UP TALL!

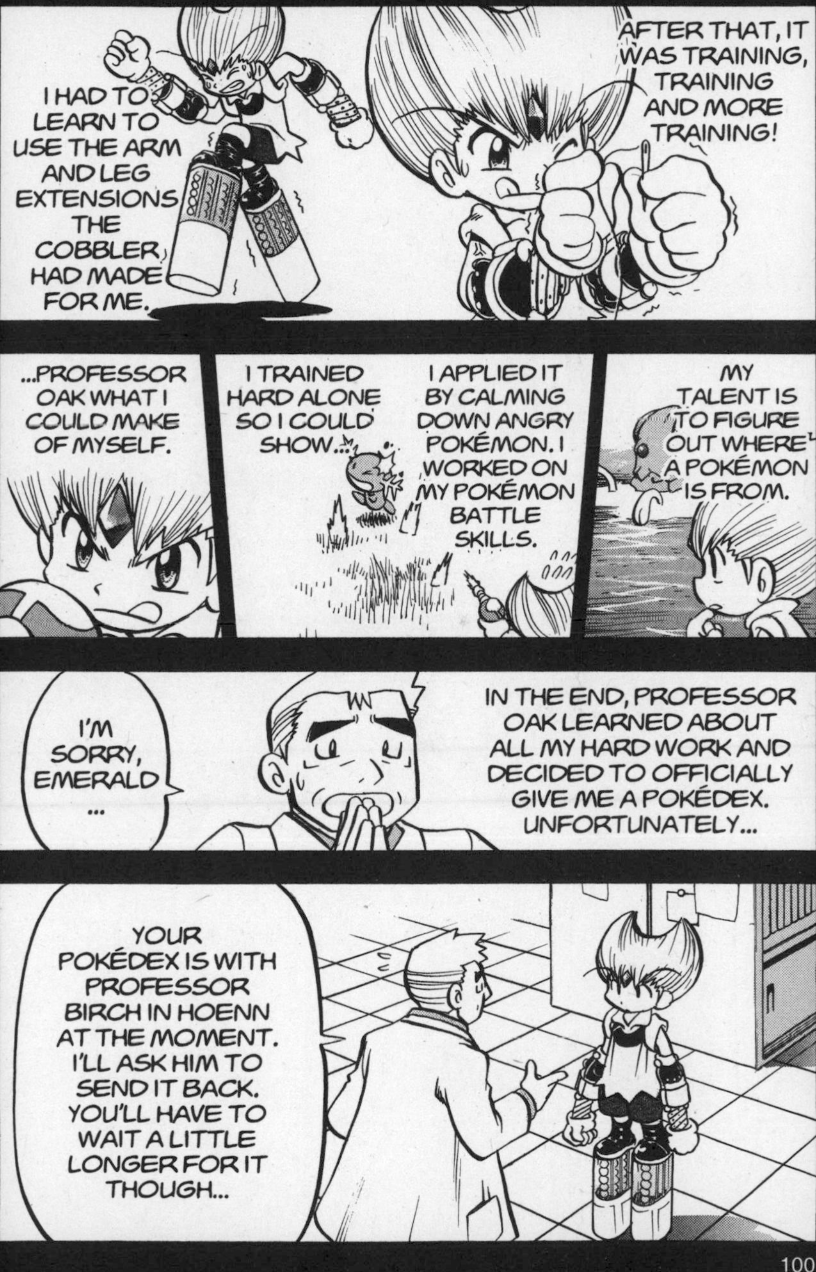
AFTER THAT, IT WAS TRAINING, TRAINING AND MORE TRAINING!
I HAD TO LEARN TO USE THE ARM AND LEG EXTENSIONS THE COBBLER HAD MADE FOR ME.
MY TALENT IS TO FIGURE OUT WHERE A POKÉMON IS FROM.
I APPLIED IT BY CALMING DOWN ANGRY POKÉMON. I WORKED ON MY POKÉMON BATTLE SKILLS.
I TRAINED HARD ALONE SO I COULD SHOW...
...PROFESSOR OAK WHAT I COULD MAKE OF MYSELF.
IN THE END, PROFESSOR OAK LEARNED ABOUT ALL MY HARD WORK AND DECIDED TO OFFICIALLY GIVE ME A POKÉDEX. UNFORTUNATELY...
I'M SORRY, EMERALD...
YOUR POKÉDEX IS WITH PROFESSOR BIRCH IN HOENN AT THE MOMENT. I'LL ASK HIM TO SEND IT BACK. YOU'LL HAVE TO WAIT A LITTLE LONGER FOR IT THOUGH...

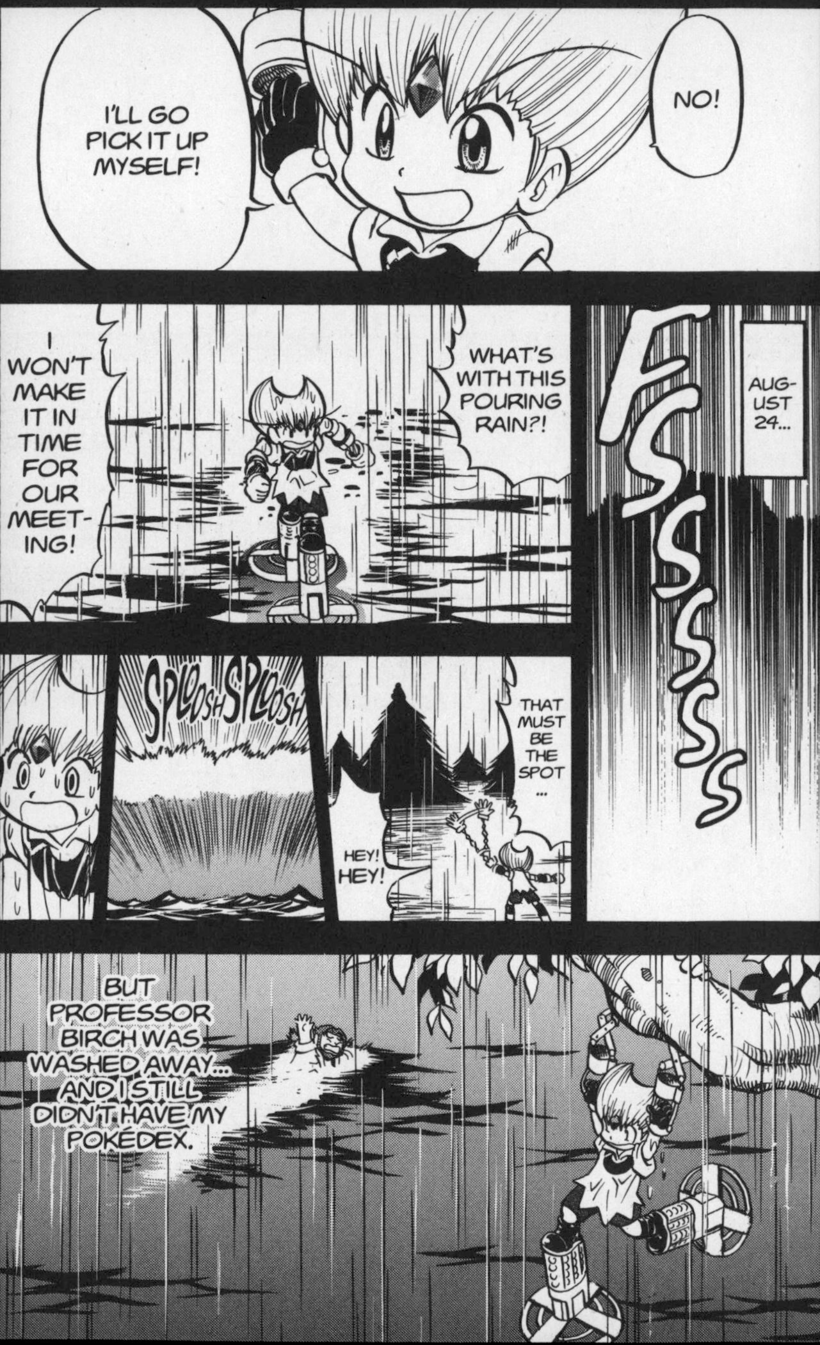
NO!
I'LL GO PICK IT UP MYSELF!
AUGUST 24...
FSSSSS
WHAT'S WITH THIS POURING RAIN?!
I WON'T MAKE IT IN TIME FOR OUR MEETING!
THAT MUST BE THE SPOT...
HEY! HEY!
SPLOOSH SPLOOSH
BUT PROFESSOR BIRCH WAS WASHED AWAY... AND I STILL DIDN'T HAVE MY POKÉDEX.

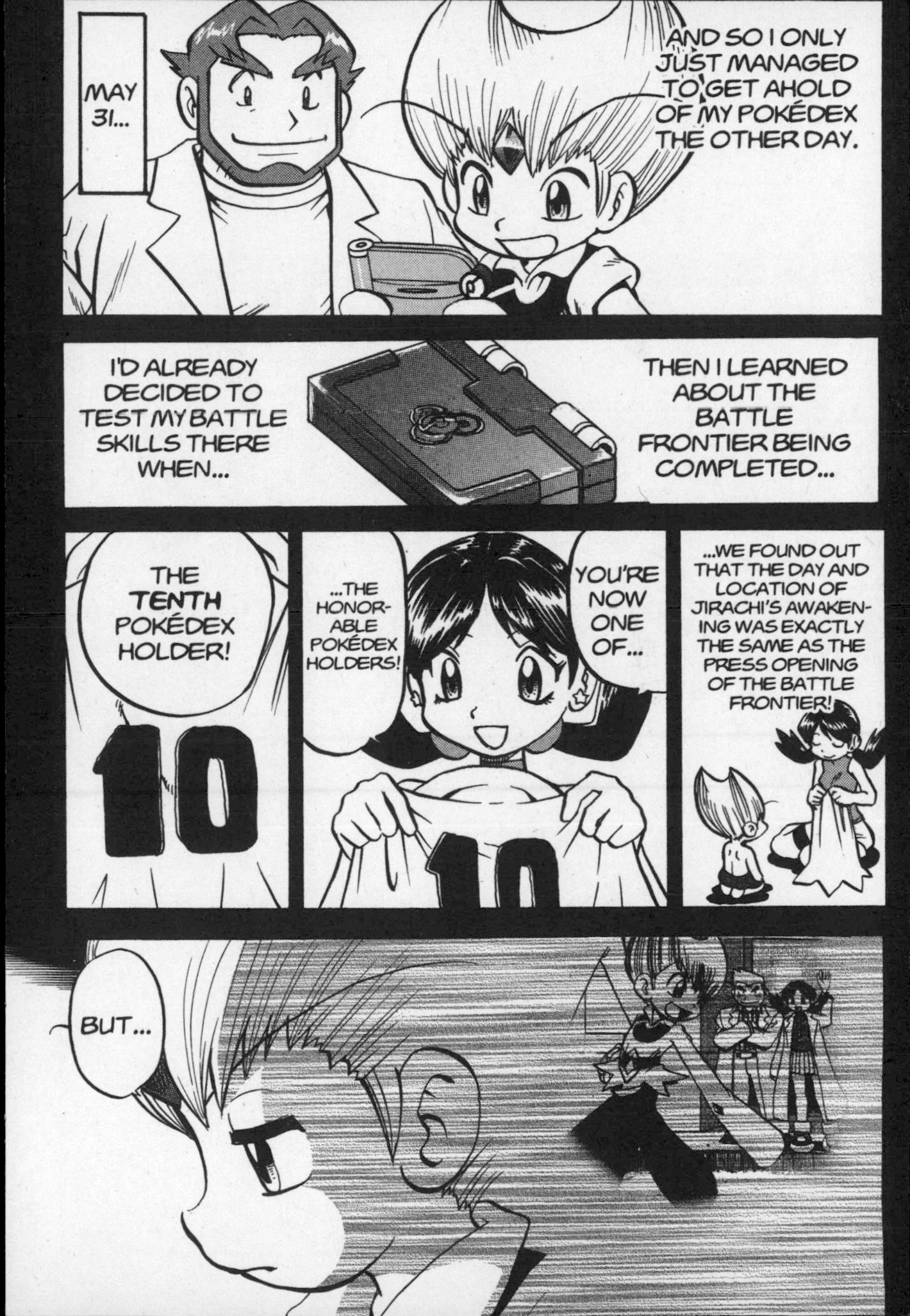
AND SO I ONLY JUST MANAGED TO GET AHOLD OF MY POKÉDEX THE OTHER DAY.
MAY 31...
THEN I LEARNED ABOUT THE BATTLE FRONTIER BEING COMPLETED...
I'D ALREADY DECIDED TO TEST MY BATTLE SKILLS THERE WHEN...
...WE FOUND OUT THAT THE DAY AND LOCATION OF JIRACHI'S AWAKENING WAS EXACTLY THE SAME AS THE PRESS OPENING OF THE BATTLE FRONTIER!
YOU'RE NOW ONE OF...
...THE HONORABLE POKÉDEX HOLDERS!
THE TENTH POKÉDEX HOLDER!
10
BUT...

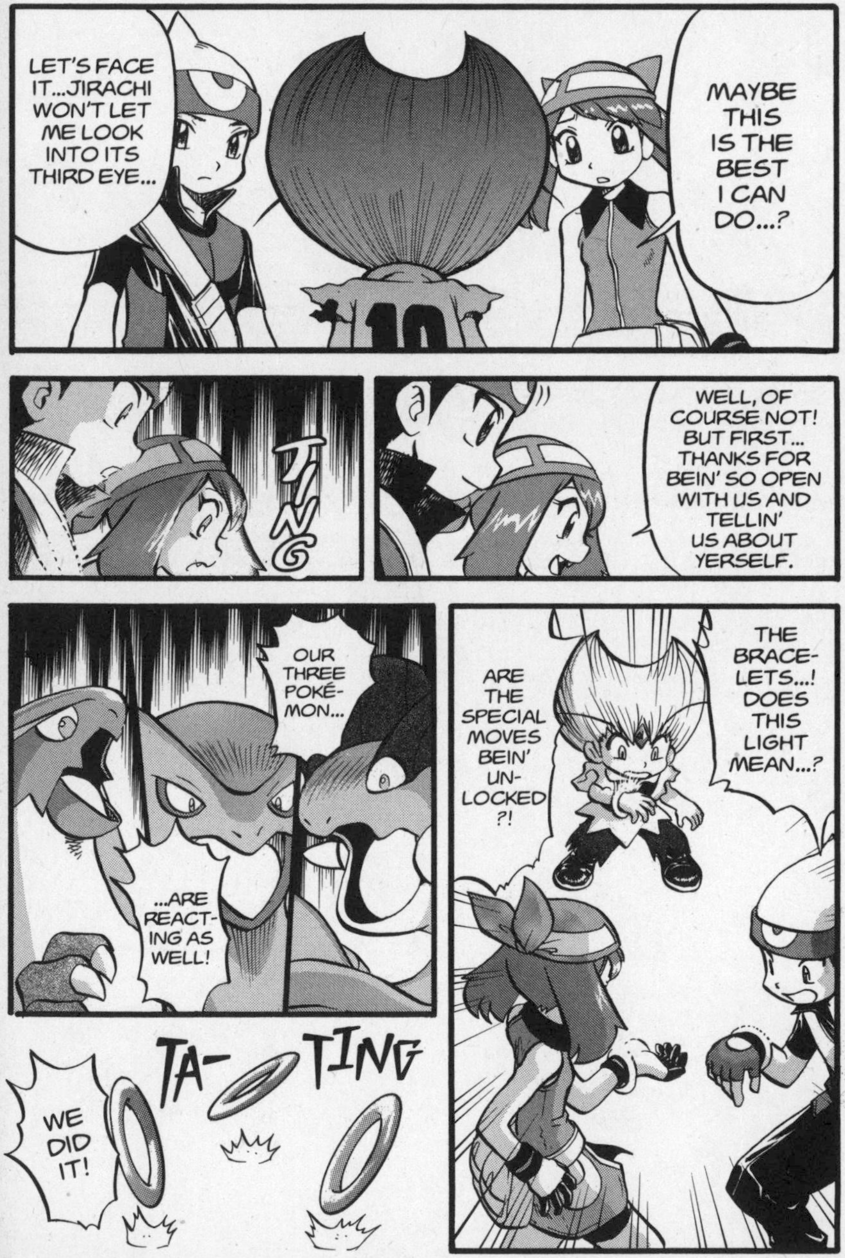
MAYBE THIS IS THE BEST I CAN DO...?
LET'S FACE IT...JIRACHI WON'T LET ME LOOK INTO ITS THIRD EYE...
WELL, OF COURSE NOT! BUT FIRST... THANKS FOR BEIN' SO OPEN WITH US AND TELLIN' US ABOUT YERSELF.
TING
THE BRACE-LETS...! DOES THIS LIGHT MEAN...?
ARE THE SPECIAL MOVES BEIN' UN-LOCKED?!
OUR THREE POKÉ-MON...
...ARE REACT-ING AS WELL!
TA-TING
WE DID IT!

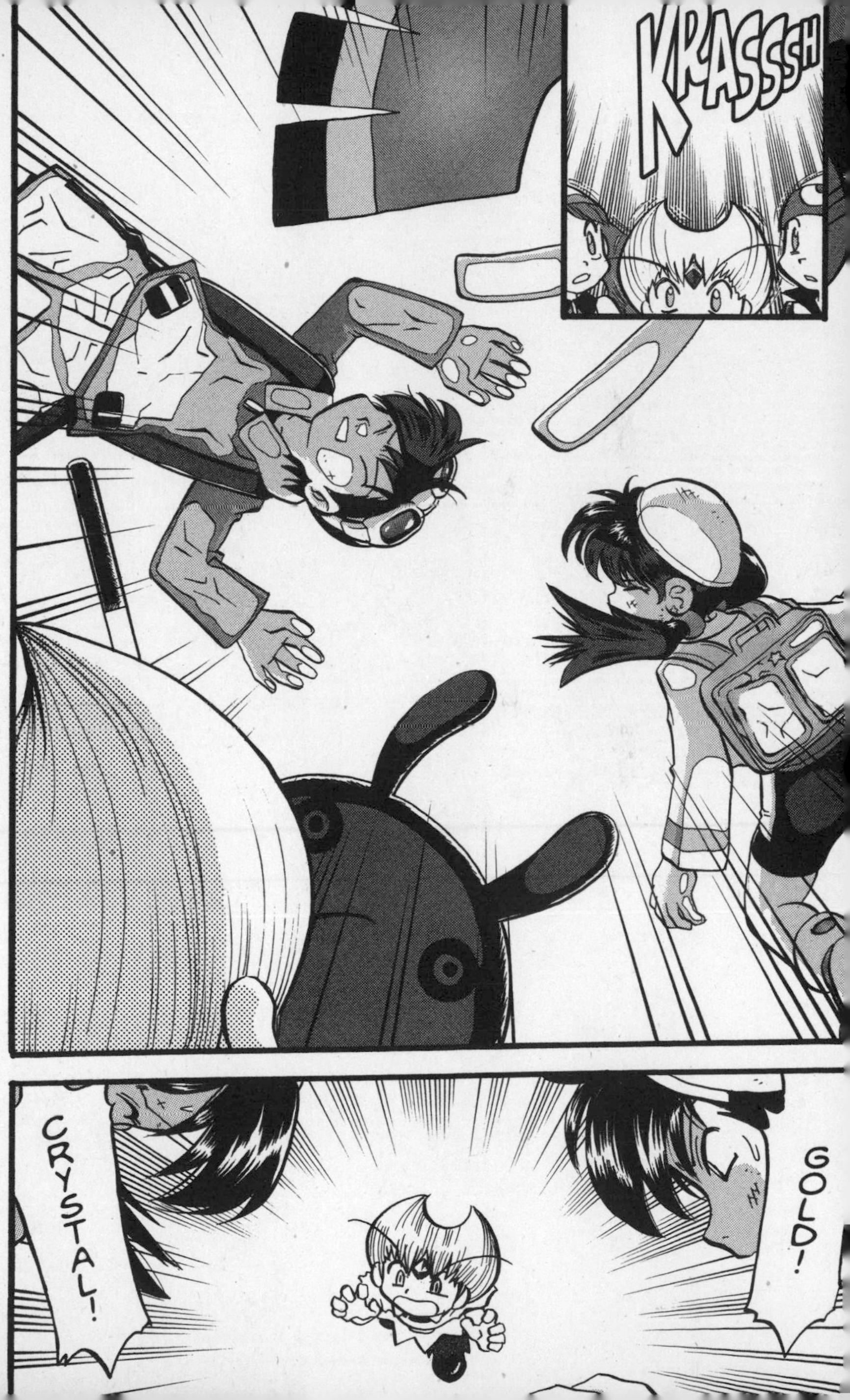
KRASSSH
GOLD!
CRYSTAL!

Character Profile Ruby

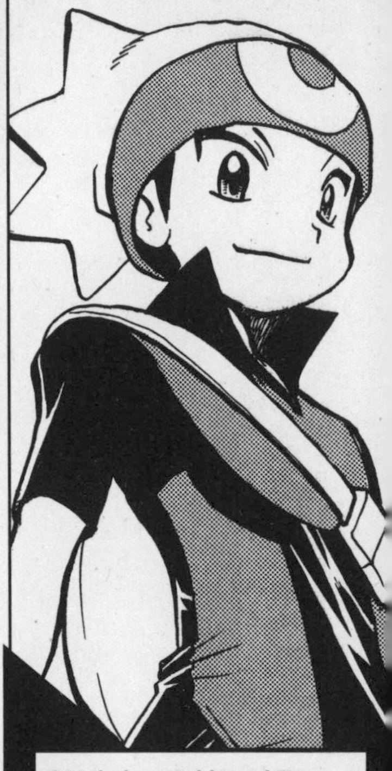

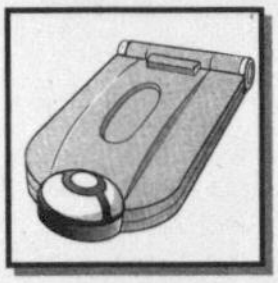

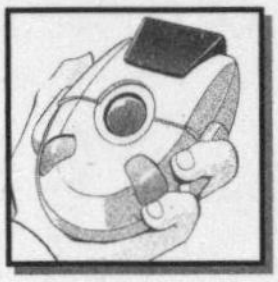

RUBY

THE POKÉDEX HOLDER WHO HAS WON EVERY POKÉMON CONTEST IN THE HOENN REGION. ORIGINALLY FROM JOHTO, HE MOVED TO HOENN WITH HIS MOTHER WHEN HIS FATHER BECAME THE PETALBURG CITY GYM LEADER. WHILE COMPETING IN THE POKÉMON CONTESTS HE LOVES, RUBY LEARNED OF A CRISIS THAT WAS TEARING HOENN APART AND DECIDED TO BATTLE TO HELP SAVE THE POPULACE, EVEN THOUGH HE ALWAYS CLAIMED TO HATE POKÉMON BATTLES BEFORE. HE SEEMS TO HAVE INHERITED THE POKÉMON BATTLE SKILLS OF HIS FATHER, NORMAN. ("BEAUTY IS BEST" IS STILL HIS MOTTO THOUGH.)

- Birthplace: Goldenrod City
- Birthday: July 2
- Blood Type: O
- Skills: Sewing, making Pokéblocks
- Family: Father (Norman), mother
- Prizes Won: Every Pokémon contest in Hoenn (Five Category x Four Cities)

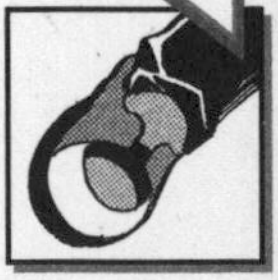

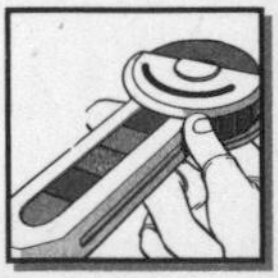

333

The Final Battle VI

OKÉMON ADVENTURES•THE SIXTH CHAPTER•EMERALD

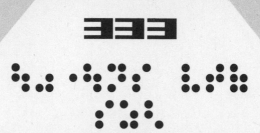

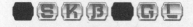

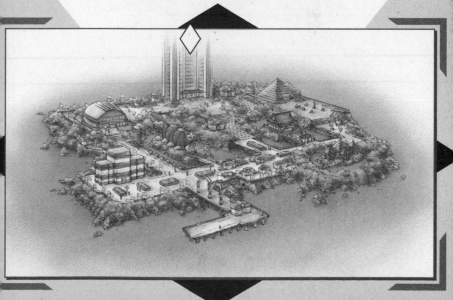

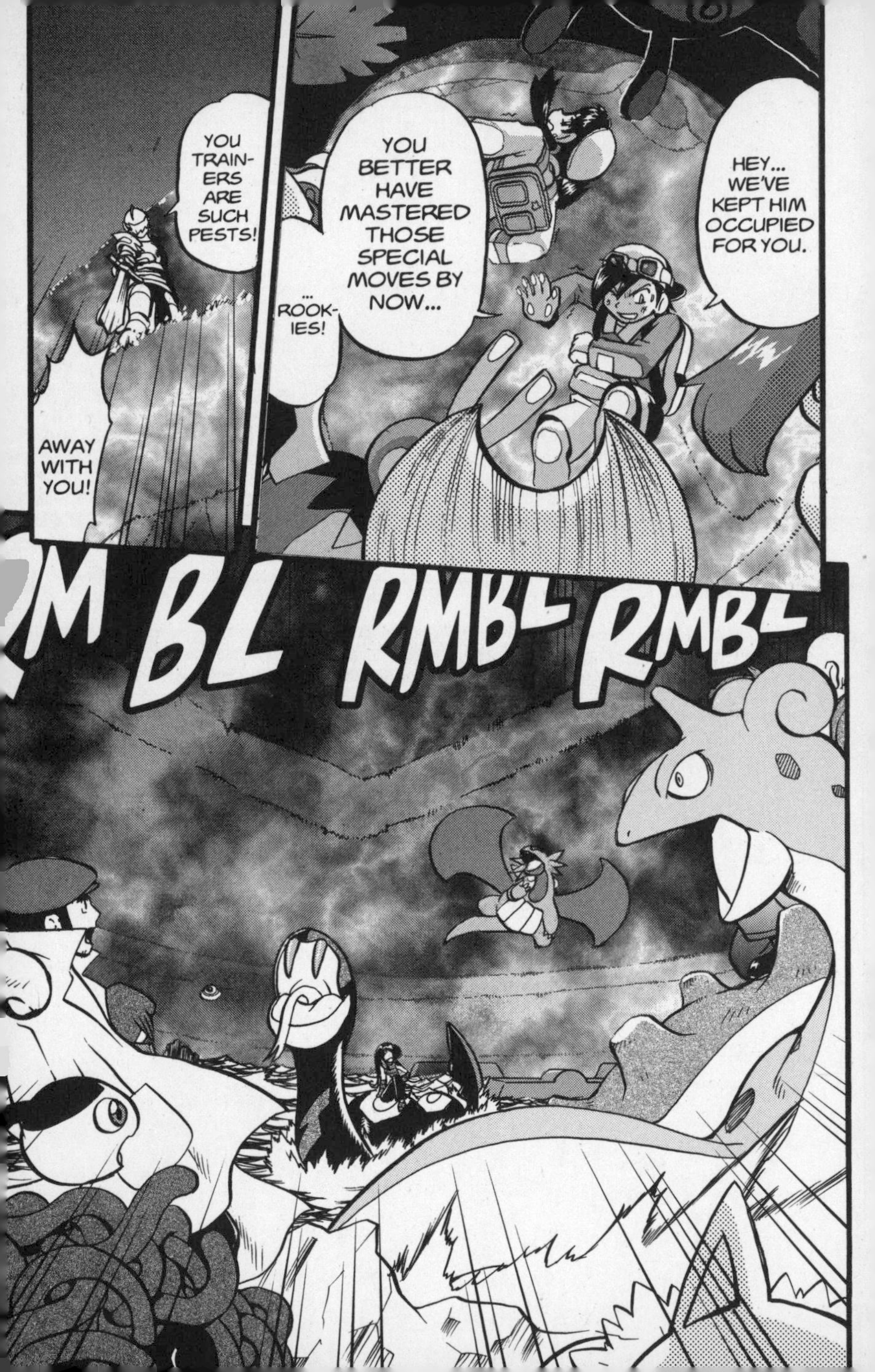
HEY... WE'VE KEPT HIM OCCUPIED FOR YOU.
YOU BETTER HAVE MASTERED THOSE SPECIAL MOVES BY NOW...
... ROOKIES!
YOU TRAINERS ARE SUCH PESTS!
AWAY WITH YOU!
RM BL RMBL RMBL

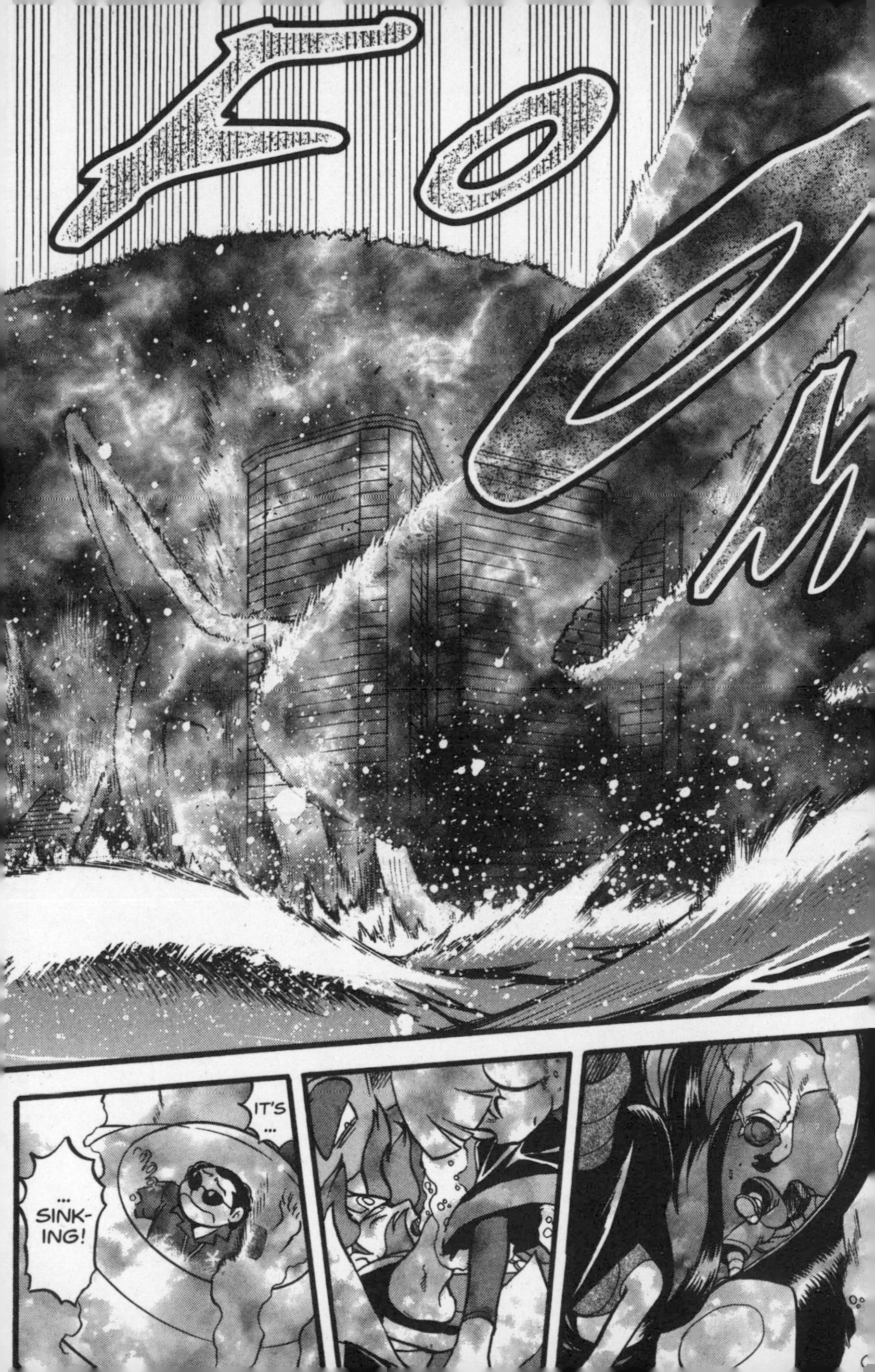
IT'S ...
... SINK-ING!

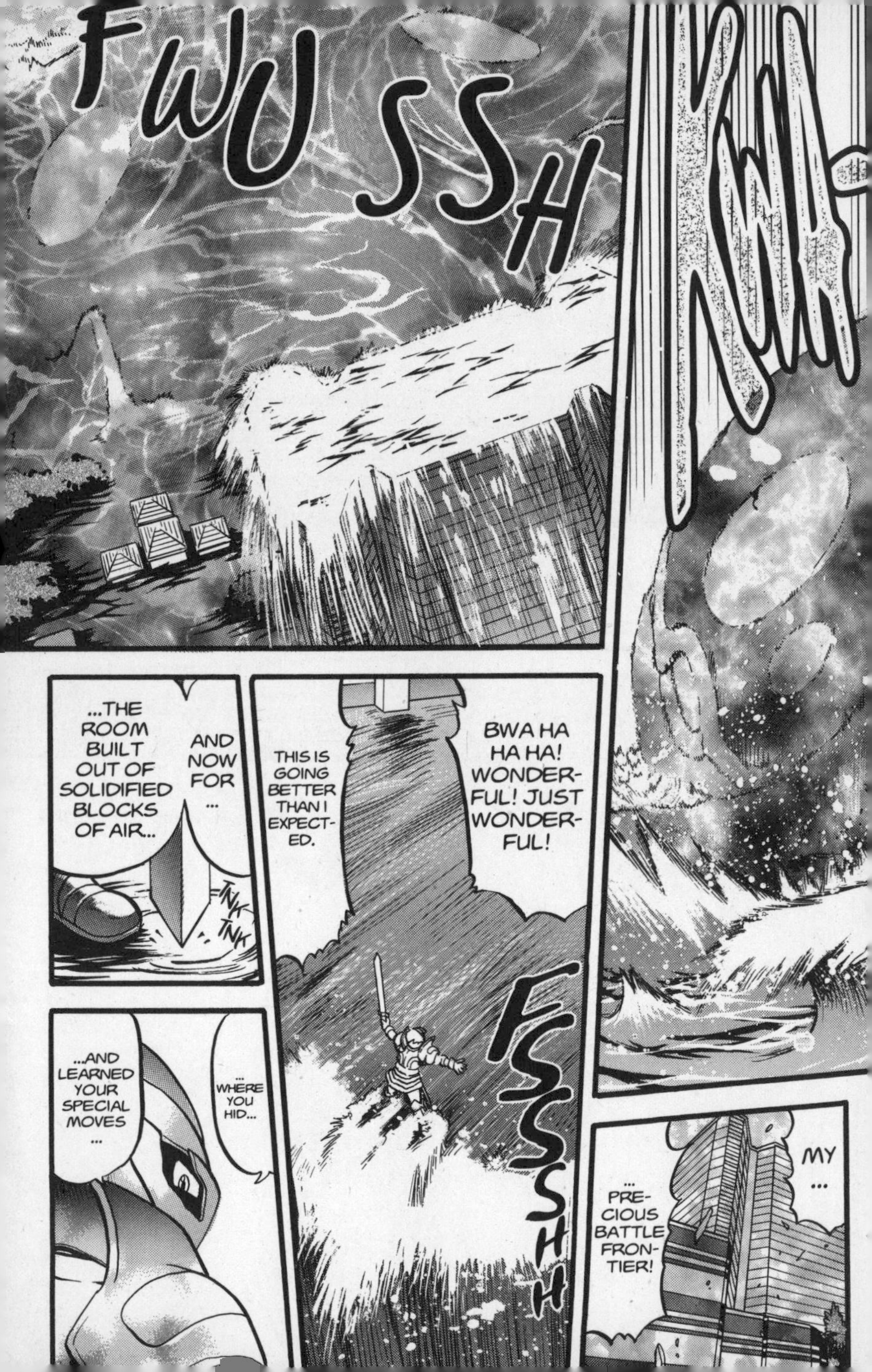
FWUSSH
MY ... PRECIOUS BATTLE FRONTIER!
BWA HA HA HA! WONDERFUL! JUST WONDERFUL!
THIS IS GOING BETTER THAN I EXPECTED.
FSSSHH
AND NOW FOR ...
...THE ROOM BUILT OUT OF SOLIDIFIED BLOCKS OF AIR...
TNK TNK
... WHERE YOU HID...
...AND LEARNED YOUR SPECIAL MOVES ...

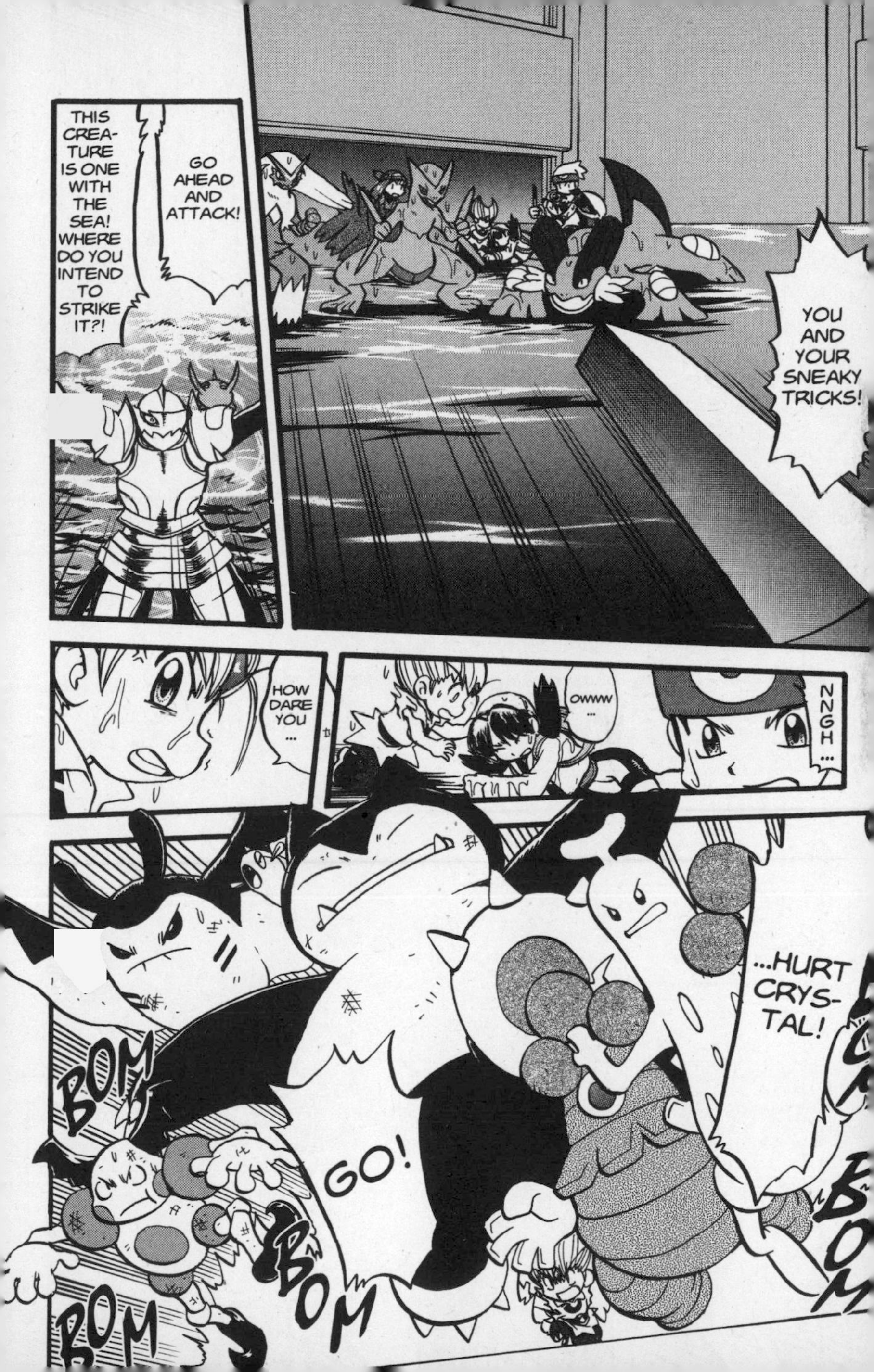
YOU AND YOUR SNEAKY TRICKS!
GO AHEAD AND ATTACK!
THIS CREATURE IS ONE WITH THE SEA! WHERE DO YOU INTEND TO STRIKE IT?!
NNGH...
OWWW...
HOW DARE YOU...
...HURT CRYSTAL!
BOM
GO!
BOM
BOM
BOM

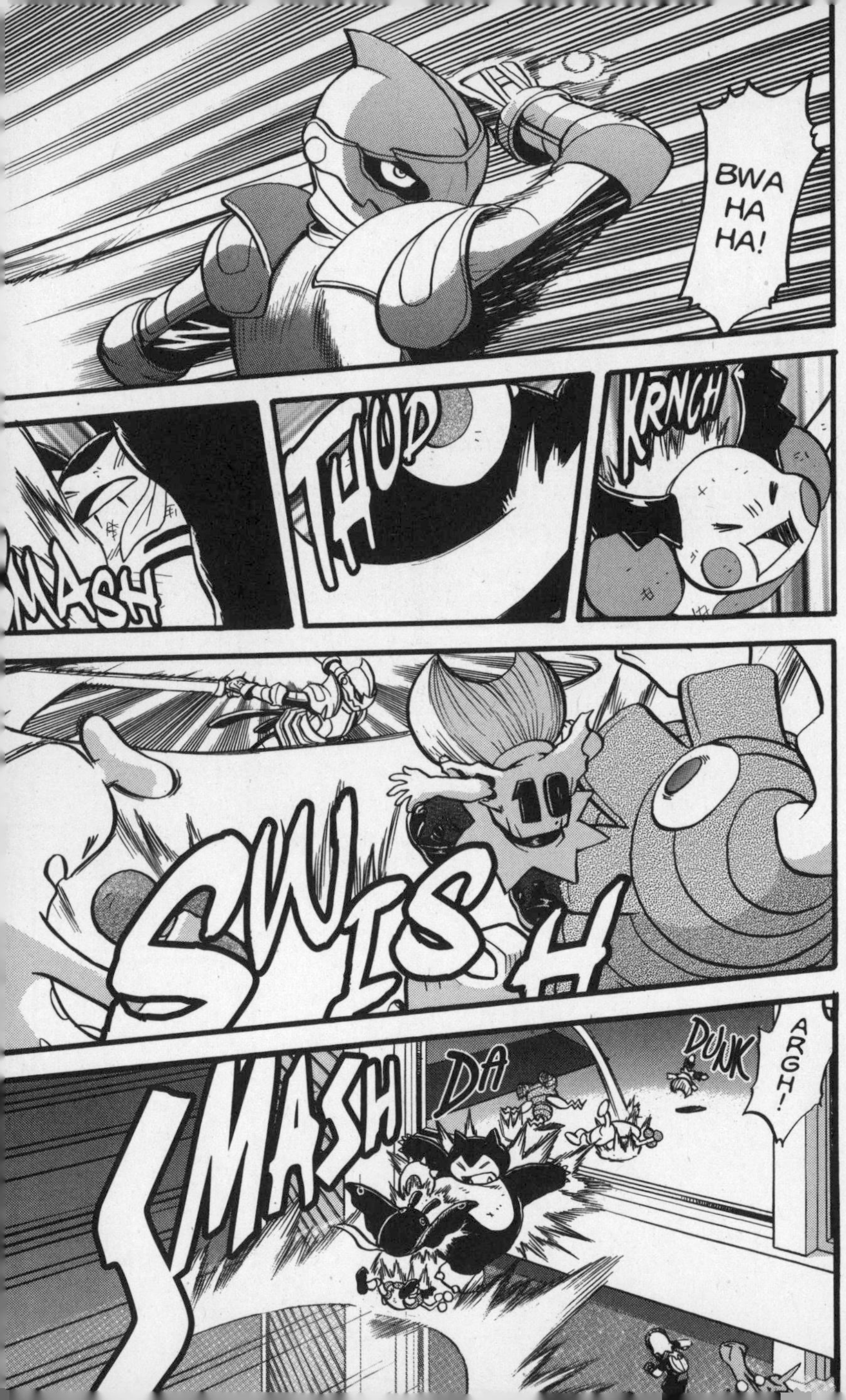
BWA HA HA!
KRNCH
THUD
MASH
SWISH
ARGH!
DUNK
DA
SMASH

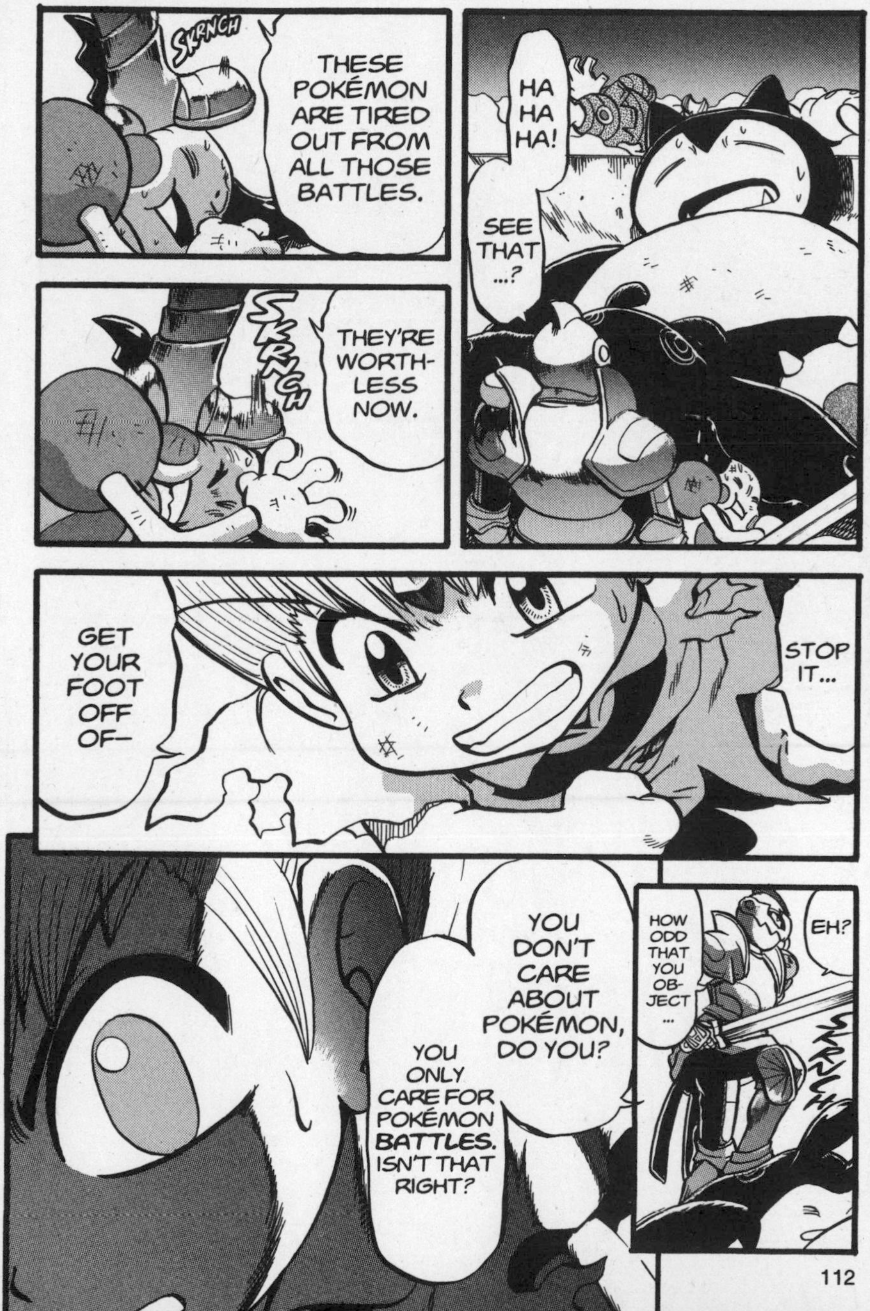
HA HA HA!
SEE THAT ...?
THESE POKÉMON ARE TIRED OUT FROM ALL THOSE BATTLES.
SKRNCH
THEY'RE WORTH-LESS NOW.
SKRNCH
STOP IT...
GET YOUR FOOT OFF OF–
EH?
HOW ODD THAT YOU OB-JECT ...
SKRNCH
YOU DON'T CARE ABOUT POKÉMON, DO YOU?
YOU ONLY CARE FOR POKÉMON **BATTLES.** ISN'T THAT RIGHT?

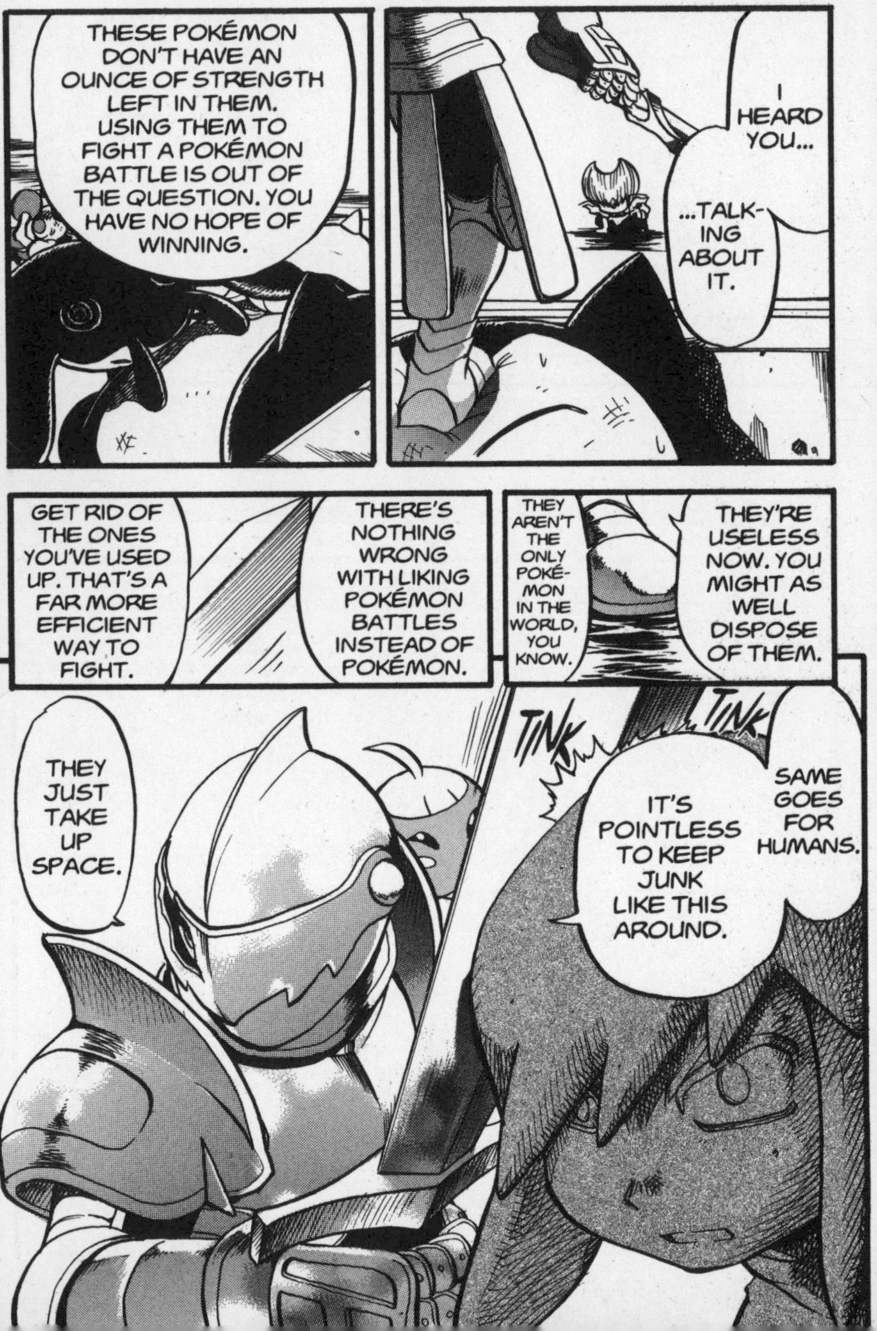
I HEARD YOU...
...TALKING ABOUT IT.
THESE POKÉMON DON'T HAVE AN OUNCE OF STRENGTH LEFT IN THEM. USING THEM TO FIGHT A POKÉMON BATTLE IS OUT OF THE QUESTION. YOU HAVE NO HOPE OF WINNING.
THEY'RE USELESS NOW. YOU MIGHT AS WELL DISPOSE OF THEM.
THEY AREN'T THE ONLY POKÉMON IN THE WORLD, YOU KNOW.
THERE'S NOTHING WRONG WITH LIKING POKÉMON BATTLES INSTEAD OF POKÉMON.
GET RID OF THE ONES YOU'VE USED UP. THAT'S A FAR MORE EFFICIENT WAY TO FIGHT.
TINK
TINK
SAME GOES FOR HUMANS.
IT'S POINTLESS TO KEEP JUNK LIKE THIS AROUND.
THEY JUST TAKE UP SPACE.

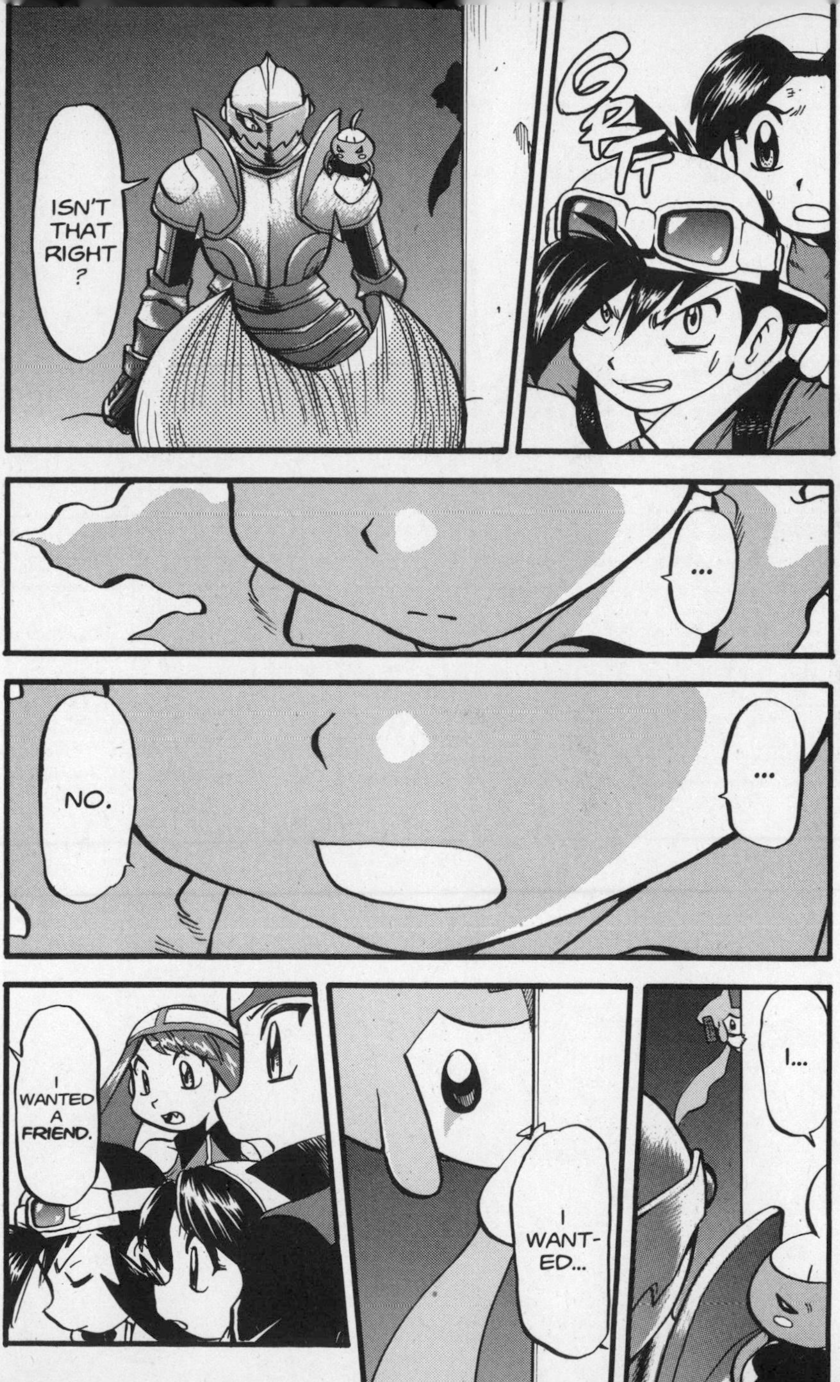
GRTT
ISN'T THAT RIGHT?
...
...
NO.
I...
I WANT-ED...
I WANTED A FRIEND.

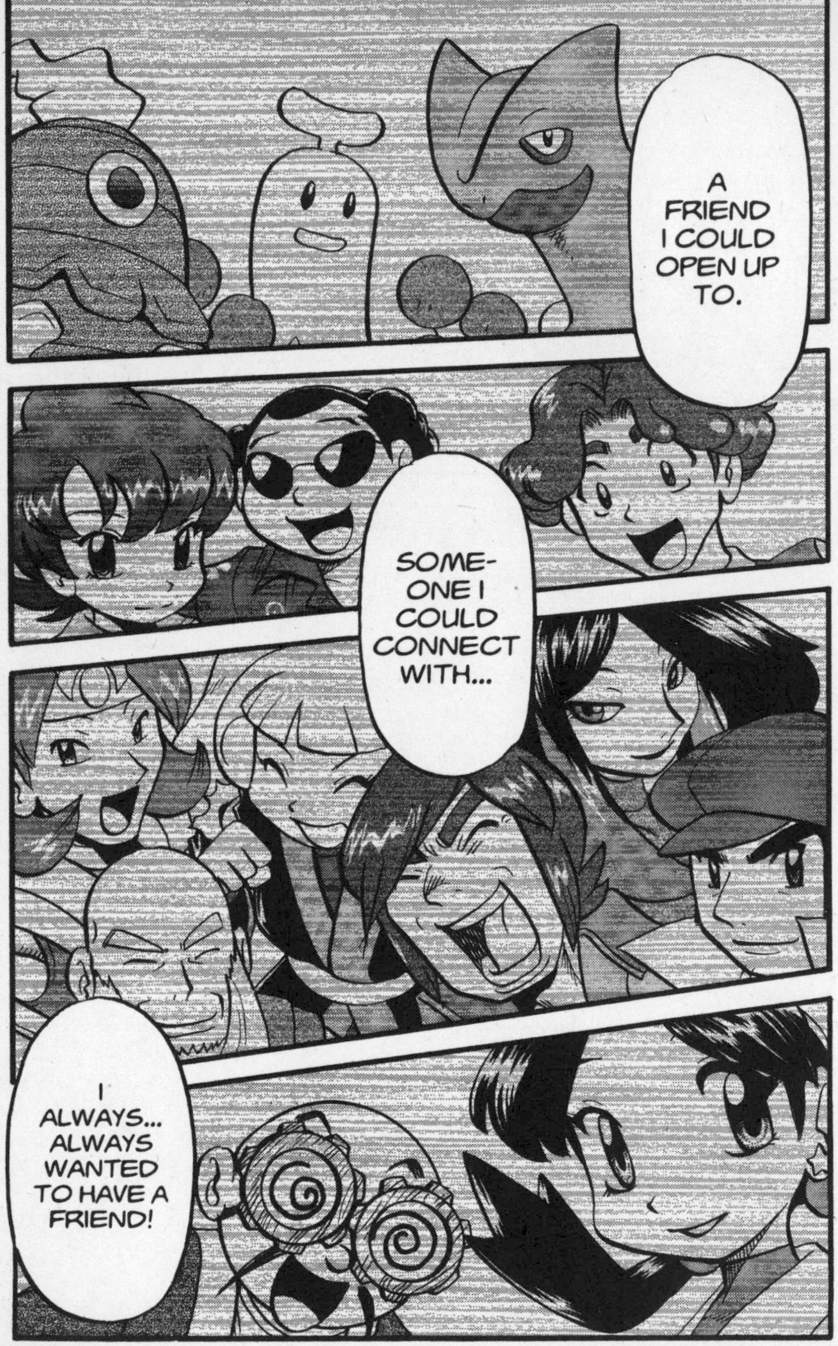
A FRIEND I COULD OPEN UP TO.
SOME-ONE I COULD CONNECT WITH...
I ALWAYS... ALWAYS WANTED TO HAVE A FRIEND!

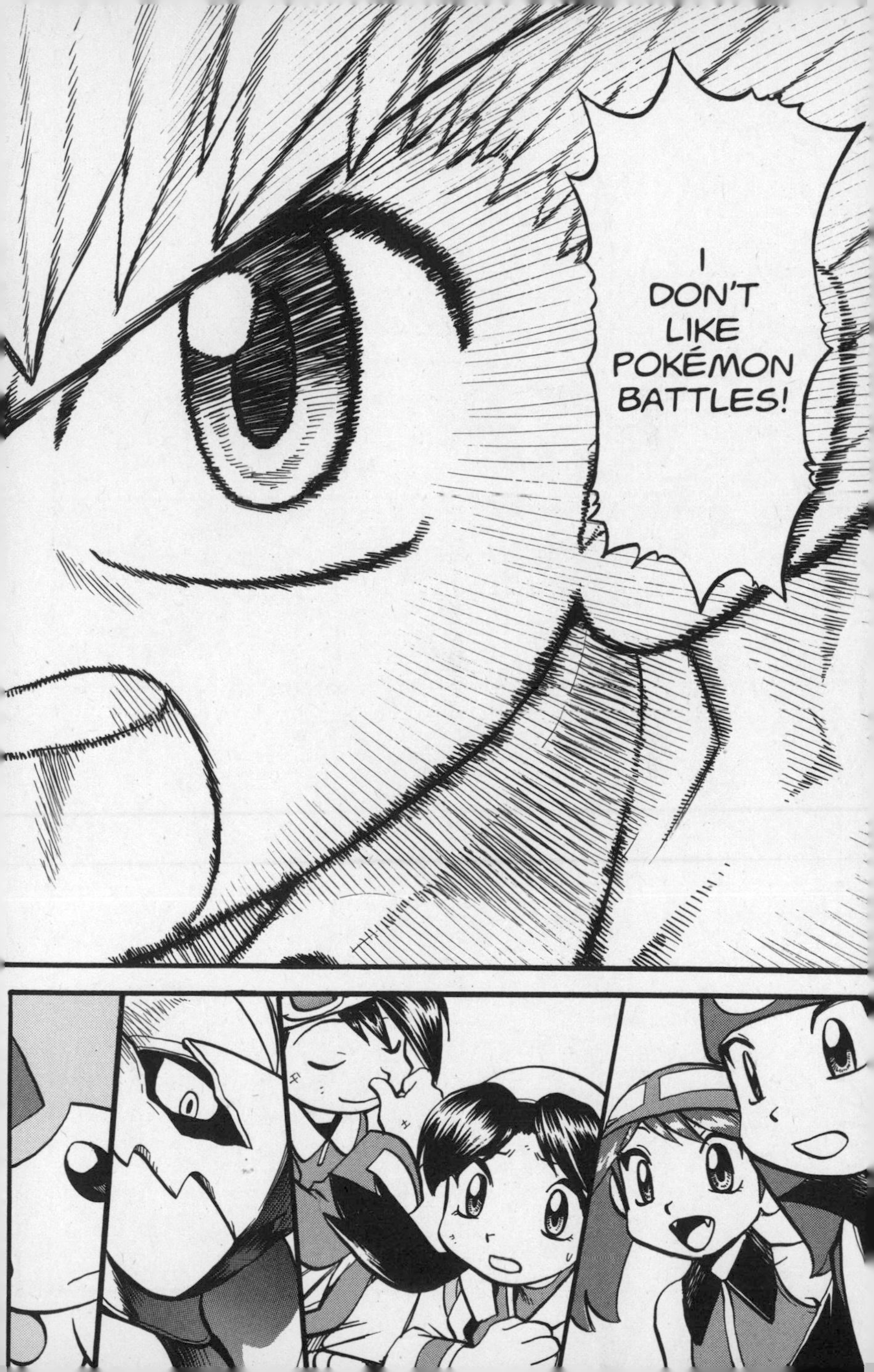
I DON'T LIKE POKÉMON BATTLES!

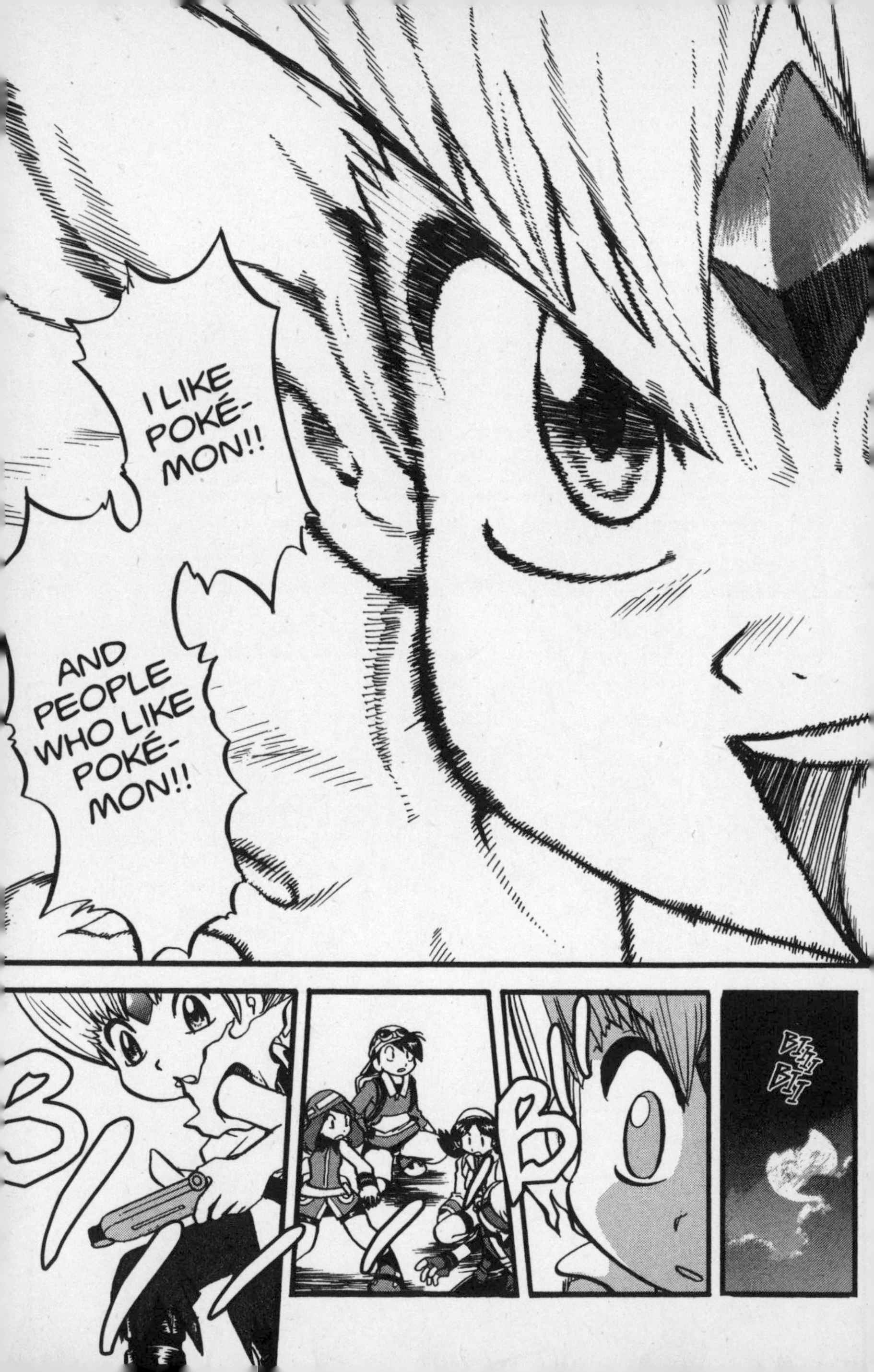
I LIKE POKÉ-MON!!
AND PEOPLE WHO LIKE POKÉ-MON!!
BIII BII

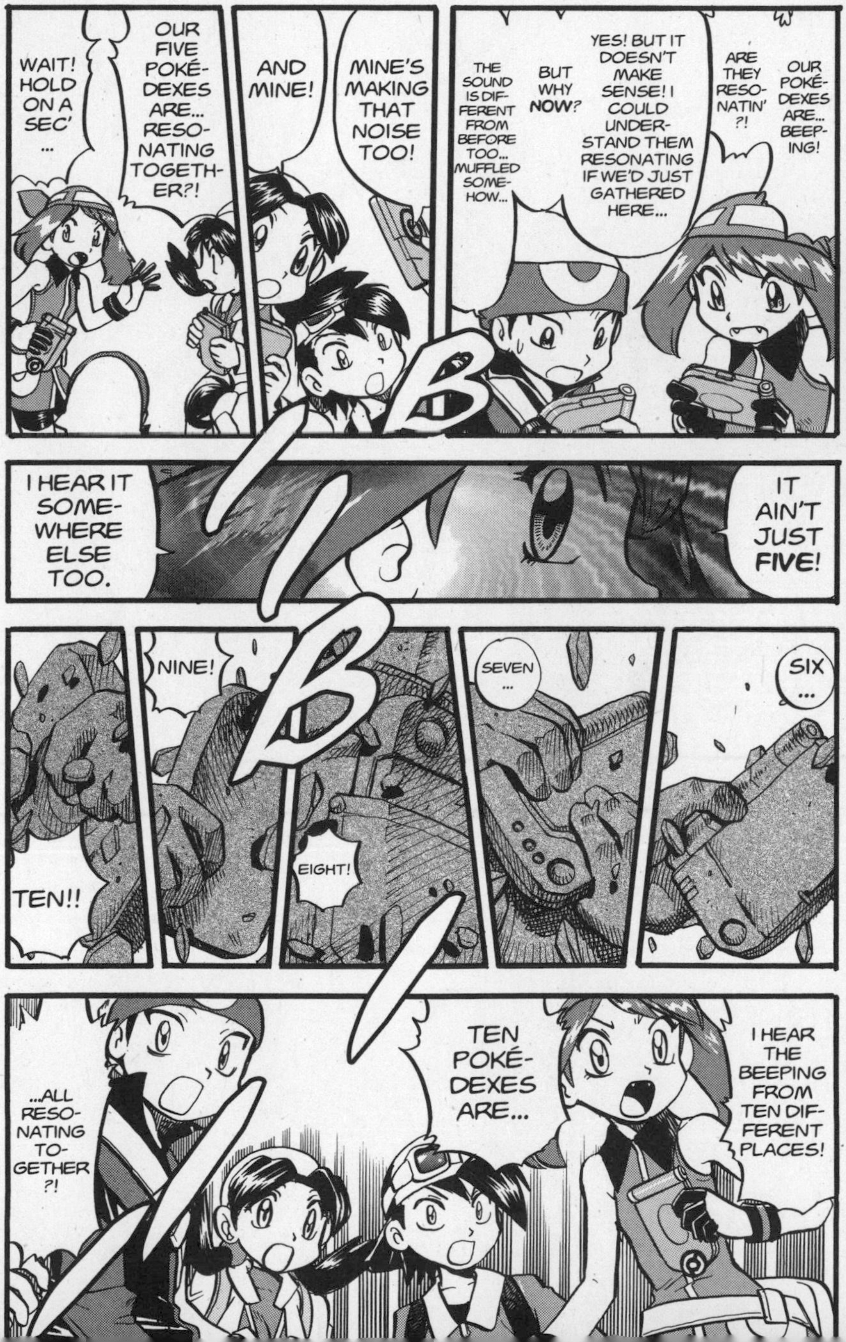
OUR POKÉ-DEXES ARE... BEEP-ING!
ARE THEY RESO-NATIN' ?!
YES! BUT IT DOESN'T MAKE SENSE! I COULD UNDER-STAND THEM RESONATING IF WE'D JUST GATHERED HERE...
BUT WHY NOW?
THE SOUND IS DIF-FERENT FROM BEFORE TOO... MUFFLED SOME-HOW...
MINE'S MAKING THAT NOISE TOO!
AND MINE!
OUR FIVE POKÉ-DEXES ARE... RESO-NATING TOGETH-ER?!
WAIT! HOLD ON A SEC' ...
IT AIN'T JUST FIVE!
I HEAR IT SOME-WHERE ELSE TOO.
SIX ...
SEVEN ...
EIGHT!
NINE!
TEN!!
I HEAR THE BEEPING FROM TEN DIF-FERENT PLACES!
TEN POKÉ-DEXES ARE...
...ALL RESO-NATING TO-GETHER ?!

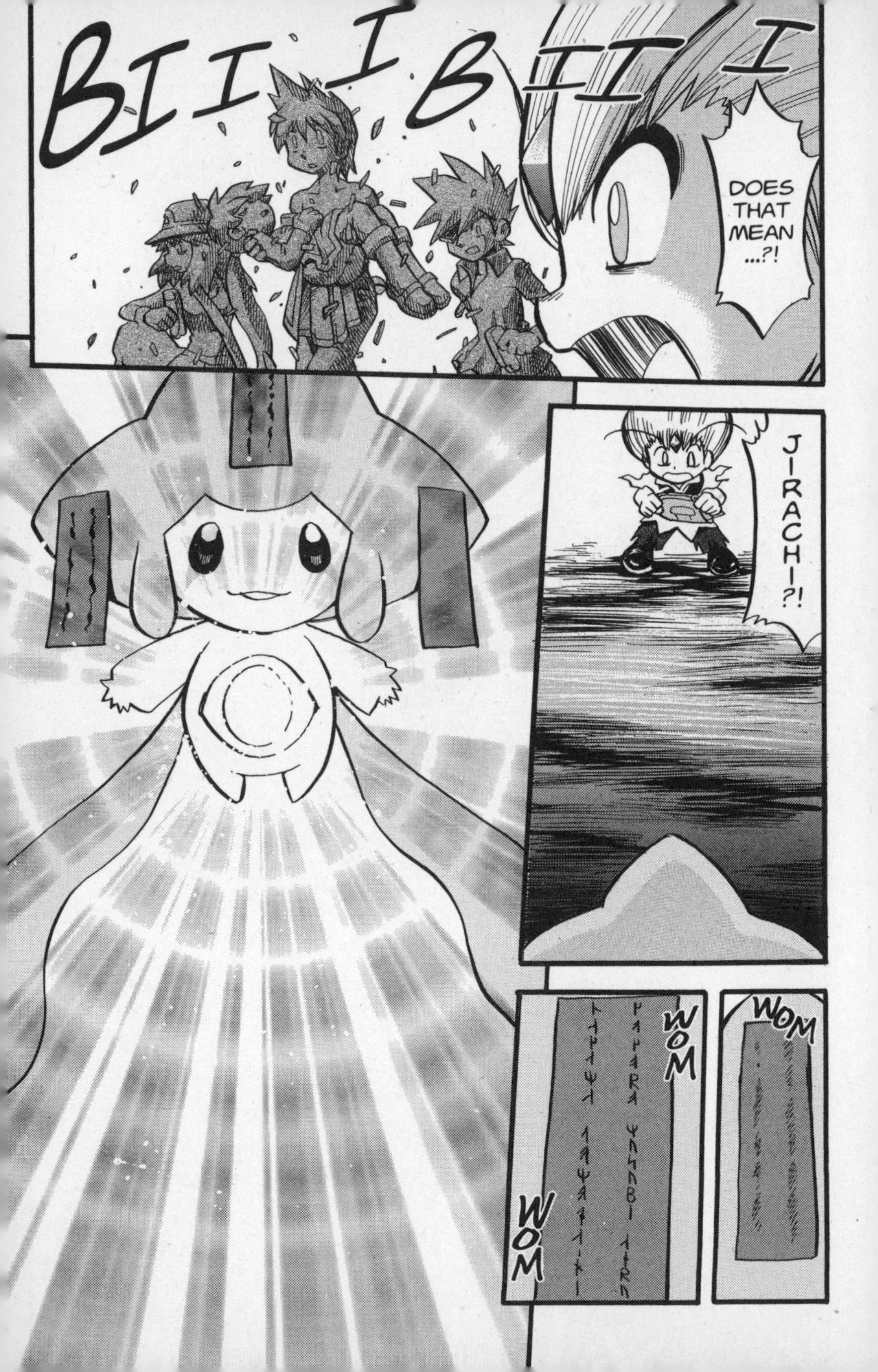
DOES THAT MEAN ...?!
BIII BIII
JIRACHI?!
WOM
WOM WOM
WOM WOM

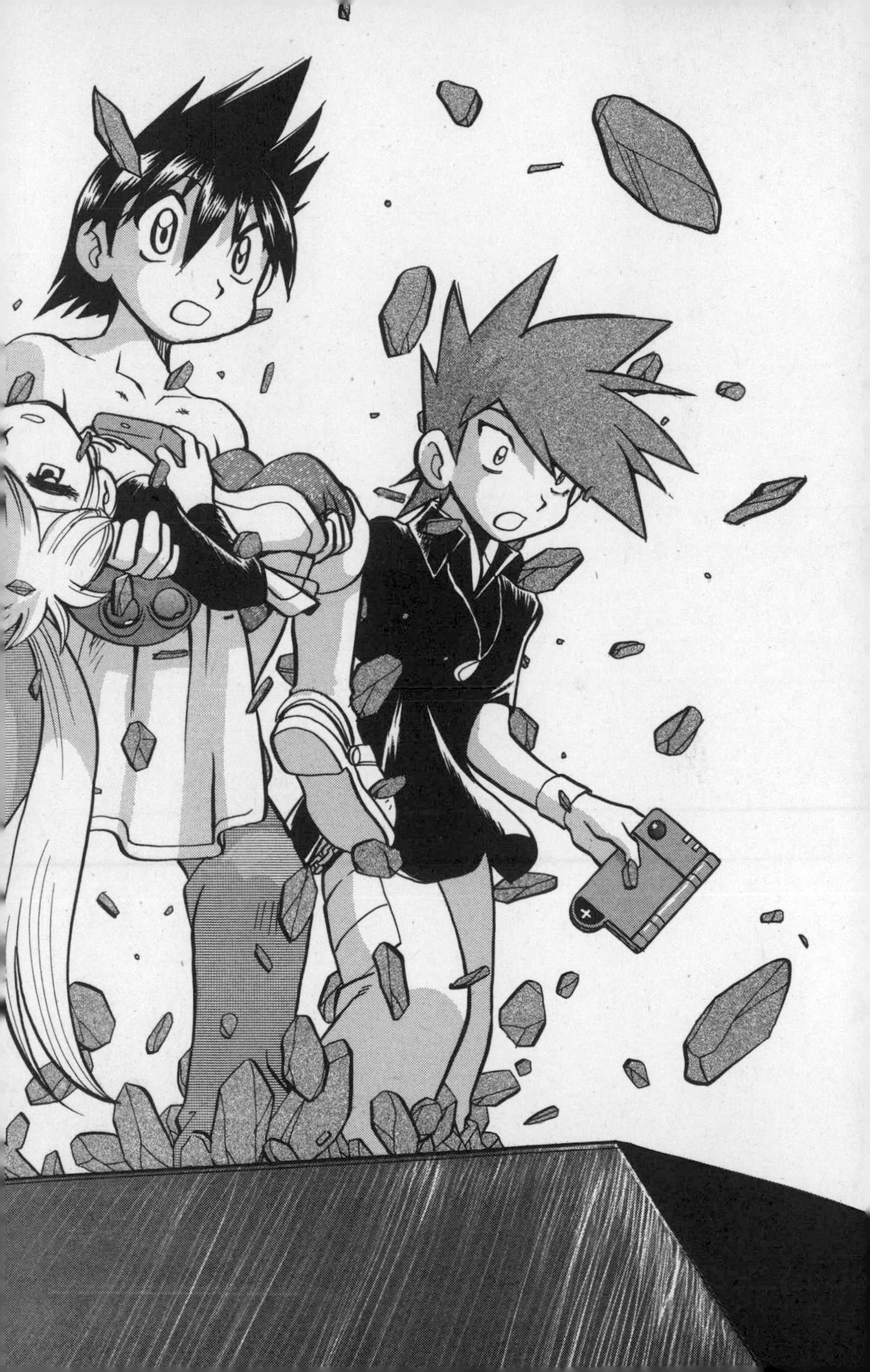

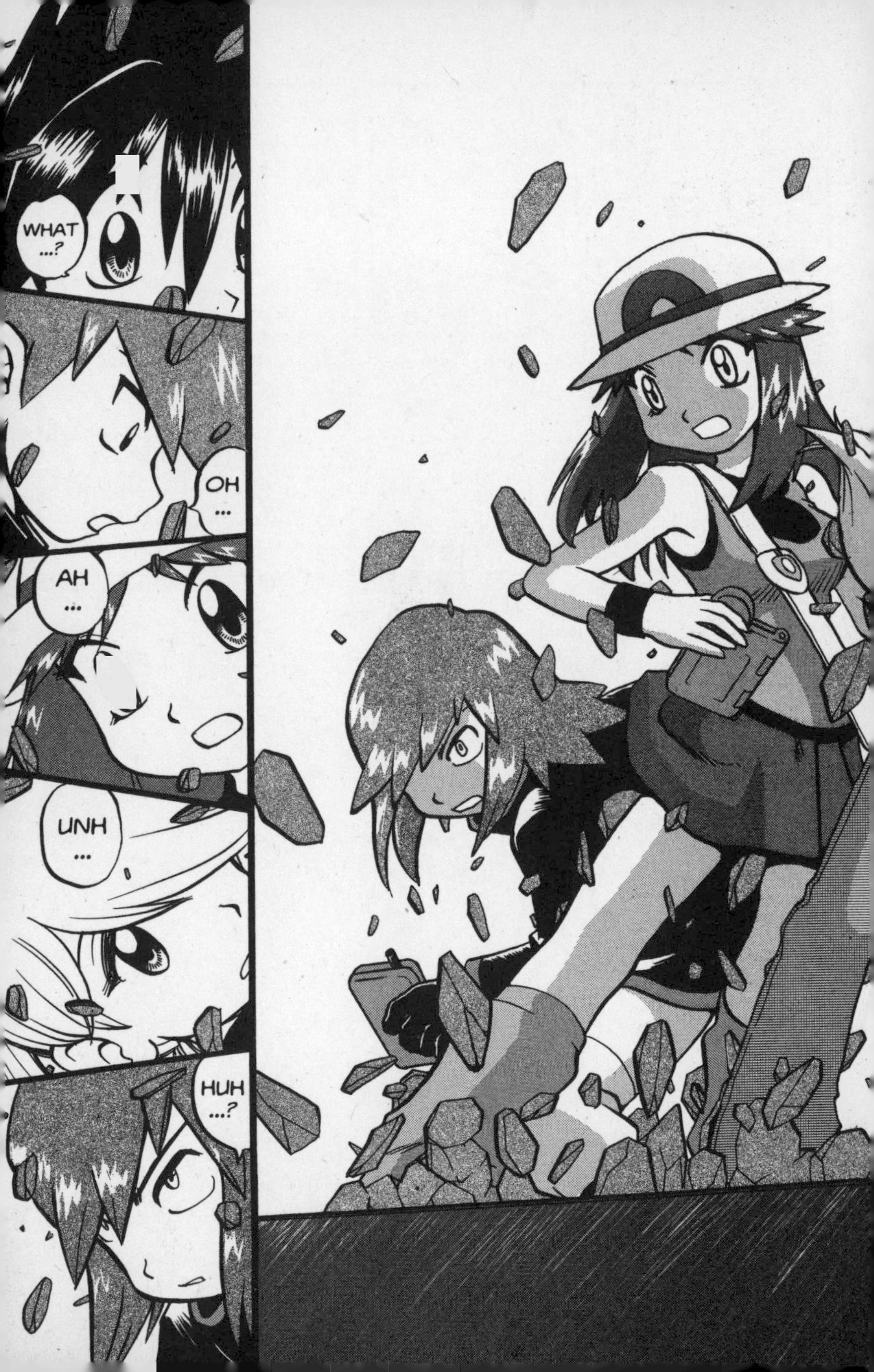
WHAT ...?
OH ...
AH ...
UNH ...
HUH ...?

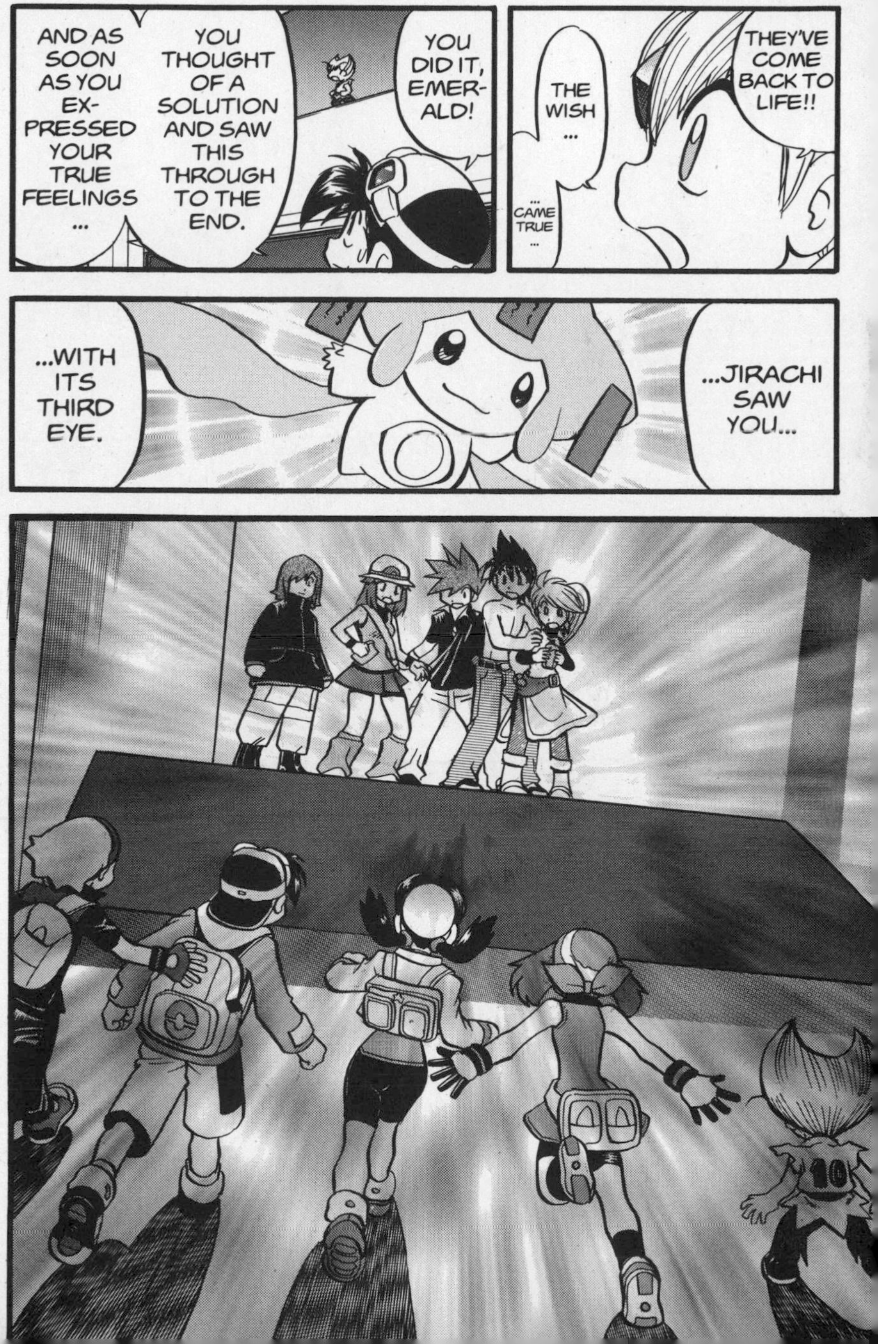
THEY'VE COME BACK TO LIFE!!
THE WISH ...
... CAME TRUE ...
YOU DID IT, EMERALD!
YOU THOUGHT OF A SOLUTION AND SAW THIS THROUGH TO THE END.
AND AS SOON AS YOU EXPRESSED YOUR TRUE FEELINGS ...
...JIRACHI SAW YOU...
...WITH ITS THIRD EYE.

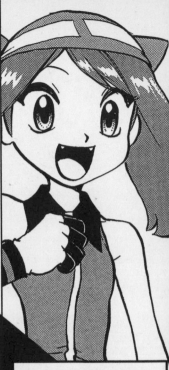

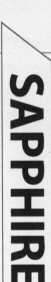

Character Profile Sapphire

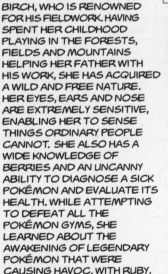

THE DAUGHTER OF POKÉMON RESEARCHER PROFESSOR BIRCH, WHO IS RENOWNED FOR HIS FIELDWORK. HAVING SPENT HER CHILDHOOD PLAYING IN THE FORESTS, FIELDS AND MOUNTAINS HELPING HER FATHER WITH HIS WORK, SHE HAS ACQUIRED A WILD AND FREE NATURE. HER EYES, EARS AND NOSE ARE EXTREMELY SENSITIVE, ENABLING HER TO SENSE THINGS ORDINARY PEOPLE CANNOT. SHE ALSO HAS A WIDE KNOWLEDGE OF BERRIES AND AN UNCANNY ABILITY TO DIAGNOSE A SICK POKÉMON AND EVALUATE ITS HEALTH. WHILE ATTEMPTING TO DEFEAT ALL THE POKÉMON GYMS, SHE LEARNED ABOUT THE AWAKENING OF LEGENDARY POKÉMON THAT WERE CAUSING HAVOC. WITH RUBY, SHE FOUGHT TO SAVE THE WORLD. ALTHOUGH SHE APPEARS WILD AT HEART, SHE IS ACTUALLY QUITE EMOTIONALLY VULNERABLE.

SAPPHIRE

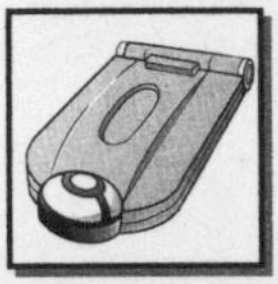

- Birthplace: Littleroot Town
- Birthday: September 20
- Blood Type: O
- Skills: Tree and cliff climbing
- Family: Father (Birch), mother
- Prizes Won: Defeated every Pokémon Gym in Hoenn

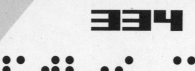

334

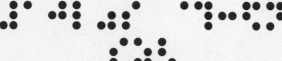

The Final Battle VII

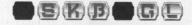

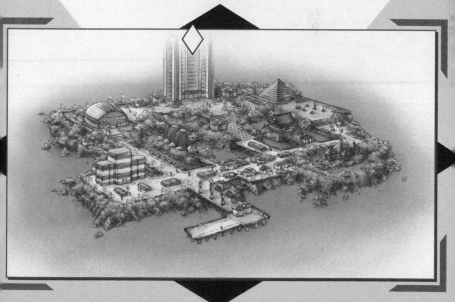

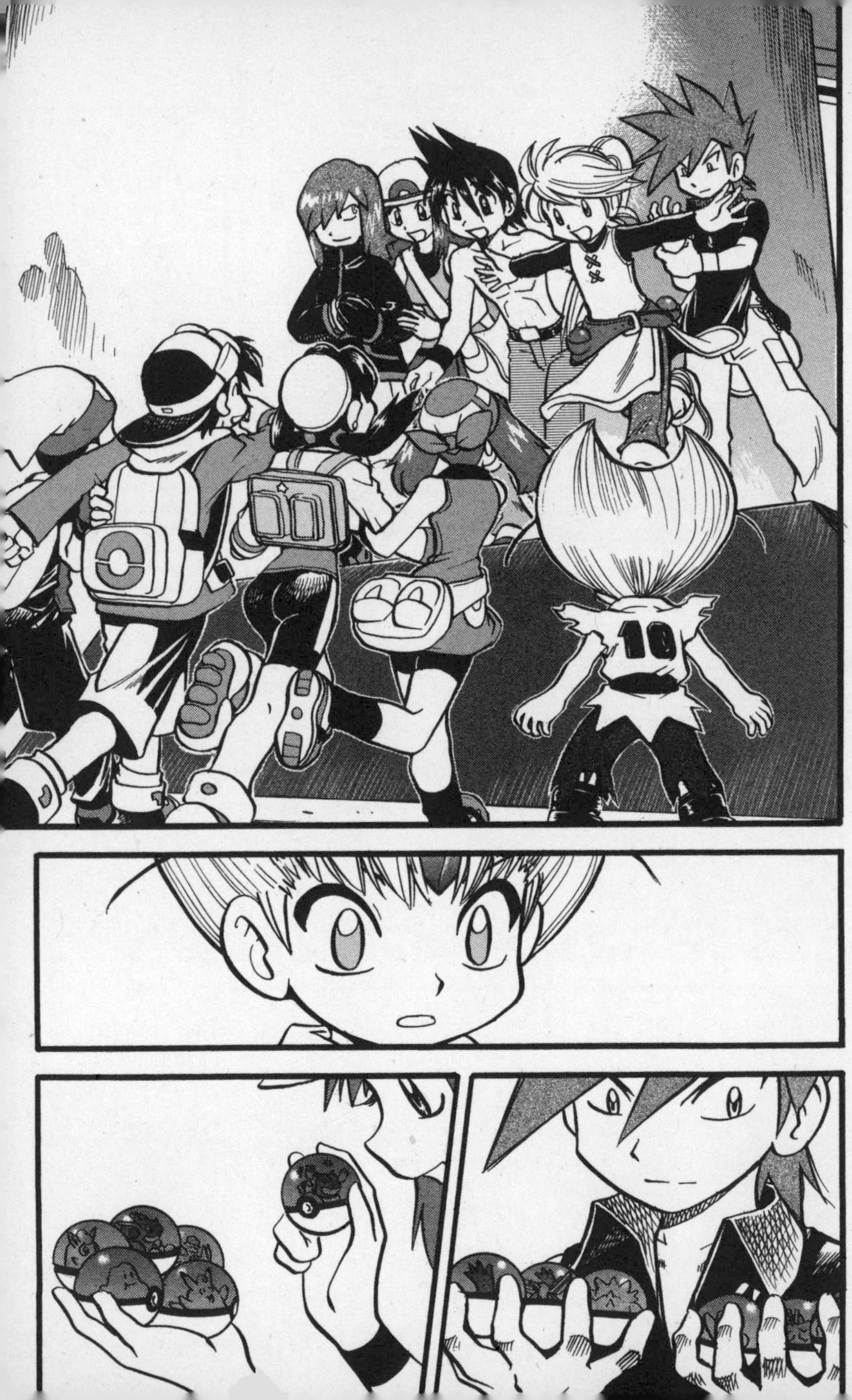
10

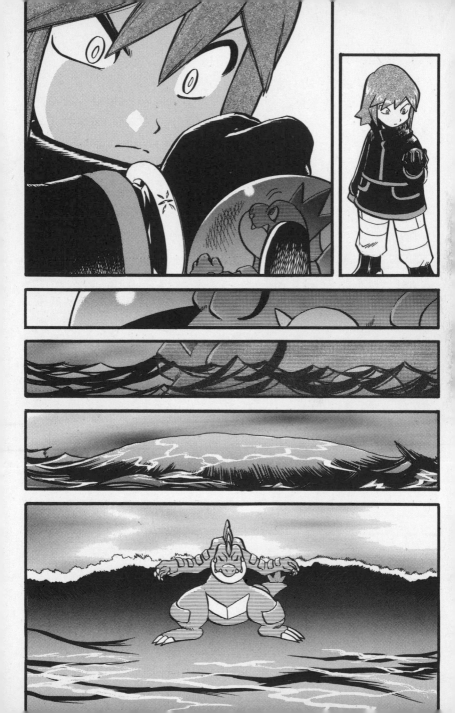

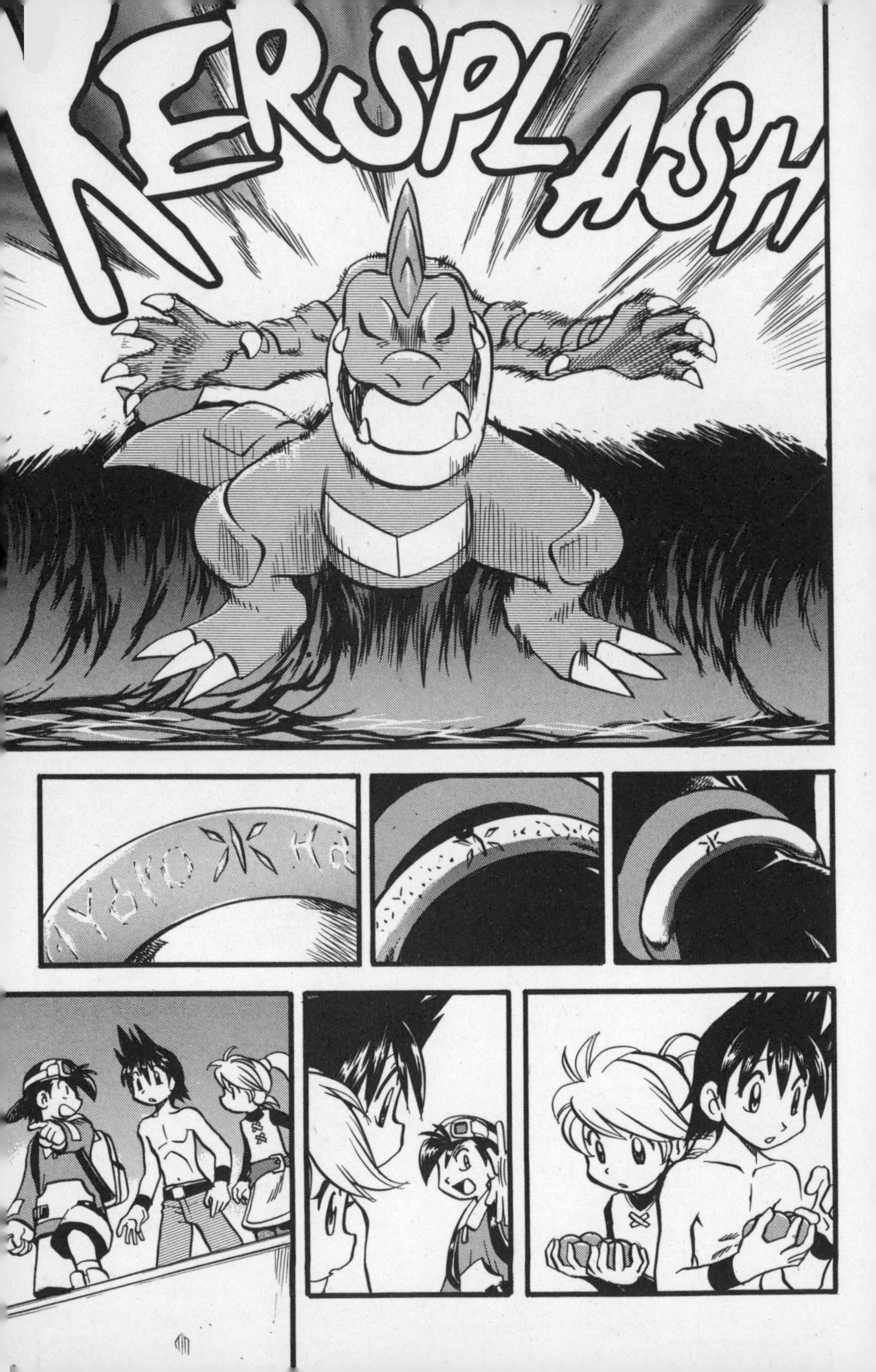
KERSPLASH

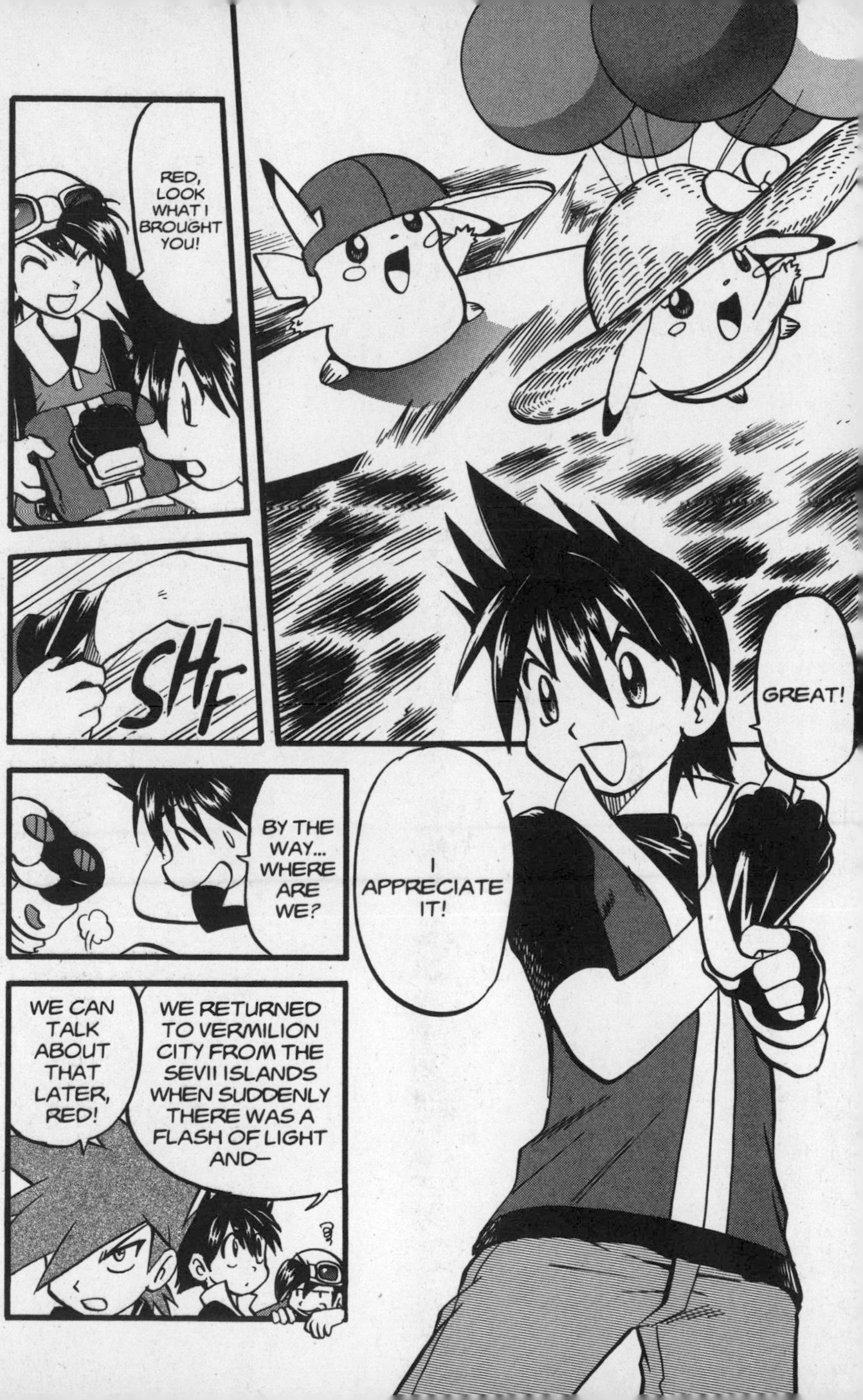
RED, LOOK WHAT I BROUGHT YOU!
GREAT!
I APPRECIATE IT!
SHF
BY THE WAY... WHERE ARE WE?
WE RETURNED TO VERMILION CITY FROM THE SEVII ISLANDS WHEN SUDDENLY THERE WAS A FLASH OF LIGHT AND–
WE CAN TALK ABOUT THAT LATER, RED!

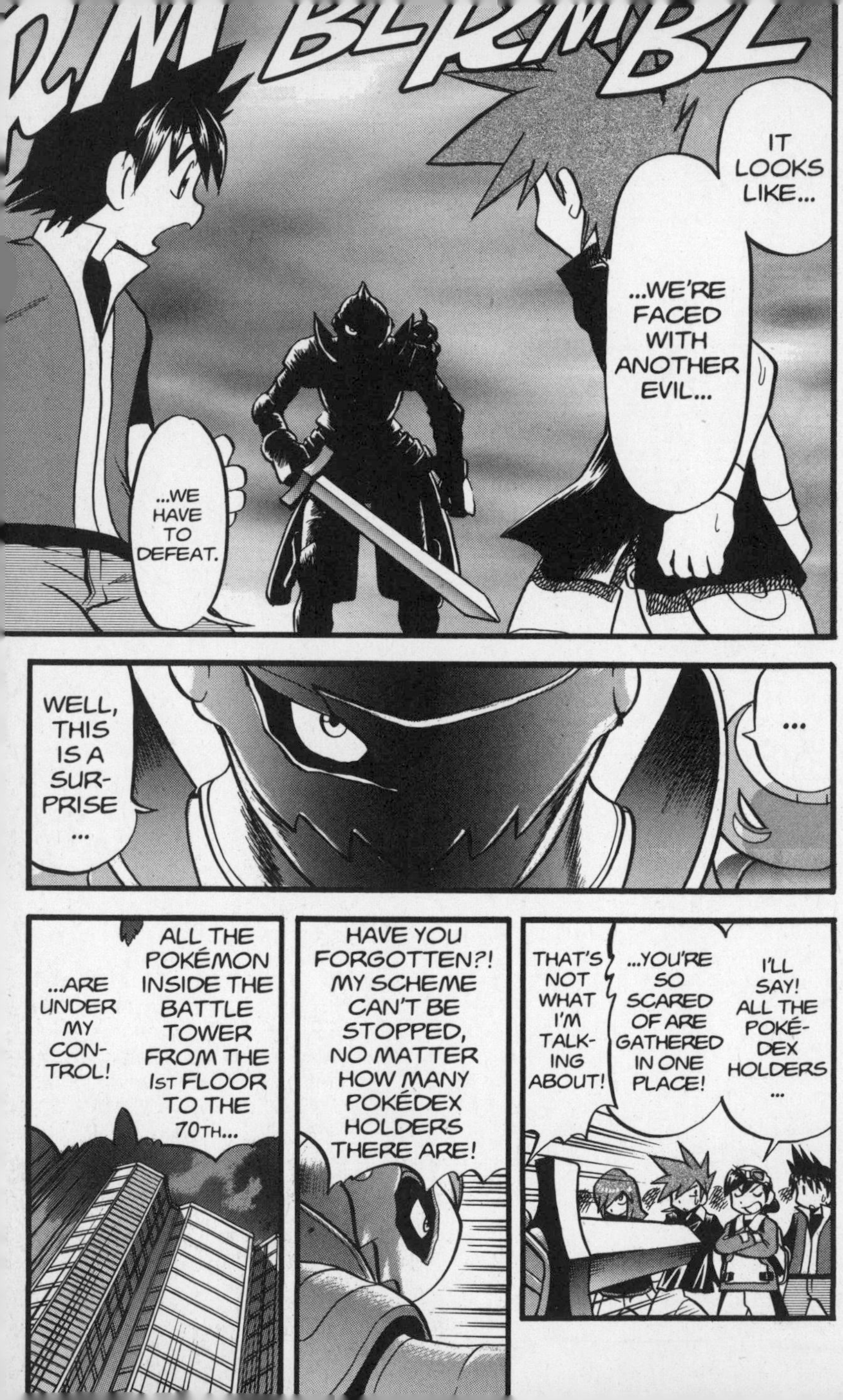
BLRMBL
IT LOOKS LIKE...
...WE'RE FACED WITH ANOTHER EVIL...
...WE HAVE TO DEFEAT.
...
WELL, THIS IS A SUR-PRISE...
I'LL SAY! ALL THE POKÉ-DEX HOLDERS...
...YOU'RE SO SCARED OF ARE GATHERED IN ONE PLACE!
THAT'S NOT WHAT I'M TALK-ING ABOUT!
HAVE YOU FORGOTTEN?! MY SCHEME CAN'T BE STOPPED, NO MATTER HOW MANY POKÉDEX HOLDERS THERE ARE!
ALL THE POKÉMON INSIDE THE BATTLE TOWER FROM THE 1ST FLOOR TO THE 70TH...
...ARE UNDER MY CONTROL!

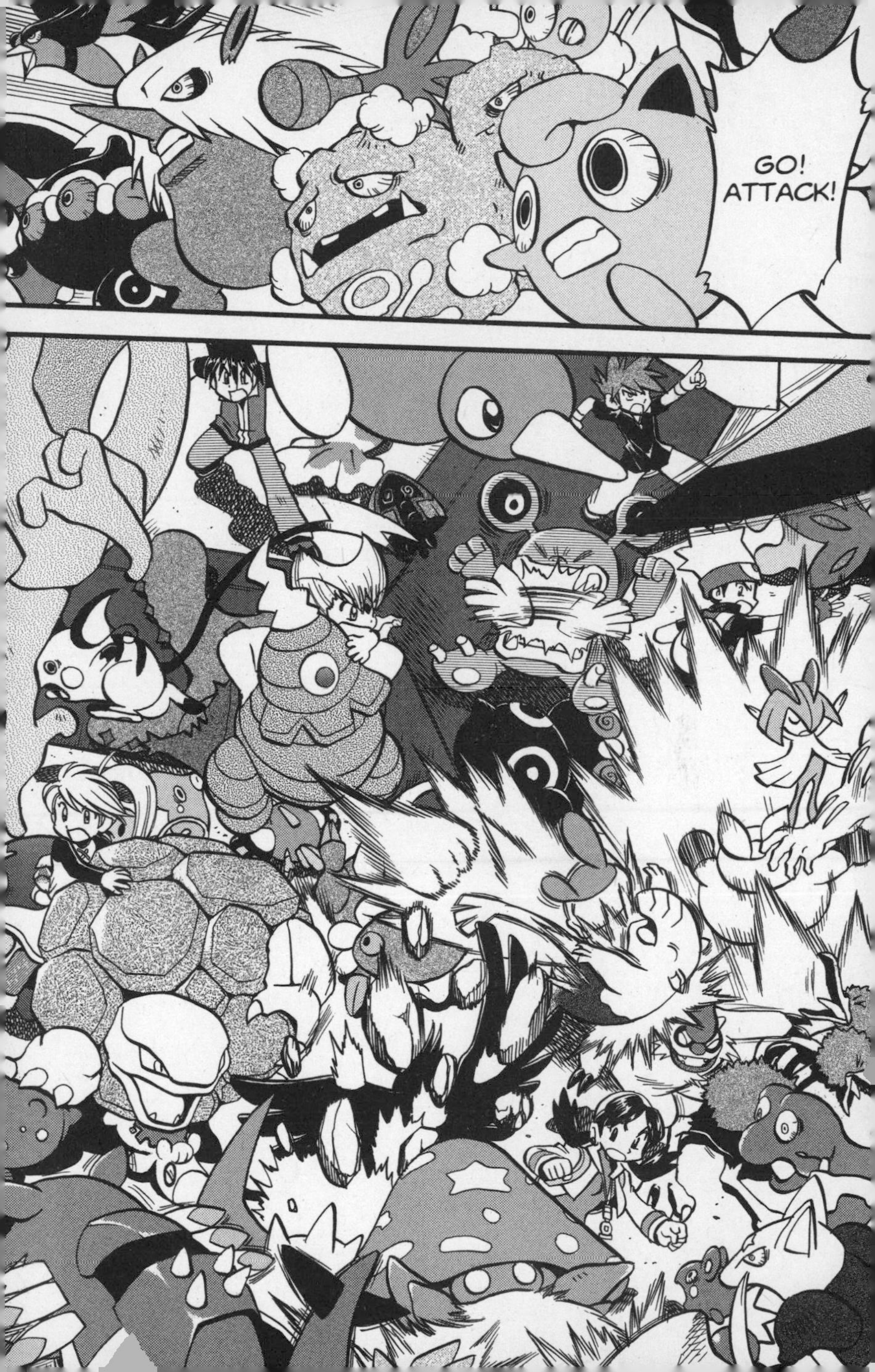
GO! ATTACK!

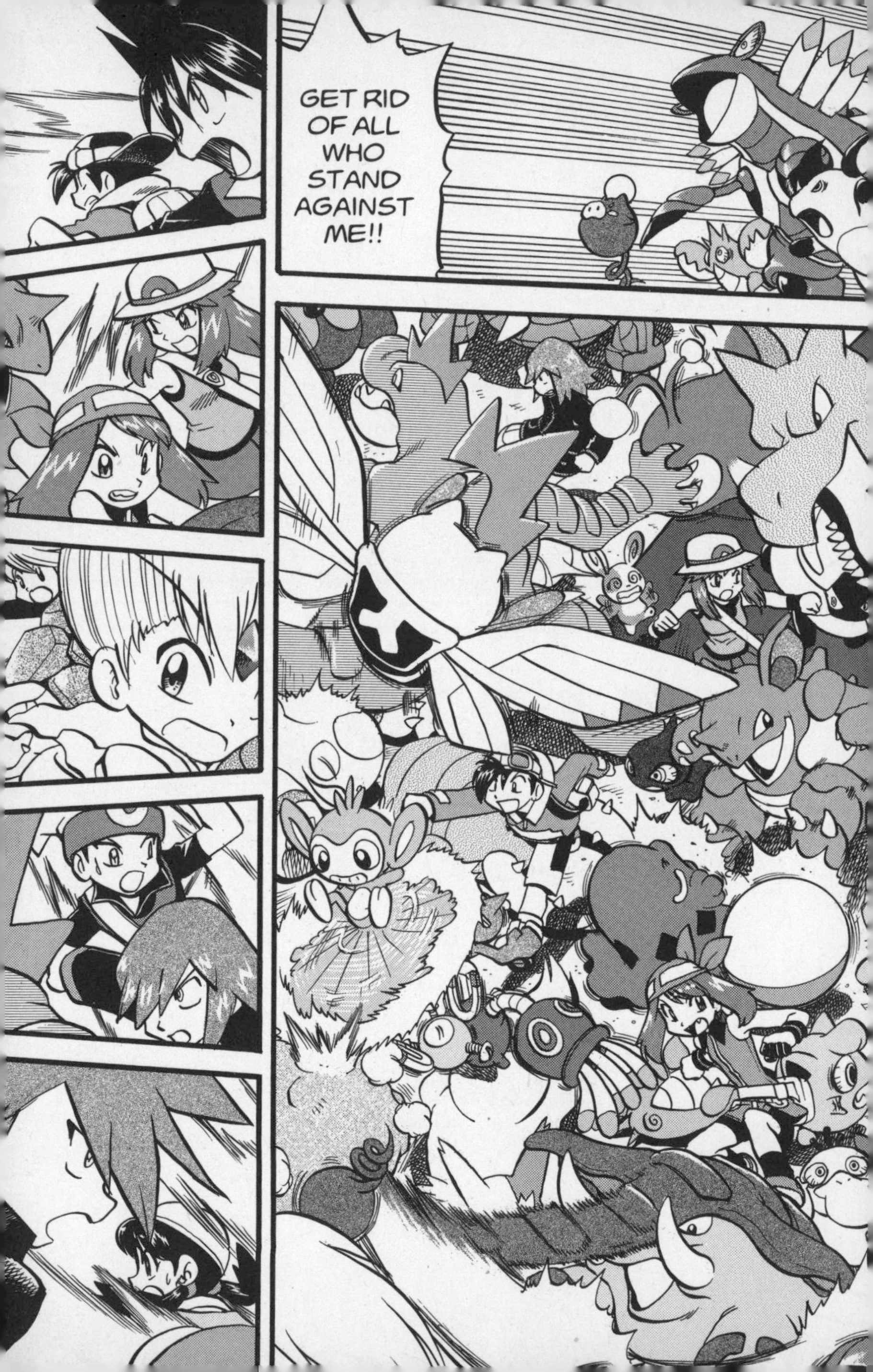
GET RID OF ALL WHO STAND AGAINST ME!!

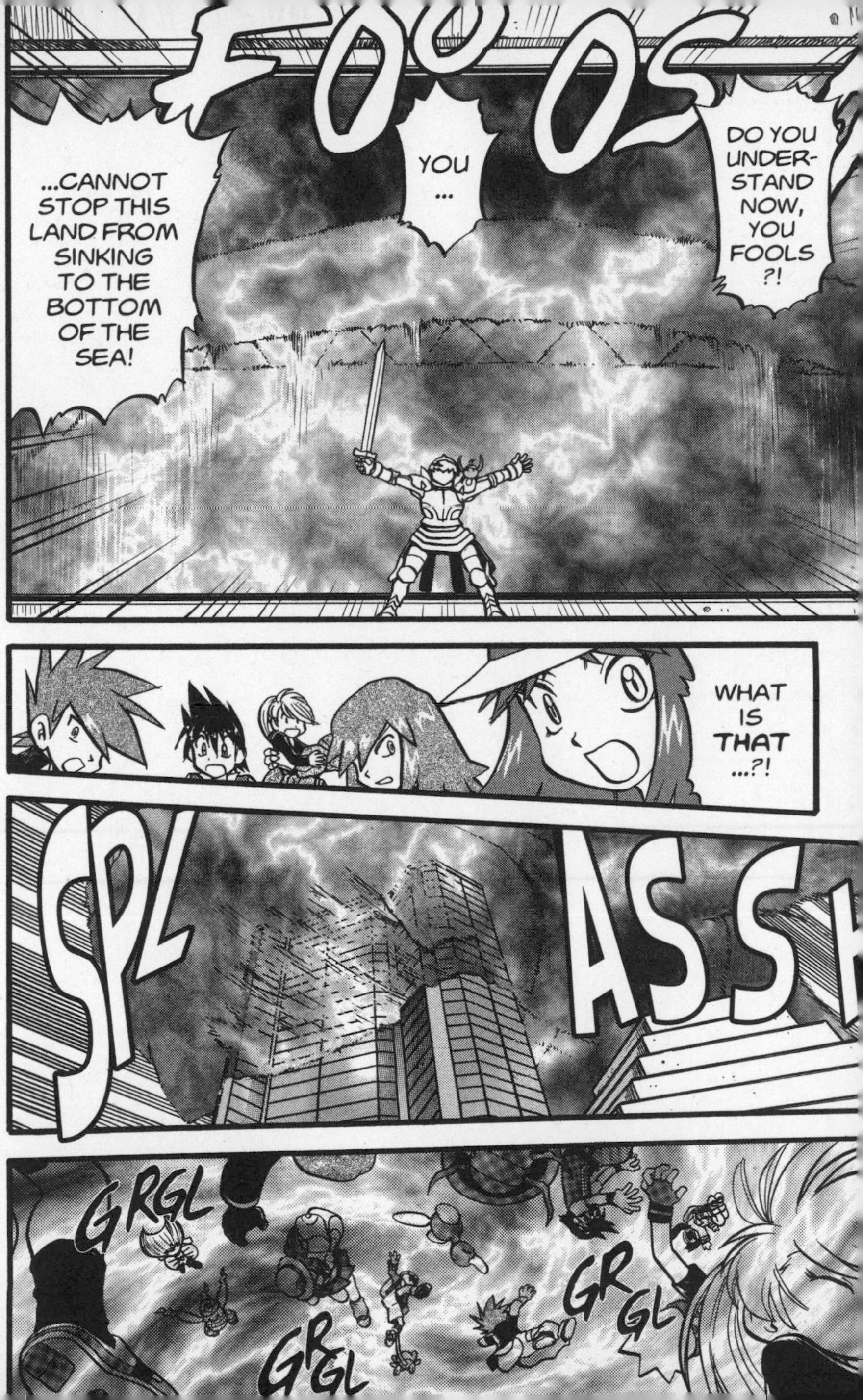
FOOOS
DO YOU UNDER-
STAND
NOW,
YOU
FOOLS
?!
YOU
...
...CANNOT
STOP THIS
LAND FROM
SINKING
TO THE
BOTTOM
OF THE
SEA!
WHAT
IS
THAT
...?!
SPL
ASS
GRGL
GRGL
GRGL

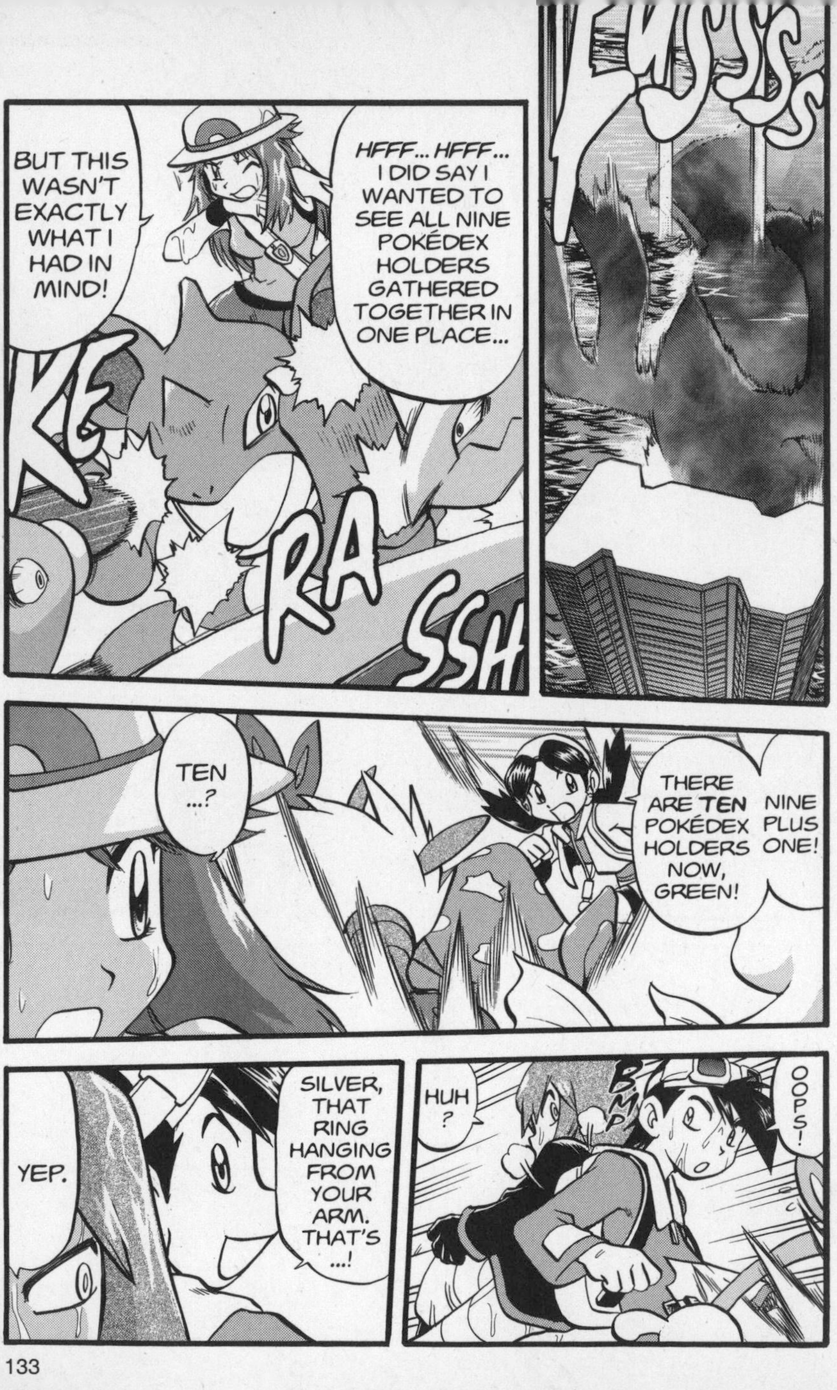
HFFF... HFFF... I DID SAY I WANTED TO SEE ALL NINE POKÉDEX HOLDERS GATHERED TOGETHER IN ONE PLACE...
BUT THIS WASN'T EXACTLY WHAT I HAD IN MIND!
KE
RA
SSH
NINE PLUS ONE!
THERE ARE TEN POKÉDEX HOLDERS NOW, GREEN!
TEN ...?
OOPS!
BMP
HUH?
SILVER, THAT RING HANGING FROM YOUR ARM. THAT'S ...!
YEP.

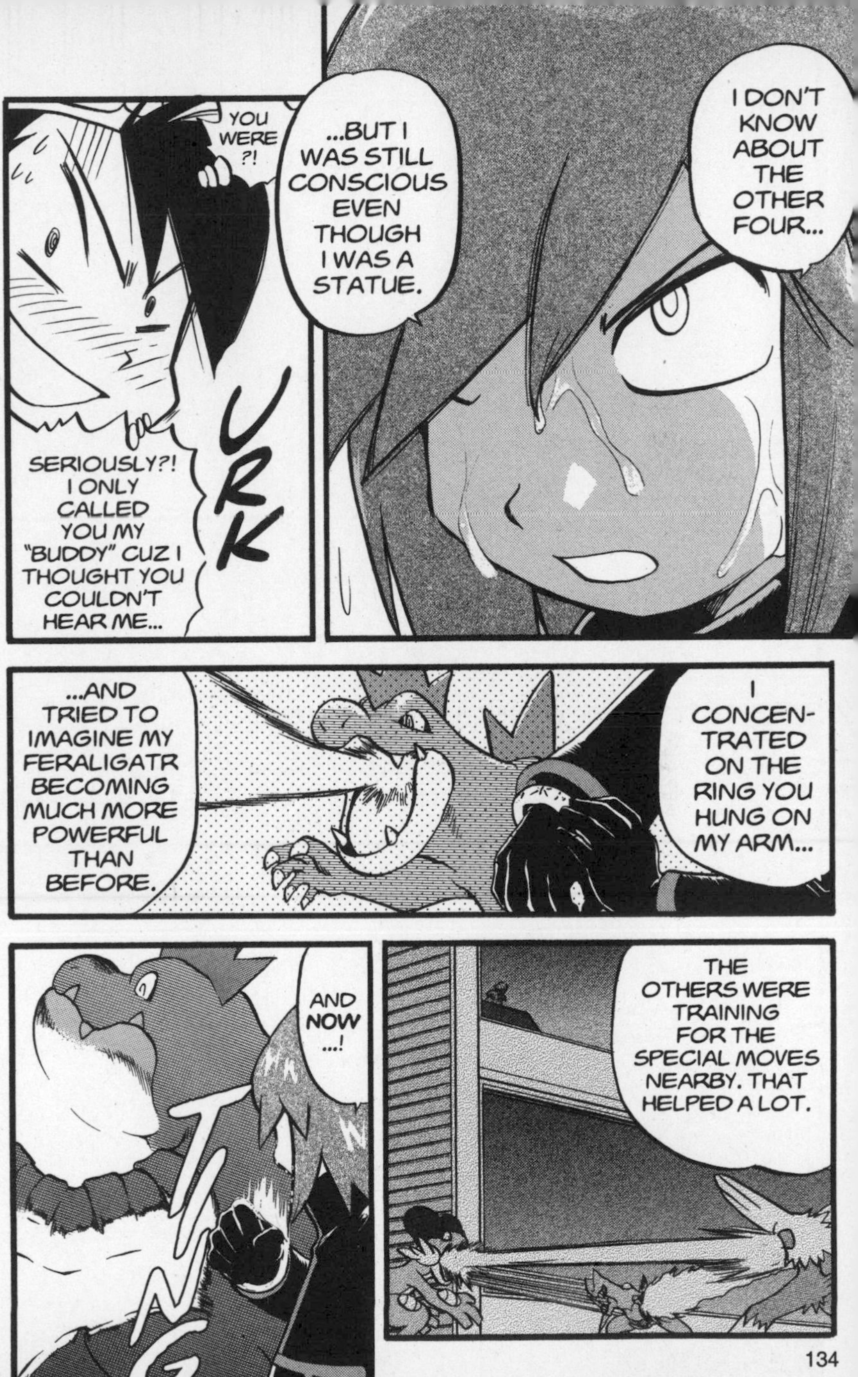
I DON'T KNOW ABOUT THE OTHER FOUR...
...BUT I WAS STILL CONSCIOUS EVEN THOUGH I WAS A STATUE.
YOU WERE?!
URK
SERIOUSLY?! I ONLY CALLED YOU MY "BUDDY" CUZ I THOUGHT YOU COULDN'T HEAR ME...
I CONCENTRATED ON THE RING YOU HUNG ON MY ARM...
...AND TRIED TO IMAGINE MY FERALIGATR BECOMING MUCH MORE POWERFUL THAN BEFORE.
THE OTHERS WERE TRAINING FOR THE SPECIAL MOVES NEARBY. THAT HELPED A LOT.
AND NOW...!
TING

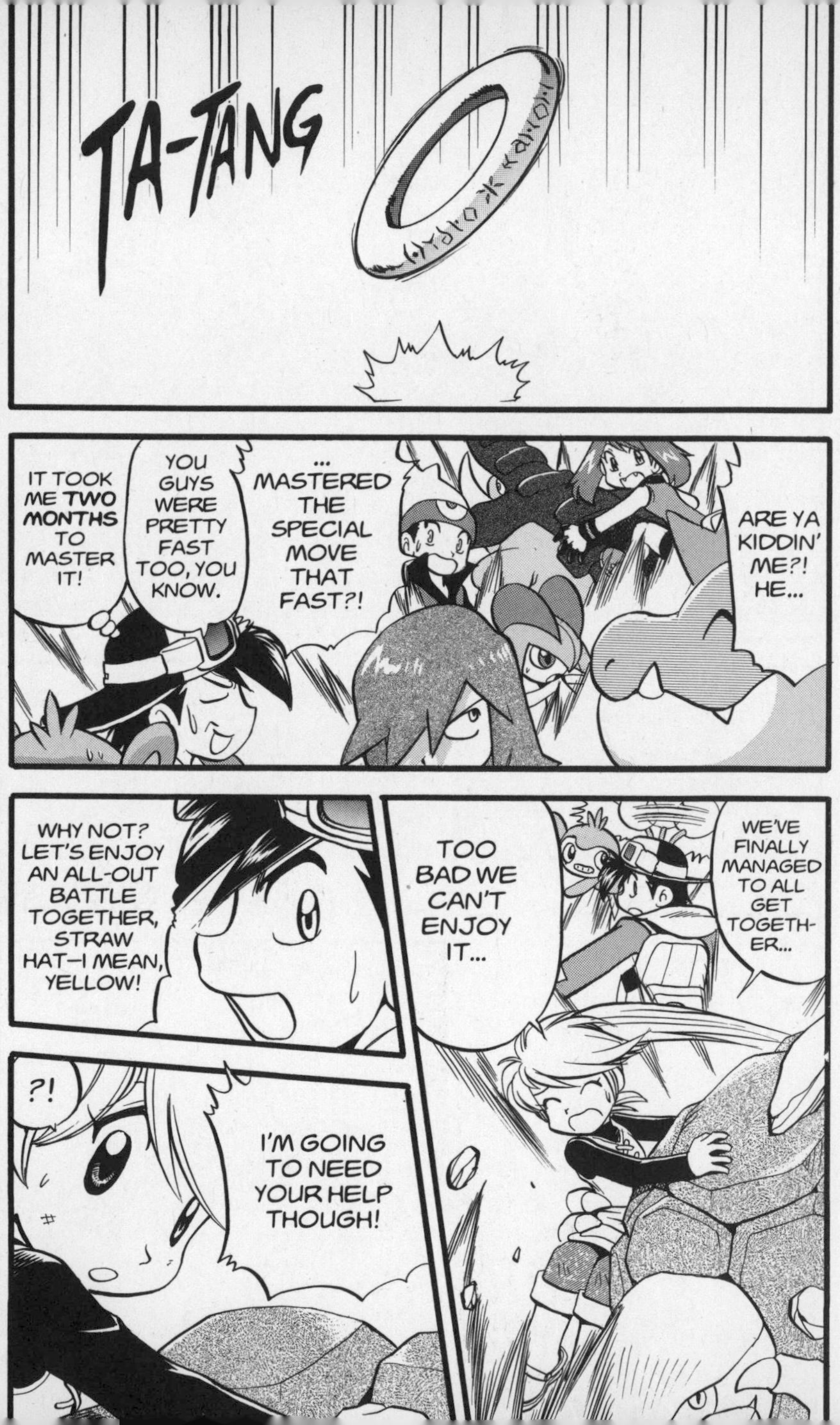
TA-TANG
ARE YA KIDDIN' ME?! HE...
... MASTERED THE SPECIAL MOVE THAT FAST?!
YOU GUYS WERE PRETTY FAST TOO, YOU KNOW.
IT TOOK ME **TWO MONTHS** TO MASTER IT!
WE'VE FINALLY MANAGED TO ALL GET TOGETH-ER...
TOO BAD WE CAN'T ENJOY IT...
WHY NOT? LET'S ENJOY AN ALL-OUT BATTLE TOGETHER, STRAW HAT—I MEAN, YELLOW!
?!
I'M GOING TO NEED YOUR HELP THOUGH!

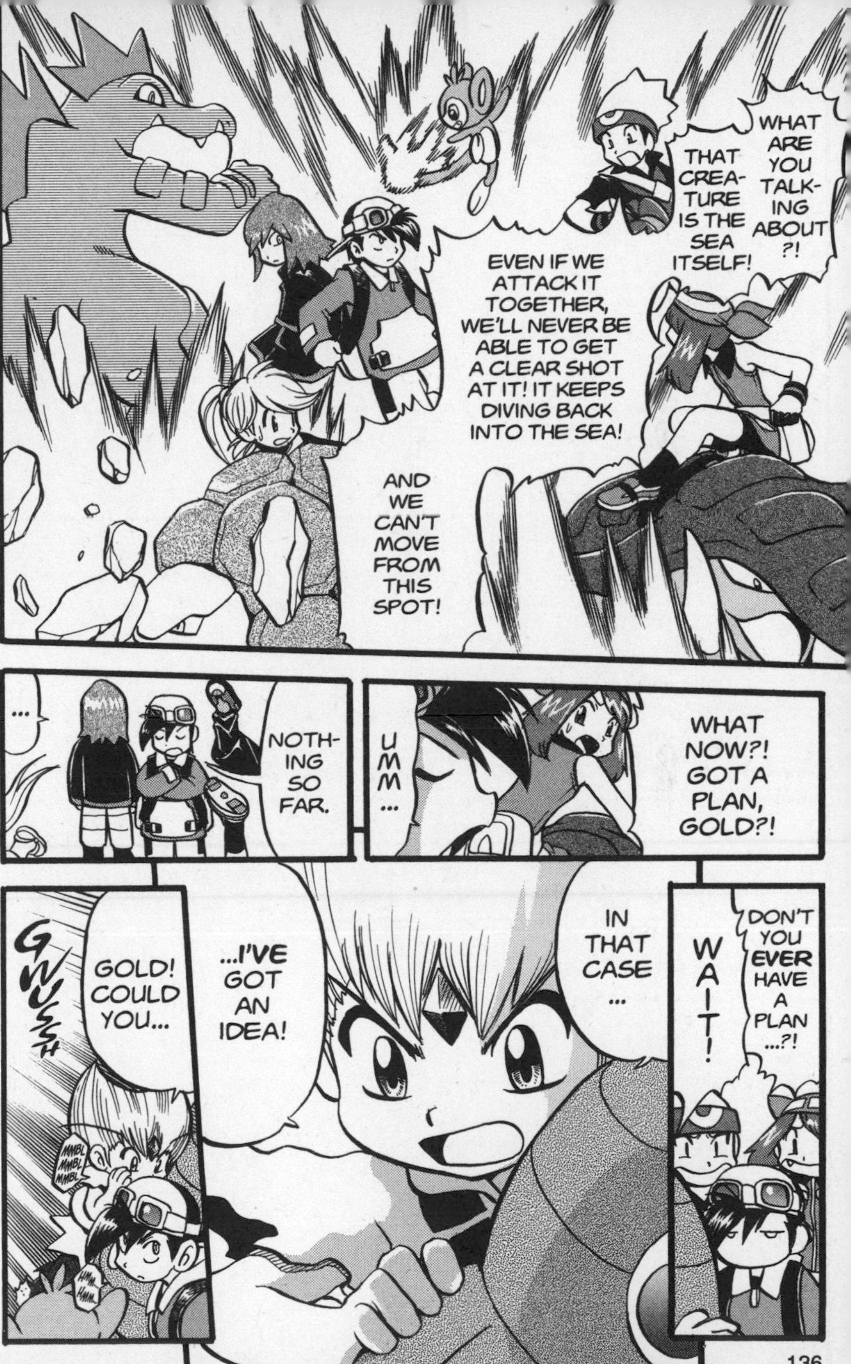
WHAT ARE YOU TALKING ABOUT?!
THAT CREATURE IS THE SEA ITSELF!
EVEN IF WE ATTACK IT TOGETHER, WE'LL NEVER BE ABLE TO GET A CLEAR SHOT AT IT! IT KEEPS DIVING BACK INTO THE SEA!
AND WE CAN'T MOVE FROM THIS SPOT!
WHAT NOW?! GOT A PLAN, GOLD?!
UMM...
NOTHING SO FAR.
...
DON'T YOU EVER HAVE A PLAN...?!
WAIT!
IN THAT CASE...
...I'VE GOT AN IDEA!
GOLD! COULD YOU...
GWUSSH
MMBL MMBL MMBL
HMM HMM.

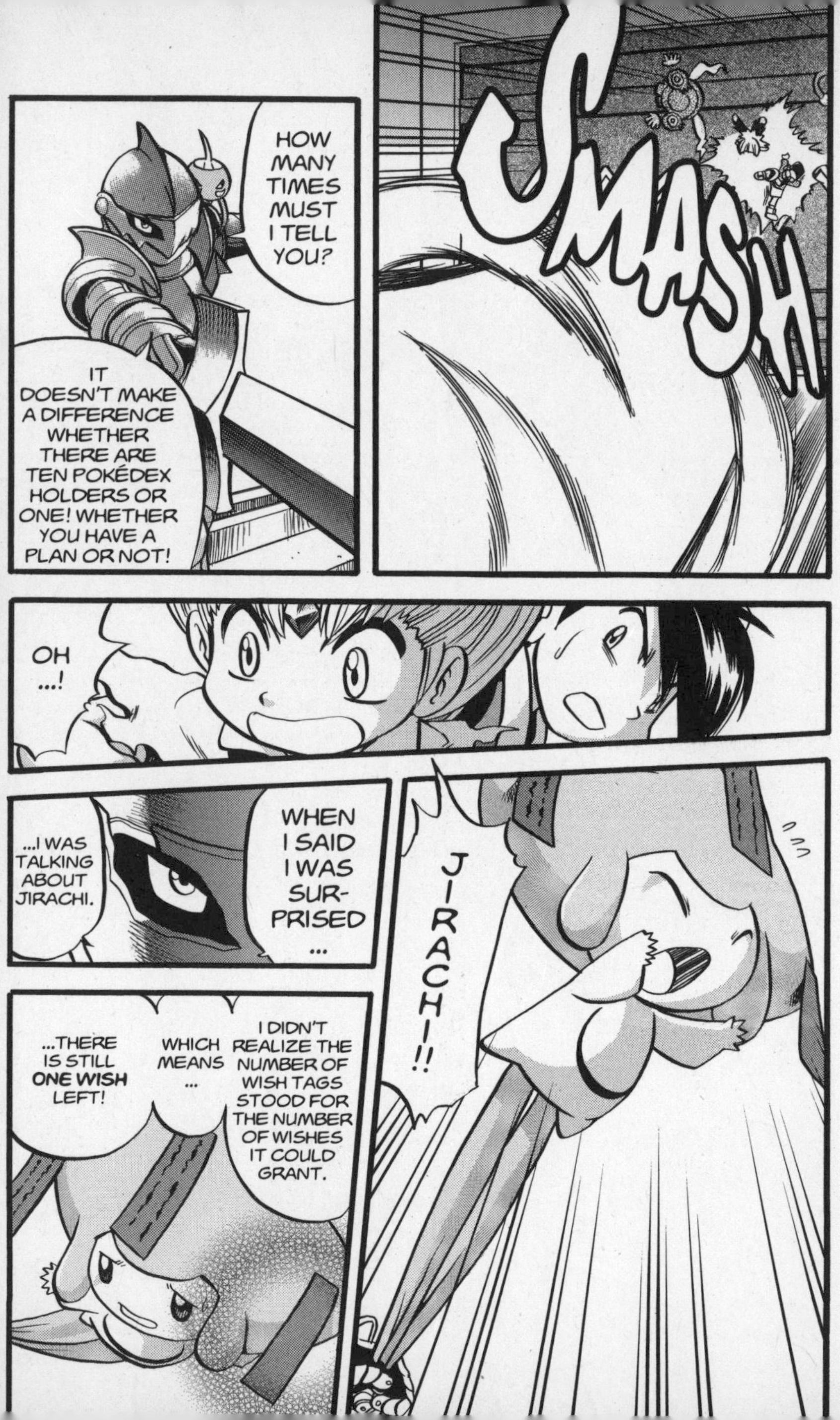
SMASH
HOW MANY TIMES MUST I TELL YOU?
IT DOESN'T MAKE A DIFFERENCE WHETHER THERE ARE TEN POKÉDEX HOLDERS OR ONE! WHETHER YOU HAVE A PLAN OR NOT!
OH ...!
JIRACHI!!
WHEN I SAID I WAS SURPRISED ...
...I WAS TALKING ABOUT JIRACHI.
I DIDN'T REALIZE THE NUMBER OF WISH TAGS STOOD FOR THE NUMBER OF WISHES IT COULD GRANT.
WHICH MEANS ...
...THERE IS STILL ONE WISH LEFT!

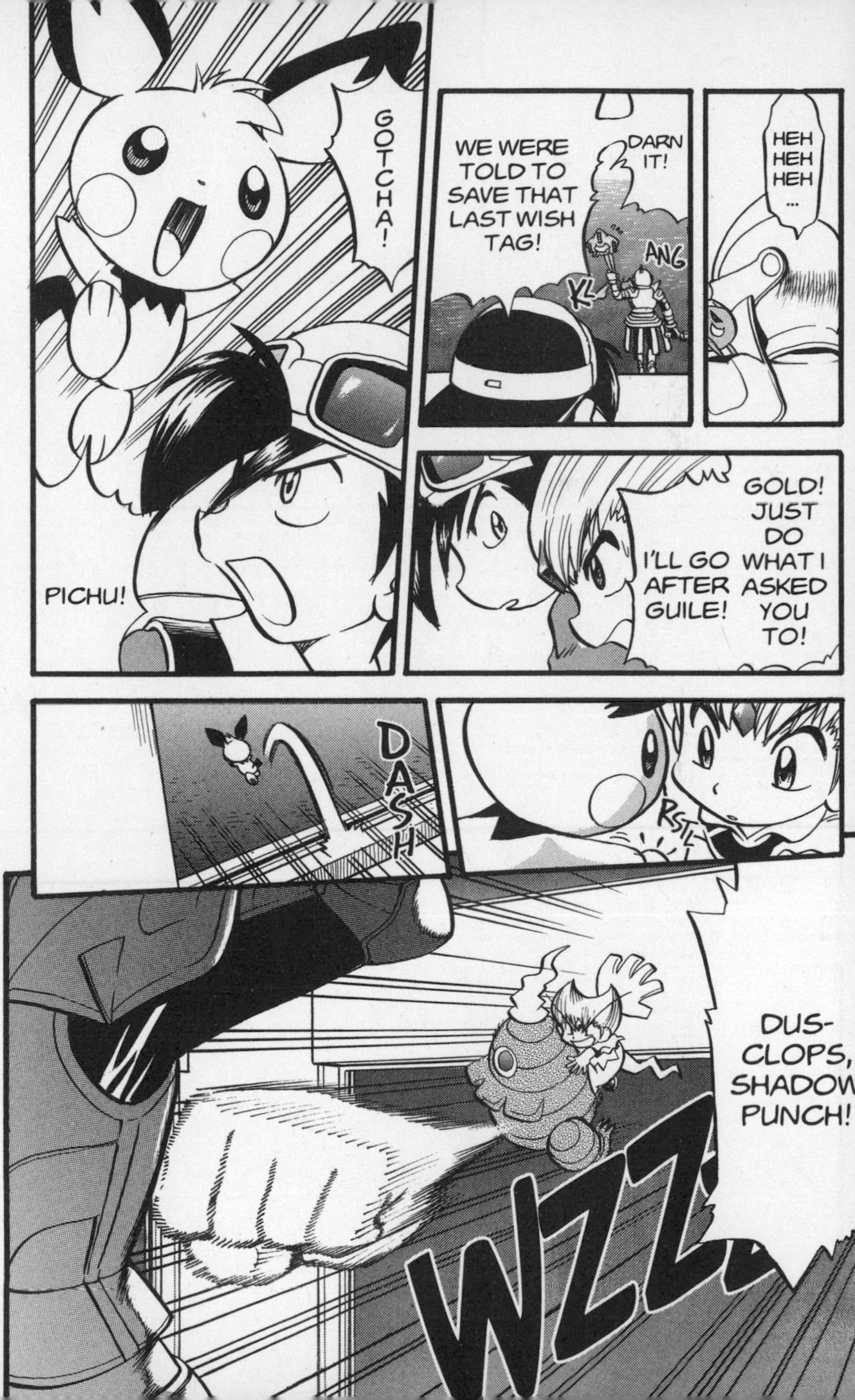
HEH HEH HEH ...
WE WERE TOLD TO SAVE THAT LAST WISH TAG!
DARN IT!
ANG
KL
GOLD! JUST DO WHAT I ASKED YOU TO!
I'LL GO AFTER GUILE!
GOTCHA!
PICHU!
RSTL
DASH
DUS-CLOPS, SHADOW PUNCH!
WZZ

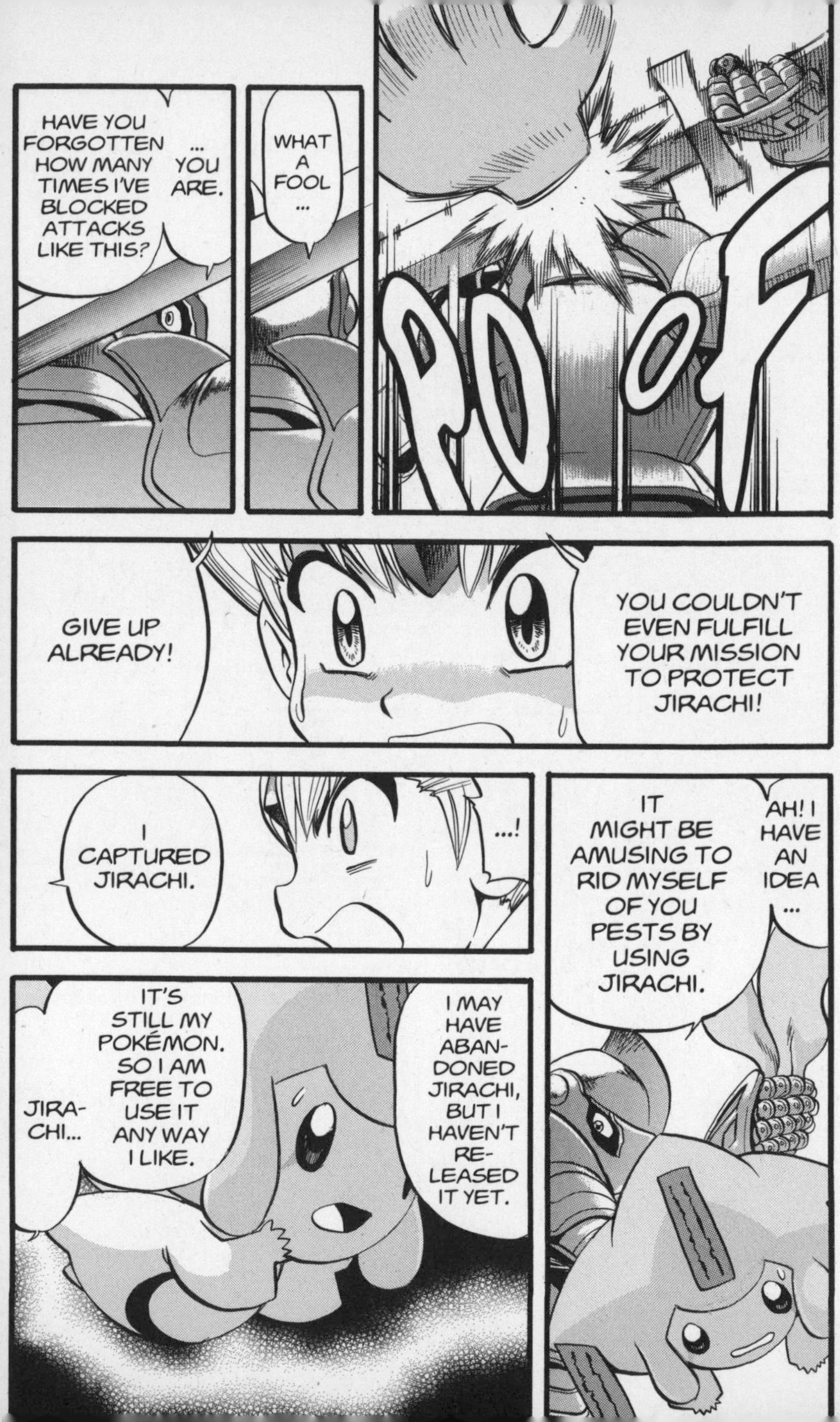
POOF
WHAT A FOOL ...
... YOU ARE.
HAVE YOU FORGOTTEN HOW MANY TIMES I'VE BLOCKED ATTACKS LIKE THIS?
YOU COULDN'T EVEN FULFILL YOUR MISSION TO PROTECT JIRACHI!
GIVE UP ALREADY!
AH! I HAVE AN IDEA ...
IT MIGHT BE AMUSING TO RID MYSELF OF YOU PESTS BY USING JIRACHI.
...!
I CAPTURED JIRACHI.
I MAY HAVE ABAN-DONED JIRACHI, BUT I HAVEN'T RE-LEASED IT YET.
IT'S STILL MY POKÉMON. SO I AM FREE TO USE IT ANY WAY I LIKE.
JIRA-CHI...

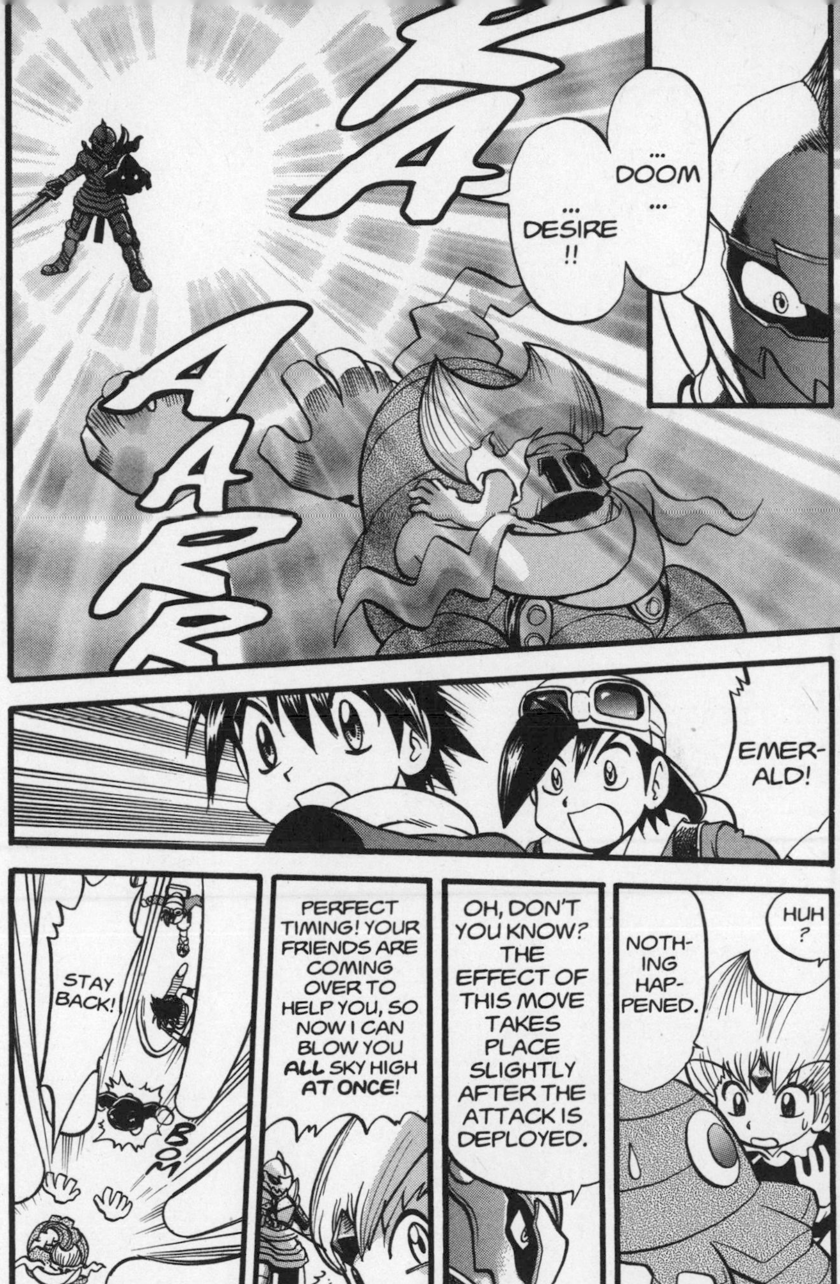
... DOOM ... ... DESIRE !!
EMER-ALD!
HUH?
NOTH-ING HAP-PENED.
OH, DON'T YOU KNOW? THE EFFECT OF THIS MOVE TAKES PLACE SLIGHTLY AFTER THE ATTACK IS DEPLOYED.
PERFECT TIMING! YOUR FRIENDS ARE COMING OVER TO HELP YOU, SO NOW I CAN BLOW YOU **ALL** SKY HIGH **AT ONCE**!
STAY BACK!
BOM

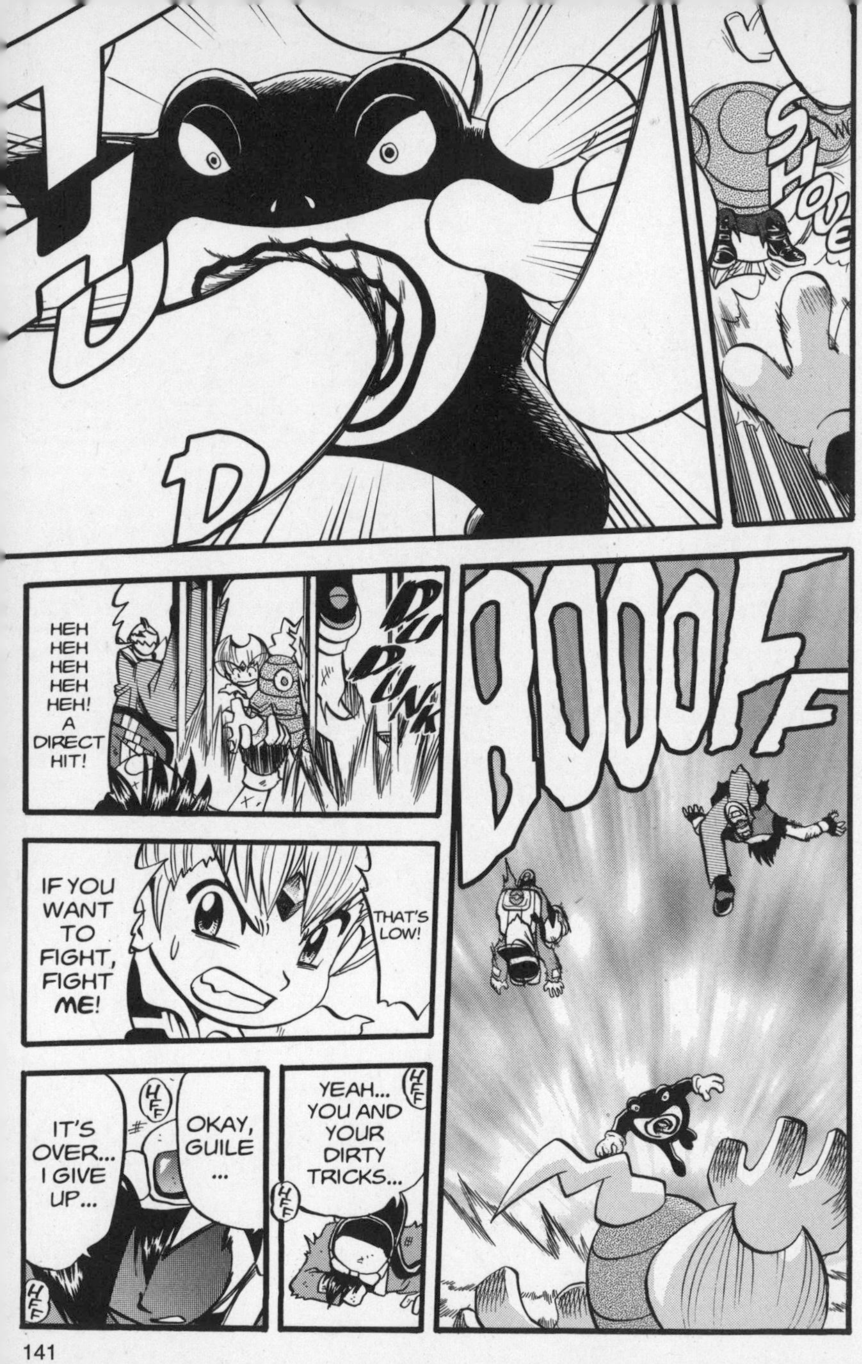
SHOVE
BOOOFF
DUDUNK
HEH HEH HEH HEH HEH! A DIRECT HIT!
THAT'S LOW!
IF YOU WANT TO FIGHT, FIGHT ME!
HFF
YEAH... YOU AND YOUR DIRTY TRICKS...
HFF
HFF
OKAY, GUILE ...
IT'S OVER... I GIVE UP...
HFF

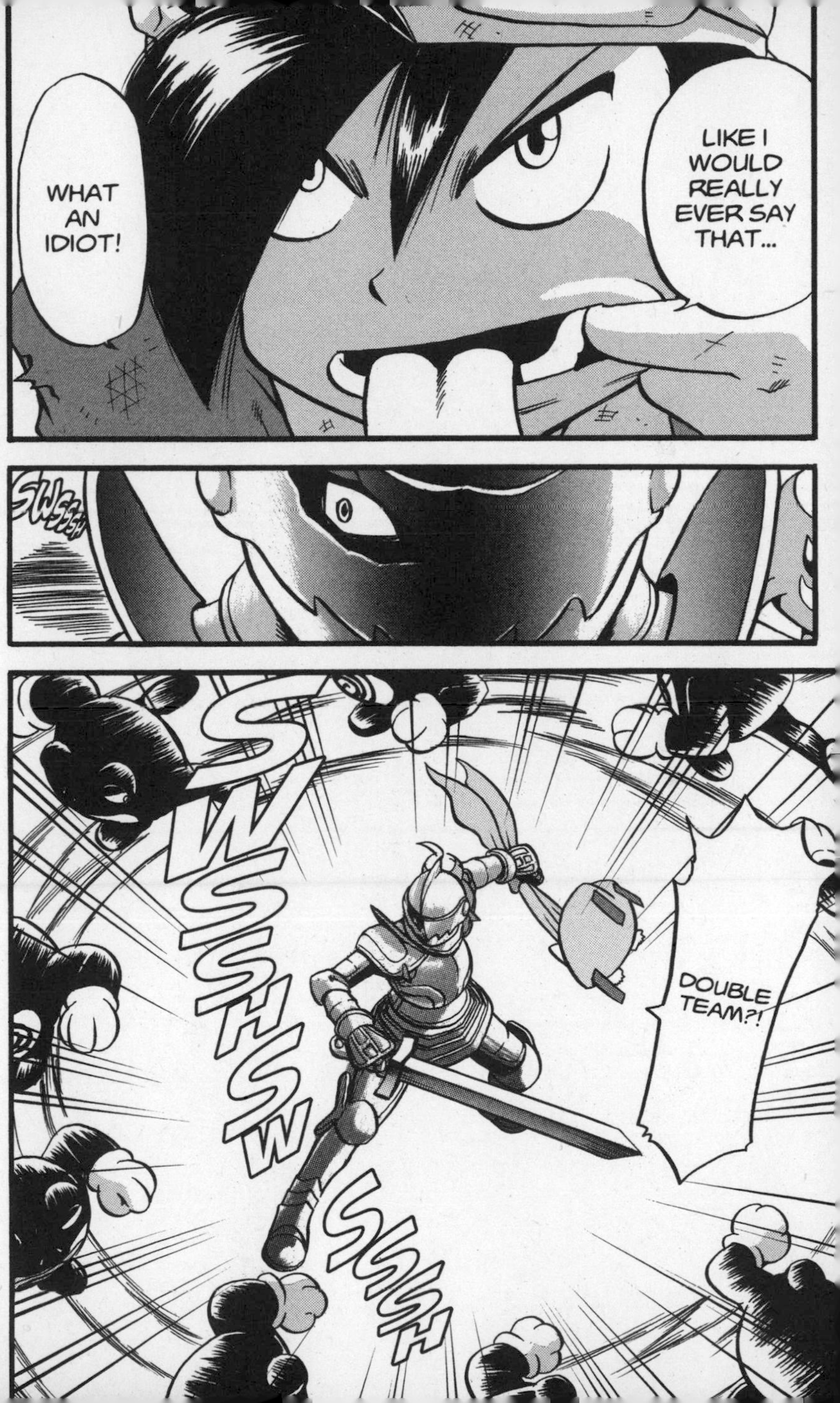
LIKE I WOULD REALLY EVER SAY THAT...
WHAT AN IDIOT!
SWSSSH
SWSHSHSW
DOUBLE TEAM?!

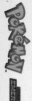

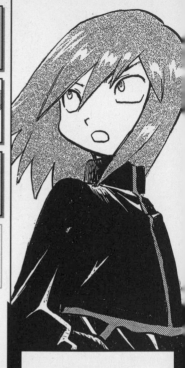

CHARACTER PROFILE SILVER

SILVER

SILVER IS A TRAINER WHO
SEARCHED LONG AND HARD
TO FIND HIS ROOTS. HE WAS
KIDNAPPED BY THE INFAMOUS
MASKED MAN AS A CHILD, SO
THE STORY OF HIS ORIGIN
REMAINED A MYSTERY FOR
QUITE SOME TIME, BUT HE
WAS FINALLY REUNITED WITH
HIS FATHER, GIOVANNI. AS A
HIGHLY SKILLED TRAINER,
HE EXCELS IN POKÉMON
BATTLES AND IS ESPECIALLY
KNOWLEDGEABLE ABOUT
TRADING POKÉMON. THUS,
HE IS KNOWN AS THE
"EXCHANGER." HE HAS
LEARNED TO FACE DIFFICULT
CHALLENGES WITH COURAGE
AND DIGNITY.

- Birthplace: Viridian City
- Birthday: December 24
  (Discovered after his reunion
  with Giovanni)
- Blood Type: AB
- Family: Father (Giovanni)

335

The Final Battle VIII

POKÉMON ADVENTURES•THE SIXTH CHAPTER•EMERALD

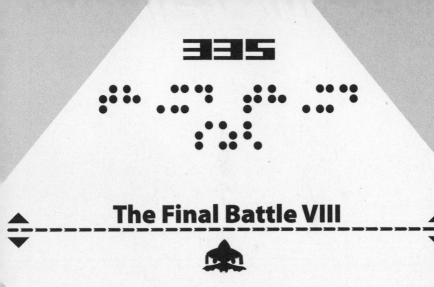

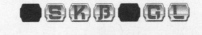

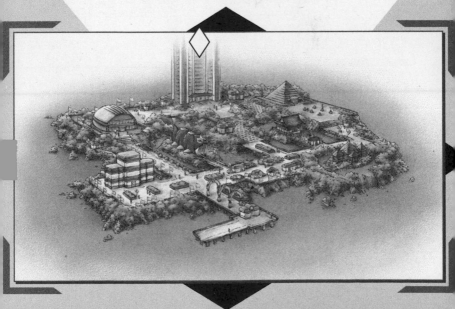

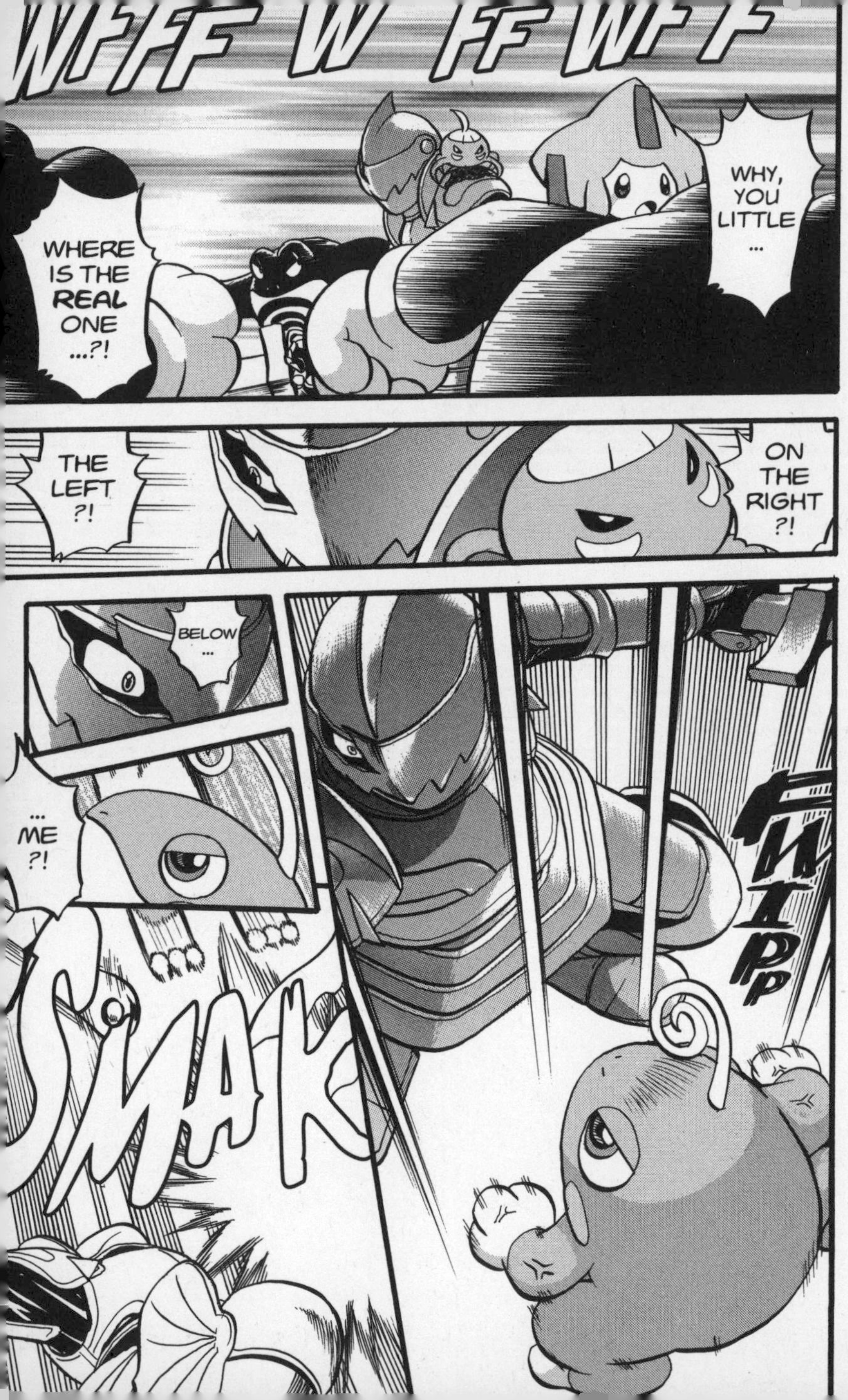
WFFF W FF WFF
WHY, YOU LITTLE ...
WHERE IS THE REAL ONE ...?!
ON THE RIGHT ?!
THE LEFT ?!
WHIPP
BELOW ...
... ME ?!
SMAK

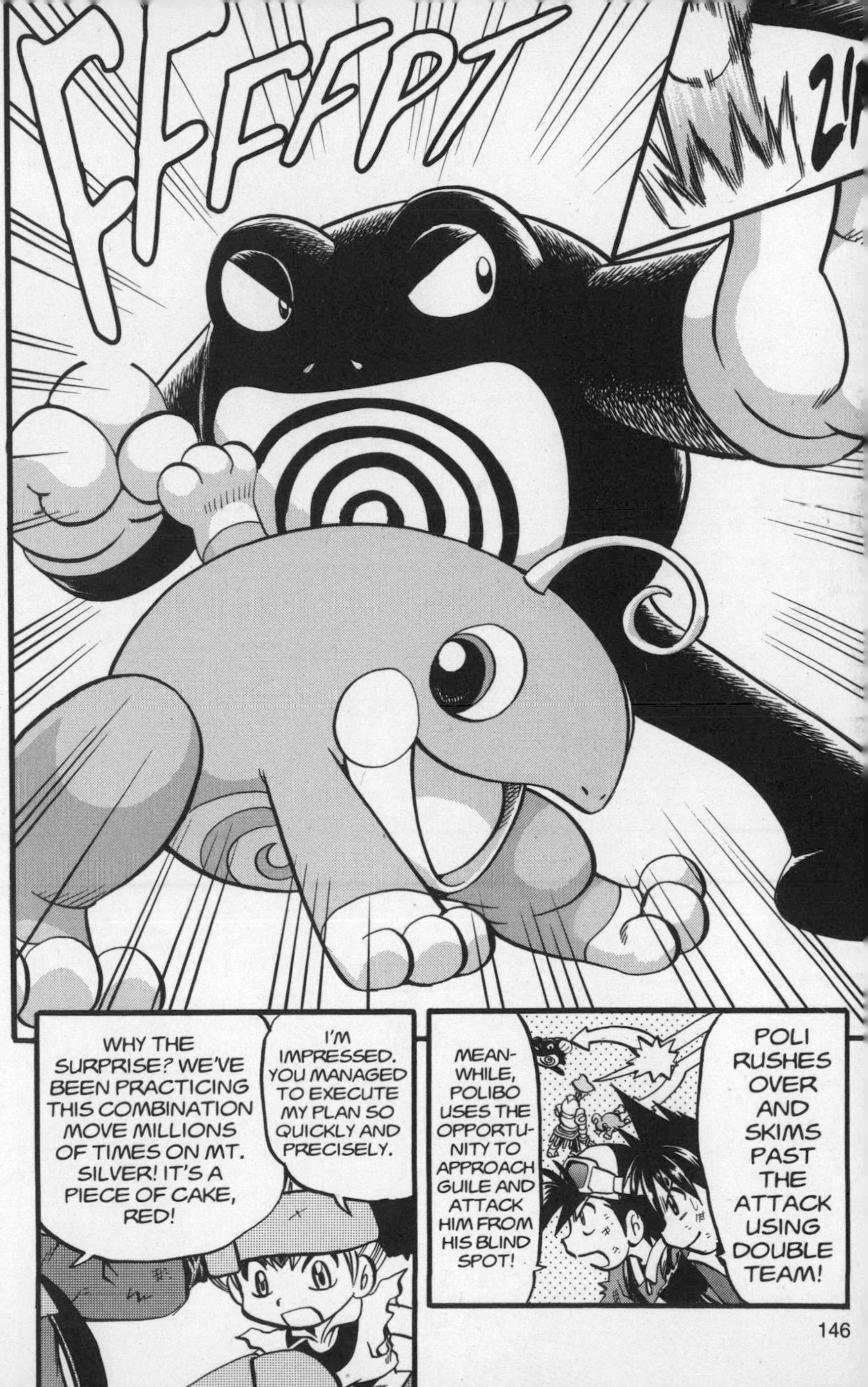
FFFPT
POLI RUSHES OVER AND SKIMS PAST THE ATTACK USING DOUBLE TEAM!
MEAN-WHILE, POLIBO USES THE OPPORTU-NITY TO APPROACH GUILE AND ATTACK HIM FROM HIS BLIND SPOT!
I'M IMPRESSED. YOU MANAGED TO EXECUTE MY PLAN SO QUICKLY AND PRECISELY.
WHY THE SURPRISE? WE'VE BEEN PRACTICING THIS COMBINATION MOVE MILLIONS OF TIMES ON MT. SILVER! IT'S A PIECE OF CAKE, RED!

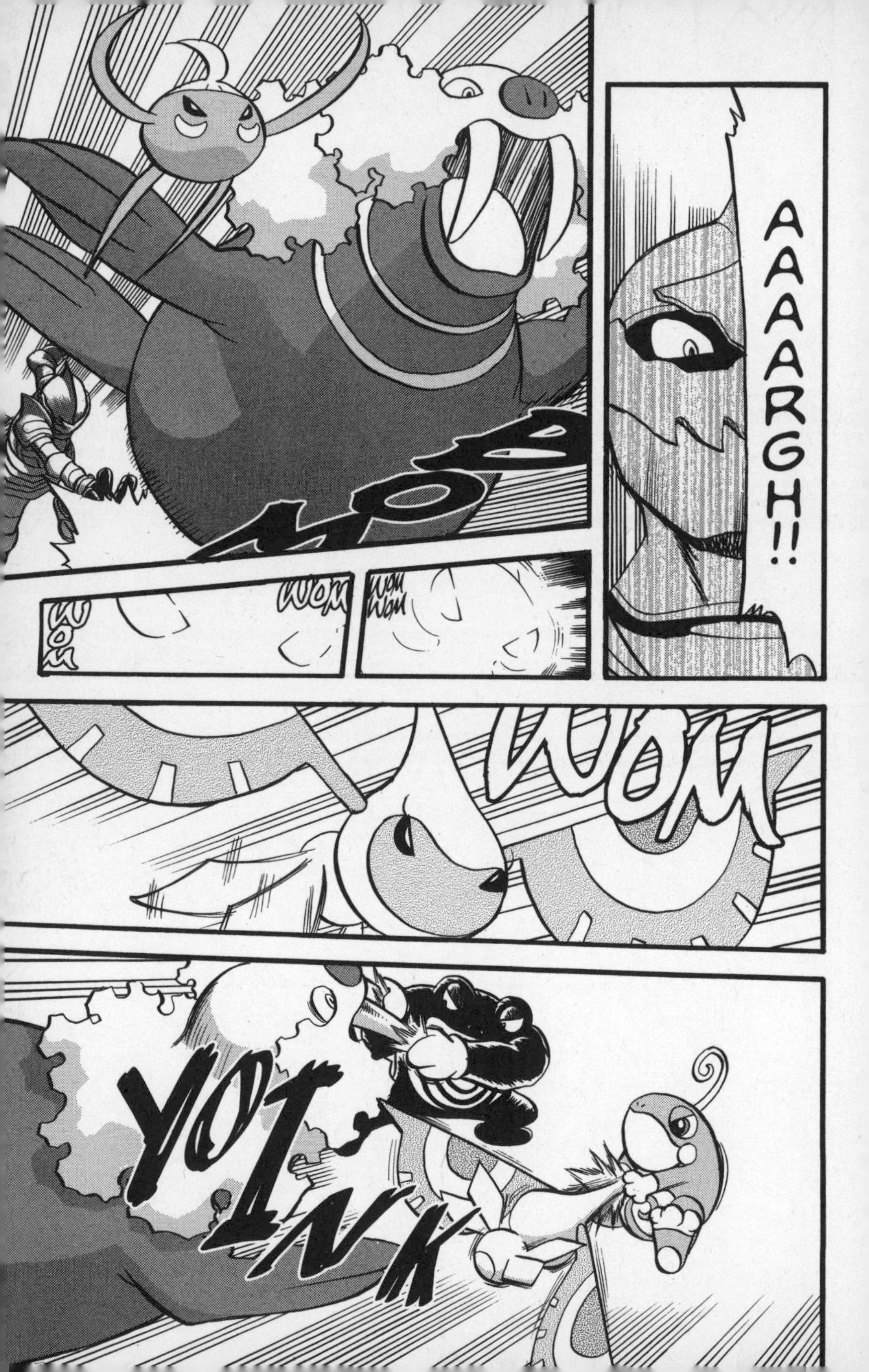
AAAARGH!!
WOM
WOM
WOM
WOM
WOM
WOM
WOM
YOINK

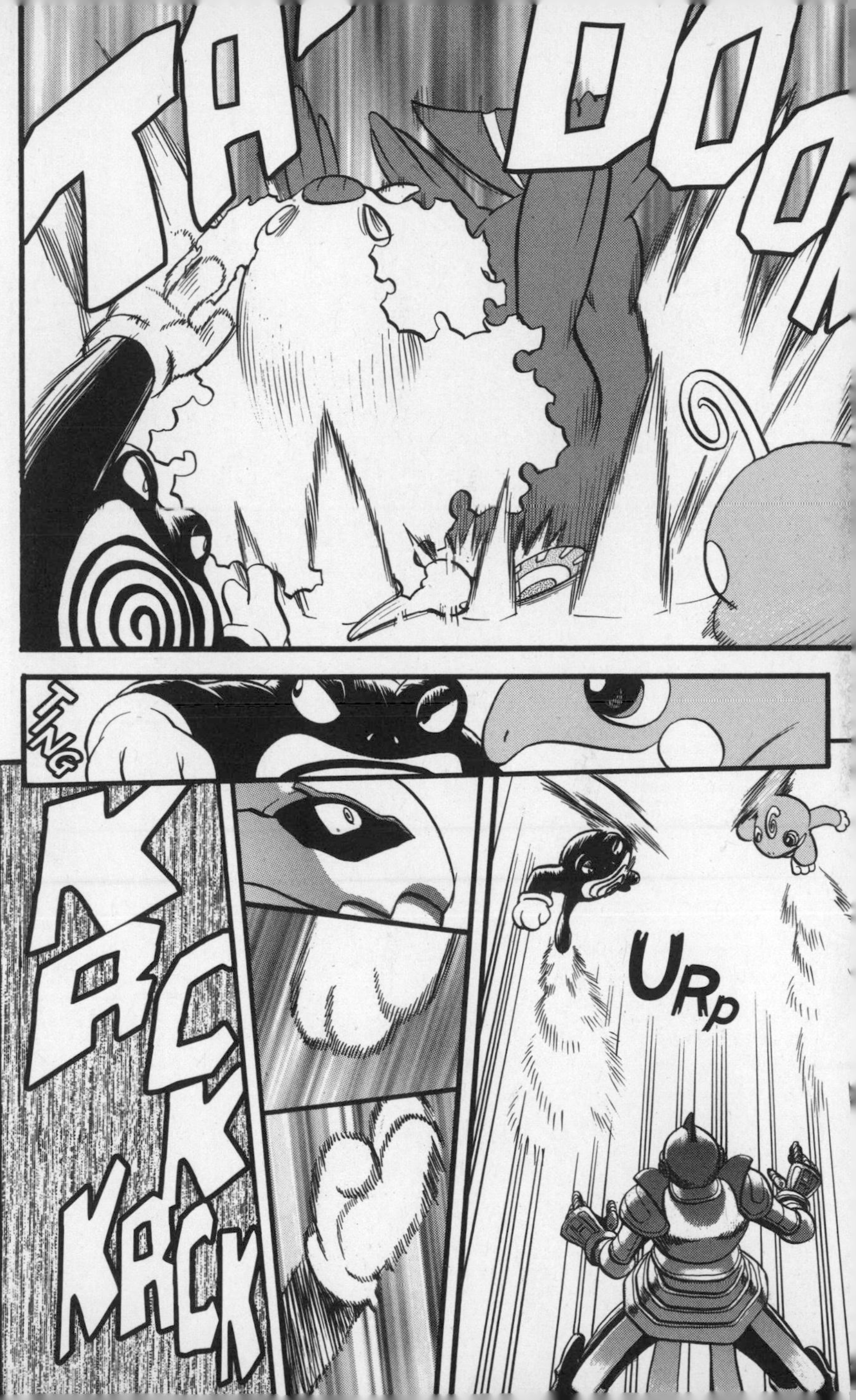
KA DOO
TING
URP
KRACK
KRACK

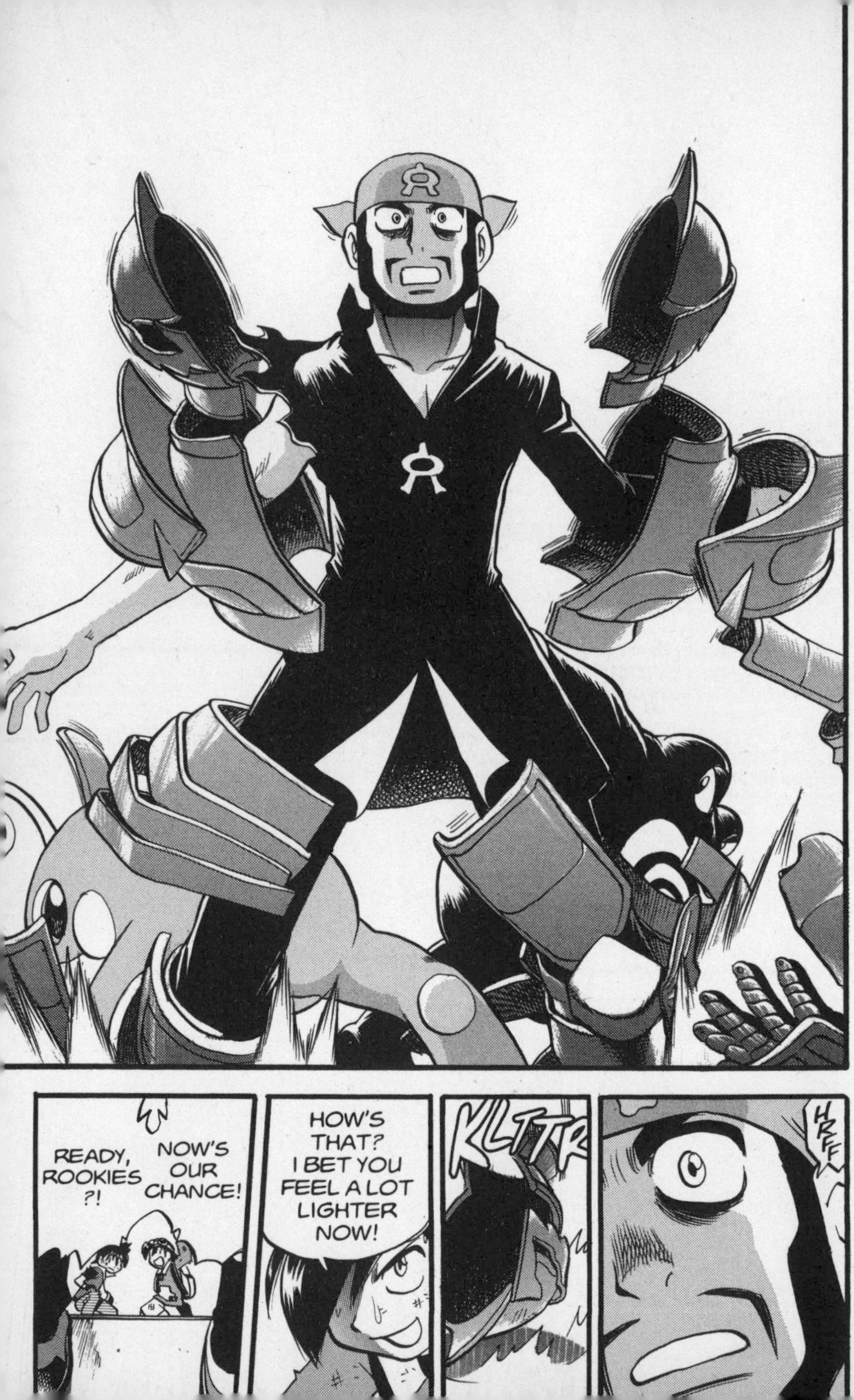
HRFF
KLTTR
HOW'S THAT? I BET YOU FEEL A LOT LIGHTER NOW!
NOW'S OUR CHANCE!
READY, ROOKIES ?!

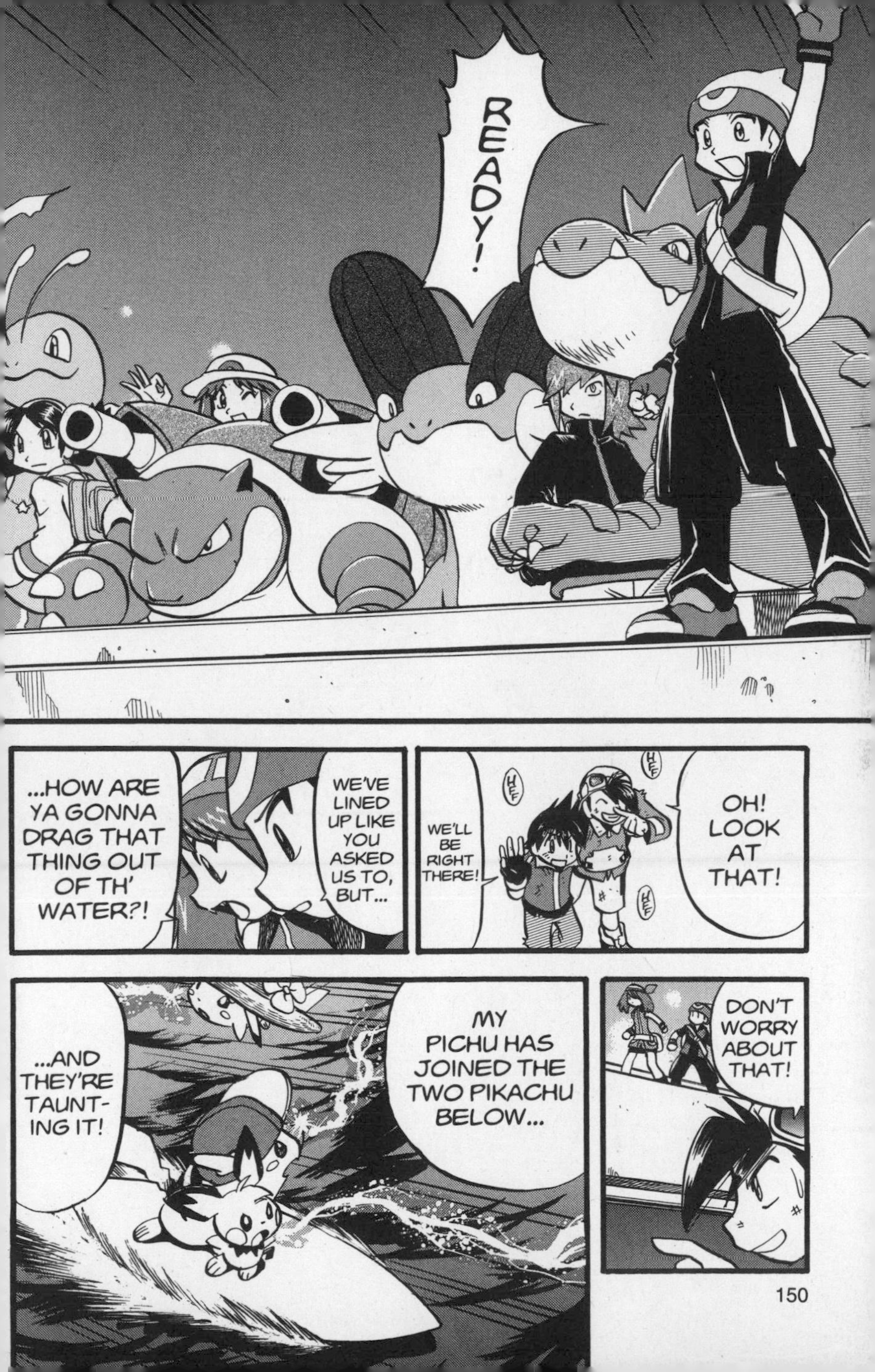
READY!
OH! LOOK AT THAT!
WE'LL BE RIGHT THERE!
WE'VE LINED UP LIKE YOU ASKED US TO, BUT...
...HOW ARE YA GONNA DRAG THAT THING OUT OF TH' WATER?!
DON'T WORRY ABOUT THAT!
MY PICHU HAS JOINED THE TWO PIKACHU BELOW...
...AND THEY'RE TAUNT-ING IT!

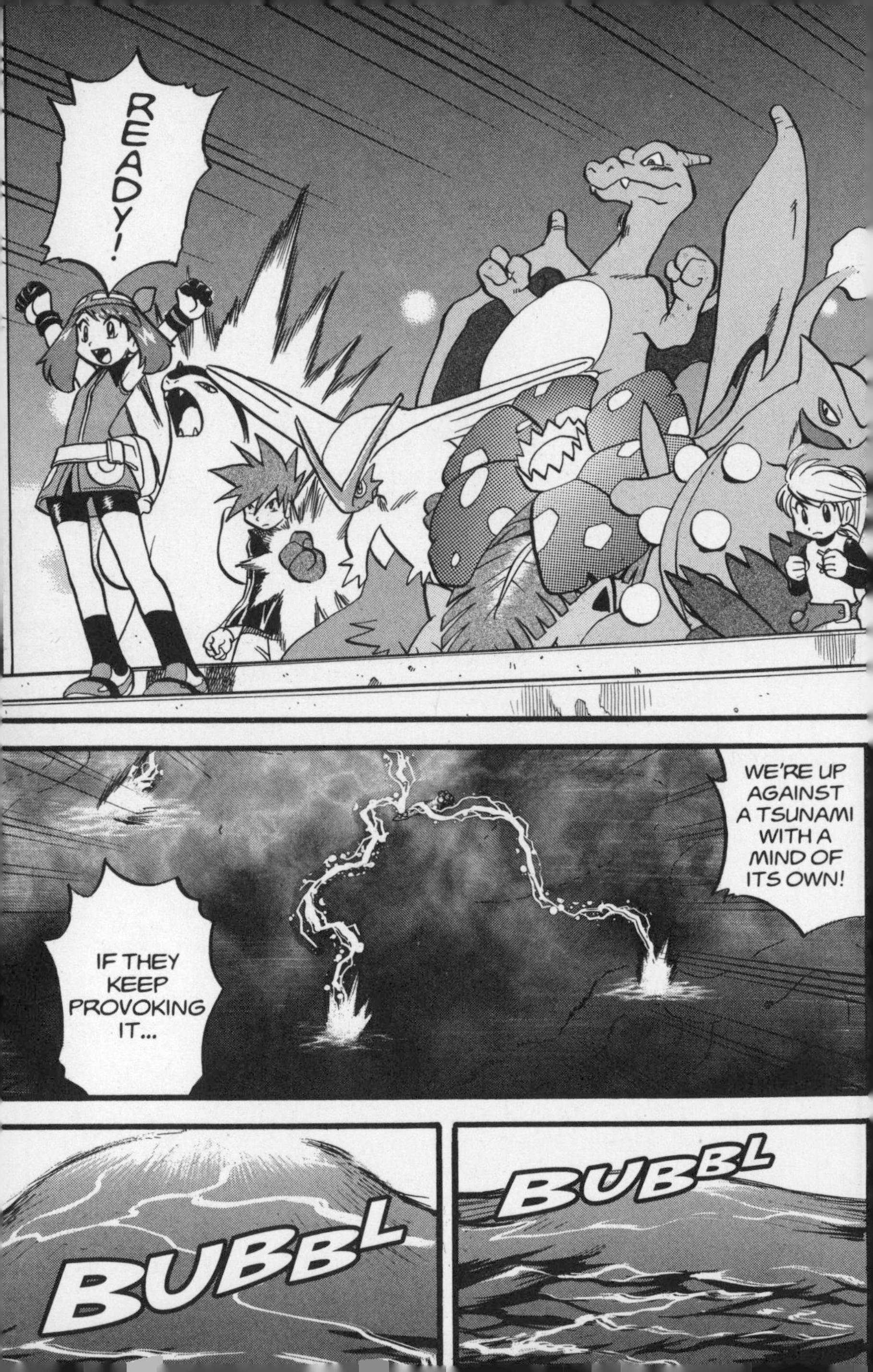
READY!
WE'RE UP AGAINST A TSUNAMI WITH A MIND OF ITS OWN!
IF THEY KEEP PROVOKING IT...
BUBBL
BUBBL

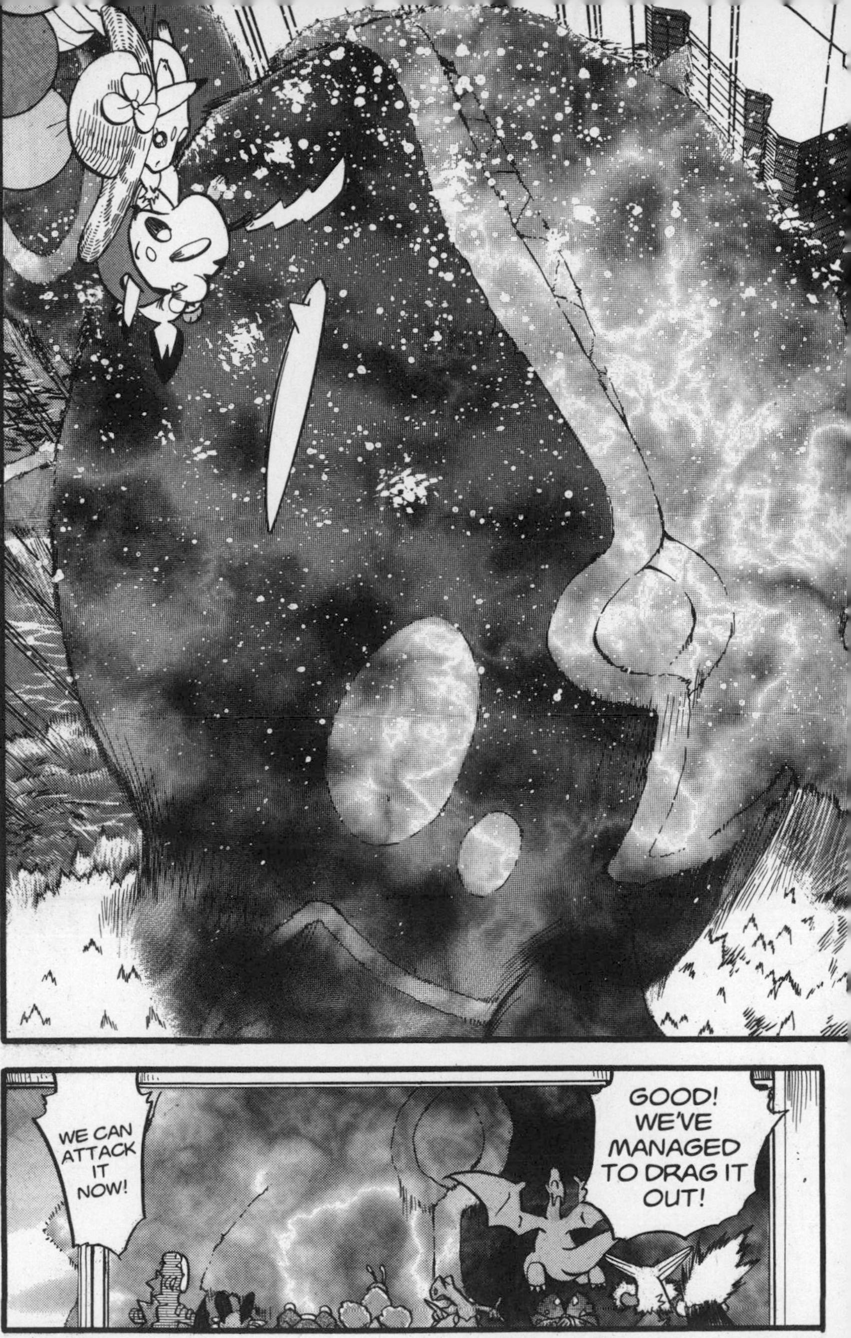
GOOD! WE'VE MANAGED TO DRAG IT OUT!
WE CAN ATTACK IT NOW!

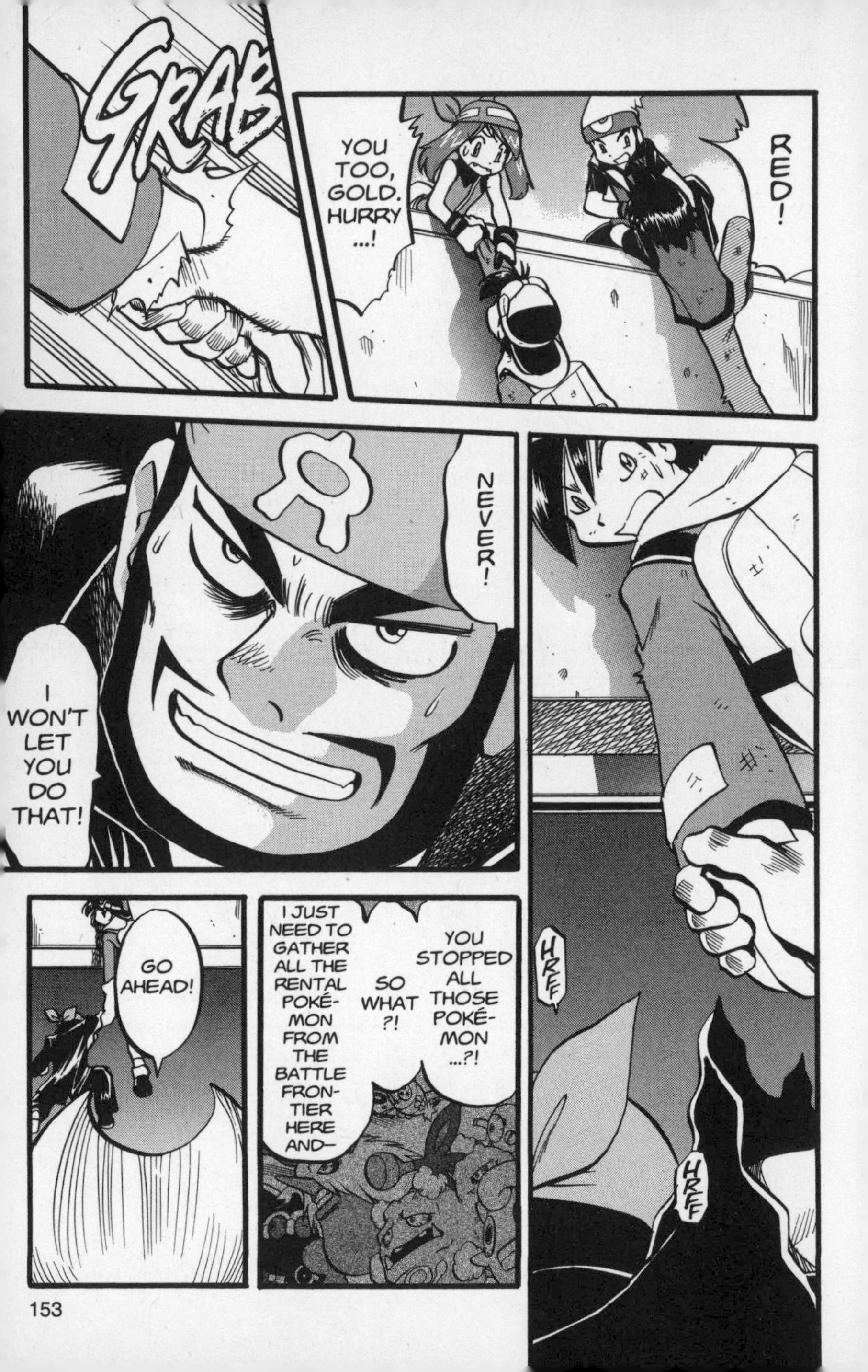
RED!
YOU TOO, GOLD. HURRY ...!
GRAB
HRFF
HRFF
NEVER!
I WON'T LET YOU DO THAT!
YOU STOPPED ALL THOSE POKÉMON ...?!
SO WHAT ?!
I JUST NEED TO GATHER ALL THE RENTAL POKÉMON FROM THE BATTLE FRONTIER HERE AND—
GO AHEAD!

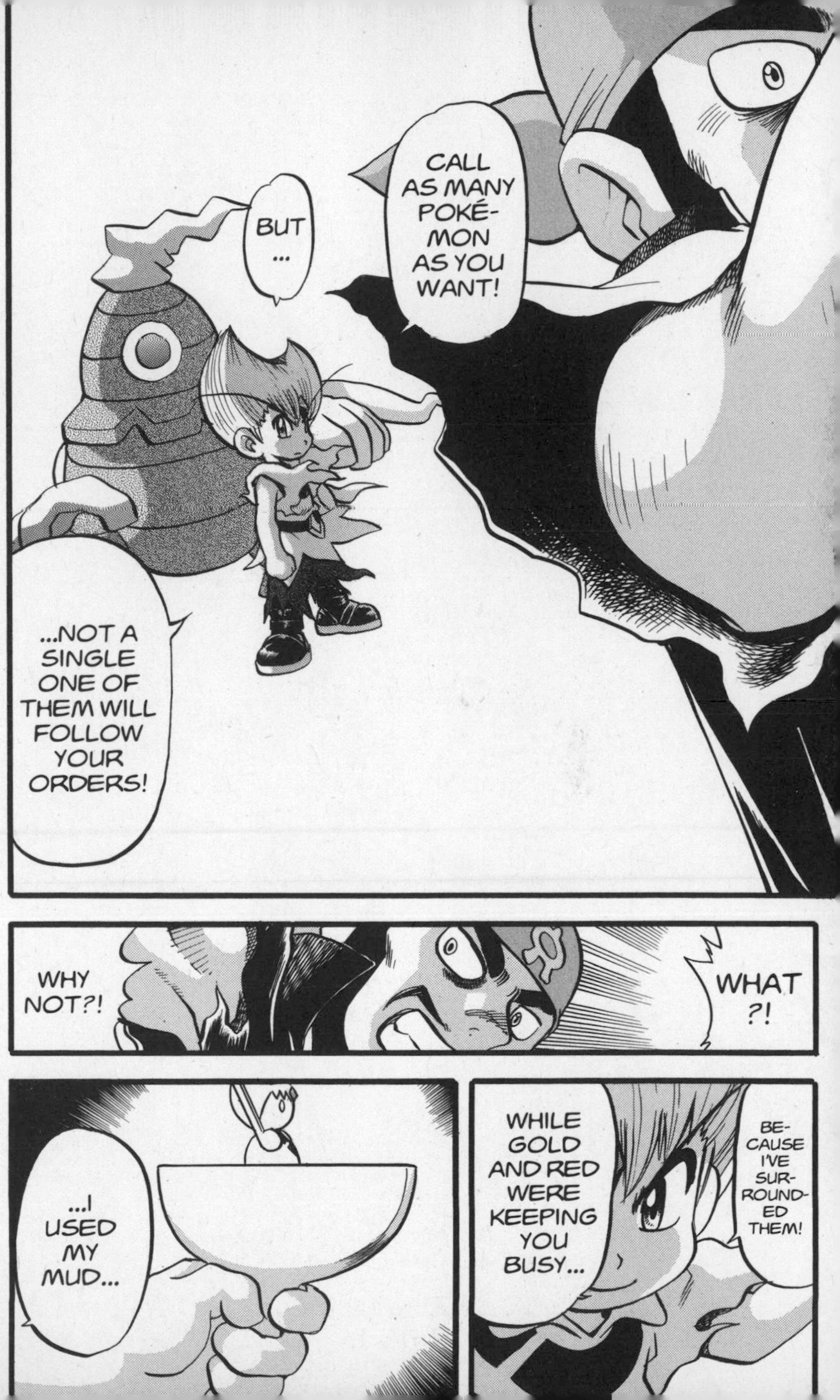
CALL AS MANY POKÉMON AS YOU WANT!
BUT ...
...NOT A SINGLE ONE OF THEM WILL FOLLOW YOUR ORDERS!
WHAT?!
WHY NOT?!
BECAUSE I'VE SURROUNDED THEM!
WHILE GOLD AND RED WERE KEEPING YOU BUSY...
...I USED MY MUD...

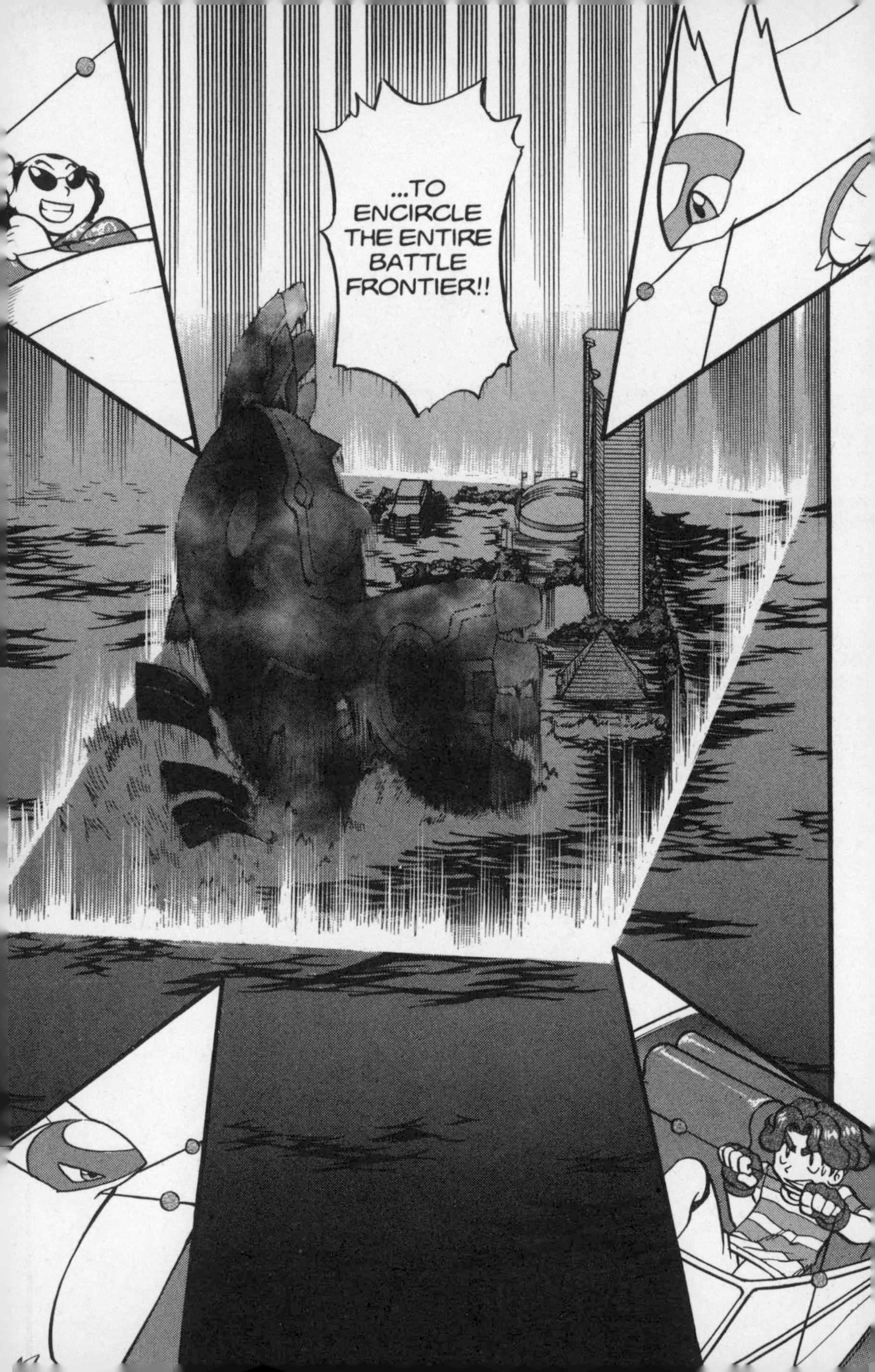
...TO ENCIRCLE THE ENTIRE BATTLE FRONTIER!!

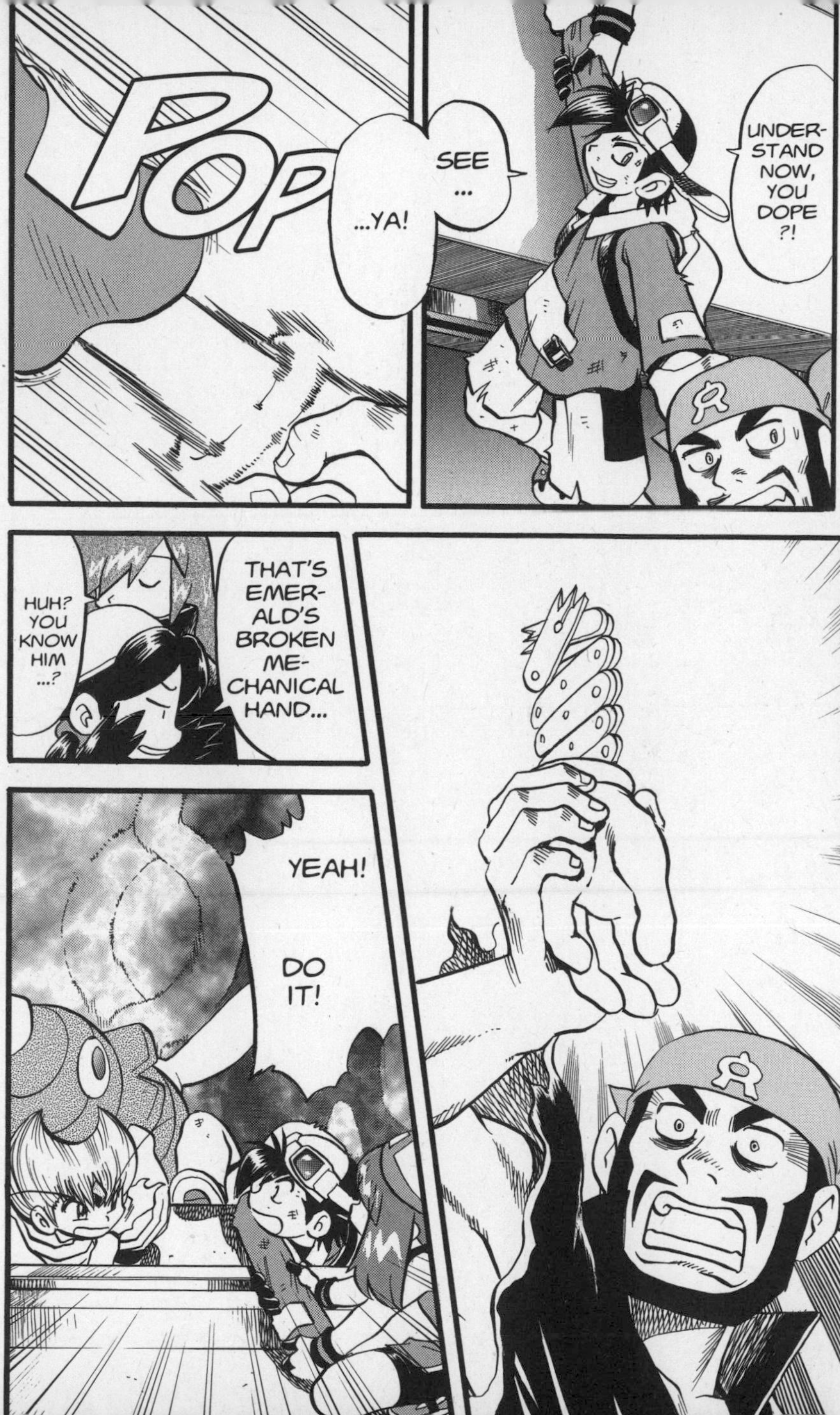
UNDER-STAND NOW, YOU DOPE?!
SEE...
...YA!
POP
THAT'S EMER-ALD'S BROKEN ME-CHANICAL HAND...
HUH? YOU KNOW HIM...?
YEAH!
DO IT!

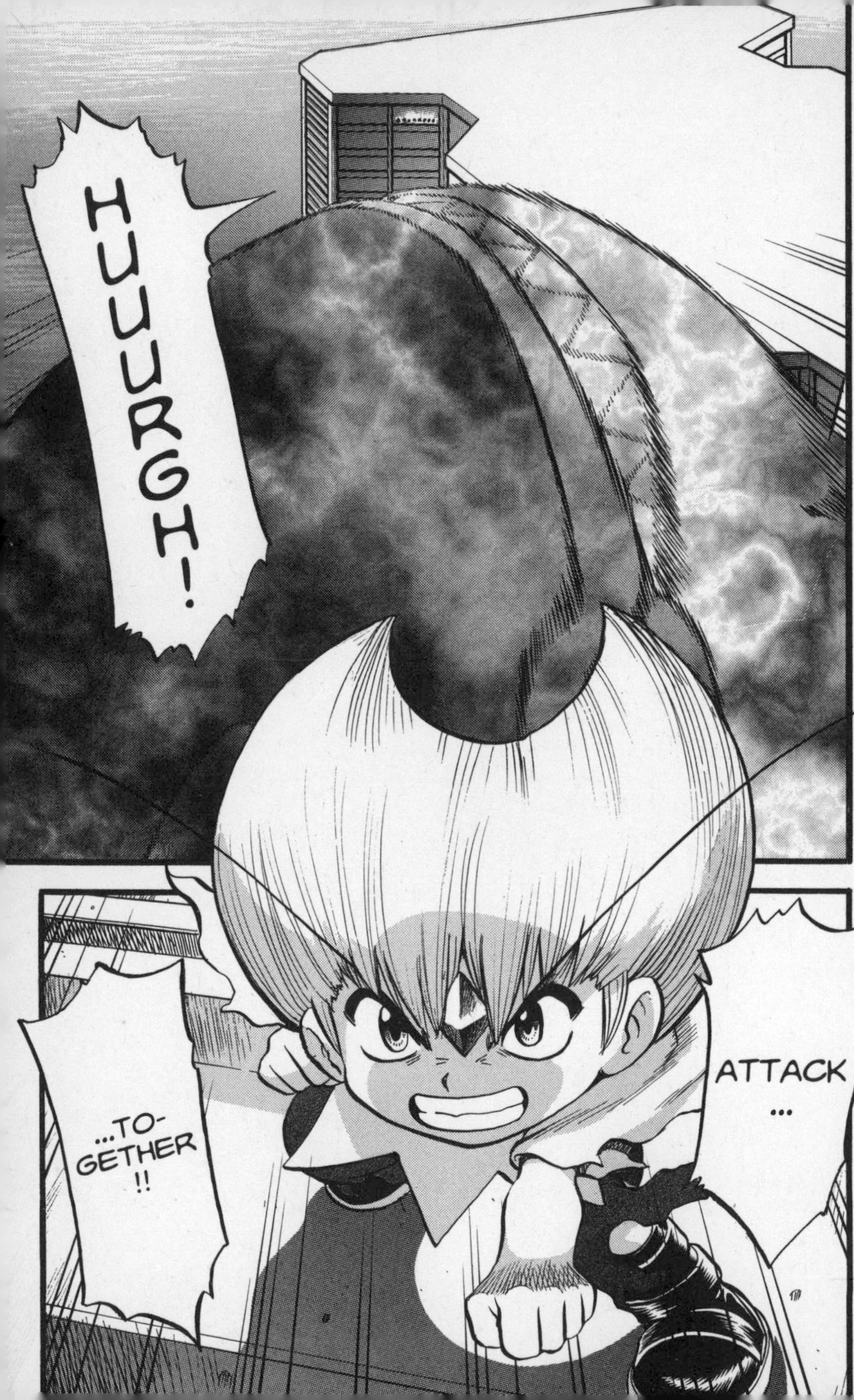
HUUURGH!
ATTACK ...
...TO-GETHER !!

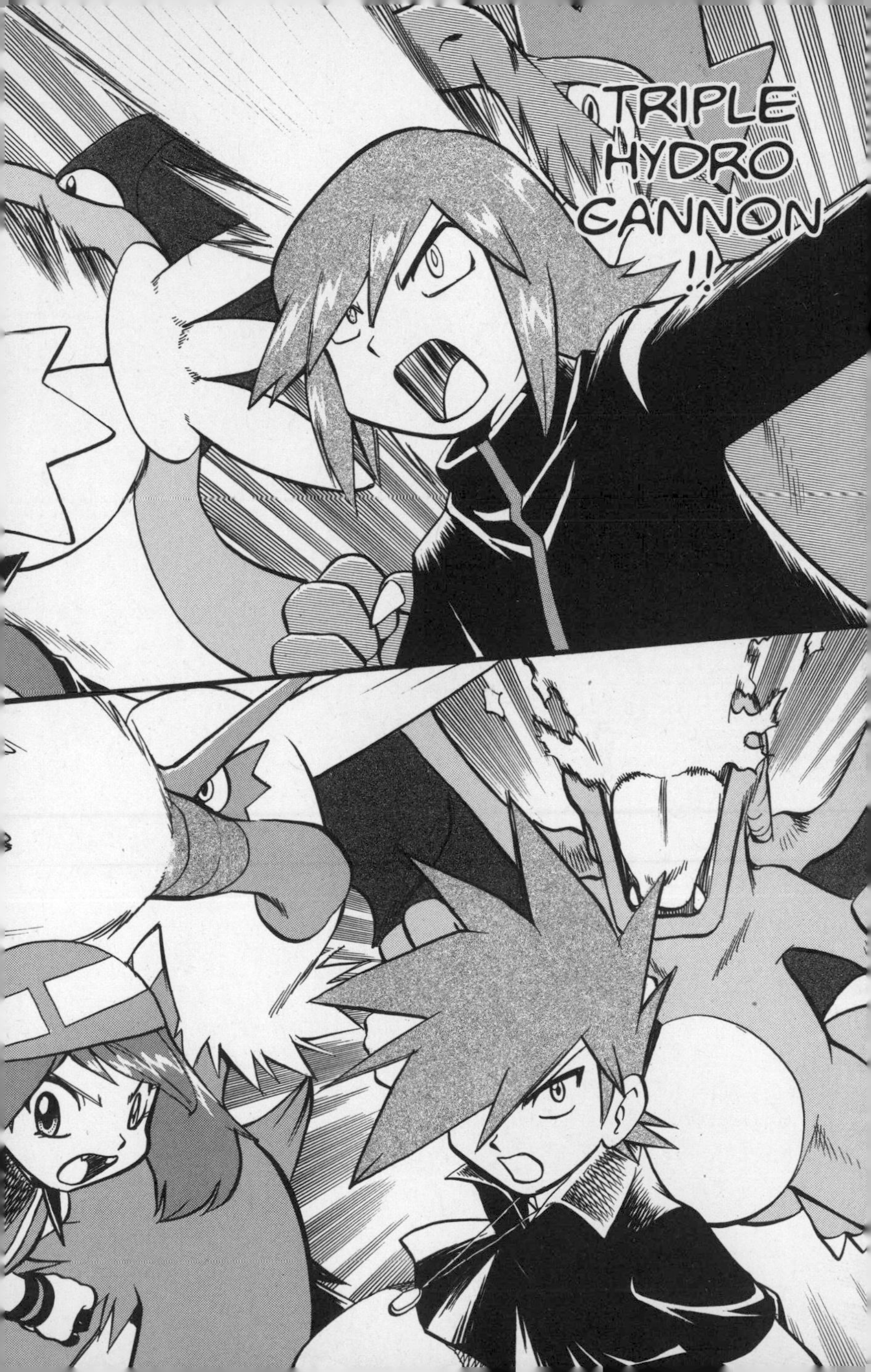
TRIPLE HYDRO CANNON !!

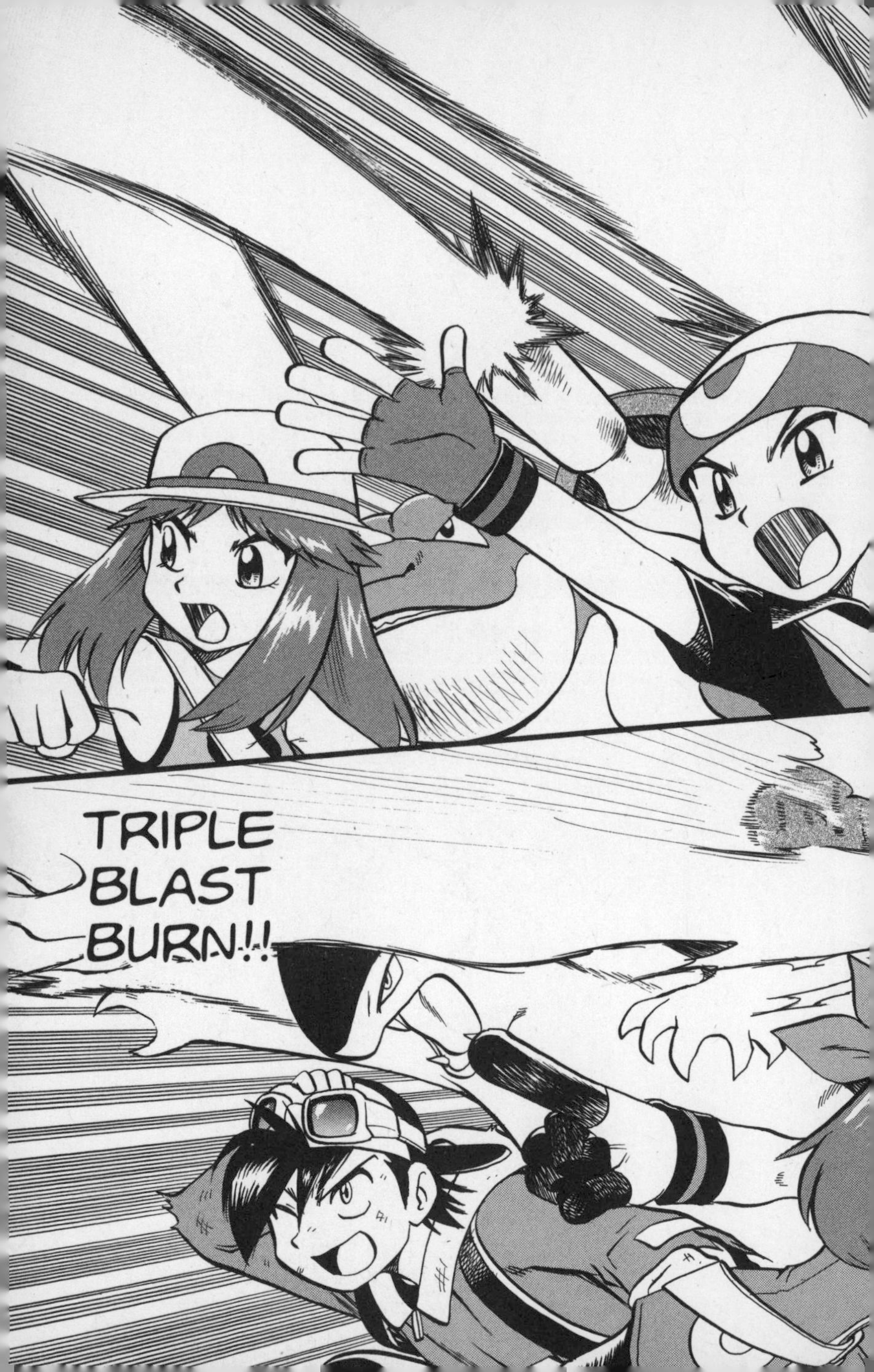
TRIPLE BLAST BURN!!

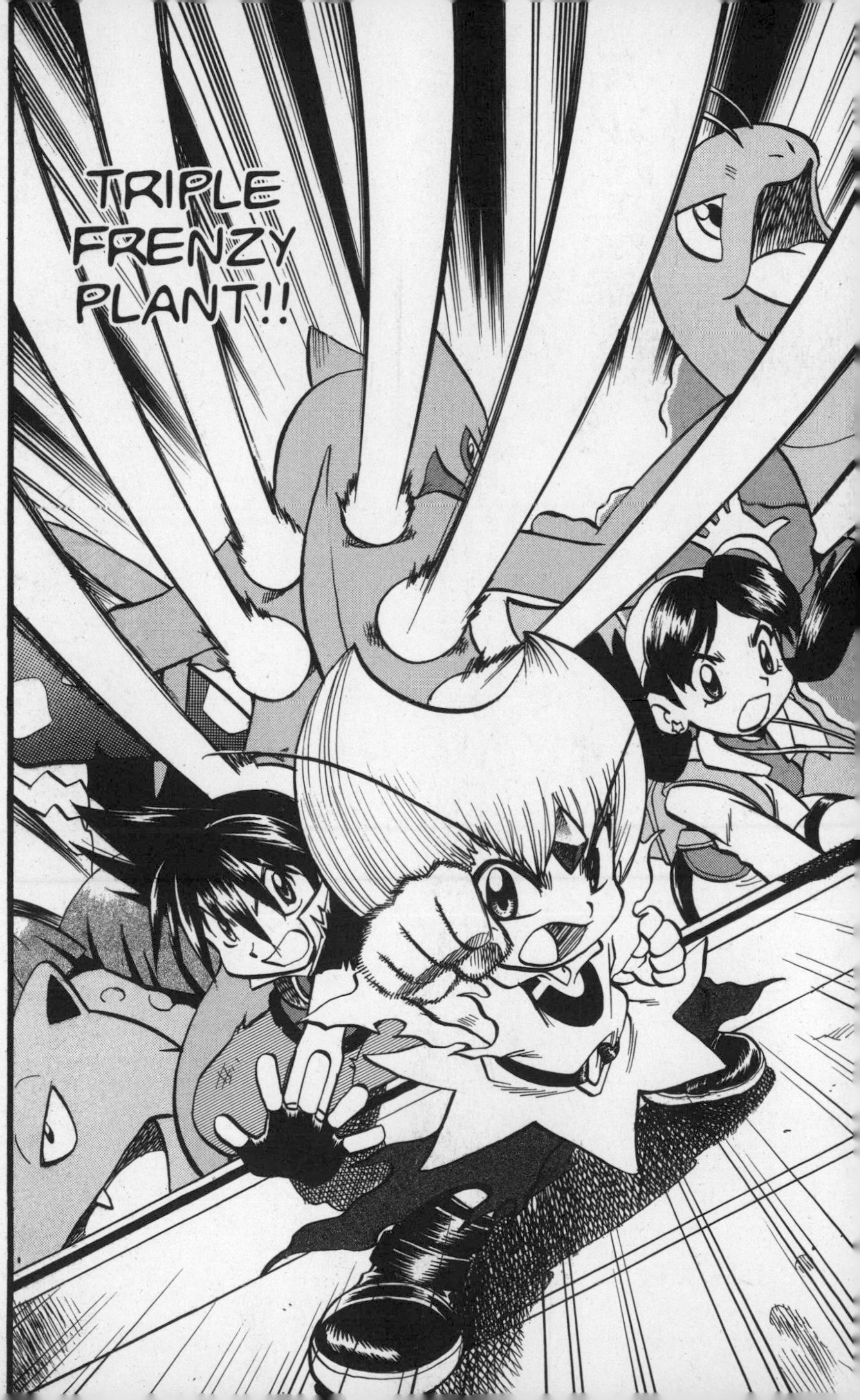
TRIPLE FRENZY PLANT!!

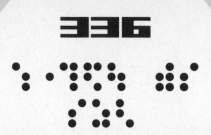

336

The Final Battle IX

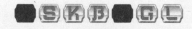

●SKB●GL

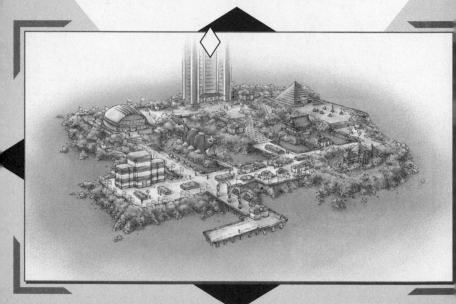

POKÉMON ADVENTURES·THE SIXTH CHAPTER·EMERAL

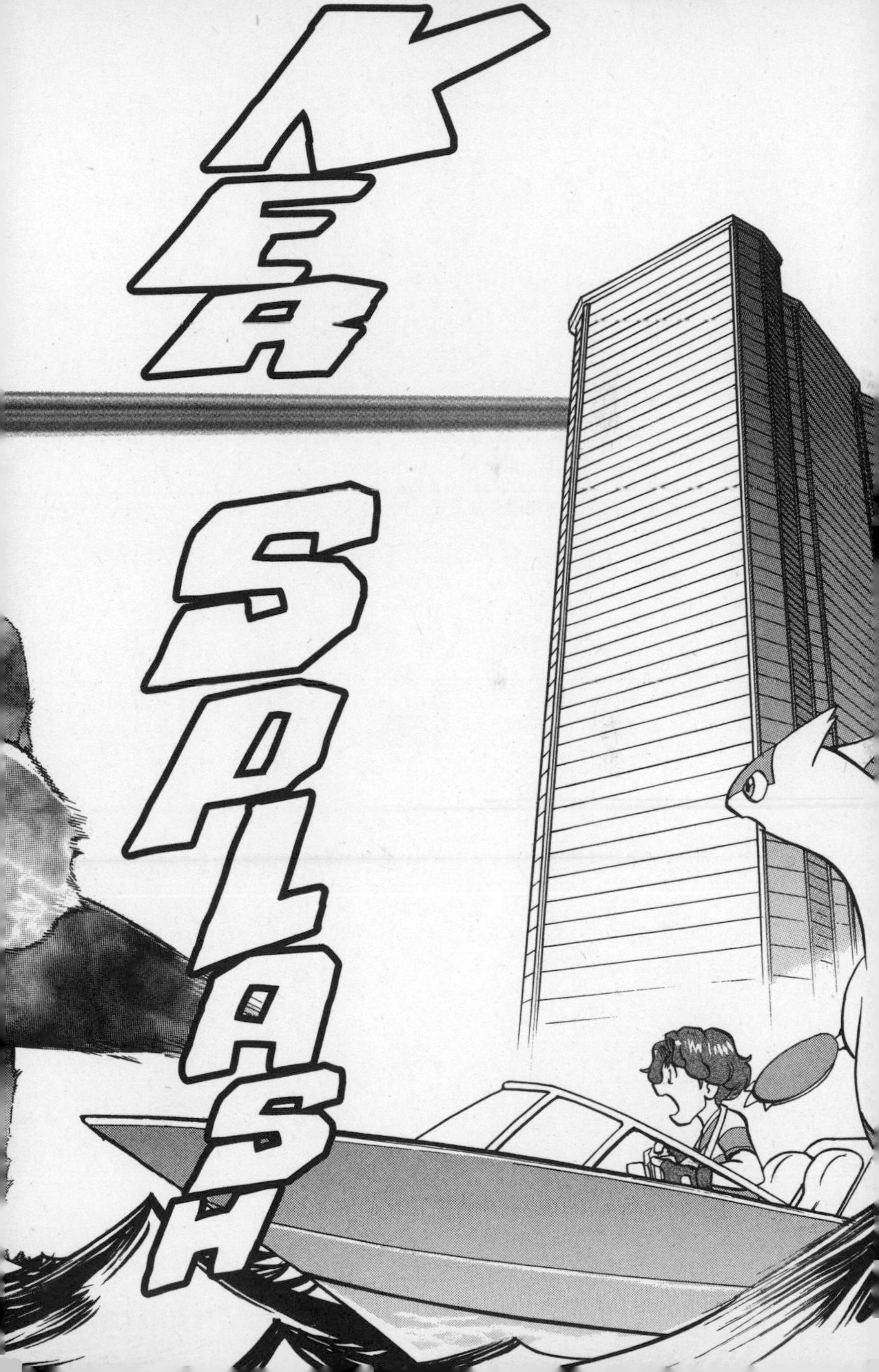
KER
SPLASH

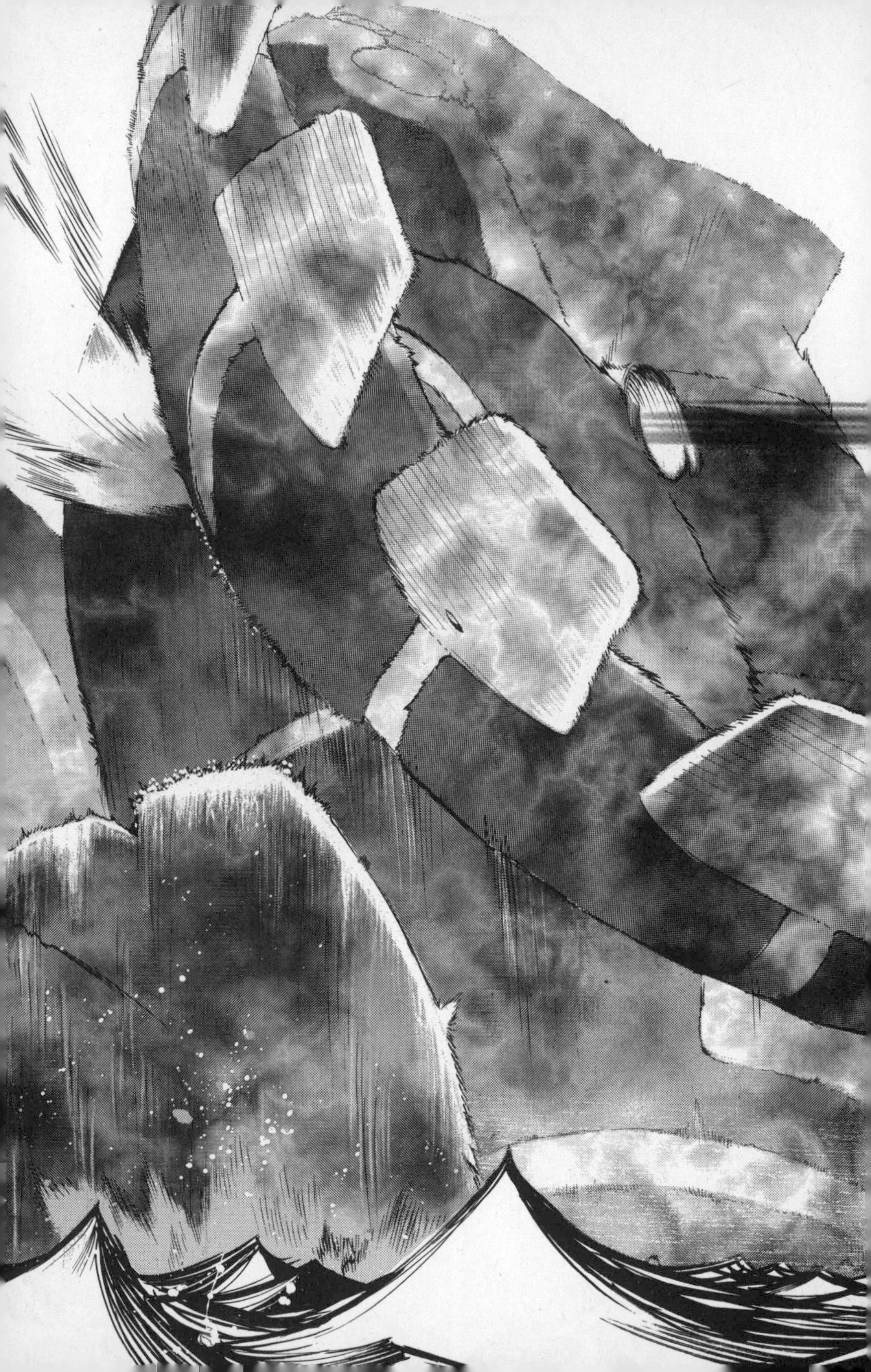

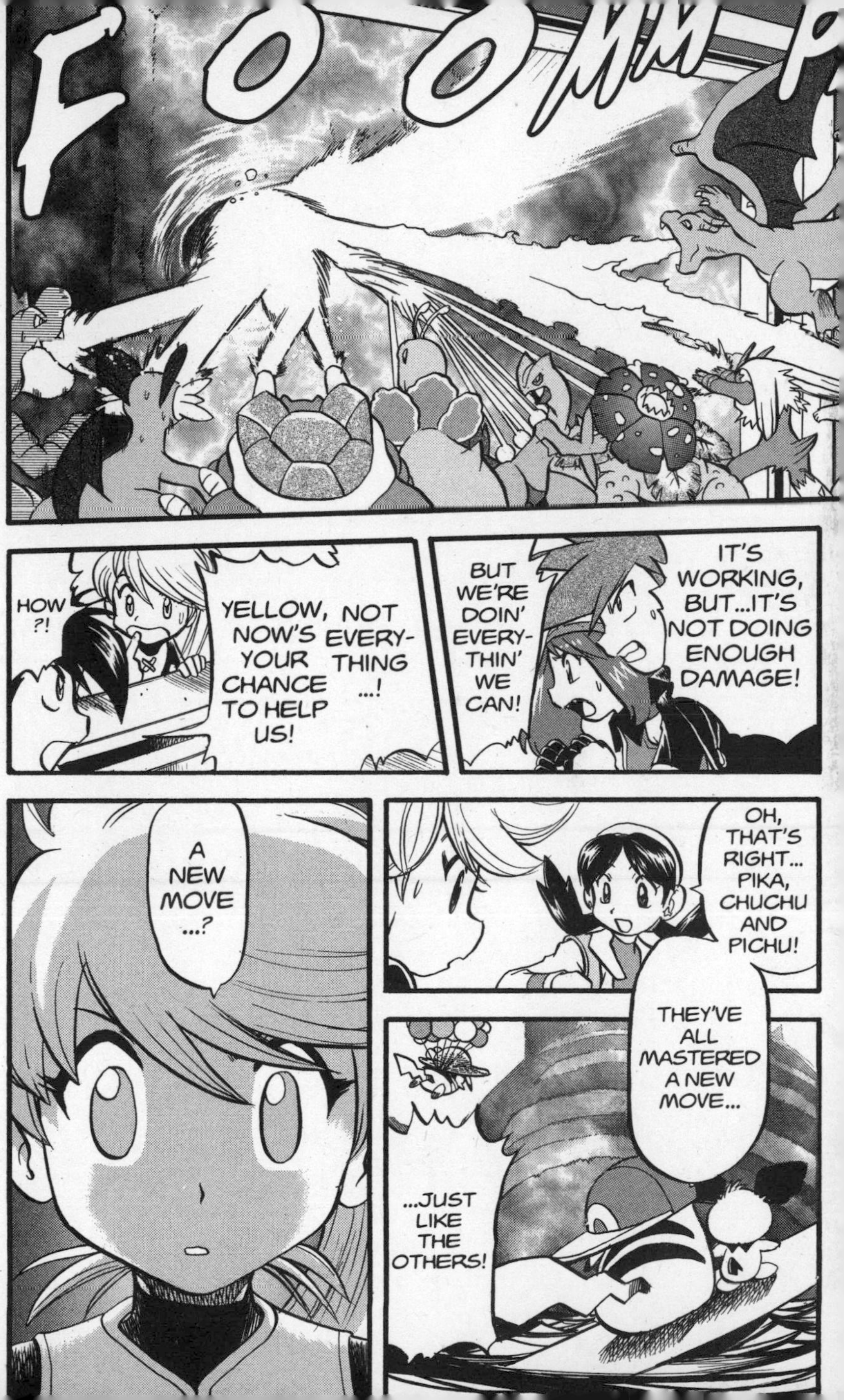
FOOMMP
IT'S WORKING, BUT...IT'S NOT DOING ENOUGH DAMAGE!
BUT WE'RE DOIN' EVERYTHIN' WE CAN!
NOT EVERYTHING...!
YELLOW, NOW'S YOUR CHANCE TO HELP US!
HOW?!
OH, THAT'S RIGHT... PIKA, CHUCHU AND PICHU!
THEY'VE ALL MASTERED A NEW MOVE...
...JUST LIKE THE OTHERS!
A NEW MOVE...?

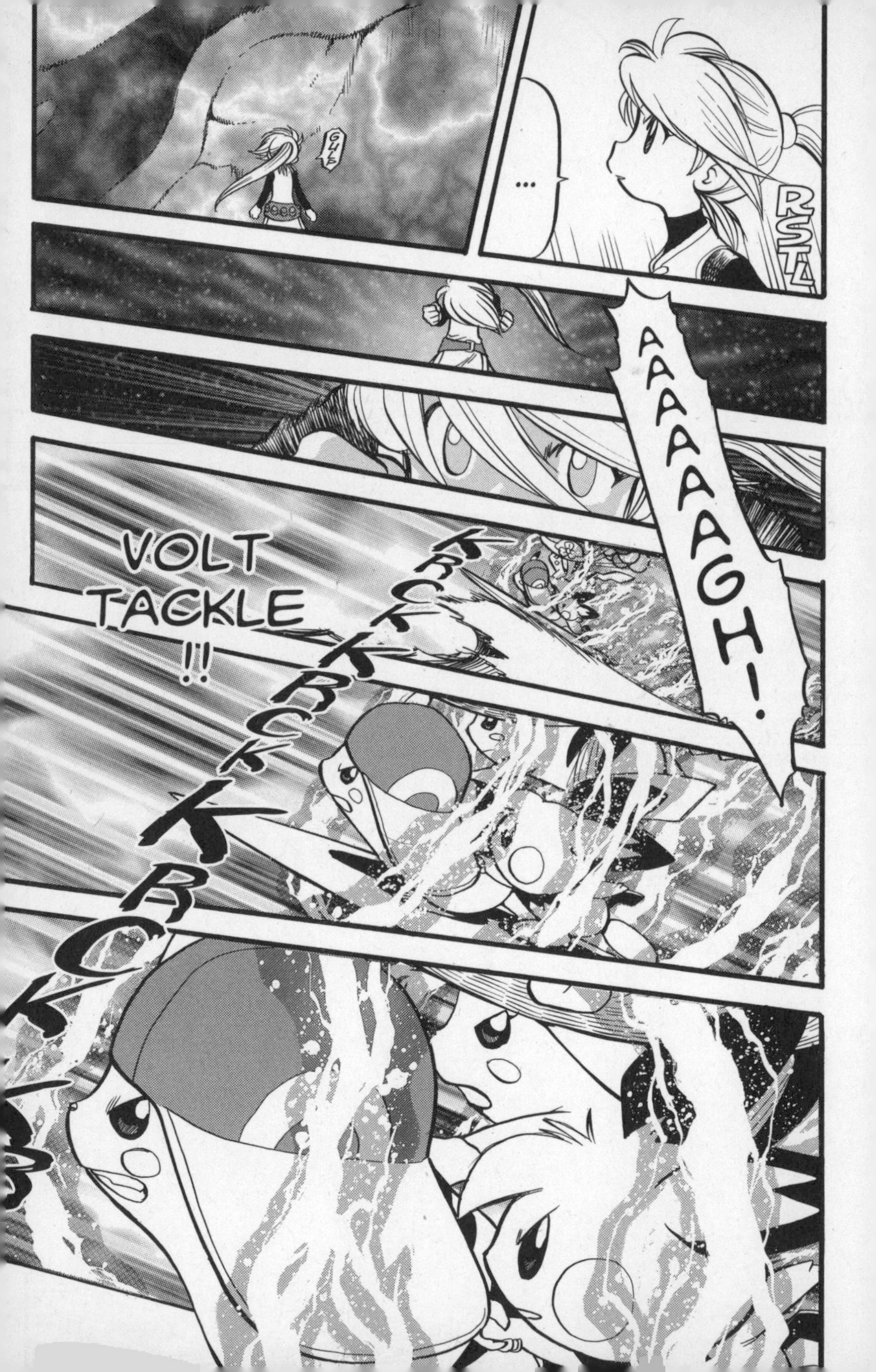
...
RSTL
GULP
AAAAAAAGH!
VOLT TACKLE!!
KRCK KRCK KRCK

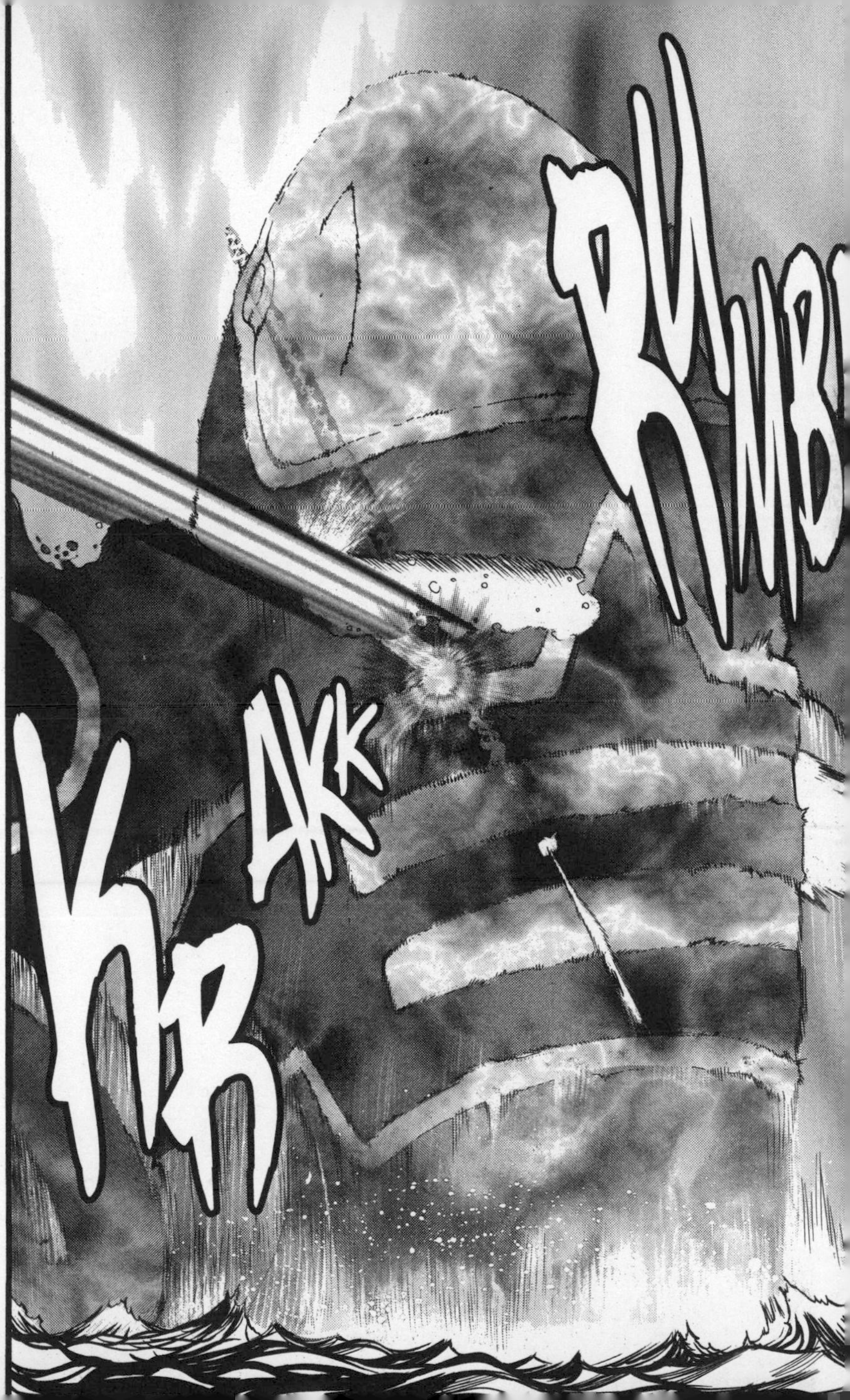
KRAKK

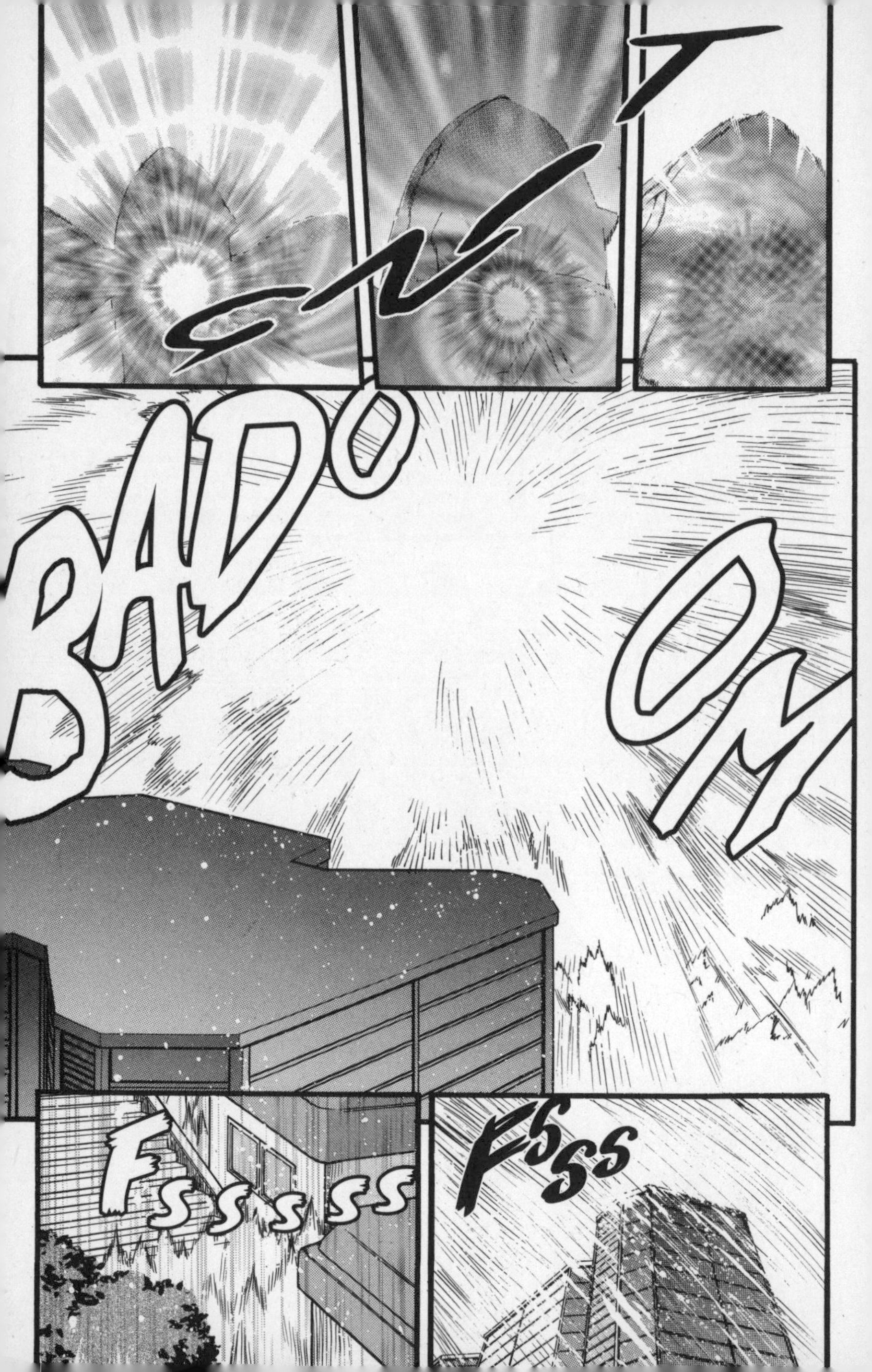
SNIT
BADOOM
FSSS
FSSSSS

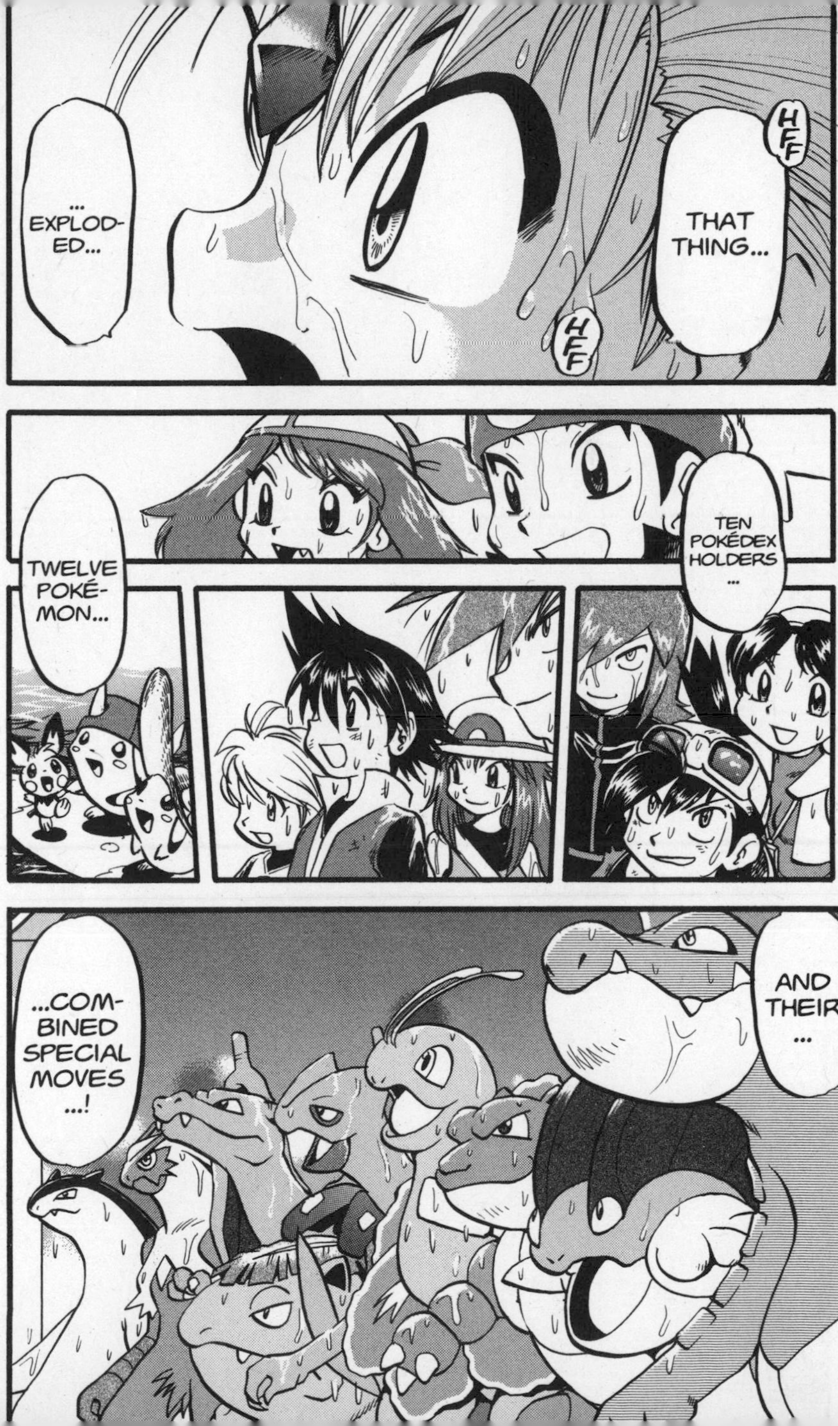
HFF
THAT THING...
HFF
...EXPLODED...
TEN POKÉDEX HOLDERS ...
TWELVE POKÉMON...
AND THEIR ...
...COMBINED SPECIAL MOVES ...!

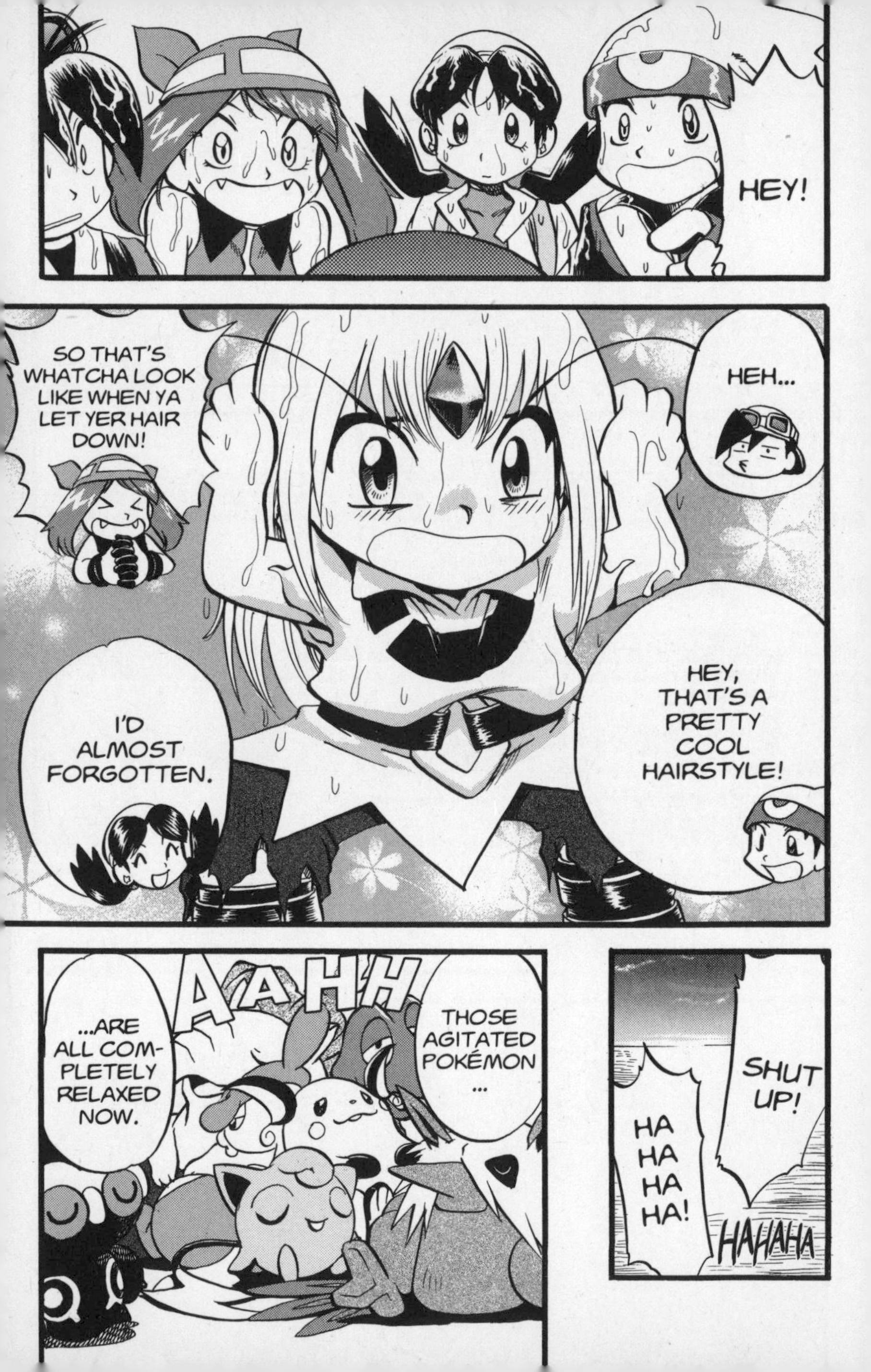
HEY!
HEH...
SO THAT'S WHATCHA LOOK LIKE WHEN YA LET YER HAIR DOWN!
HEY, THAT'S A PRETTY COOL HAIRSTYLE!
I'D ALMOST FORGOTTEN.
SHUT UP!
HA HA HA HA!
HAHAHA
THOSE AGITATED POKÉMON ...
AAHH
...ARE ALL COM-PLETELY RELAXED NOW.

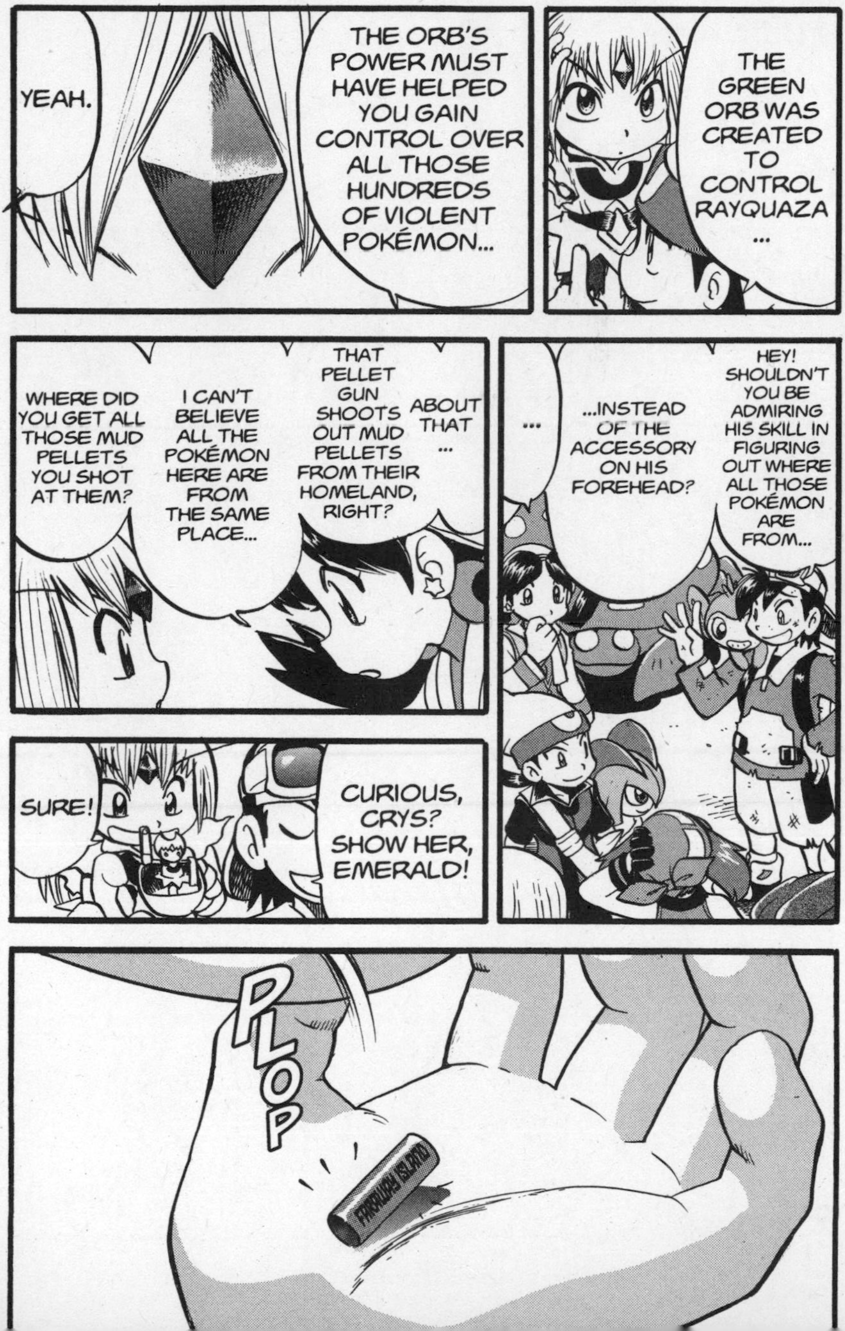
THE GREEN ORB WAS CREATED TO CONTROL RAYQUAZA ...
THE ORB'S POWER MUST HAVE HELPED YOU GAIN CONTROL OVER ALL THOSE HUNDREDS OF VIOLENT POKÉMON...
YEAH.
HEY! SHOULDN'T YOU BE ADMIRING HIS SKILL IN FIGURING OUT WHERE ALL THOSE POKÉMON ARE FROM...
...INSTEAD OF THE ACCESSORY ON HIS FOREHEAD?
...
ABOUT THAT ...
THAT PELLET GUN SHOOTS OUT MUD PELLETS FROM THEIR HOMELAND, RIGHT?
I CAN'T BELIEVE ALL THE POKÉMON HERE ARE FROM THE SAME PLACE...
WHERE DID YOU GET ALL THOSE MUD PELLETS YOU SHOT AT THEM?
CURIOUS, CRYS? SHOW HER, EMERALD!
SURE!
PLOP
FARAWAY ISLAND

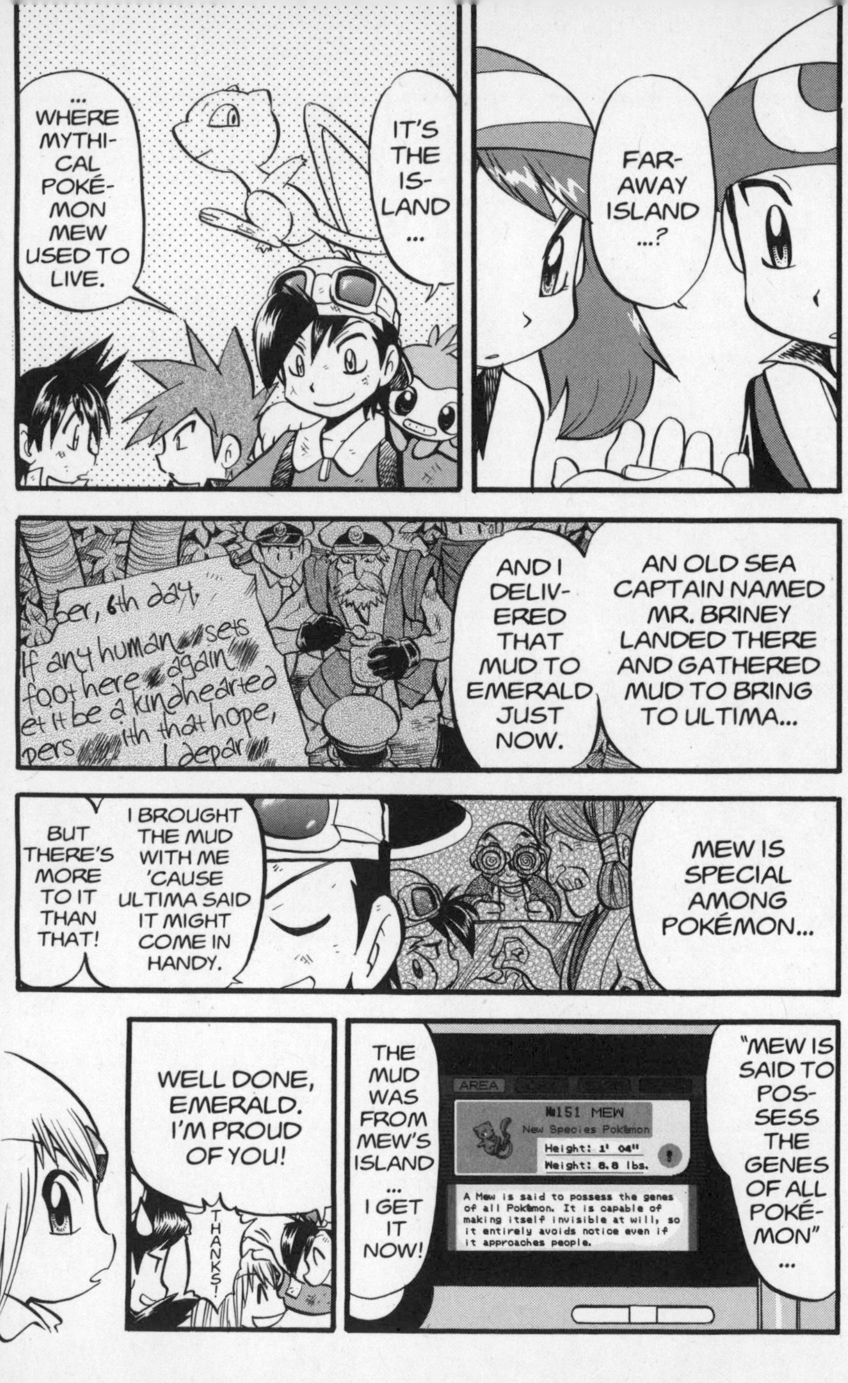
FAR-AWAY ISLAND ...?
IT'S THE ISLAND ...
... WHERE MYTHICAL POKÉMON MEW USED TO LIVE.
AN OLD SEA CAPTAIN NAMED MR. BRINEY LANDED THERE AND GATHERED MUD TO BRING TO ULTIMA...
AND I DELIVERED THAT MUD TO EMERALD JUST NOW.
ber, 6th day,
If any human sets
foot here again
et it be a kindhearted
pers ith that hope,
I depar
MEW IS SPECIAL AMONG POKÉMON...
I BROUGHT THE MUD WITH ME 'CAUSE ULTIMA SAID IT MIGHT COME IN HANDY.
BUT THERE'S MORE TO IT THAN THAT!
"MEW IS SAID TO POSSESS THE GENES OF ALL POKÉMON" ...
AREA
№151 MEW
New Species Pokémon
Height: 1' 04"
Weight: 8.8 lbs.
A Mew is said to possess the genes of all Pokémon. It is capable of making itself invisible at will, so it entirely avoids notice even if it approaches people.
THE MUD WAS FROM MEW'S ISLAND ... I GET IT NOW!
WELL DONE, EMERALD. I'M PROUD OF YOU!
THANKS!

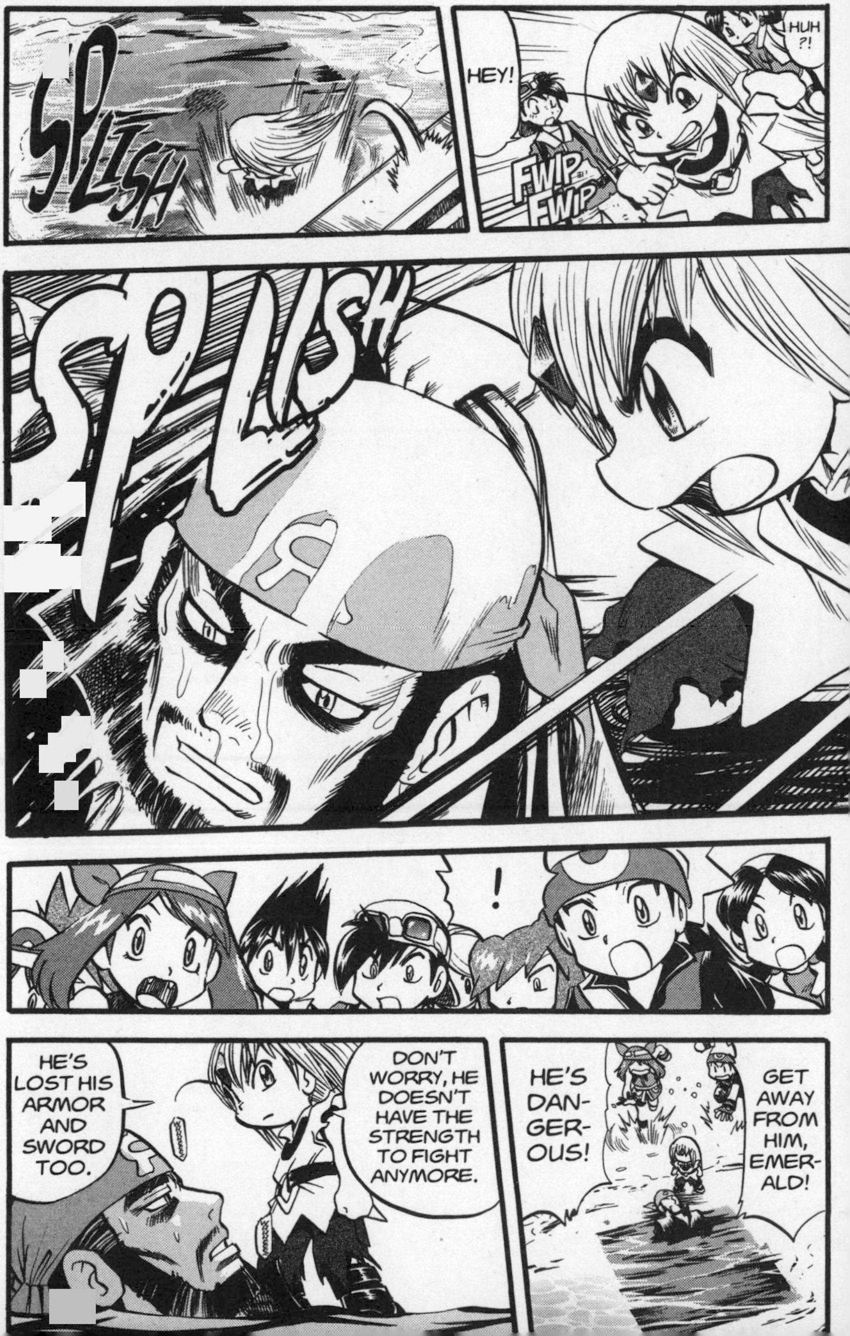
HUH ?!
HEY!
FWIP FWIP
SPLISH
SPLISH
!
GET AWAY FROM HIM, EMER- ALD!
HE'S DAN- GER- OUS!
DON'T WORRY, HE DOESN'T HAVE THE STRENGTH TO FIGHT ANYMORE.
HE'S LOST HIS ARMOR AND SWORD TOO.

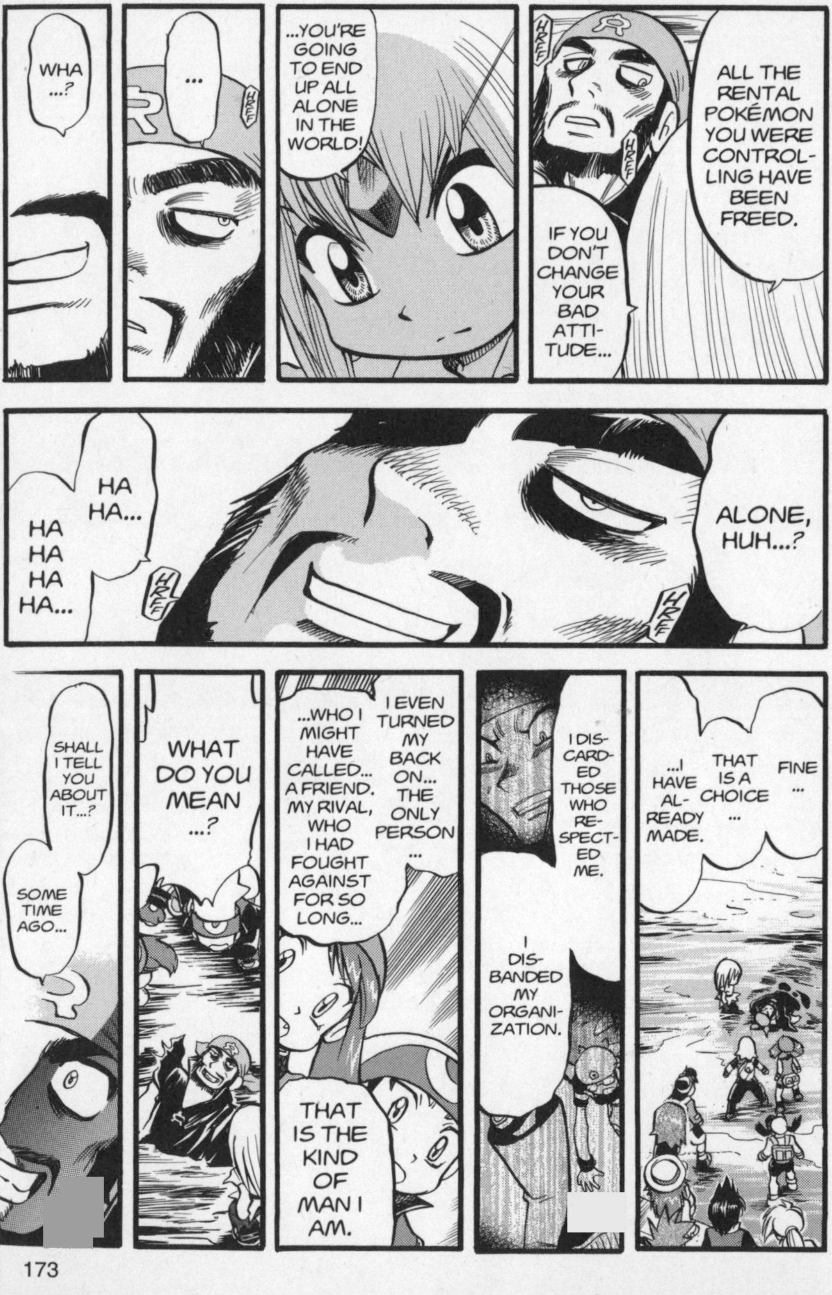
HREFF
ALL THE RENTAL POKÉMON YOU WERE CONTROL-LING HAVE BEEN FREED.
HREFF
IF YOU DON'T CHANGE YOUR BAD ATTI-TUDE...
...YOU'RE GOING TO END UP ALL ALONE IN THE WORLD!
...
HREFF
WHA ...?
ALONE, HUH...?
HREFF
HA HA...
HA HA HA HA...
HREFF
FINE ...
THAT IS A CHOICE ...
...I HAVE AL-READY MADE.
I DIS-CARD-ED THOSE WHO RE-SPECT-ED ME.
I DIS-BANDED MY ORGANI-ZATION.
I EVEN TURNED MY BACK ON... THE ONLY PERSON ...
...WHO I MIGHT HAVE CALLED... A FRIEND. MY RIVAL, WHO I HAD FOUGHT AGAINST FOR SO LONG...
THAT IS THE KIND OF MAN I AM.
WHAT DO YOU MEAN ...?
SHALL I TELL YOU ABOUT IT...?
SOME TIME AGO...

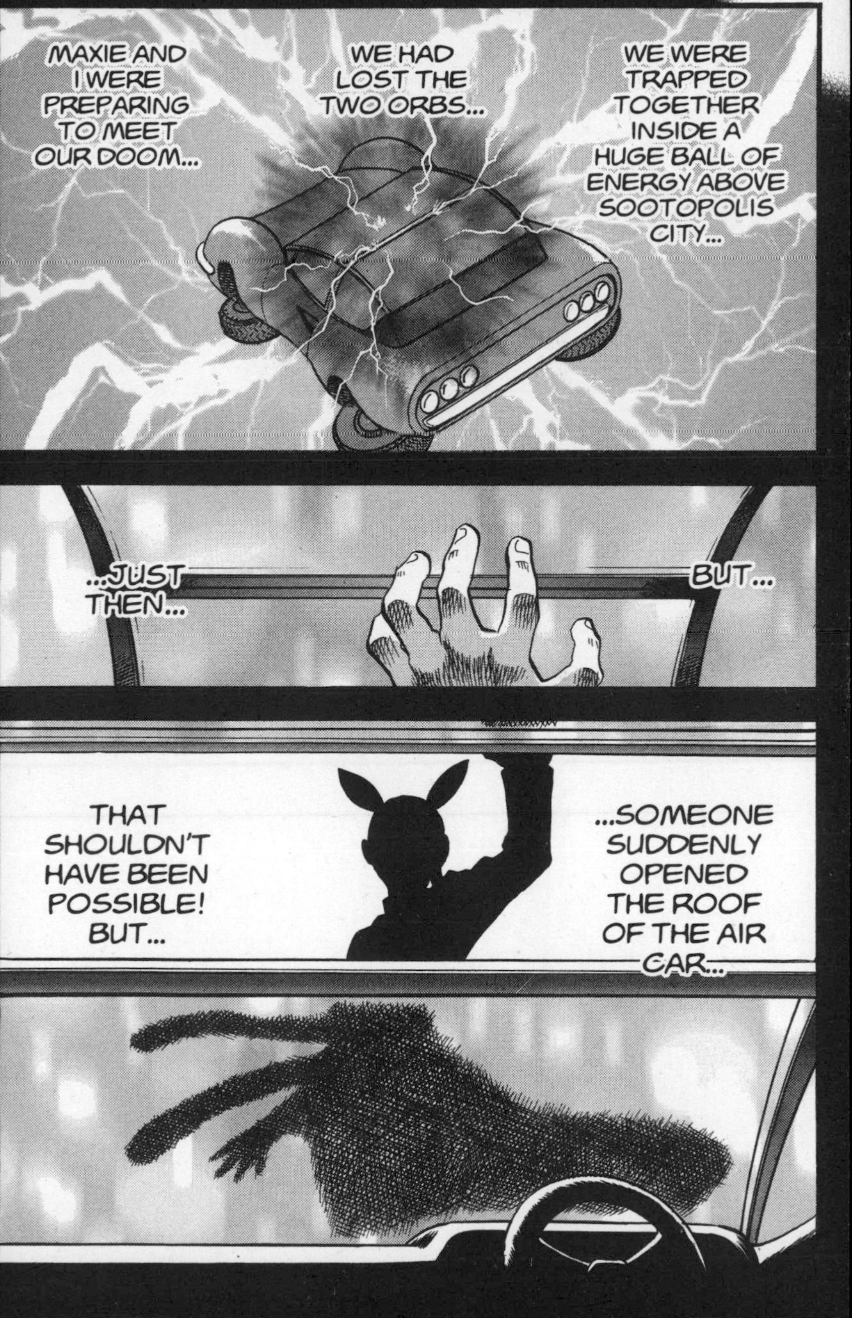
WE WERE TRAPPED TOGETHER INSIDE A HUGE BALL OF ENERGY ABOVE SOOTOPOLIS CITY...
WE HAD LOST THE TWO ORBS...
MAXIE AND I WERE PREPARING TO MEET OUR DOOM...
BUT...
...JUST THEN...
...SOMEONE SUDDENLY OPENED THE ROOF OF THE AIR CAR...
THAT SHOULDN'T HAVE BEEN POSSIBLE! BUT...

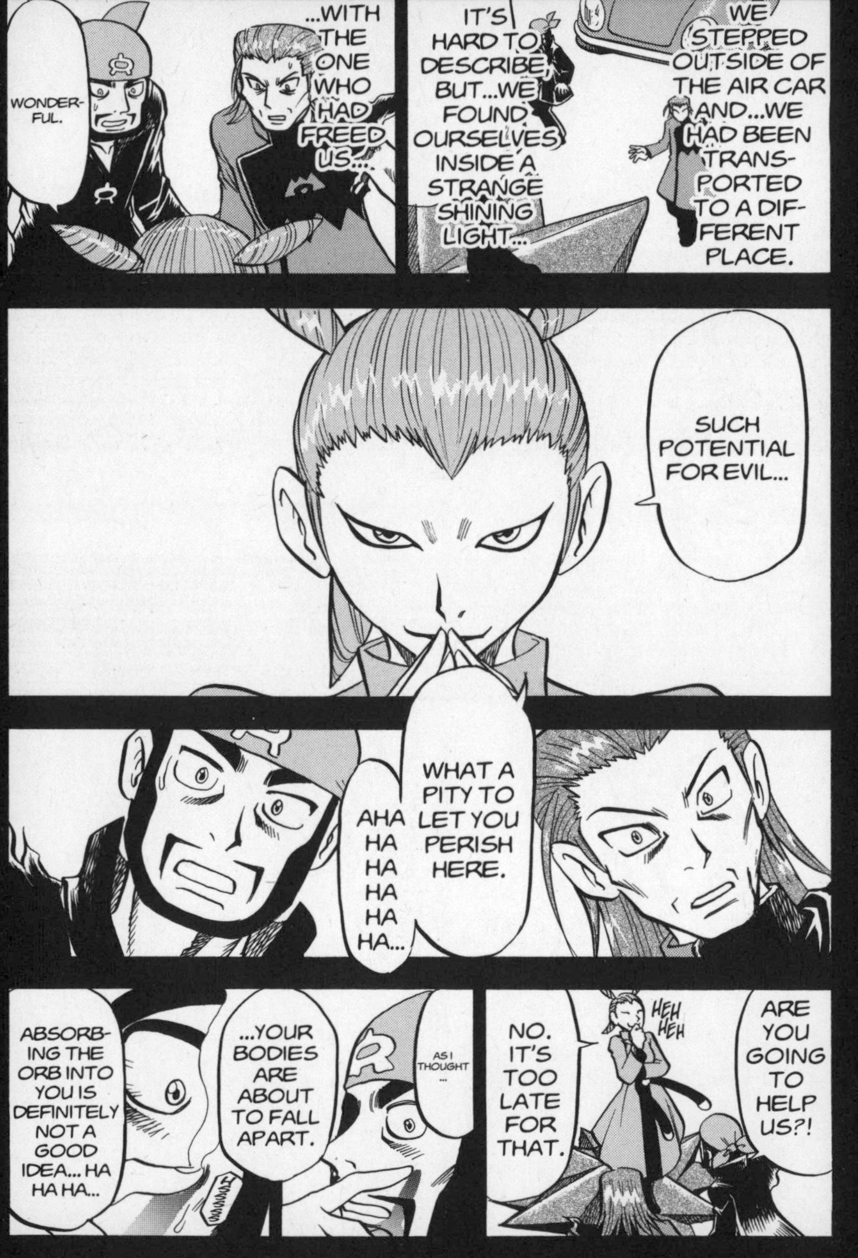
WE STEPPED OUTSIDE OF THE AIR CAR AND...WE HAD BEEN TRANS-PORTED TO A DIF-FERENT PLACE.
IT'S HARD TO DESCRIBE, BUT...WE FOUND OURSELVES INSIDE A STRANGE SHINING LIGHT...
...WITH THE ONE WHO HAD FREED US....
WONDER-FUL.
SUCH POTENTIAL FOR EVIL...
WHAT A PITY TO LET YOU PERISH HERE.
AHA HA HA HA HA HA...
ARE YOU GOING TO HELP US?!
HEH HEH
NO. IT'S TOO LATE FOR THAT.
AS I THOUGHT...
...YOUR BODIES ARE ABOUT TO FALL APART.
ABSORB-ING THE ORB INTO YOU IS DEFINITELY NOT A GOOD IDEA... HA HA HA...

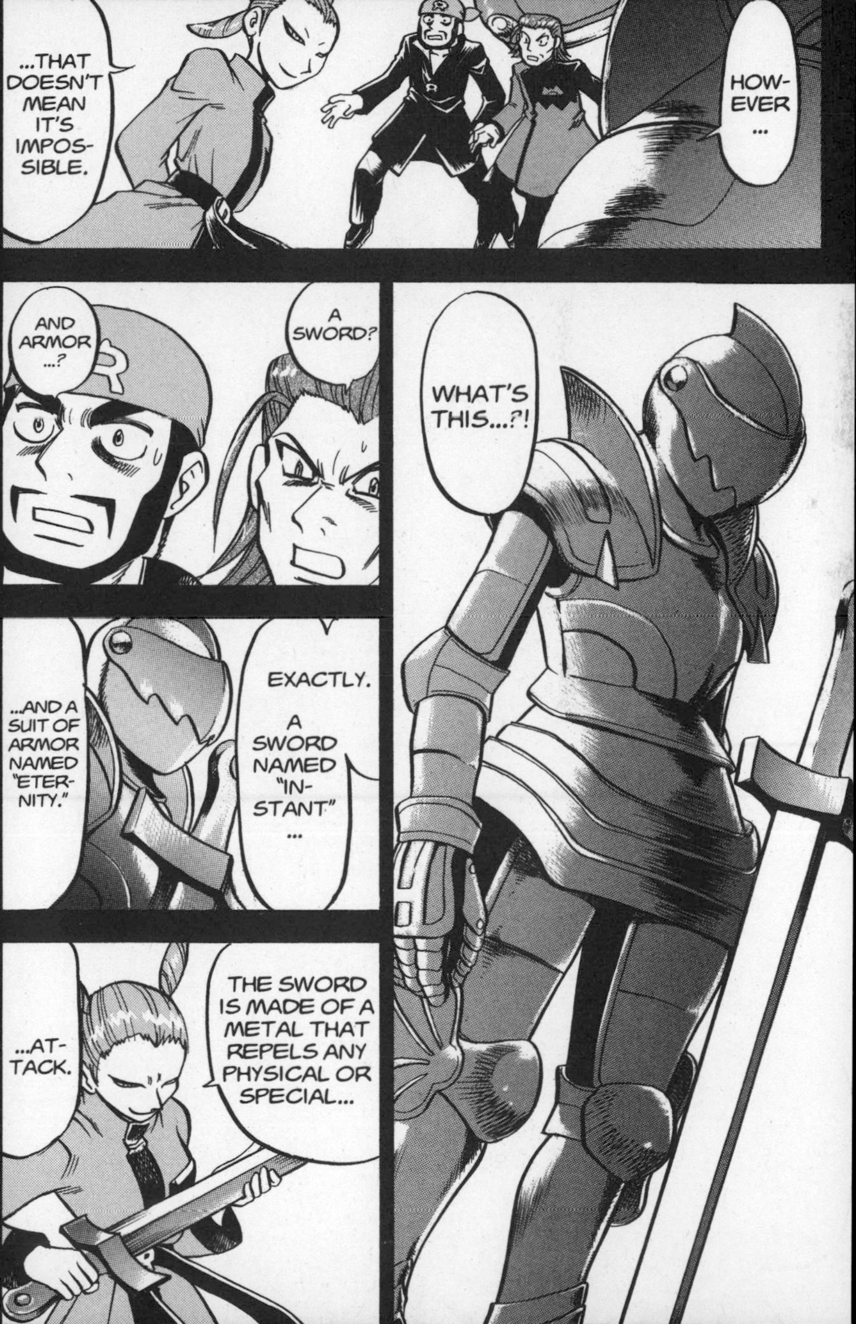
HOW-EVER...
...THAT DOESN'T MEAN IT'S IMPOSSIBLE.
WHAT'S THIS...?!
A SWORD?
AND ARMOR...?
EXACTLY. A SWORD NAMED "IN-STANT"...
...AND A SUIT OF ARMOR NAMED "ETER-NITY."
THE SWORD IS MADE OF A METAL THAT REPELS ANY PHYSICAL OR SPECIAL...
...AT-TACK.

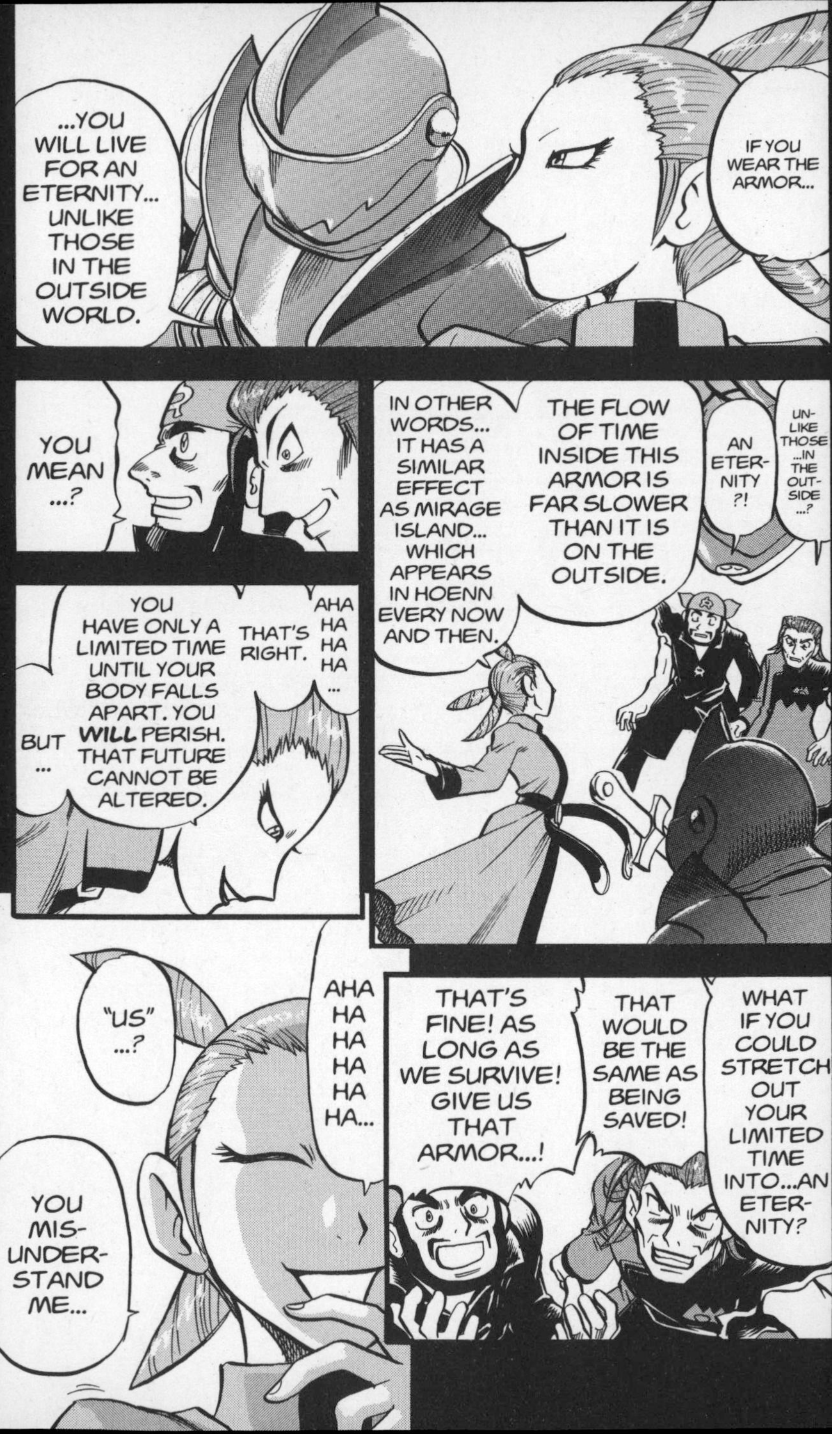
IF YOU WEAR THE ARMOR...
...YOU WILL LIVE FOR AN ETERNITY... UNLIKE THOSE IN THE OUTSIDE WORLD.
UN-LIKE THOSE ...IN THE OUT-SIDE ...?
AN ETER-NITY ?!
THE FLOW OF TIME INSIDE THIS ARMOR IS FAR SLOWER THAN IT IS ON THE OUTSIDE.
IN OTHER WORDS... IT HAS A SIMILAR EFFECT AS MIRAGE ISLAND... WHICH APPEARS IN HOENN EVERY NOW AND THEN.
YOU MEAN ...?
AHA HA HA HA ...
THAT'S RIGHT.
YOU HAVE ONLY A LIMITED TIME UNTIL YOUR BODY FALLS APART. YOU **WILL** PERISH. THAT FUTURE CANNOT BE ALTERED.
BUT ...
WHAT IF YOU COULD STRETCH OUT YOUR LIMITED TIME INTO...AN ETER-NITY?
THAT WOULD BE THE SAME AS BEING SAVED!
THAT'S FINE! AS LONG AS WE SURVIVE! GIVE US THAT ARMOR...!
AHA HA HA HA HA HA...
"US" ...?
YOU MIS-UNDER-STAND ME...

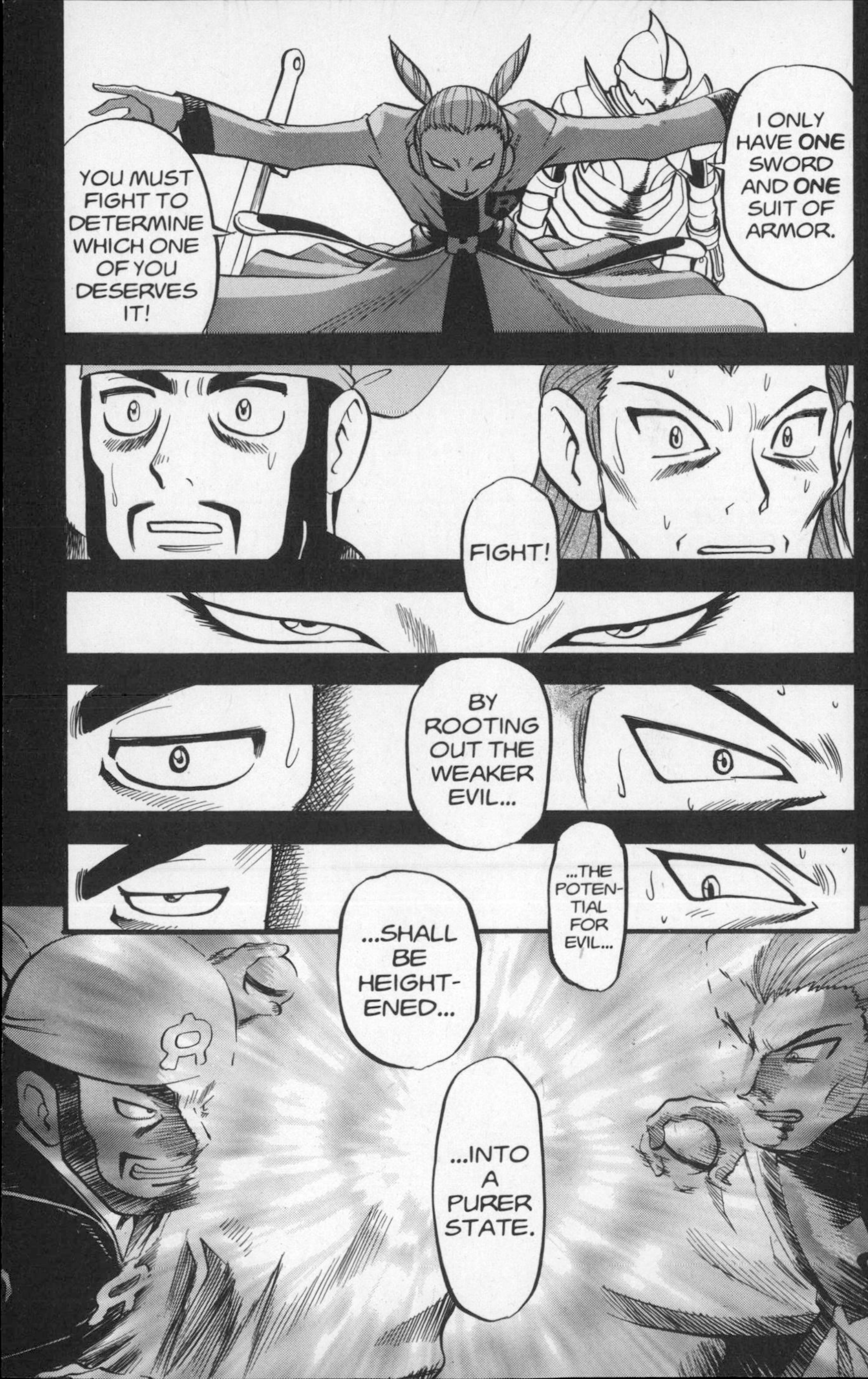
I ONLY HAVE **ONE** SWORD AND **ONE** SUIT OF ARMOR.
YOU MUST FIGHT TO DETERMINE WHICH ONE OF YOU DESERVES IT!
FIGHT!
BY ROOTING OUT THE WEAKER EVIL...
...THE POTEN-TIAL FOR EVIL...
...SHALL BE HEIGHT-ENED...
...INTO A PURER STATE.

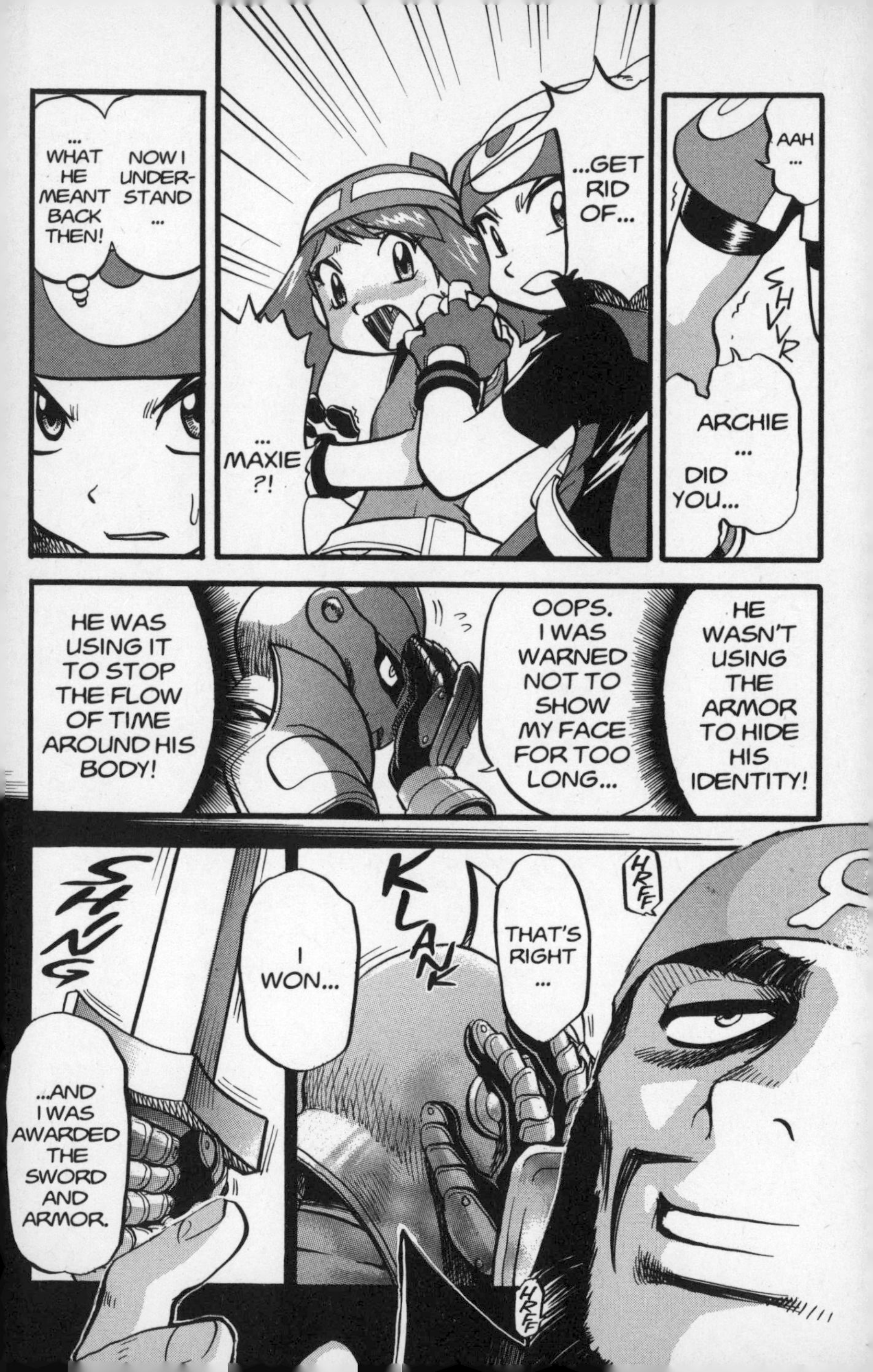
AAH ...
SHVVR
ARCHIE ... DID YOU...
...GET RID OF...
... MAXIE ?!
NOW I UNDERSTAND ...
... WHAT HE MEANT BACK THEN!
HE WASN'T USING THE ARMOR TO HIDE HIS IDENTITY!
OOPS. I WAS WARNED NOT TO SHOW MY FACE FOR TOO LONG...
HE WAS USING IT TO STOP THE FLOW OF TIME AROUND HIS BODY!
HRFF
THAT'S RIGHT ...
KLANK
I WON...
HRFF
SHING
...AND I WAS AWARDED THE SWORD AND ARMOR.

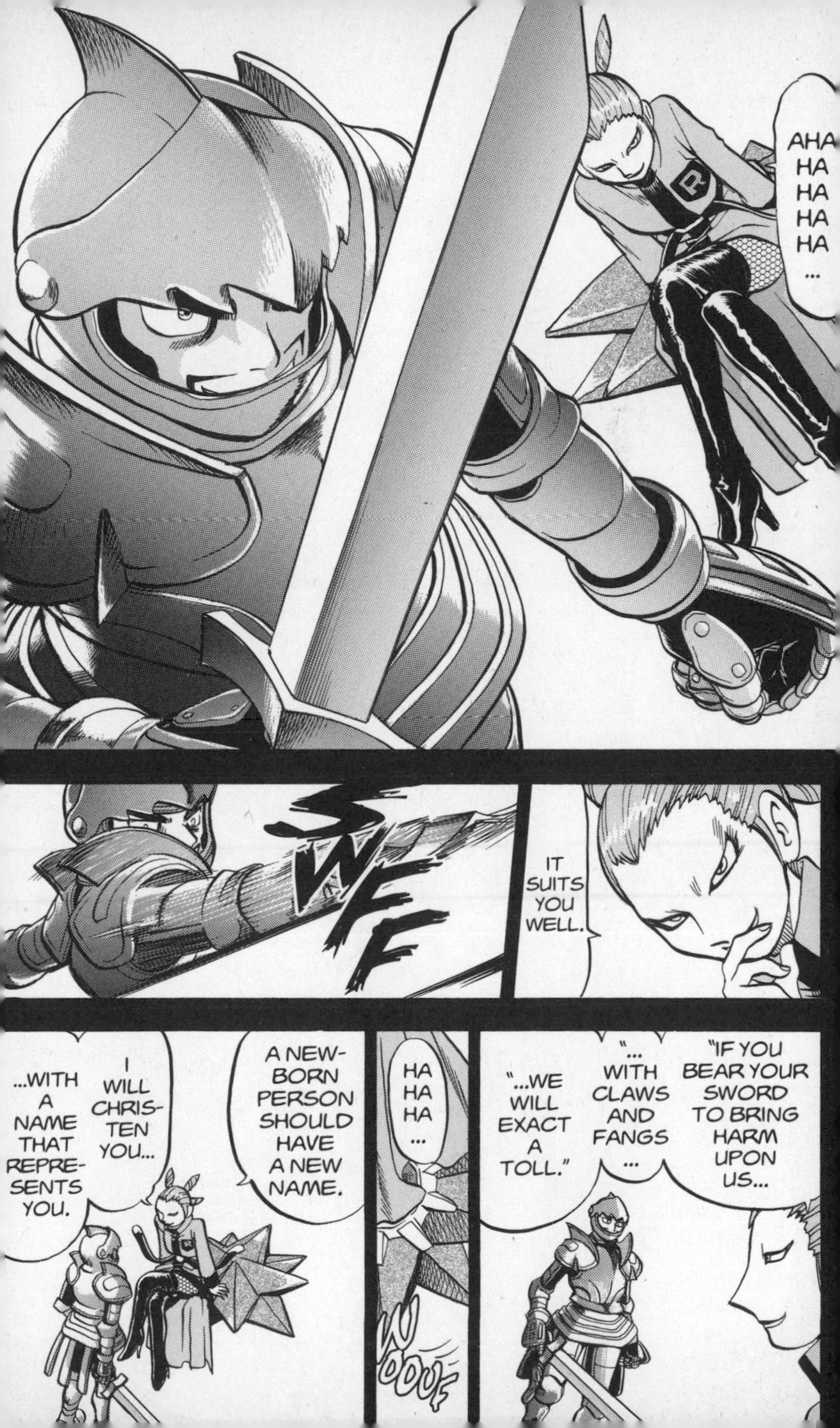

AHA HA HA HA HA ...
IT SUITS YOU WELL.
SWF
"IF YOU BEAR YOUR SWORD TO BRING HARM UPON US...
"... WITH CLAWS AND FANGS ...
"...WE WILL EXACT A TOLL."
HA HA HA ...
A NEW-BORN PERSON SHOULD HAVE A NEW NAME.
I WILL CHRISTEN YOU...
...WITH A NAME THAT REPRESENTS YOU.

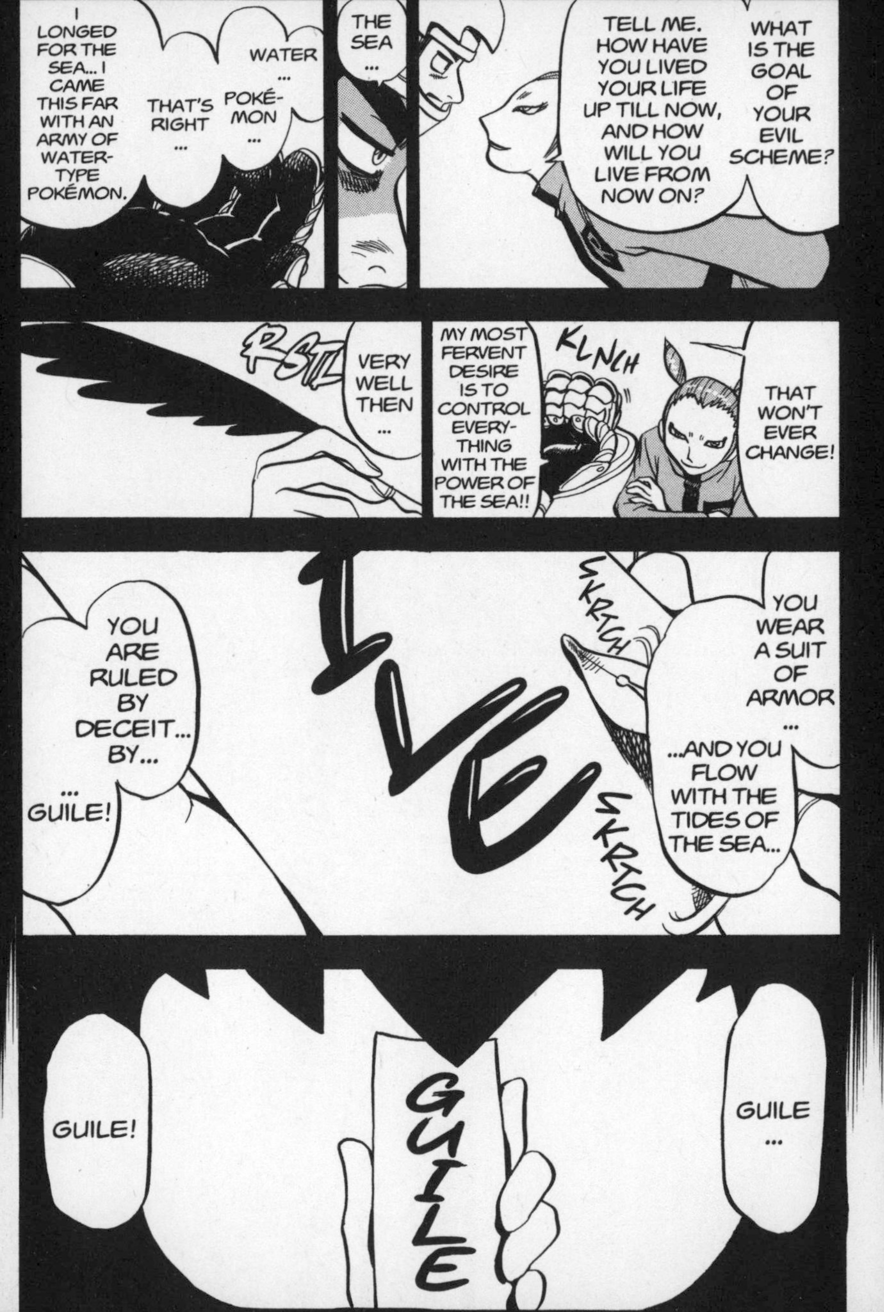
WHAT IS THE GOAL OF YOUR EVIL SCHEME?
TELL ME. HOW HAVE YOU LIVED YOUR LIFE UP TILL NOW, AND HOW WILL YOU LIVE FROM NOW ON?
THE SEA ...
WATER ...
POKÉ-MON ...
THAT'S RIGHT ...
I LONGED FOR THE SEA... I CAME THIS FAR WITH AN ARMY OF WATER-TYPE POKÉMON.
THAT WON'T EVER CHANGE!
KLNCH
MY MOST FERVENT DESIRE IS TO CONTROL EVERY-THING WITH THE POWER OF THE SEA!!
VERY WELL THEN ...
RSTL
YOU WEAR A SUIT OF ARMOR ...
...AND YOU FLOW WITH THE TIDES OF THE SEA...
SKRTCH
SKRTCH
YOU ARE RULED BY DECEIT... BY...
... GUILE!
GUILE ...
GUILE
GUILE!

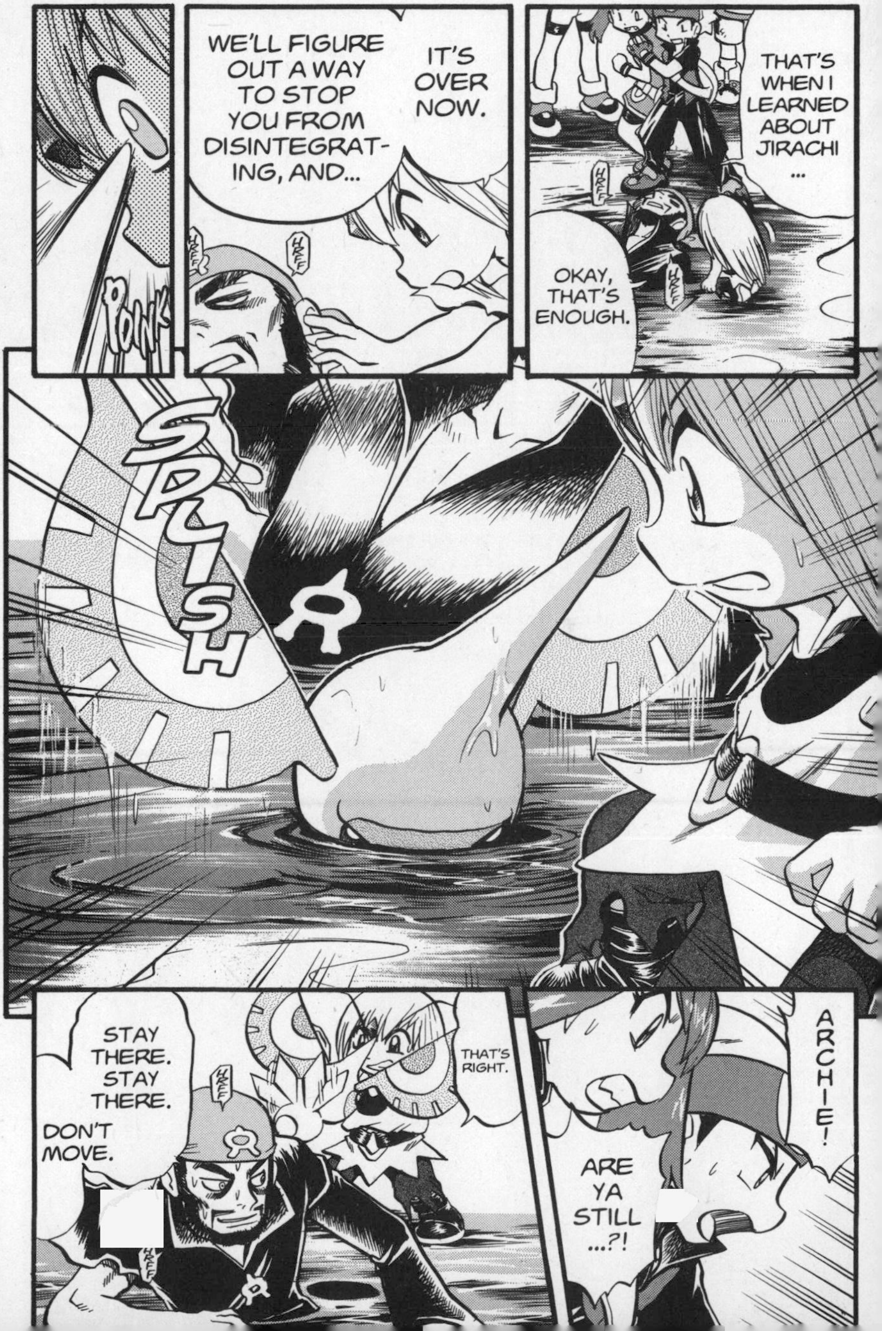
THAT'S WHEN I LEARNED ABOUT JIRACHI ...
HRFF
HRFF
OKAY, THAT'S ENOUGH.
IT'S OVER NOW.
WE'LL FIGURE OUT A WAY TO STOP YOU FROM DISINTEGRAT-ING, AND...
HRFF
HRFF
POINK
SPLISH
ARCHIE!
ARE YA STILL ...?!
THAT'S RIGHT.
STAY THERE. STAY THERE.
DON'T MOVE.
HRFF
HRFF

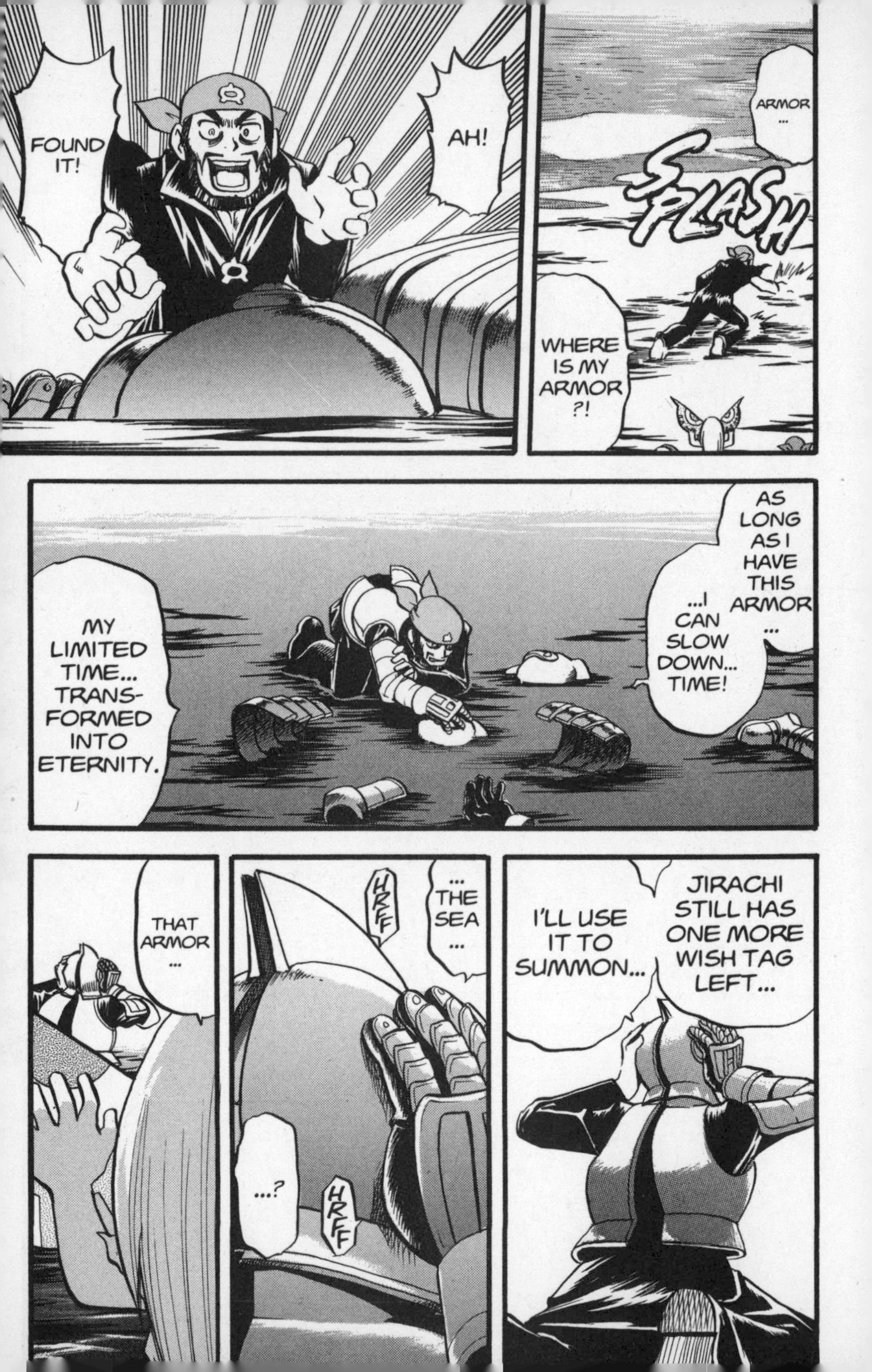
ARMOR...
SPLASH
WHERE IS MY ARMOR?!
AH!
FOUND IT!
AS LONG AS I HAVE THIS ARMOR...
...I CAN SLOW DOWN... TIME!
MY LIMITED TIME... TRANS-FORMED INTO ETERNITY.
JIRACHI STILL HAS ONE MORE WISH TAG LEFT...
I'LL USE IT TO SUMMON...
...THE SEA...
HRFF
...?
HRFF
THAT ARMOR...

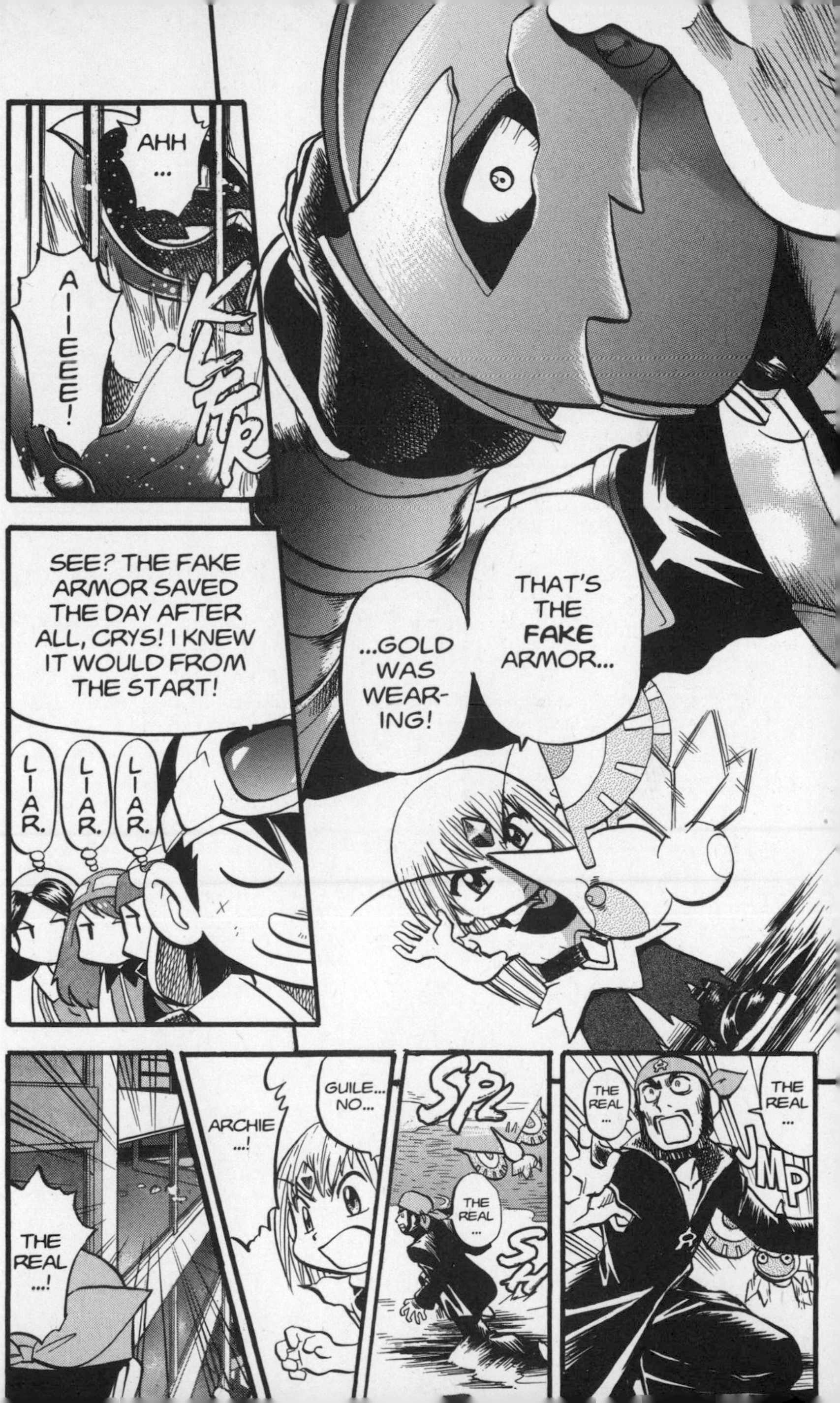
THAT'S THE **FAKE** ARMOR...
...GOLD WAS WEARING!
AHH ...
AIIEEE!
SEE? THE FAKE ARMOR SAVED THE DAY AFTER ALL, CRYS! I KNEW IT WOULD FROM THE START!
LIAR.
LIAR.
LIAR.
THE REAL ...
THE REAL ...
JMP
SPL
THE REAL ...
SH
GUILE... NO...
ARCHIE ...!
THE REAL ...!

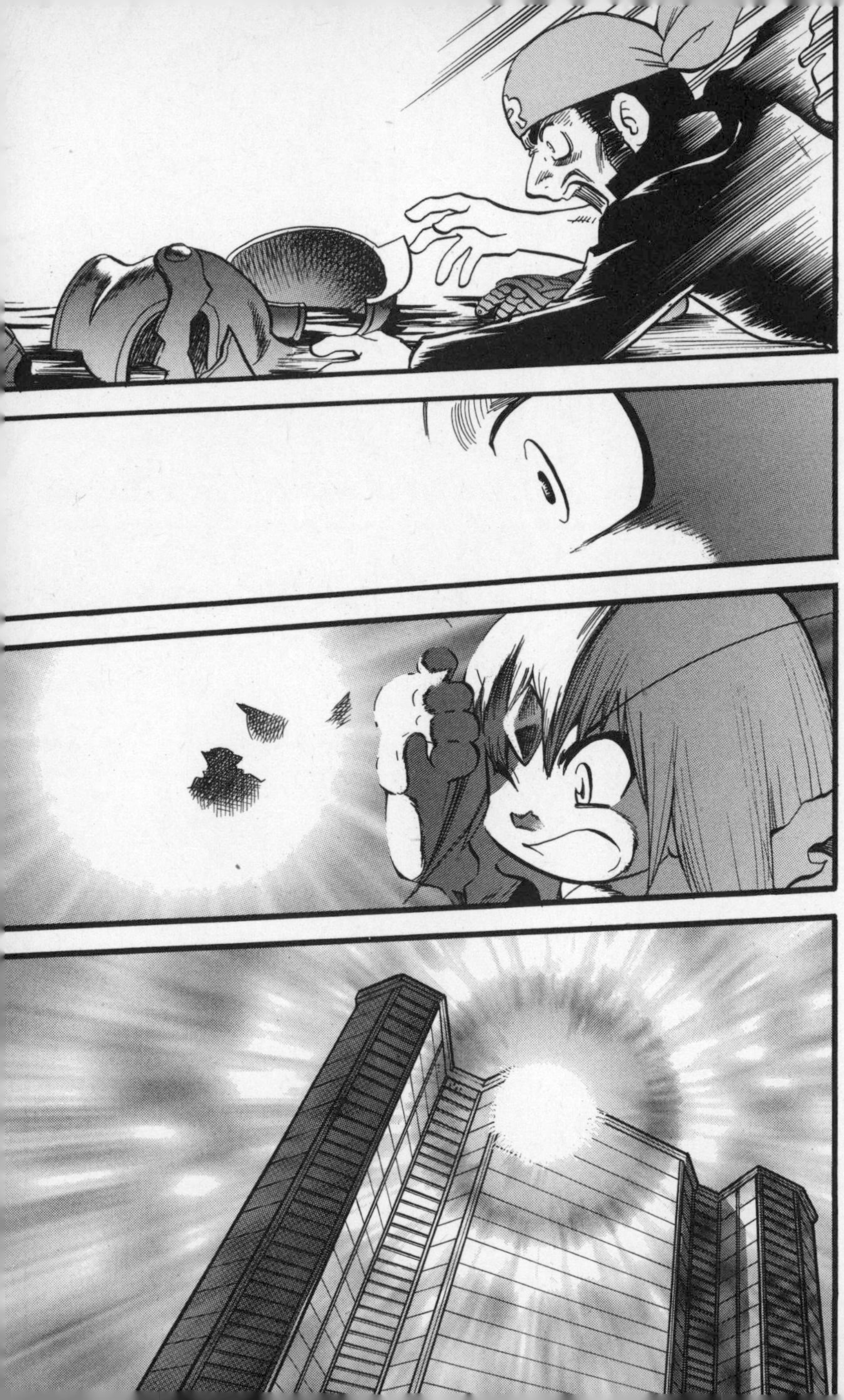

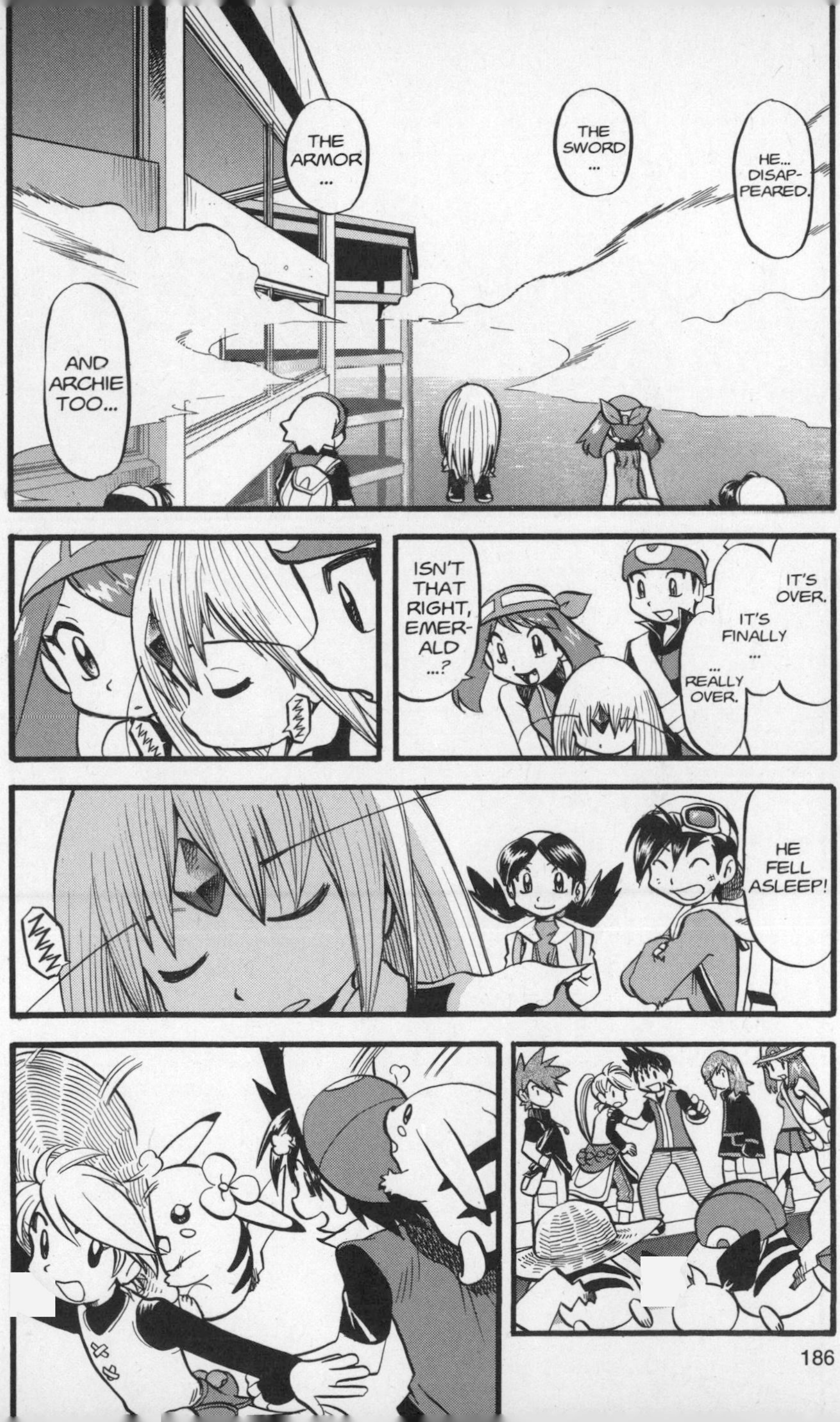
HE... DISAP-PEARED.
THE SWORD...
THE ARMOR...
AND ARCHIE TOO...
IT'S OVER.
IT'S FINALLY...
...REALLY OVER.
ISN'T THAT RIGHT, EMERALD...?
HE FELL ASLEEP!

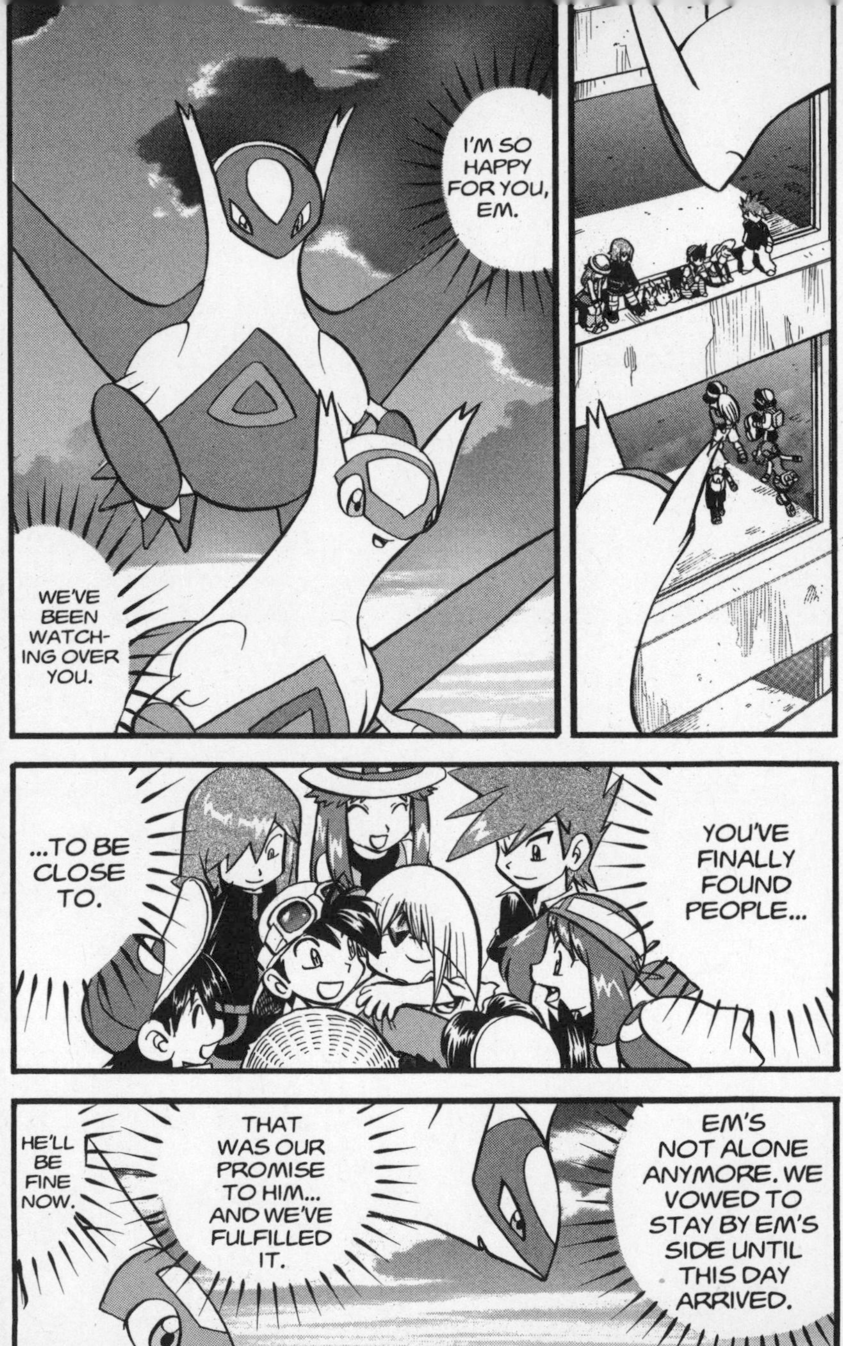
I'M SO HAPPY FOR YOU, EM.
WE'VE BEEN WATCHING OVER YOU.
YOU'VE FINALLY FOUND PEOPLE...
...TO BE CLOSE TO.
EM'S NOT ALONE ANYMORE. WE VOWED TO STAY BY EM'S SIDE UNTIL THIS DAY ARRIVED.
THAT WAS OUR PROMISE TO HIM... AND WE'VE FULFILLED IT.
HE'LL BE FINE NOW.

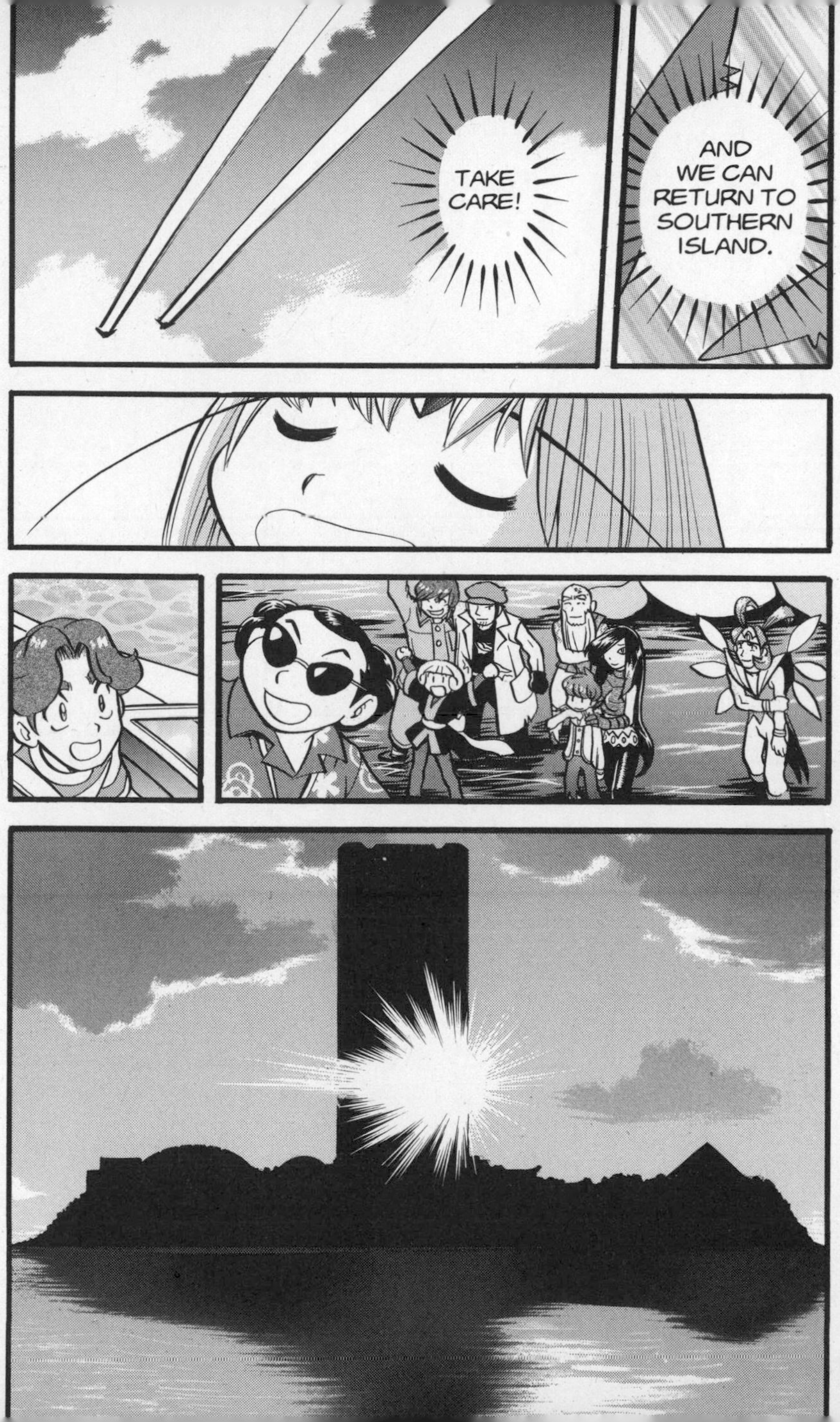
AND WE CAN RETURN TO SOUTHERN ISLAND.
TAKE CARE!

337

Epilogue

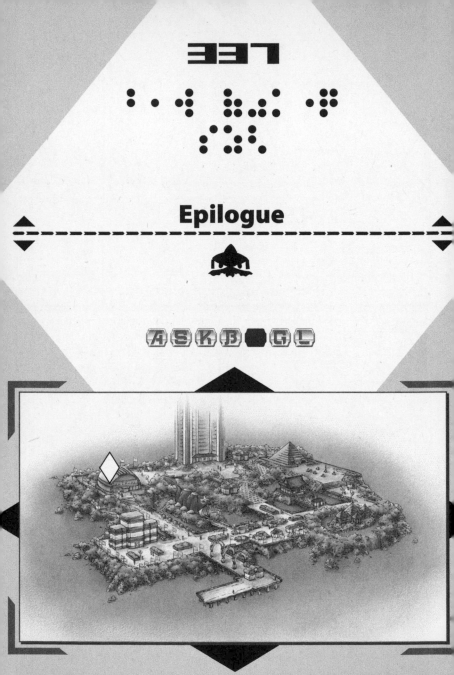

ASKB■GL

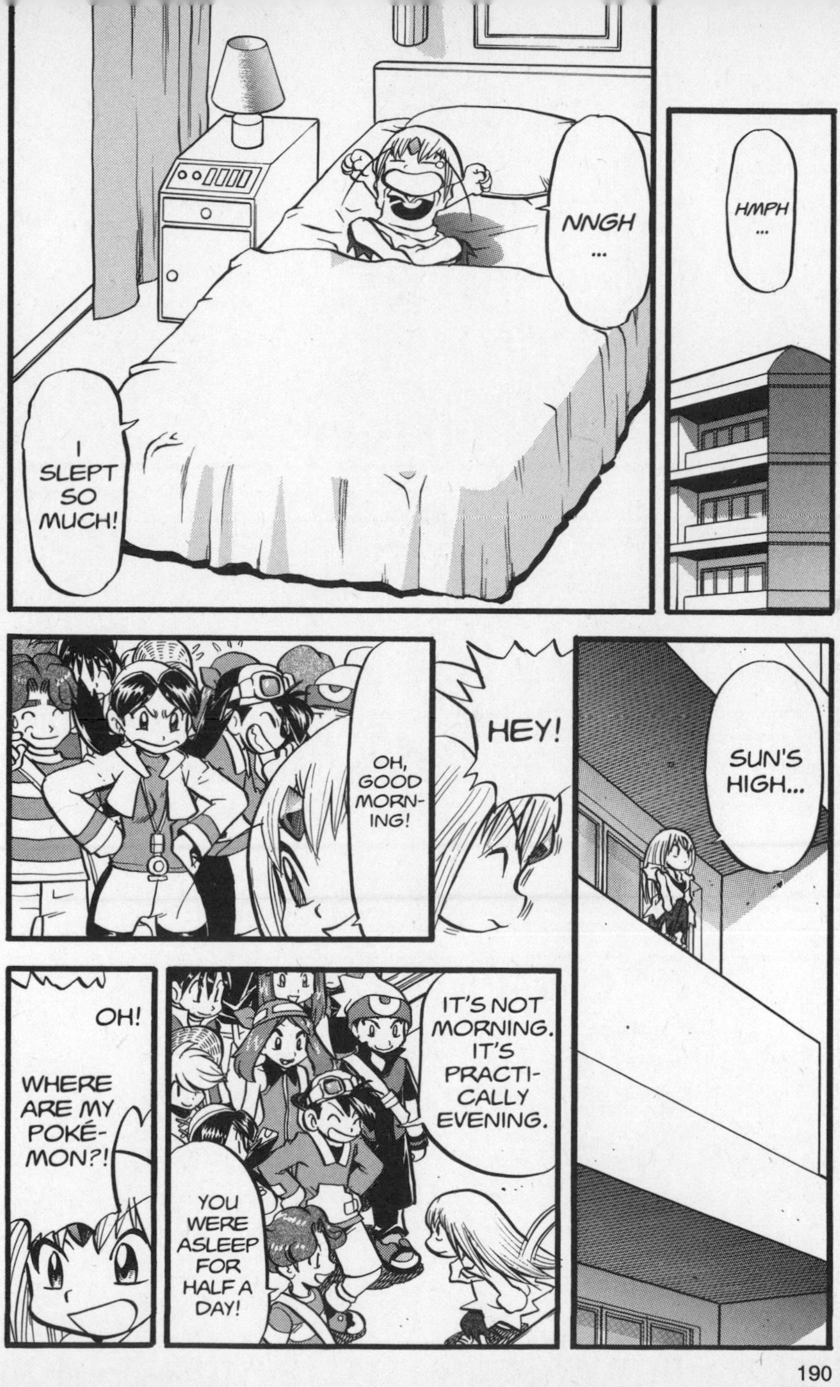
HMPH ...
NNGH ...
I SLEPT SO MUCH!
SUN'S HIGH...
HEY!
OH, GOOD MORN-ING!
IT'S NOT MORNING. IT'S PRACTI-CALLY EVENING.
YOU WERE ASLEEP FOR HALF A DAY!
OH!
WHERE ARE MY POKÉ-MON?!

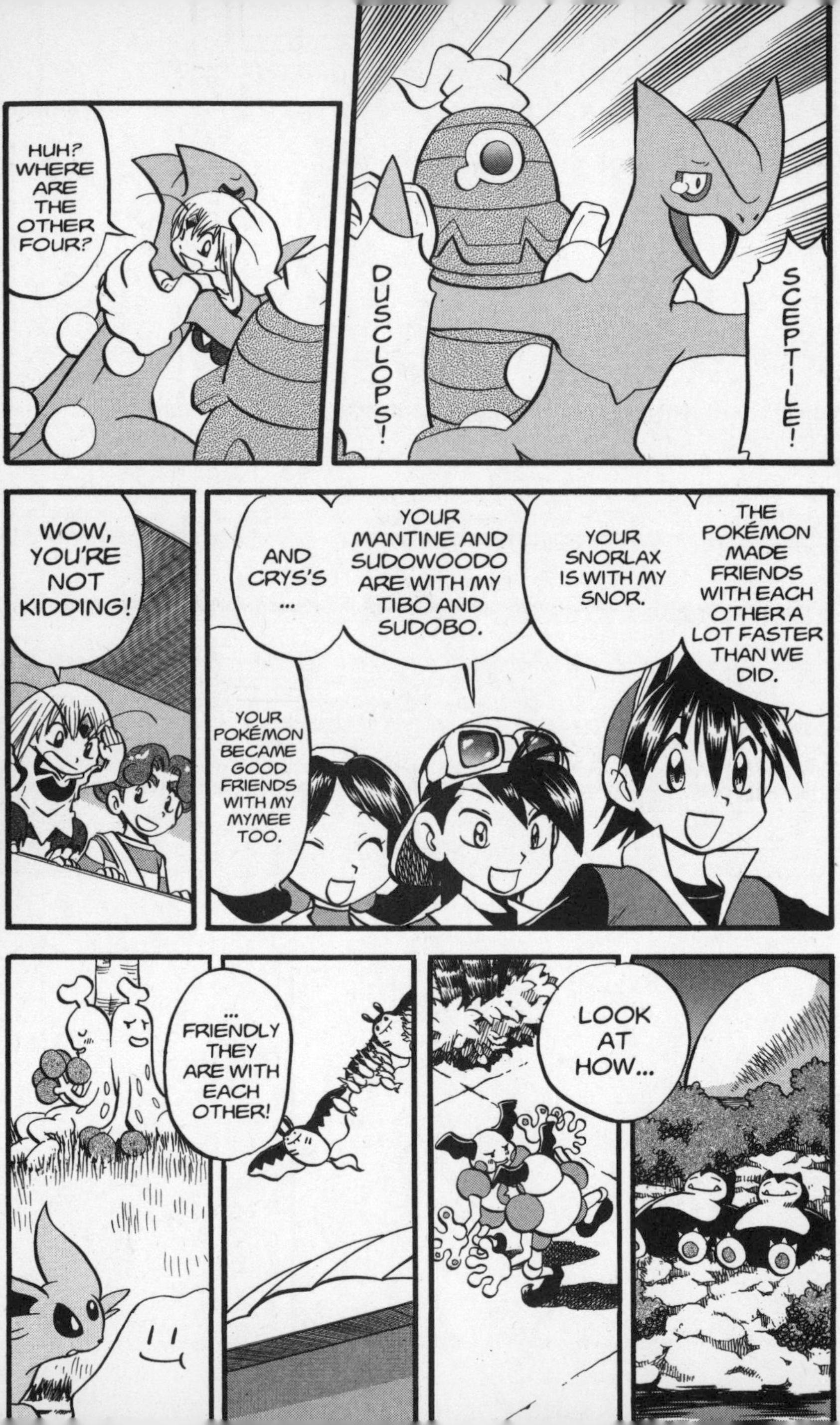
SCEPTILE!
DUSCLOPS!
HUH? WHERE ARE THE OTHER FOUR?
THE POKéMON MADE FRIENDS WITH EACH OTHER A LOT FASTER THAN WE DID.
YOUR SNORLAX IS WITH MY SNOR.
YOUR MANTINE AND SUDOWOODO ARE WITH MY TIBO AND SUDOBO.
AND CRYS'S ...
YOUR POKéMON BECAME GOOD FRIENDS WITH MY MYMEE TOO.
WOW, YOU'RE NOT KIDDING!
LOOK AT HOW...
... FRIENDLY THEY ARE WITH EACH OTHER!

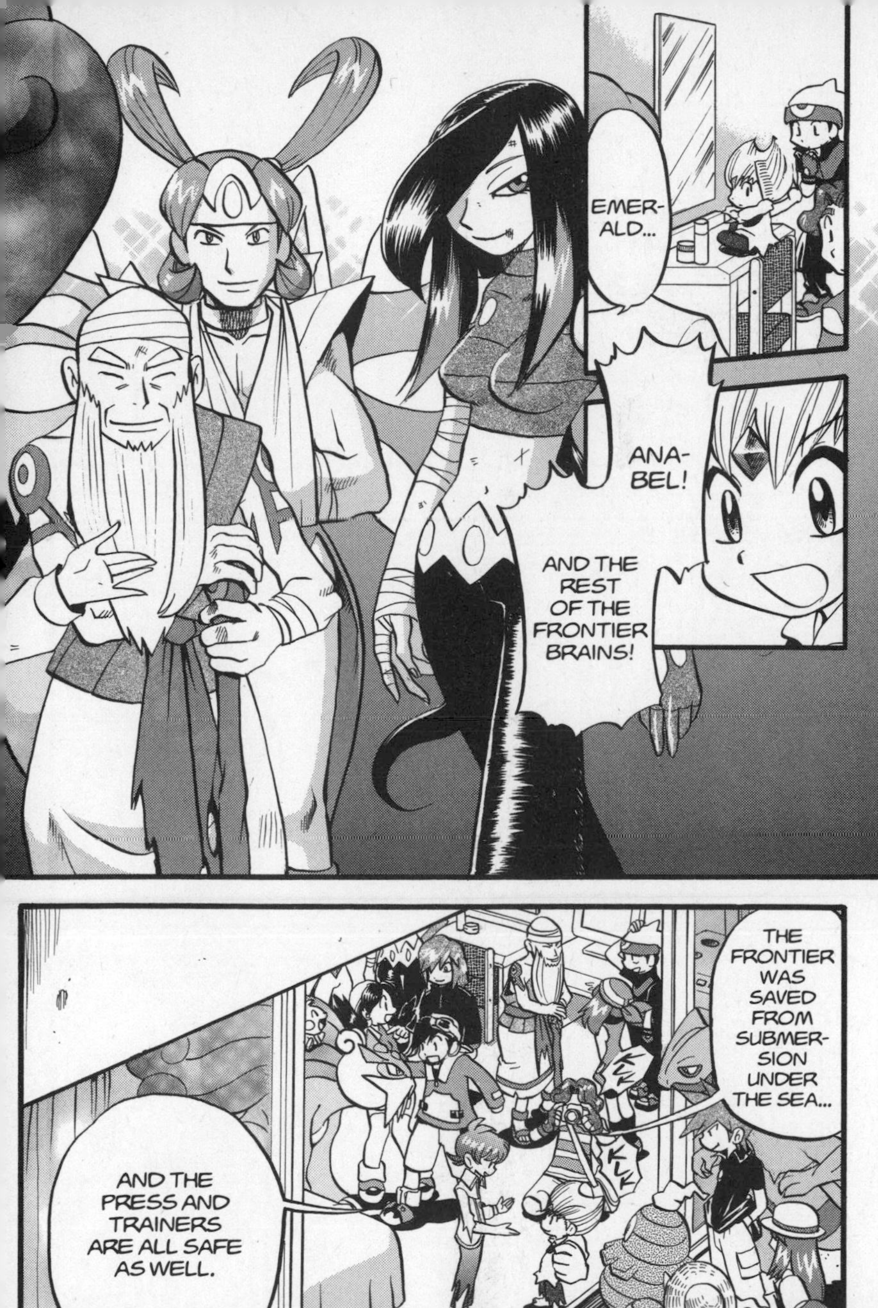
EMER-ALD...
ANA-BEL!
AND THE REST OF THE FRONTIER BRAINS!
THE FRONTIER WAS SAVED FROM SUBMER-SION UNDER THE SEA...
AND THE PRESS AND TRAINERS ARE ALL SAFE AS WELL.

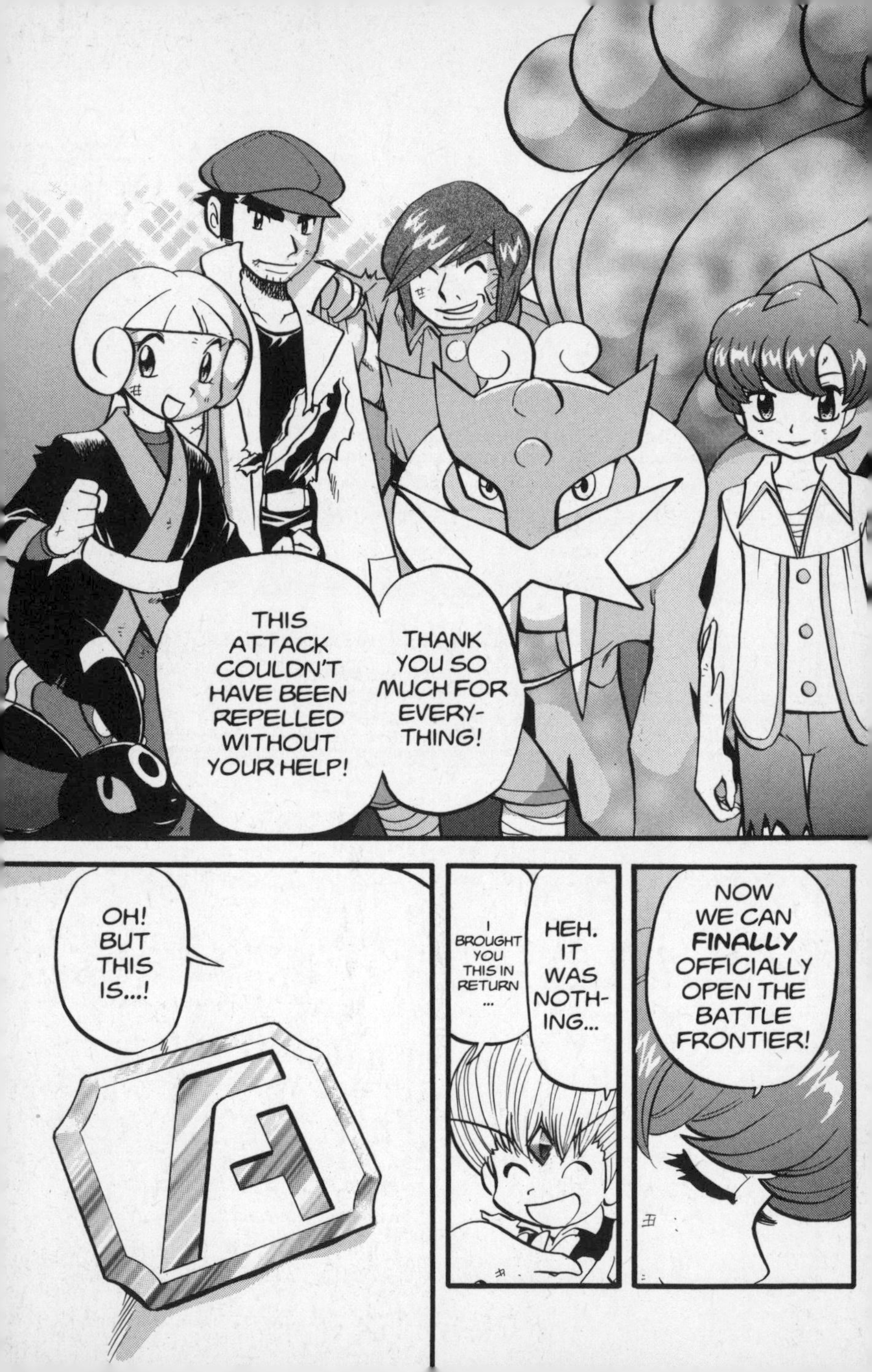
THANK YOU SO MUCH FOR EVERY-THING!
THIS ATTACK COULDN'T HAVE BEEN REPELLED WITHOUT YOUR HELP!
NOW WE CAN **FINALLY** OFFICIALLY OPEN THE BATTLE FRONTIER!
HEH. IT WAS NOTH-ING...
I BROUGHT YOU THIS IN RETURN...
OH! BUT THIS IS...!

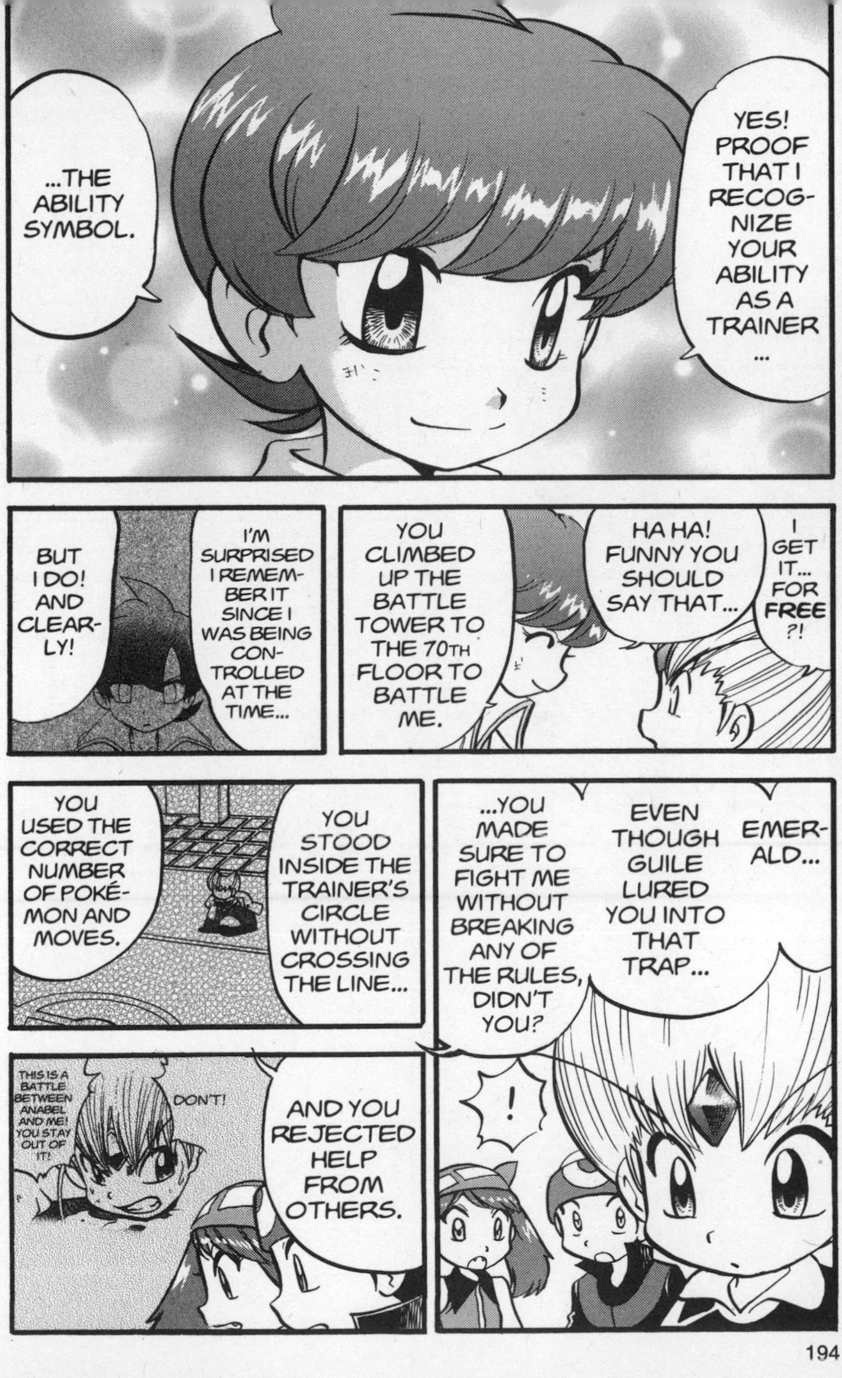
YES! PROOF THAT I RECOGNIZE YOUR ABILITY AS A TRAINER...
...THE ABILITY SYMBOL.
I GET IT... FOR FREE?!
HA HA! FUNNY YOU SHOULD SAY THAT...
YOU CLIMBED UP THE BATTLE TOWER TO THE 70TH FLOOR TO BATTLE ME.
I'M SURPRISED I REMEMBER IT SINCE I WAS BEING CONTROLLED AT THE TIME...
BUT I DO! AND CLEARLY!
EMERALD...
EVEN THOUGH GUILE LURED YOU INTO THAT TRAP...
...YOU MADE SURE TO FIGHT ME WITHOUT BREAKING ANY OF THE RULES, DIDN'T YOU?
YOU STOOD INSIDE THE TRAINER'S CIRCLE WITHOUT CROSSING THE LINE...
YOU USED THE CORRECT NUMBER OF POKÉMON AND MOVES.
!
AND YOU REJECTED HELP FROM OTHERS.
DON'T!
THIS IS A BATTLE BETWEEN ANABEL AND ME! YOU STAY OUT OF IT!

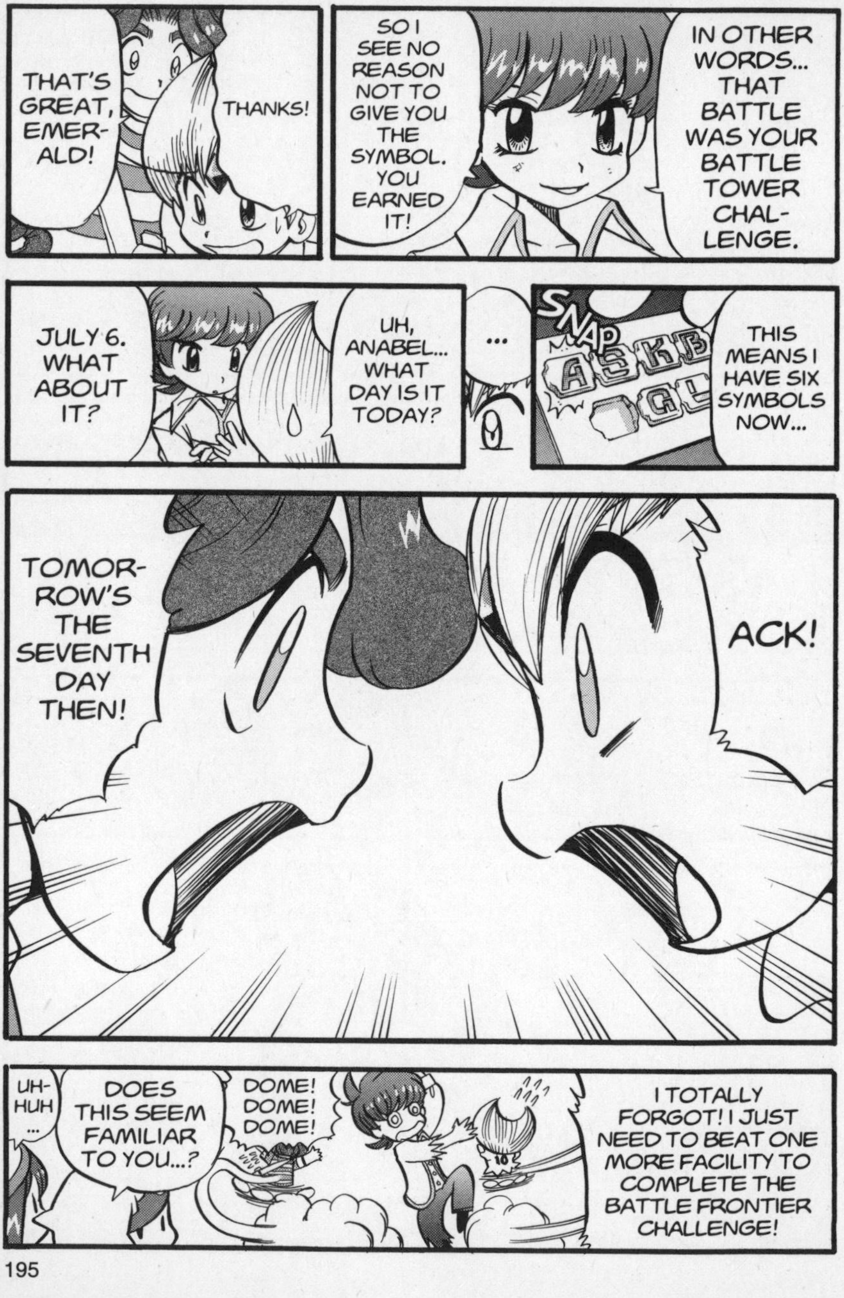
IN OTHER WORDS... THAT BATTLE WAS YOUR BATTLE TOWER CHALLENGE.
SO I SEE NO REASON NOT TO GIVE YOU THE SYMBOL. YOU EARNED IT!
THANKS!
THAT'S GREAT, EMERALD!
SNAP
THIS MEANS I HAVE SIX SYMBOLS NOW...
...
UH, ANABEL... WHAT DAY IS IT TODAY?
JULY 6. WHAT ABOUT IT?
ACK!
TOMORROW'S THE SEVENTH DAY THEN!
I TOTALLY FORGOT! I JUST NEED TO BEAT ONE MORE FACILITY TO COMPLETE THE BATTLE FRONTIER CHALLENGE!
DOME! DOME! DOME!
DOES THIS SEEM FAMILIAR TO YOU...?
UH-HUH ...

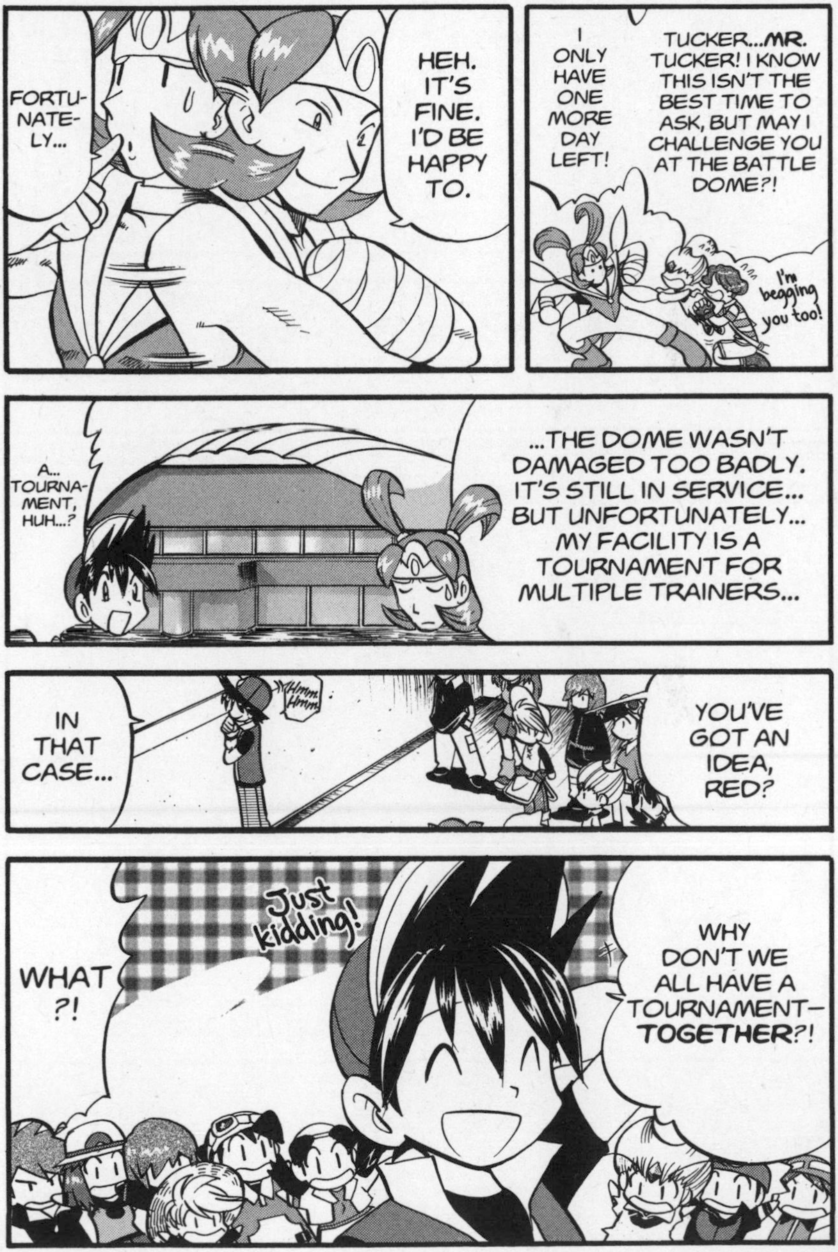
TUCKER...**MR.** TUCKER! I KNOW THIS ISN'T THE BEST TIME TO ASK, BUT MAY I CHALLENGE YOU AT THE BATTLE DOME?!
I ONLY HAVE ONE MORE DAY LEFT!
I'm begging you too!
HEH. IT'S FINE. I'D BE HAPPY TO.
FORTU-NATE-LY...
...THE DOME WASN'T DAMAGED TOO BADLY. IT'S STILL IN SERVICE... BUT UNFORTUNATELY... MY FACILITY IS A TOURNAMENT FOR MULTIPLE TRAINERS...
A... TOURNA-MENT, HUH...?
YOU'VE GOT AN IDEA, RED?
Hmm Hmm
IN THAT CASE...
WHY DON'T WE ALL HAVE A TOURNAMENT—**TOGETHER**?!
Just kidding!
WHAT?!

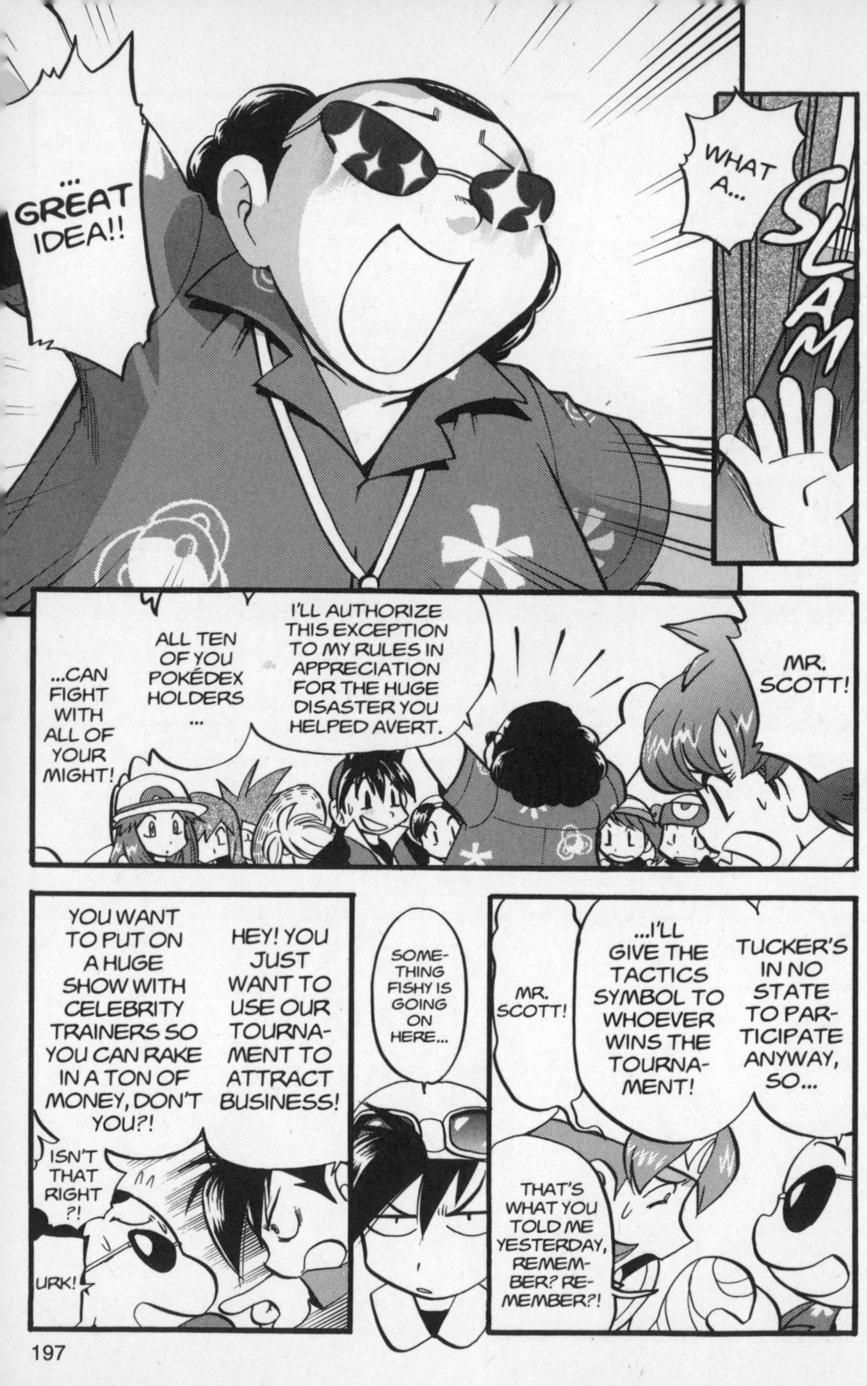
WHAT A...
SLAM
...GREAT IDEA!!
MR. SCOTT!
I'LL AUTHORIZE THIS EXCEPTION TO MY RULES IN APPRECIATION FOR THE HUGE DISASTER YOU HELPED AVERT.
ALL TEN OF YOU POKÉDEX HOLDERS...
...CAN FIGHT WITH ALL OF YOUR MIGHT!
TUCKER'S IN NO STATE TO PARTICIPATE ANYWAY, SO...
...I'LL GIVE THE TACTICS SYMBOL TO WHOEVER WINS THE TOURNAMENT!
MR. SCOTT!
THAT'S WHAT YOU TOLD ME YESTERDAY, REMEMBER? REMEMBER?!
SOMETHING FISHY IS GOING ON HERE...
HEY! YOU JUST WANT TO USE OUR TOURNAMENT TO ATTRACT BUSINESS!
YOU WANT TO PUT ON A HUGE SHOW WITH CELEBRITY TRAINERS SO YOU CAN RAKE IN A TON OF MONEY, DON'T YOU?!
ISN'T THAT RIGHT?!
URK!

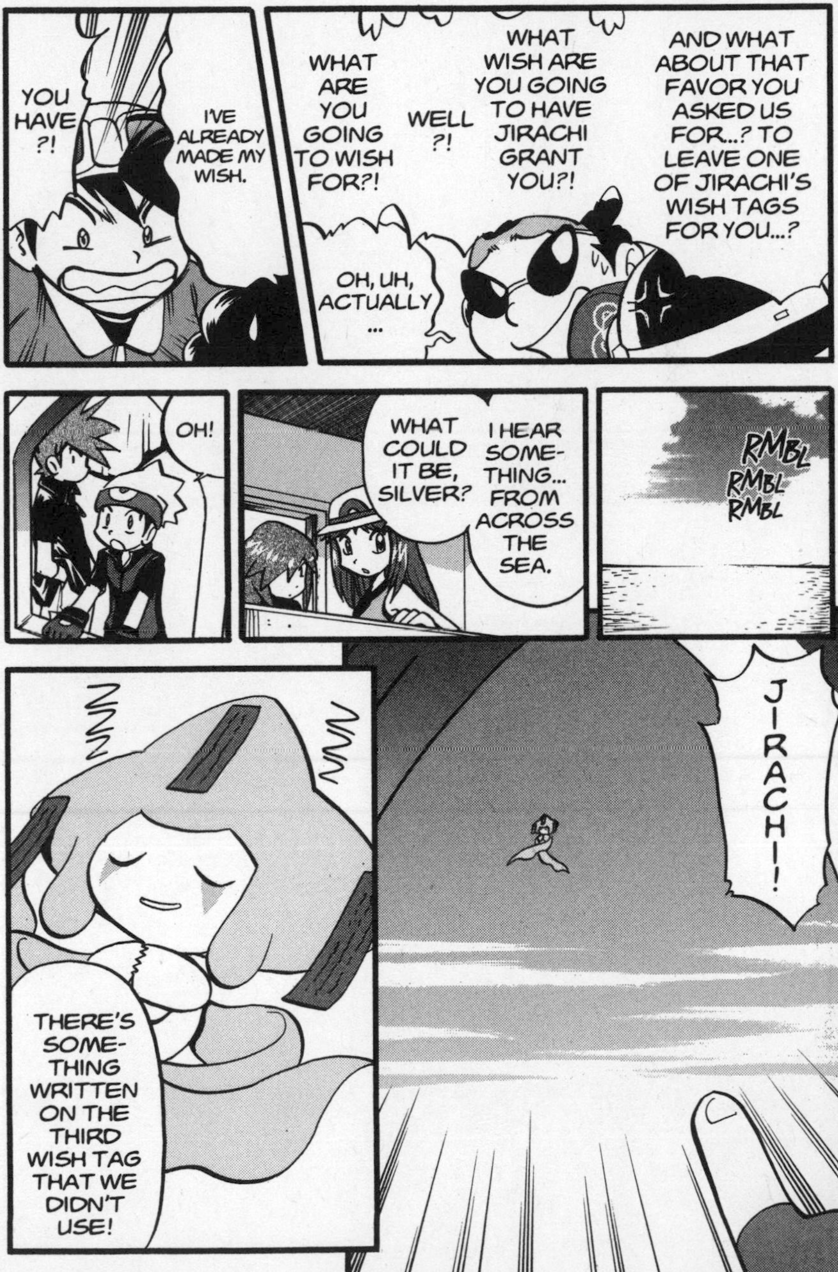
AND WHAT ABOUT THAT FAVOR YOU ASKED US FOR...? TO LEAVE ONE OF JIRACHI'S WISH TAGS FOR YOU...?
WHAT WISH ARE YOU GOING TO HAVE JIRACHI GRANT YOU?!
WELL ?!
WHAT ARE YOU GOING TO WISH FOR?!
OH, UH, ACTUALLY ...
I'VE ALREADY MADE MY WISH.
YOU HAVE ?!
RMBL RMBL RMBL
I HEAR SOME-THING... FROM ACROSS THE SEA.
WHAT COULD IT BE, SILVER?
OH!
JIRACHI!
THERE'S SOME-THING WRITTEN ON THE THIRD WISH TAG THAT WE DIDN'T USE!

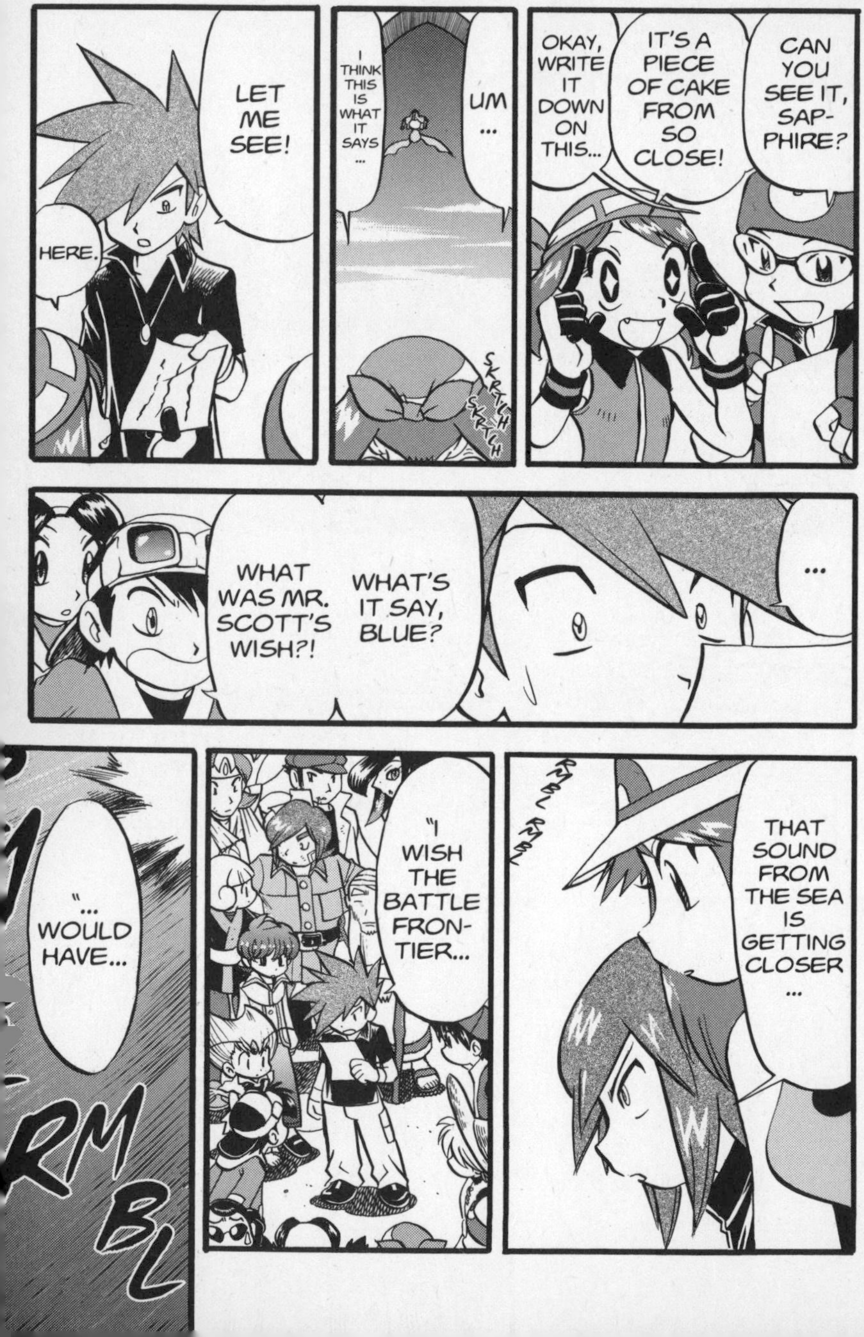
CAN YOU SEE IT, SAP-PHIRE?
IT'S A PIECE OF CAKE FROM SO CLOSE!
OKAY, WRITE IT DOWN ON THIS...
UM ...
I THINK THIS IS WHAT IT SAYS ...
SKRTCH SKRTCH
LET ME SEE!
HERE.
...
WHAT'S IT SAY, BLUE?
WHAT WAS MR. SCOTT'S WISH?!
RMBL RMBL
THAT SOUND FROM THE SEA IS GETTING CLOSER ...
"I WISH THE BATTLE FRON-TIER...
"... WOULD HAVE...
RMBL

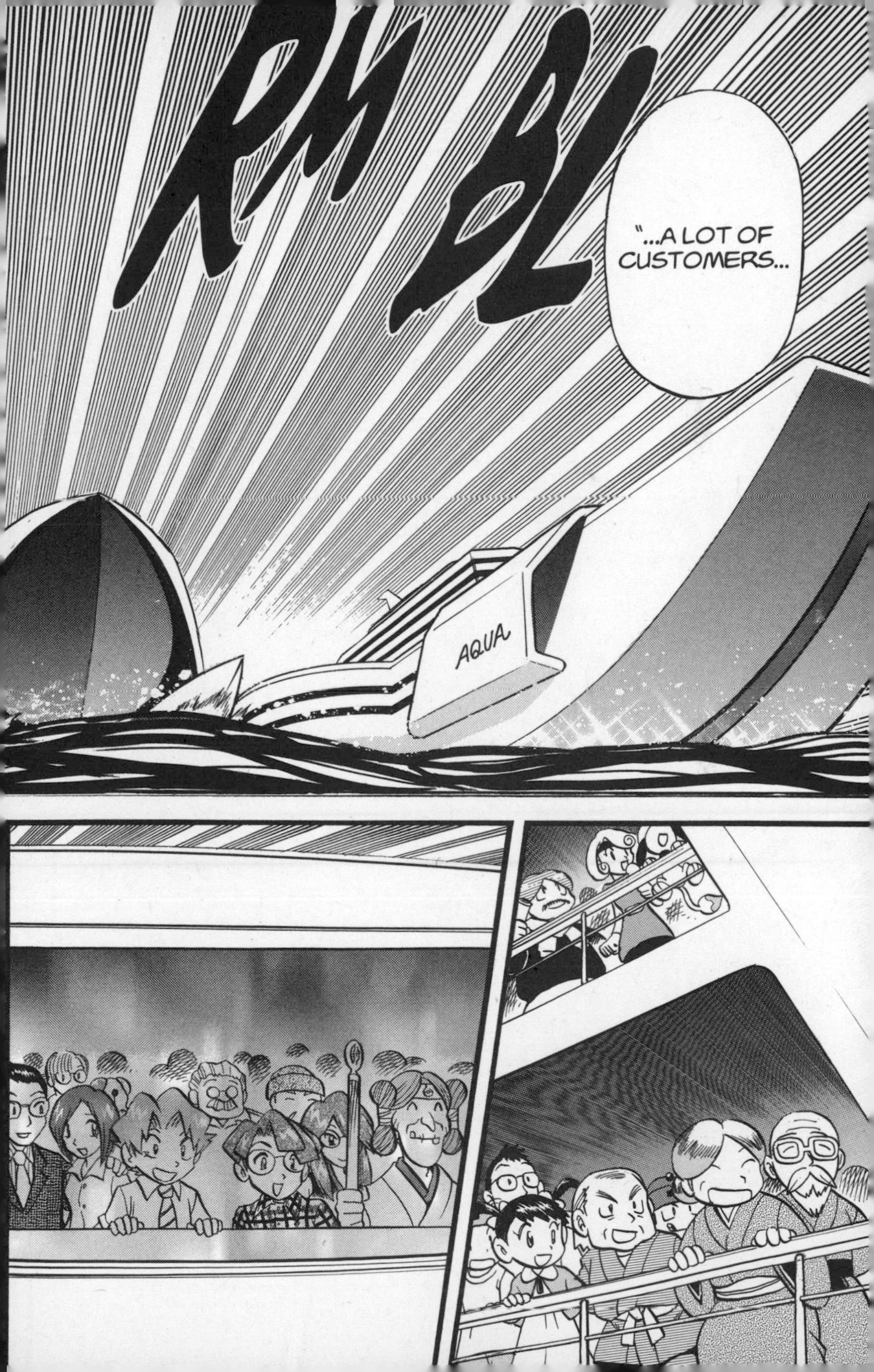
"...A LOT OF CUSTOMERS...
AQUA

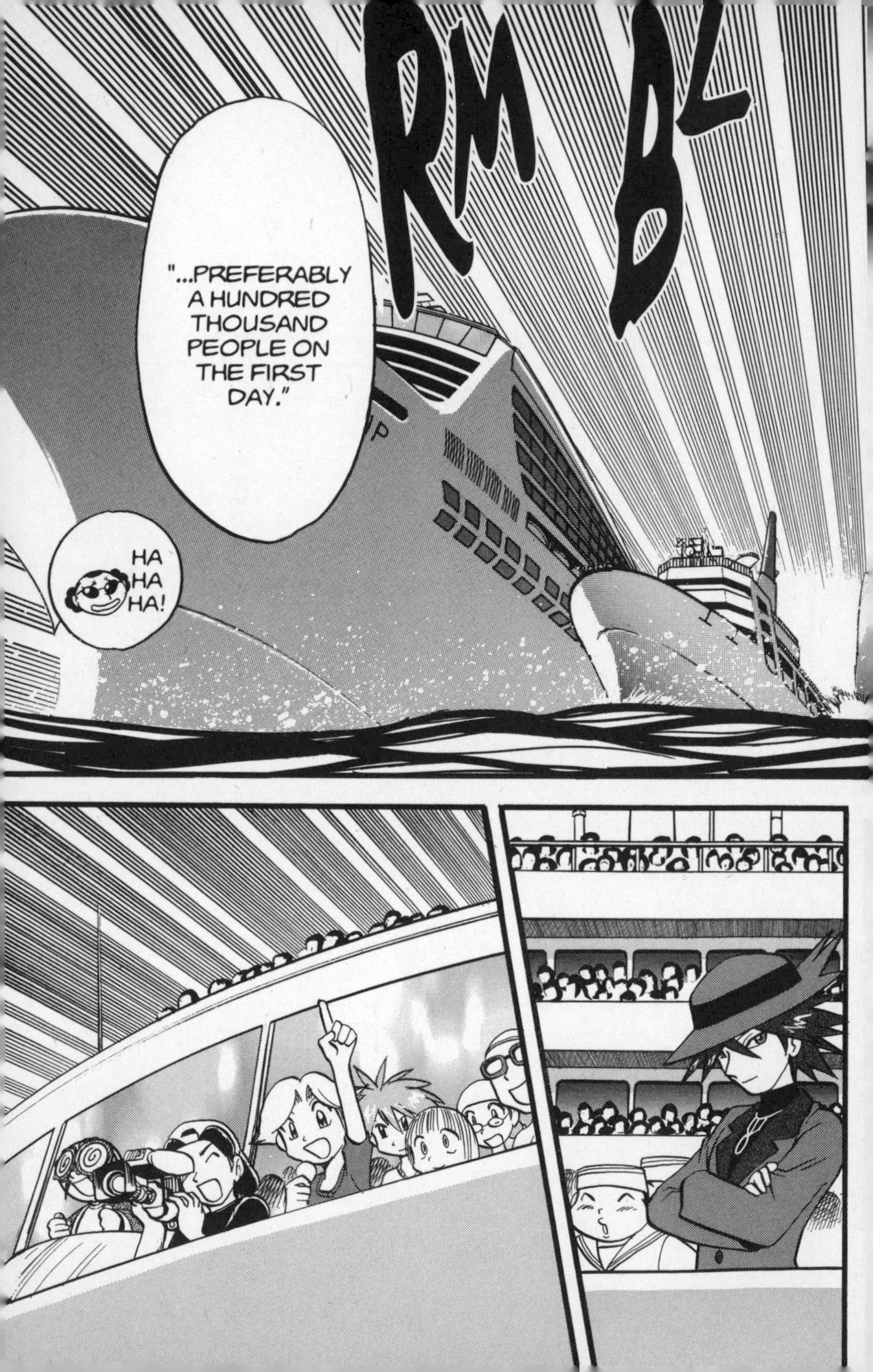
"...PREFERABLY A HUNDRED THOUSAND PEOPLE ON THE FIRST DAY."
HA HA HA!

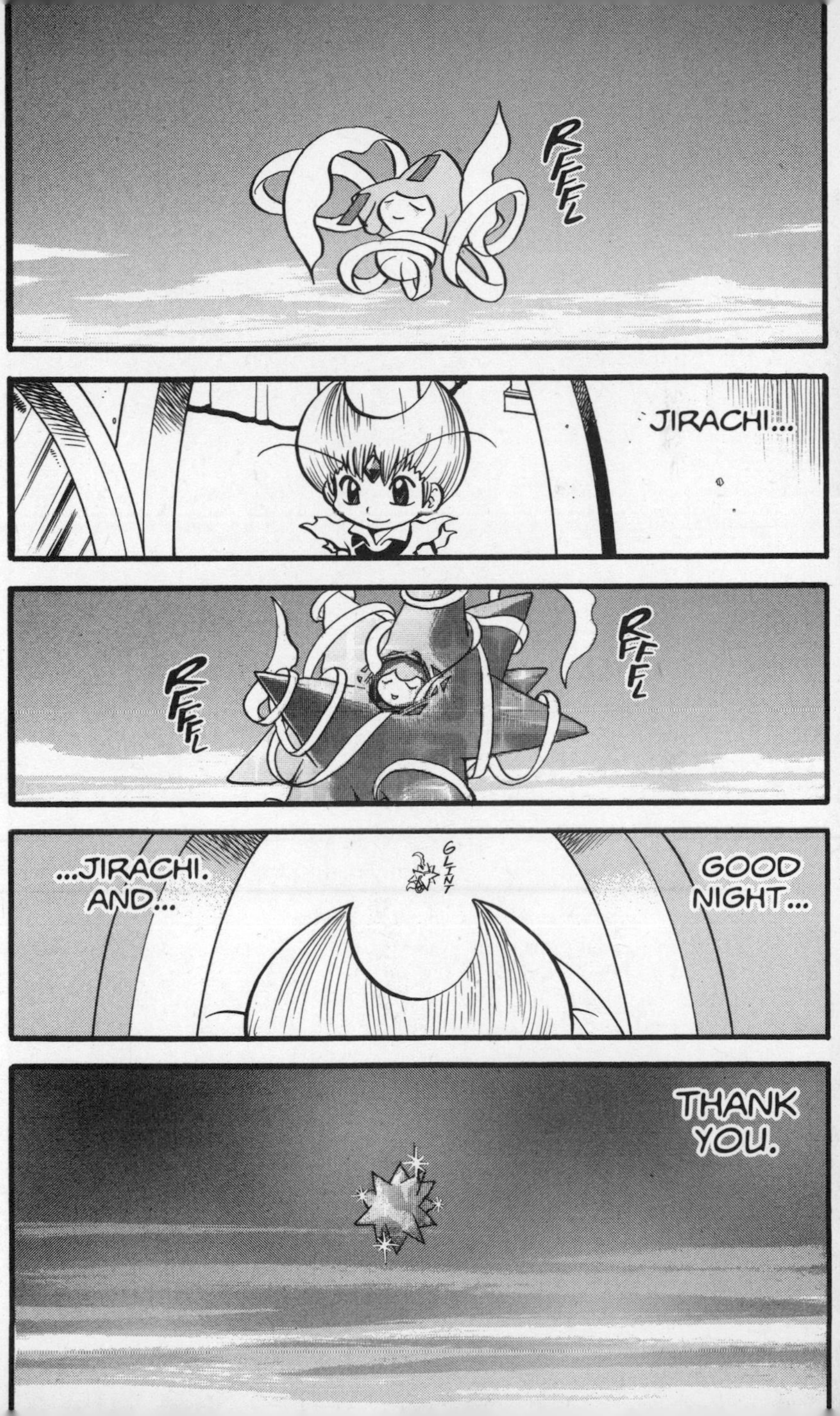
RFFFL
JIRACHI...
RFFFL
RFFFL
GOOD NIGHT...
GLINT
...JIRACHI. AND...
THANK YOU.

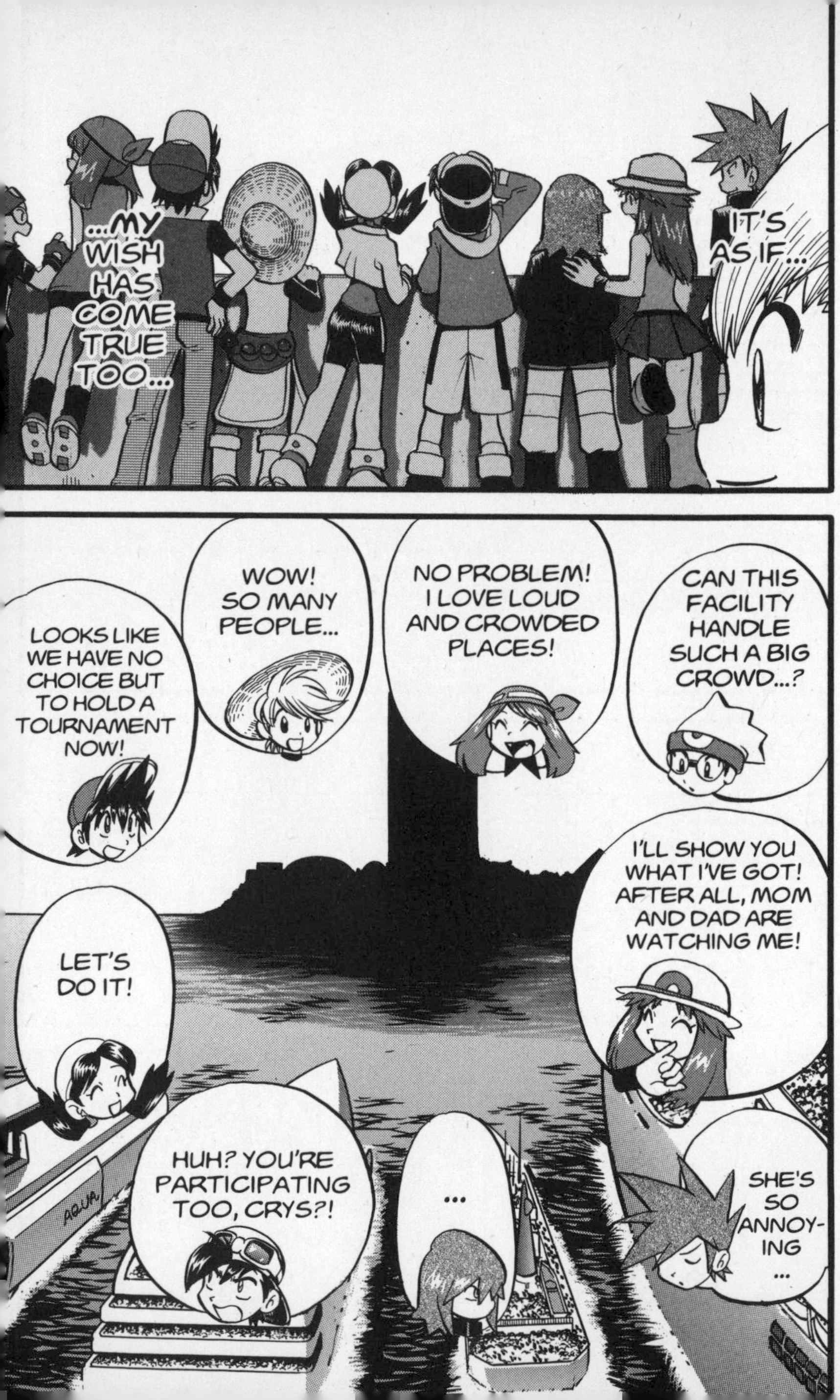
IT'S AS IF...
...MY WISH HAS COME TRUE TOO...
CAN THIS FACILITY HANDLE SUCH A BIG CROWD...?
NO PROBLEM! I LOVE LOUD AND CROWDED PLACES!
WOW! SO MANY PEOPLE...
LOOKS LIKE WE HAVE NO CHOICE BUT TO HOLD A TOURNAMENT NOW!
I'LL SHOW YOU WHAT I'VE GOT! AFTER ALL, MOM AND DAD ARE WATCHING ME!
LET'S DO IT!
SHE'S SO ANNOY-ING...
...
HUH? YOU'RE PARTICIPATING TOO, CRYS?!

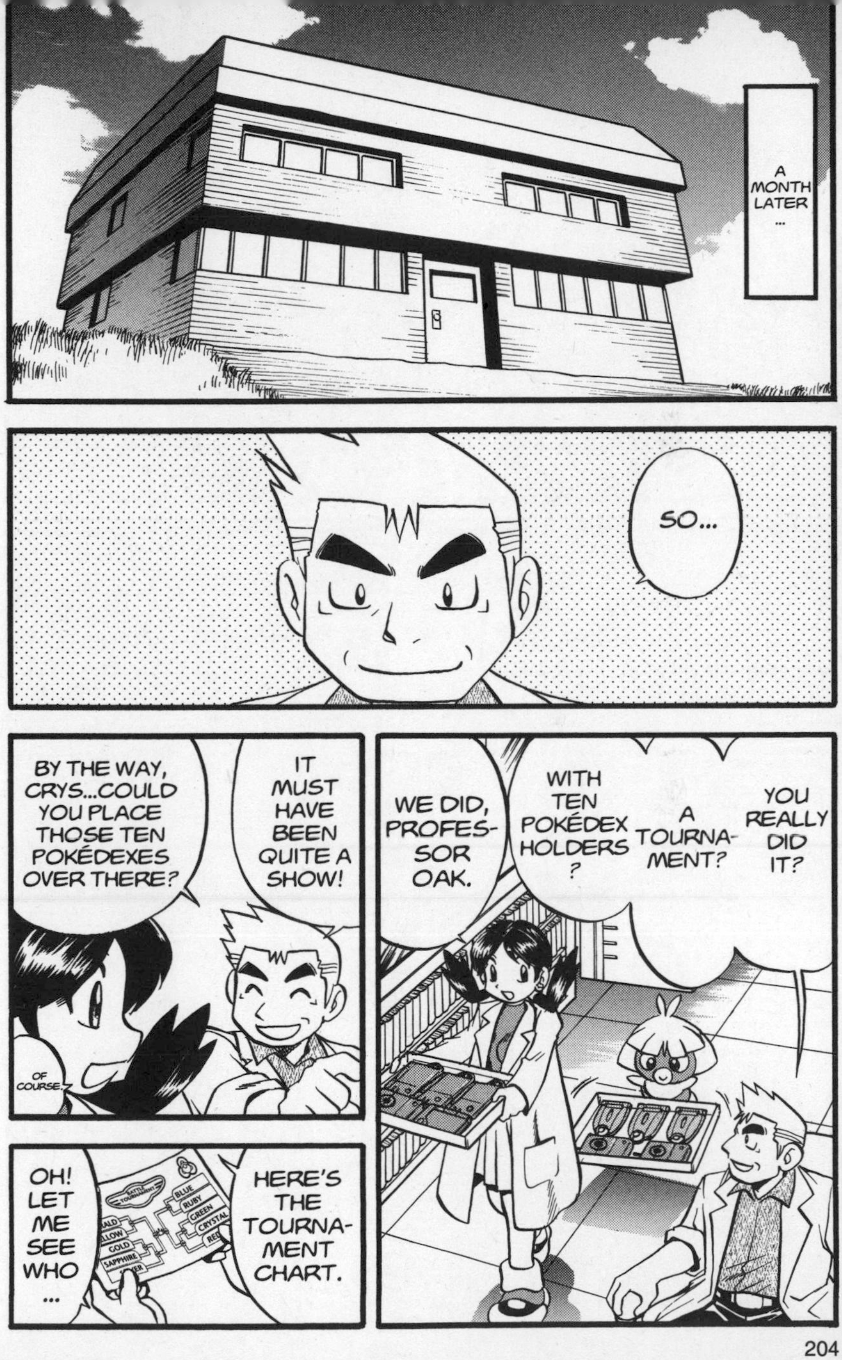
A MONTH LATER ...
SO...
YOU REALLY DID IT?
A TOURNAMENT?
WITH TEN POKÉDEX HOLDERS?
WE DID, PROFESSOR OAK.
IT MUST HAVE BEEN QUITE A SHOW!
BY THE WAY, CRYS...COULD YOU PLACE THOSE TEN POKÉDEXES OVER THERE?
OF COURSE.
HERE'S THE TOURNAMENT CHART.
OH! LET ME SEE WHO ...
BLUE
RUBY
GREEN
CRYSTAL
GOLD
SAPPHIRE

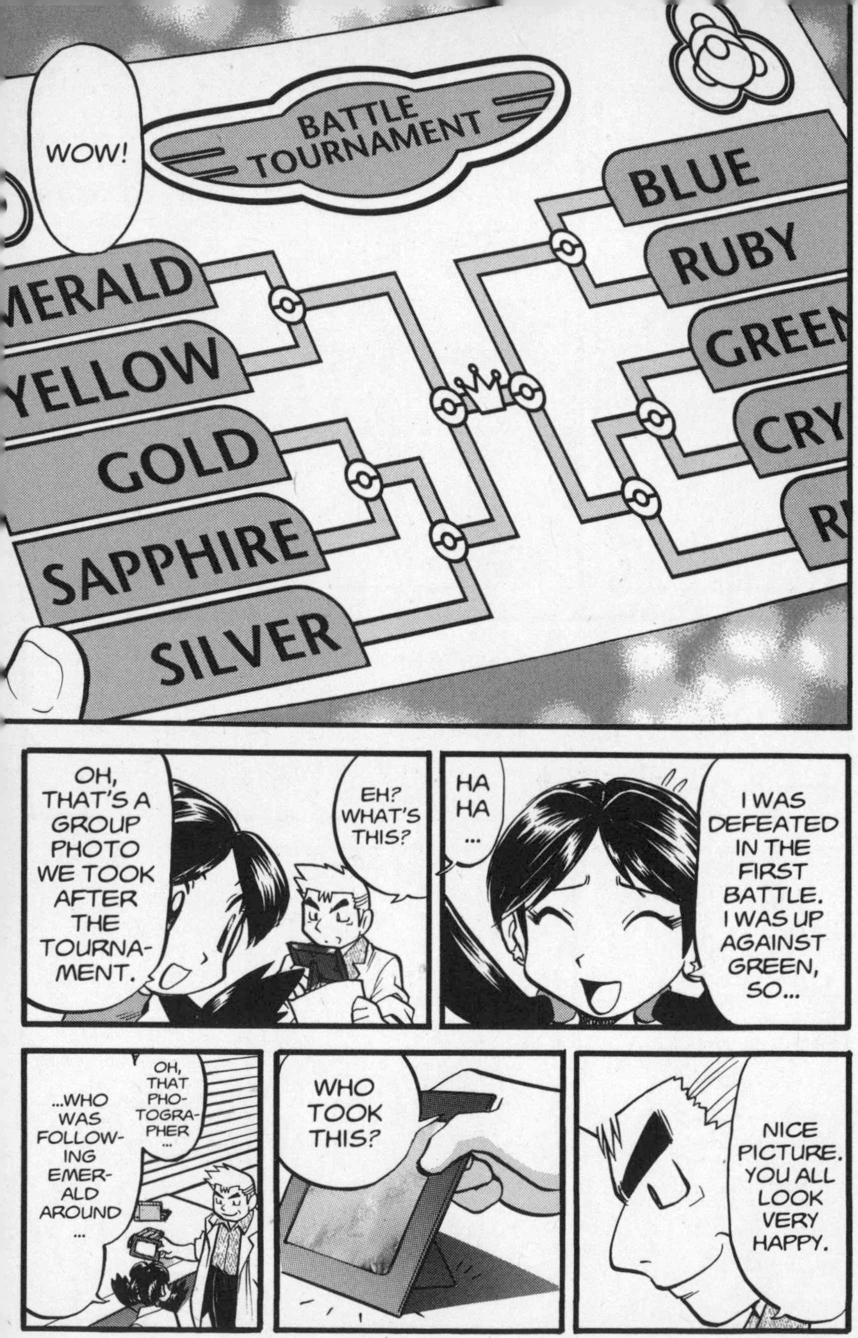
WOW!
BATTLE TOURNAMENT
BLUE
RUBY
GREE
CRY
R
MERALD
YELLOW
GOLD
SAPPHIRE
SILVER
I WAS DEFEATED IN THE FIRST BATTLE. I WAS UP AGAINST GREEN, SO...
HA HA ...
EH? WHAT'S THIS?
OH, THAT'S A GROUP PHOTO WE TOOK AFTER THE TOURNAMENT.
NICE PICTURE. YOU ALL LOOK VERY HAPPY.
WHO TOOK THIS?
OH, THAT PHOTOGRAPHER ...
...WHO WAS FOLLOWING EMERALD AROUND ...

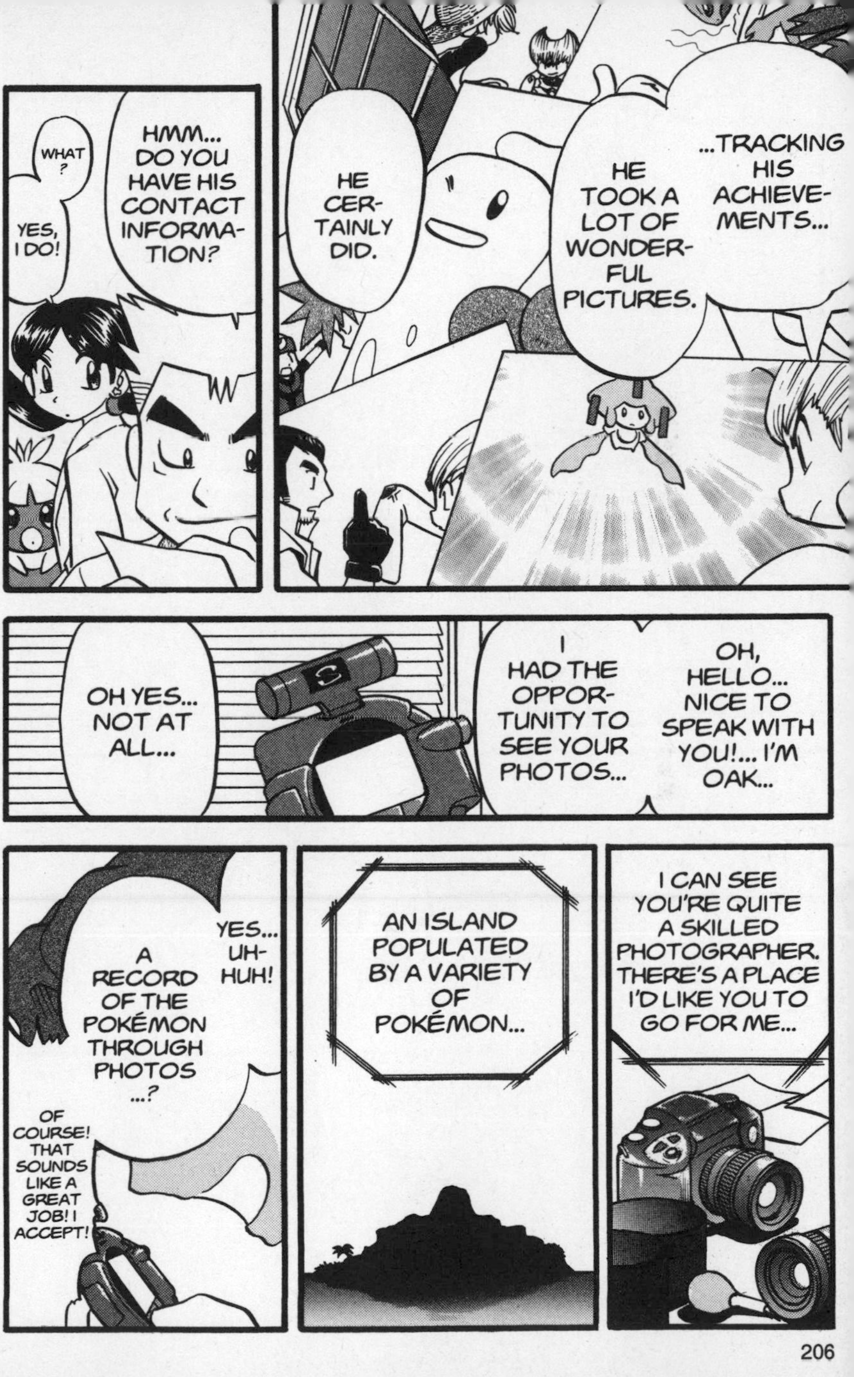
...TRACKING HIS ACHIEVEMENTS...
HE TOOK A LOT OF WONDERFUL PICTURES.
HE CERTAINLY DID.
HMM... DO YOU HAVE HIS CONTACT INFORMATION?
WHAT?
YES, I DO!
OH, HELLO... NICE TO SPEAK WITH YOU!... I'M OAK...
I HAD THE OPPORTUNITY TO SEE YOUR PHOTOS...
OH YES... NOT AT ALL...
I CAN SEE YOU'RE QUITE A SKILLED PHOTOGRAPHER. THERE'S A PLACE I'D LIKE YOU TO GO FOR ME...
AN ISLAND POPULATED BY A VARIETY OF POKÉMON...
YES... UH-HUH!
A RECORD OF THE POKÉMON THROUGH PHOTOS ...?
OF COURSE! THAT SOUNDS LIKE A GREAT JOB! I ACCEPT!

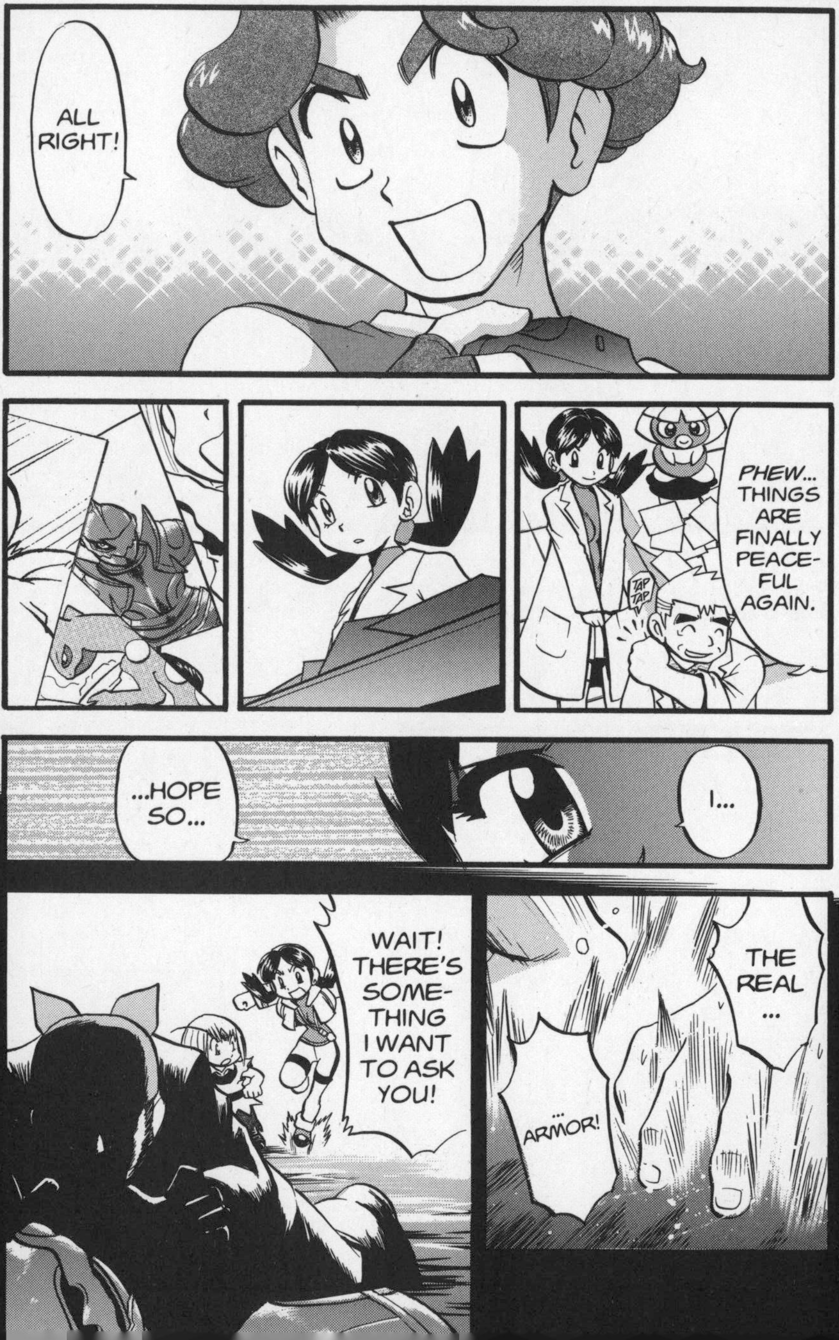
ALL RIGHT!
PHEW... THINGS ARE FINALLY PEACE-FUL AGAIN.
TAP TAP
I...
...HOPE SO...
THE REAL ...
... ARMOR!
WAIT! THERE'S SOME-THING I WANT TO ASK YOU!

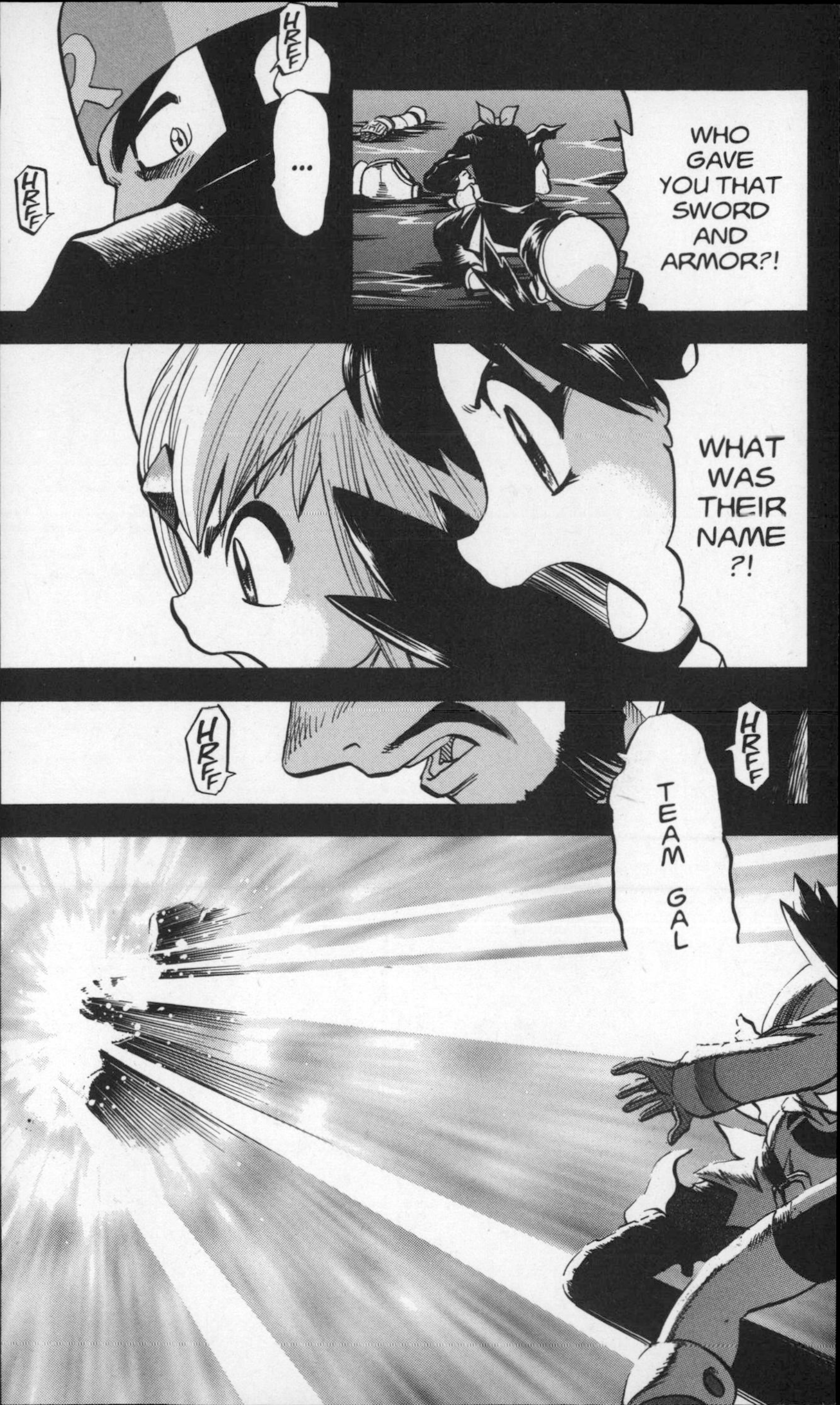
WHO GAVE YOU THAT SWORD AND ARMOR?!
HREFF
...
HREFF
WHAT WAS THEIR NAME?!
HREFF
HREFF
TEAM GAL

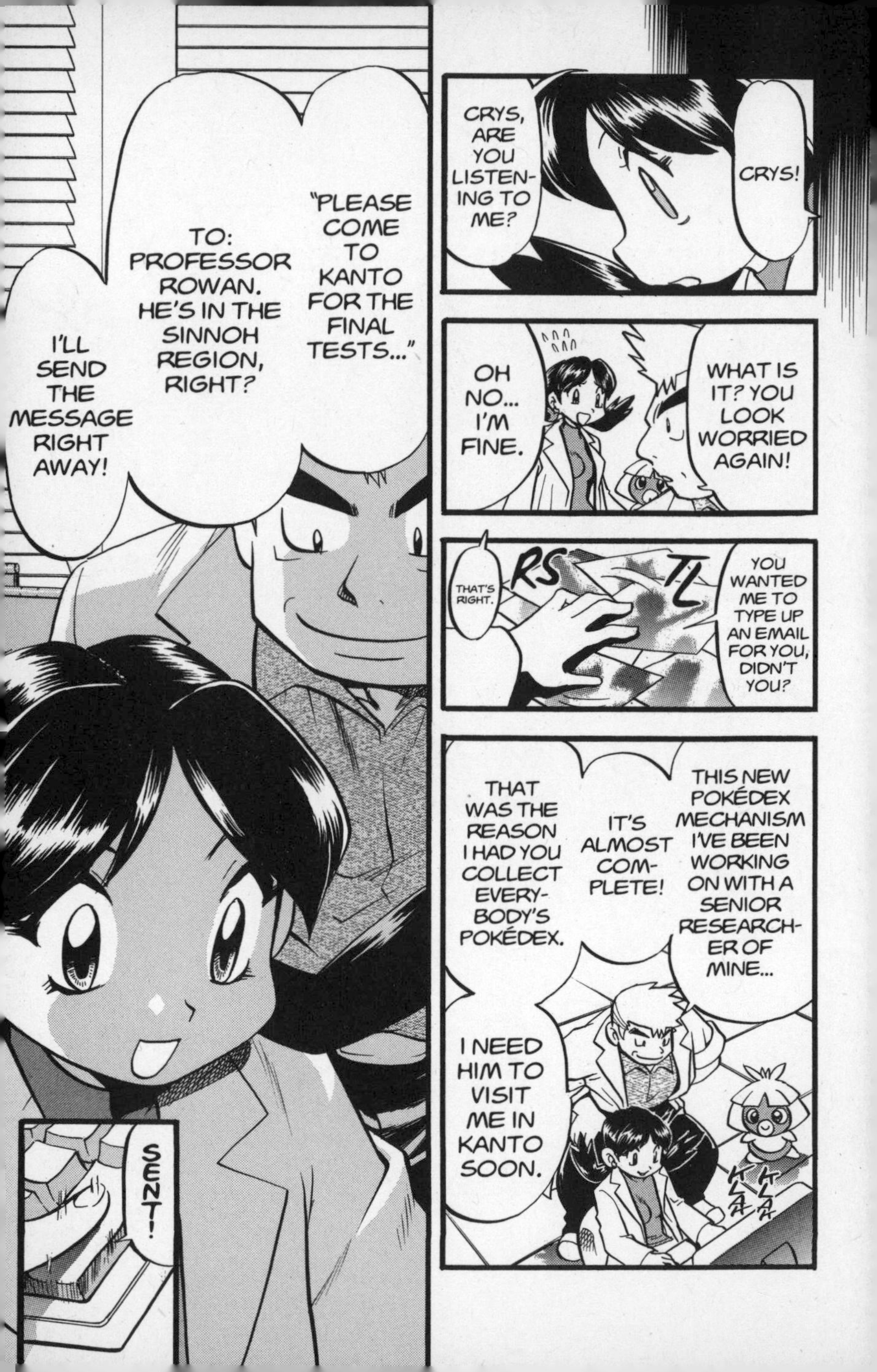
CRYS!
CRYS, ARE YOU LISTENING TO ME?
WHAT IS IT? YOU LOOK WORRIED AGAIN!
OH NO... I'M FINE.
YOU WANTED ME TO TYPE UP AN EMAIL FOR YOU, DIDN'T YOU?
RSTL
THAT'S RIGHT.
THIS NEW POKÉDEX MECHANISM I'VE BEEN WORKING ON WITH A SENIOR RESEARCHER OF MINE...
IT'S ALMOST COMPLETE!
THAT WAS THE REASON I HAD YOU COLLECT EVERYBODY'S POKÉDEX.
I NEED HIM TO VISIT ME IN KANTO SOON.
KLAK KLAK
"PLEASE COME TO KANTO FOR THE FINAL TESTS..."
TO: PROFESSOR ROWAN. HE'S IN THE SINNOH REGION, RIGHT?
I'LL SEND THE MESSAGE RIGHT AWAY!
SENT!

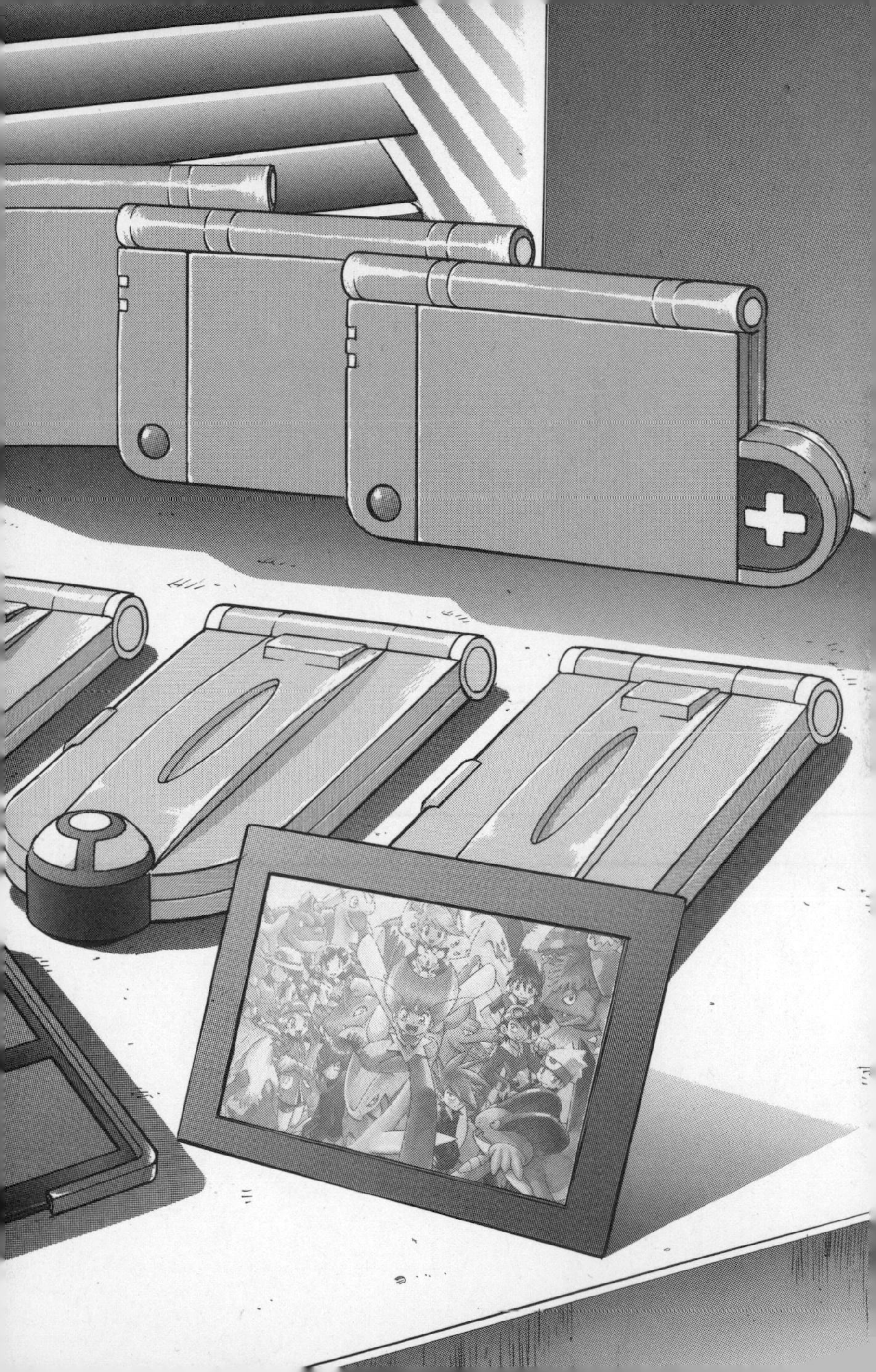

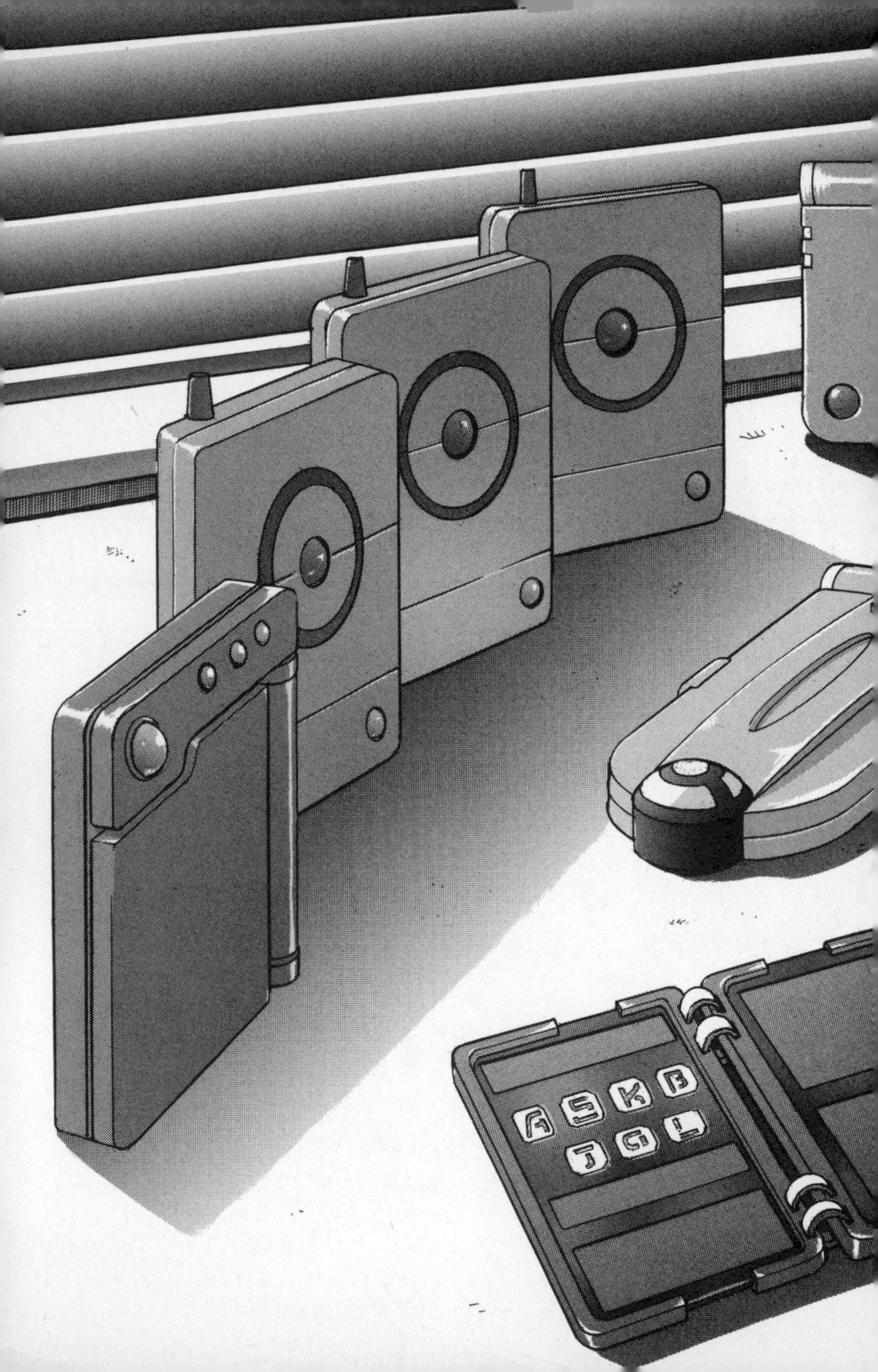

Pokémon™ Adventures Emerald

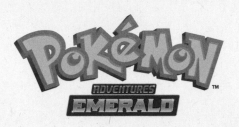

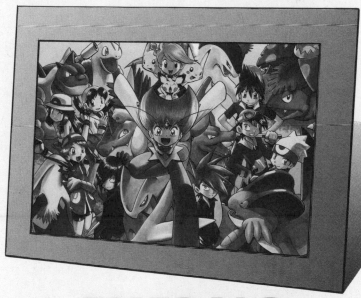

EMERALD

RED • GREEN • BLUE • YELLOW • GOLD • SILVER • CRYSTAL
RUBY • SAPPHIRE

Fin

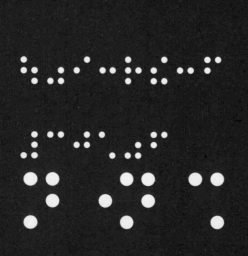

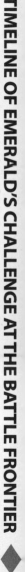

TIMELINE OF EMERALD'S CHALLENGE AT THE BATTLE FRONTIER

DAY 4	DAY 3	DAY 2	DAY 1	DAY 0
$\frac{7}{4}$	$\frac{7}{3}$	$\frac{7}{2}$	$\frac{7}{1}$	$\frac{6}{30}$

DAY 0 — 6/30

OPENING CEREMONY

(DEMONSTRATION BATTLE AND PRESS CONFERENCE)

DAY 1 — 7/1

BATTLE FACTORY

(CHALLENGE→WIN) Ⓚ

DAY 2 — 7/2

BATTLE PIKE

(CHALLENGE→WIN) Ⓛ

DAY 3 — 7/3

BATTLE PYRAMID

(CHALLENGE→WIN) Ⓑ

DAY 4 — 7/4

(MORNING) BATTLE AT THE ARTISAN CAVE

(AFTERNOON) BATTLE ARENA

(CHALLENGE→WIN) Ⓖ

HOENN

BATTLE FRONTIER

Day	Date		
DAY 5	7/5	**BATTLE DOME** (CHALLENGE-DEFEAT)	(AFTERNOON/EVENING) **BATTLE PALACE** (CHALLENGE-WIN) S (NIGHT) **BATTLE TOWER** (FINAL BATTLE AGAINST GUILE BEGINS)
DAY 6	7/6	**BATTLE TOWER** (END OF BATTLE WITH GUILE BEGUN ON DAY 5)	A
DAY 7	7/7	**BATTLE DOME** (REMATCH–TOURNAMENT DO-OVER)	J

Pokémon Adventures Emerald™

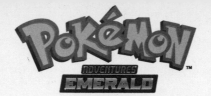

6

The Sixth Chapter

Secret Japanese-Braille Subtitles Decoded!

VOL. 27

Adventure 309: Pike Queen
Adventure 310: If You're Lucky
Adventure 311: Homeland Mud
Adventure 312: Pyramid Adventure
Adventure 313: Flying Star
Adventure 314: Artisan Cave
Adventure 315: The Armor-Clad Man
Adventure 316: Skills of the Salon Maiden
Adventure 317: Scott's Intentions

The Loss of the Wishing Star
Continues in Vol. 28…

27

VOL. 26

Adventure 303: The Shining Frontier
Adventure 304: The Calming Mud Pellet
Adventure 305: Challenge the Seven Facilities
Adventure 306: The Frontier Brain of Knowledge
Adventure 307: A Suspicious Shadow
Adventure 308: Sending a Request

The Awakening After 1,000 Years
Continues in Vol. 27…

26

The Sixth Chapter

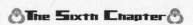

29

28

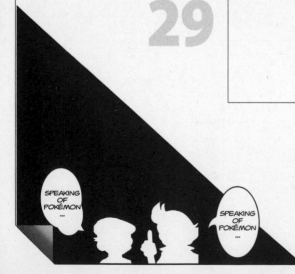

SPEAKING
OF
POKÉMON
...

SPEAKING
OF
POKÉMON
...

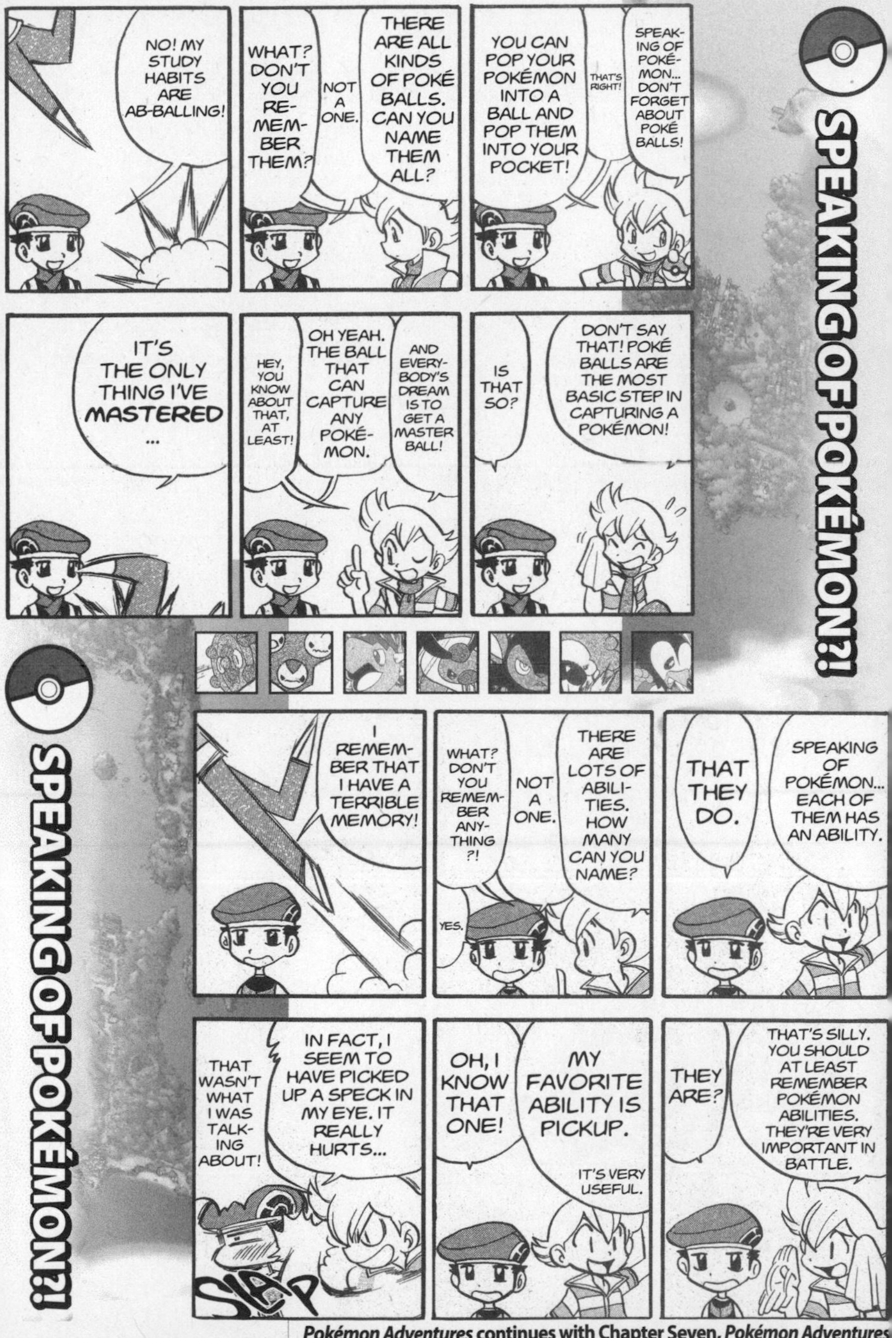
SPEAKING OF POKÉMON?!
SPEAKING OF POKÉMON... DON'T FORGET ABOUT POKÉ BALLS!
THAT'S RIGHT!
YOU CAN POP YOUR POKÉMON INTO A BALL AND POP THEM INTO YOUR POCKET!
THERE ARE ALL KINDS OF POKÉ BALLS. CAN YOU NAME THEM ALL?
NOT A ONE.
WHAT? DON'T YOU REMEMBER THEM?
NO! MY STUDY HABITS ARE AB-BALLING!
DON'T SAY THAT! POKÉ BALLS ARE THE MOST BASIC STEP IN CAPTURING A POKÉMON!
IS THAT SO?
AND EVERYBODY'S DREAM IS TO GET A MASTER BALL!
OH YEAH. THE BALL THAT CAN CAPTURE ANY POKÉMON.
HEY, YOU KNOW ABOUT THAT, AT LEAST!
IT'S THE ONLY THING I'VE MASTERED ...
SPEAKING OF POKÉMON?!
SPEAKING OF POKÉMON... EACH OF THEM HAS AN ABILITY.
THAT THEY DO.
THERE ARE LOTS OF ABILITIES. HOW MANY CAN YOU NAME?
NOT A ONE.
WHAT? DON'T YOU REMEMBER ANYTHING?!
YES.
I REMEMBER THAT I HAVE A TERRIBLE MEMORY!
THAT'S SILLY. YOU SHOULD AT LEAST REMEMBER POKÉMON ABILITIES. THEY'RE VERY IMPORTANT IN BATTLE.
THEY ARE?
MY FAVORITE ABILITY IS PICKUP.
IT'S VERY USEFUL.
OH, I KNOW THAT ONE!
IN FACT, I SEEM TO HAVE PICKED UP A SPECK IN MY EYE. IT REALLY HURTS...
THAT WASN'T WHAT I WAS TALKING ABOUT!
SLAP

Pokémon Adventures **continues with Chapter Seven,** ***Pokémon Adventures Diamond and Pearl/Platinum*****, all available now individually or as a box set!**

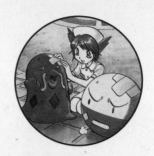

Message from
Hidenori Kusaka

I played *Pokémon Ruby/Sapphire* to complete the
National Pokédex for *Platinum*.* I was filling in the
Pokédex using the Dual-slot mode and Pal Park,
but I still couldn't complete it, so I dragged out the
GameCube games, including *Pokémon Box* and
Pokémon Coliseum. For Lugia, I snagged Shadow Lugia,
purified it, sent it to my GBA and then challenged
myself on *XD* again so I could send the data to
Platinum. It was a reunion with the Pokémon I raised...
not just in my memories but in reality too. That's what
makes Pokémon so much fun!

*This volume was originally published in Japan in 2008.

Message from
Satoshi Yamamoto

This is the final volume of the Emerald story arc! As I
first read the script for the end of this story I began to
shake with excitement. I got goose bumps on my skin
and tears in my eyes. I think everyone should read it.
I worked extra hard on the chapters for this volume. If
you're a new reader to the series who is thinking about
starting from this volume, I advise you to go back and
start with volume 1. I can assure you, you'll enjoy this
one a million times better!

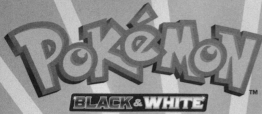
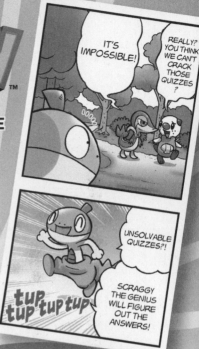
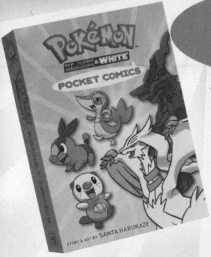

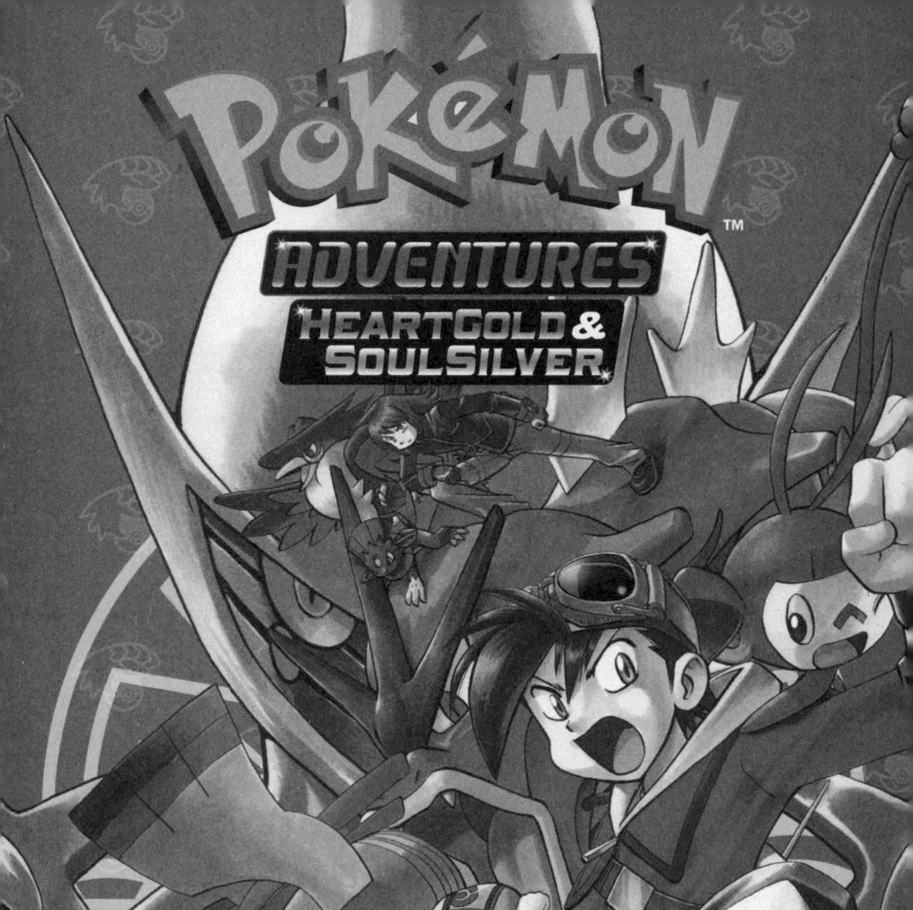

POKéMON™
ADVENTURES
HEARTGOLD & SOULSILVER
Story by HIDENORI KUSAKA
Art by SATOSHI YAMAMOTO

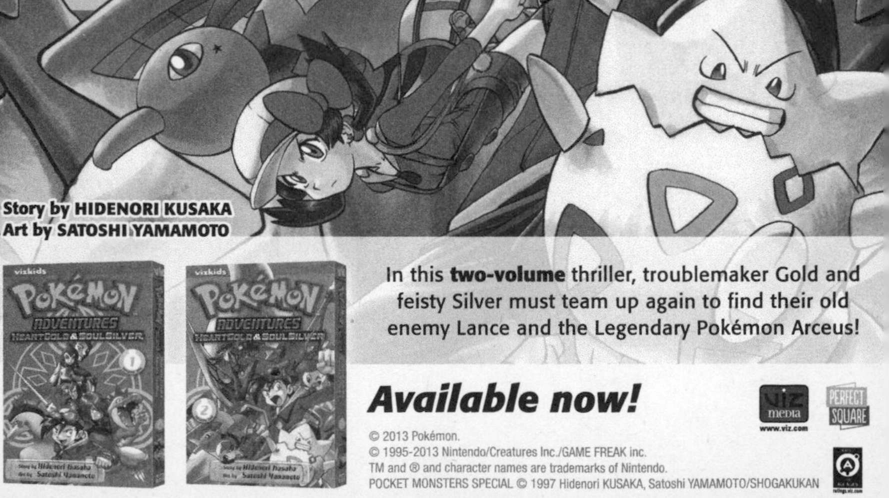

The adventure continues in the Johto region!

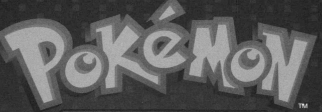

POKÉMON™ ADVENTURES

GOLD & SILVER BOX SET

Includes POKÉMON ADVENTURES Vols. 8-14 and a collectible poster!

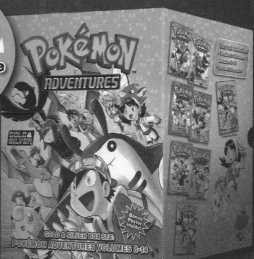

Story by
HIDENORI KUSAKA

Art by
MATO, SATOSHI YAMAMOTO

POKÉMON
ADVENTURES
GOLD & SILVER
Bonus Poster Inside!
GOLD & SILVER BOX SET:
POKÉMON ADVENTURES VOLUMES 8-14

More exciting Pokémon adventures starring Gold and his rival Silver! First someone steals Gold's backpack full of Poké Balls (and Pokémon!). Then someone steals Prof. Elm's Totodile. Can Gold catch the thief—or thieves?!

Keep an eye on Team Rocket, Gold... Could they be behind this crime wave?

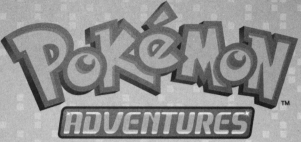
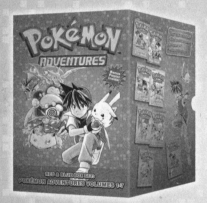

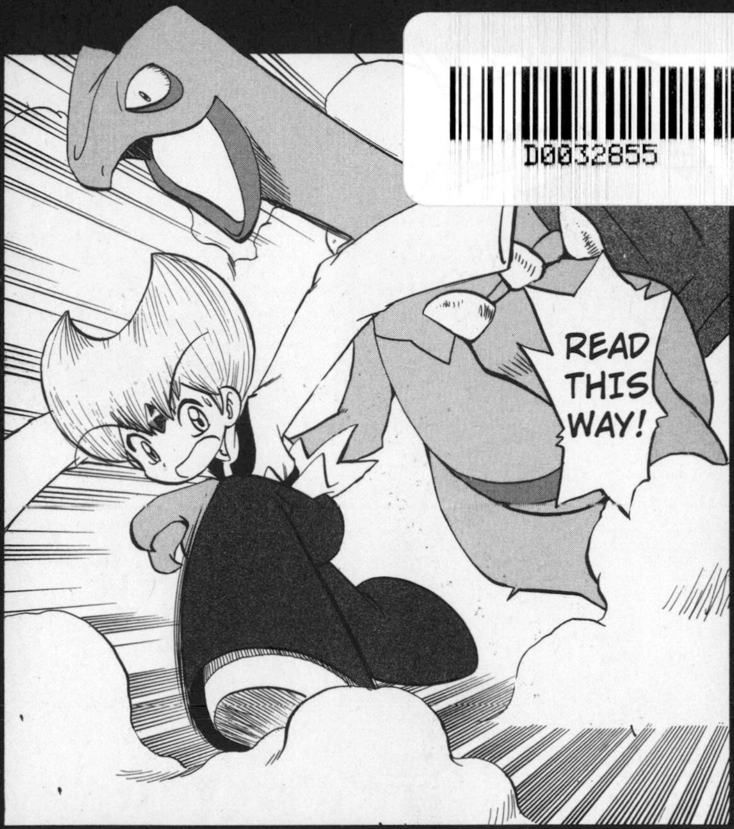
READ THIS WAY!

THIS IS THE END OF THIS GRAPHIC NOVEL!

To properly enjoy this VIZ Media graphic novel, please turn it around and begin reading from right to left.

This book has been printed in the original Japanese format in order to preserve the orientation of the original artwork.

Have fun with it!

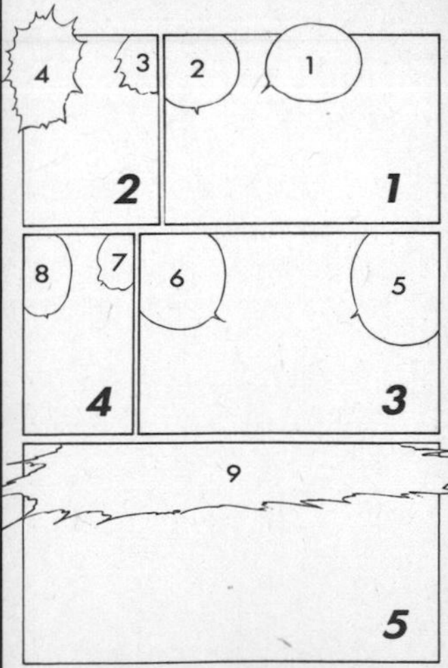
1
2
3
4
5
6
7
8
9

FOLLOW THE ACTION THIS WAY.